TALES OF MYSTERY & THE SUPERNATURAL

General Editor: David Stuart Davies

**SHERLOCK HOLMES:
THE GAME'S AFOOT**

Sherlock Holmes:
The Game's Afoot

New Sherlock Holmes stories collected by
David Stuart Davies

WORDSWORTH EDITIONS

In loving memory of
MICHAEL TRAYLER
the founder of Wordsworth Editions

1

Readers who are interested in other titles from
Wordsworth Editions are invited to visit our website at
www.wordsworth-editions.com

For our latest list and a full mail-order service contact
Bibliophile Books, 5 Thomas Road, London E14 7BN
Tel: +44 0207 515 9222 Fax: +44 0207 538 4115
e-mail: orders@bibliophilebooks.com

This edition published 2008 by
Wordsworth Editions Limited
8B East Street, Ware, Hertfordshire SG12 9HJ

ISBN 978 1 84022 071 1

Typeset in Great Britain by Roperford Editorial
Printed by Clays Ltd, St Ives plc

CONTENTS

INTRODUCTION

When the young doctor Arthur Conan Doyle sat down in his surgery in Southsea in 1886 and set about making notes for a novel involving a mystery which would be solved by a detective character called Sherrinford Holmes he could have had little idea of the phenomenon he was about to unleash on the world. (He changed the first name to Sherlock once he began writing the story). To be fair, it took some time before the public took much notice of the thin, hawk-nosed sleuth who shared rooms in Baker Street with a Dr Watson, who narrated his adventures. Holmes first appeared in *A Study in Scarlet*, a novella which was included in *Beeton's Christmas Annual* for 1887. The story and the character passed by virtually unnoticed. Even Holmes's second appearance in *The Sign of Four* (1890) failed to raise much interest amongst the reading public. But when the detective's adventures began appearing in the new publication *The Strand Magazine* in 1891, he became a rip-roaring success. Within a few months, the Sherlock Holmes short story was the main reason people purchased *The Strand* and the sales rocketed. Overnight it seemed that Sherlock Holmes and his creator Conan Doyle became household names.

It is difficult to imagine at this distance the effect Doyle's magical character had on the public at the time. There was no radio, television or movies and so reading was one of the main leisure activities, and the Holmes stories were lapped up by an eager populace. The detective achieved the status one today might equate with a pop star, a world-class footballer, a famous film star – or Harry Potter!

But Doyle soon tired of his character. He found the chore of having to create a baffling mystery for Holmes to solve every month too demanding, and so he killed him off at the Reichenbach Falls in the story *The Final Problem* (1893). There was a public outcry. It is said that men wore black armbands in the City as a mark of mourning, and Doyle received many abusive letters from his readers. One woman wrote calling the author a 'brute' for killing Holmes.

It is well known that some years later Doyle brought Holmes back to solve the mystery of *The Hound of the Baskervilles* (1902), claiming at the time that Holmes had not returned to life but that this was an investigation from an earlier period in his career. However, pressure from publishers and financial inducements eventually led Doyle to relent and he brought the detective back permanently in the story *The Empty House* (1904), explaining that Holmes had escaped death at the Reichenbach Falls and had been travelling for some years before returning to London, to Baker Street, to Dr Watson and to solving crime once more. It was a less than credible explanation, but neither publishers nor the readers cared. The thing that mattered was the return of the Great Detective. Doyle's Holmes stories appeared sporadically and, it has to be said, with lessening effect and quality, until 1927, a few years before the author's death in 1930.

However, before the end of the nineteenth century, there were already parodies, plays and even music hall songs about the deer-stalkered one. And by the time Doyle died, there had been many films featuring Holmes's detective exploits. He had not only become a national institution but an international one as well. The silhouette of the sharp-featured fellow in a deerstalker cap smoking a curly pipe became recognised around the world. For the greater part of the twentieth century, the cinema, radio and later television carried the Sherlockian torch forward. Most of these productions were based on Doyle's original tales but in particular the radio series featuring Basil Rathbone (and Nigel Bruce as Dr Watson) in the 1940s included many new plots. When they ran out of Doyle's stories, other writers were employed to come up with fresh tales 'in the style of'. This approach was also reflected in Rathbone and Bruce's famous film series for Universal, which ran concurrently with the radio shows. Gradually, the detective began to have a career independent of Arthur Conan Doyle's stories.

In the early 1950s, Doyle's son Adrian collaborated with the crime writer John Dickson Carr to create an enchanting set of new stories, *The Exploits of Sherlock Holmes*, which really captured the flavour, mood and piquancy of the originals. However, it has to be said that it was not until the mid-1970s that the Holmes pastiche bandwagon started rolling in a considerable way. This was down to one book: *The Seven-Per-Cent Solution* (1976) by Nicholas Meyer. This novel attempted to explain the real relationship between Holmes and Professor Moriarty and why Holmes disappeared from London for some time after his encounter with the Moriarty at the Reichenbach Falls. For some reason the book hit a nerve with the reading public at the time, became a worldwide bestseller, and was made into a Hollywood movie. Suddenly, Sherlock Holmes was in vogue once more.

In essence the novel *The Seven-Per-Cent Solution* opened the floodgates. There was interest in Holmes again as a literary character and in 1980, when Doyle's work came out of copyright, others – many others in fact – attempted to emulate Meyer's success. Since the publication of *The Seven Percent Solution*, there has been a steady stream – no, let's be honest, there has been a deluge of pastiches featuring Sherlock Holmes, Dr Watson and indeed various of the satellites of his Baker Street world such as Mrs Hudson, Lestrade, Moriarty and even the Baker Street Irregulars, the little street arabs who occasionally helped the sleuth in his investigations. Even I am guilty of penning five Holmes novels and two one-man plays, *Sherlock Holmes – The Last Act* and *The Death and Life of Sherlock Holmes*. (Two of my novels: *The Tangled Skein* & *Sherlock Holmes and The Hentzau Affair* are currently available in Wordworth's Mystery & The Supernatural series). It would seem that the appetite for Holmes is insatiable. Arthur Conan Doyle wrote only 56 short stories and four novels featuring the character; but now there are thousands of his exploits penned by numerous hands from all continents of the world. Harry Potter eat your heart out.

It is impossible to explain fully why this character has such a mesmeric hold on the public. There are even statues erected to him in London, Edinburgh and Japan. There are many other brilliant detectives in fiction who, while having a certain popularity, come nowhere near to accruing the fanatical following that Sherlock Holmes generates. Why is this? Let us consider the elements which make up a Holmes story. There are the mysteries, of course: the conundrums which baffle not only Watson but the reader, and are clearly explained at the end when Holmes demonstrates his detective brilliance. Then there is the wonderful Victorian period with its pea-souper fogs, hansom cabs and gas-lit cobbled streets. This period is of course fascinating to the modern reader. Victorian London now seems another world with almost fairytale resonances, but it must be remembered that when these stories were first written this was the contemporary scene. The settings, the characters and the everyday details would be as familiar to Doyle's original readers as motorways, iPods and computers would be to us today. That is one reason why the period detail seems so natural and presents itself in an unobtrusive fashion in the original stories, unlike many modern writers who, when setting their mysteries in the past, tend to burden their writing with period detail they have unearthed in their research.

Another attraction of the Holmes stories is the wonderful set of bizarre and remarkable characters who people their pages, such as the blackmailer Charles Augustus Milverton, the worst man in London; the vengeful one-legged murderer, Jonathan Small; the avaricious red-headed pawnbroker, Jabez Wilson; and the strange creeping Professor Presbury, to name but a few. Then there is the friendship between Holmes and Watson. Here Doyle carries out a wonderful balancing act of presenting this relationship as both reserved, in keeping with the Victorian modes of conduct, and yet emotional. We weep with Watson when he believes that he has lost his friend – 'the best and wisest man I have ever known' – at the Reichenbach Falls; and we are touched by Holmes's sudden and unexpected display of emotion towards Watson in 'The Three Garridebs': 'For God's sake, say you're not hurt, Watson. For God's sake say you are not hurt.' Holmes and Watson are not only one of the great partnerships in literature, but one of the great friendships also.

All these aspects combine to make the Holmes stories magical and somehow enable them to speak to readers of many nations. But there is something more, something else that, in truth, beggars description. Something, I suspect, that even Conan Doyle could not explain. When reading the stories, we feel it, we comprehend it, but we cannot describe it. It is the X factor, an intangible ingredient, which appeals to both the mind and the heart but defies recognition. I, for one, do not want to find out what it is. When the mysterious is explained, the magic dissolves. Holmes makes a similar observation to Watson when he explains one of his deductions in *A Study in Scarlet*:

> You know a conjuror gets no credit when once he has explained his trick; and if I show you too much of my method of working, you will come to the conclusion that I am a very ordinary individual after all.

So let us just accept that these stories are unique, as are the characters of Sherlock Holmes and Dr John H. Watson, and be content that they still fascinate and entertain. And here in *The Game's Afoot* we have a new batch of twenty adventures to do just that: to fascinate and entertain you. These stories, collected together for the first time, have been penned by authors who not only are skilled storytellers but also have great knowledge and understanding of the Holmes canon and so can replicate in the best possible way the mood, tone and fidelity of the original tales. (Brief biographies of the contributors to this collection can be found at the back of the book.)

Indeed, apart from a few exceptions, entertaining divertissements to add a little variety along the way, the majority of the stories in this collection aim to provide the reader with a traditional Sherlock Holmes story containing all the elements we have already referred to, including that mysterious X factor. That does not mean that they are slavish copies of Doyle with no spark of their own or that there will be no surprises for the reader along the way; it means that there is no attempt to introduce elements into the stories that are at odds with the original conception. There are no instances where Watson reveals himself to be Moriarty after all, or that Mycroft is a woman or that Holmes is in fact an alien. Neither is there a parade of other literary figures such as Dorian Gray, Raffles or Count Dracula calling on Holmes for assistance. In other words, there is little in these tales that Arthur Conan Doyle would not have penned himself.

I like to think of these stories as new vintage Holmes. I hope you agree.

So settle down, allow your mind to travel back to the London of very long ago, to those foggy, gas-lit streets with the sound of the lonely cab clip-clopping through the gloom, and get ready to join Sherlock Holmes and Dr Watson investigating another baffling mystery because, my friend, once more, the game's afoot.

DAVID STUART DAVIES

THE AUTHORS

MATTHEW BOOTH

Matthew Booth is the author of *Sherlock Holmes and The Giant's Hand* (Breese Books, 2004), and is a regular scriptwriter for the American radio network, Imagination Theatre, contributing particularly to their series, *The Further Adventures of Sherlock Holmes*. Matthew is also the creator of Anthony Rathe, a former barrister and sleuth, who features in a series of radio plays also produced by Imagination Theatre. Along with David Stuart Davies, Matthew is co-founder and co-performer of The Mystery Men, a literary performance group, whose informative and entertaining dramatic presentations on crime and popular fiction regularly tour literary festivals across the country. He is currently working on a contemporary crime novel called *Ties That Bind*, featuring Manchester-based private detective John Dakin.

DAVID STUART DAVIES

David Stuart Davies is the general editor of the Wordsworth Mystery and Supernatural Series and the author of five Holmes pastiches, two of which, *The Tangled Skein* and *Sherlock Holmes and the Hentzau Affair*, are available in this series. He has also written widely about the films of the famous detective. His survey of the detective's screen career *Starring Sherlock Holmes* was published by Titan in 2007. D.S.D. edited the crime fiction magazine *Sherlock* for ten years. He is a member of the national committee of the Crime Writers' Association and edits their monthly publication, *Red Herrings*. His play *Sherlock Holmes – The Last Act* has been touring since 1999 and was joined in the spring of 2008 by his revolutionary new play *The Death and Life of Sherlock Holmes*, which examines the nature of this famous literary character and premièred at the Yvonne Arnaud Theatre in Guildford. D.S.D. has his own detective character, Johnny Hawke, who operates in London during World War II. He has featured in three novels so far; the latest, *Without Conscience*, was published in the spring of 2008.

www.davidstuartdavies.com

M. J. ELLIOTT

M. J. Elliott is a member of the Crime Writers' Association. His Holmesian fiction has appeared in the UK in *Sherlock* magazine and in Canada in the collections *Curious Incidents 2* and *Gaslight Grimoires*. His radio scriptwriting credits include episodes of *The Classic Adventures of Sherlock Holmes* and *The Further Adventures of Sherlock Holmes*.

www.myspace.com/matthewjelliott

JOHN HALL

John Hall is well known in the Sherlockian world as an astute scholar of the genre. He has a regular column in the journal of the Sherlock Holmes Society of London. He has also written several Holmes novels including *Sherlock Holmes and the Telephone Murder Mystery*, *The Travels of Sherlock Holmes* and *Sherlock Holmes and the Disgraced Inspector*. John is a member of The International Pipe Smokers' Hall of Fame.

JOHN HOWARD

John Howard was born in London in 1961. His short fiction, solo and in collaboration, has appeared in the anthologies *Beneath the Ground* and *Strange Tales*; as well as the collection *Masques & Citadels* (with Mark Valentine). John has published many articles and reviews in the science fiction and horror fields, especially on the work of classic authors such as Fritz Leiber, Arthur Machen, August Derleth, M. R. James, and the writers of the pulp era.

www.waldeneast.com.

RAFE McGREGOR

Rafe McGregor was born in 1973 and worked in law enforcement for eleven years before deciding he wanted to write for a living. He lives with his wife in a village near York. Since the end of 2005 he has had thirty short stories and feature articles published in magazines, journals, or online. Credits include the *London Magazine*, *Military Illustrated*, *The Dalesman*, and two crime fiction novellas. He is a member of the Sherlock Holmes Society of London and The Musgraves, reviews for Tangled Web UK, and edits *Cobwebby Bottles*, an online Sherlockian newsletter.

www.rafemcgregor.co.uk

CHISTOPHER SEQUEIRA

Christopher Sequueira is a Australian writer who works predominantly in the speculative fiction realm, especially in the horror, science fiction and mystery genres. His published work includes poetry, short fiction and comic-book scripts (including some *Justice League* stories for DC Comics). Sequeira is a long-time member of the Sherlockian society, The Sydney Passengers, and he has played both Holmes and Professor Moriarty for that group in various dramatic re-enactments including Moriarty's plunge to his death in battle with Holmes at Reichenbach Falls, which was shown on national TV in Australia. Sequeira has also contributed many essays and articles on Holmesian matters to the journal of the Sydney Passengers, *Passengers' Log*. One of these, 'No Stranger to the Knife: Sherlock Holmes vs Jack the Ripper', was praised by eminent Sherlock Holmes scholar Leslie S. Klinger as 'a brilliant paper' in his *Return of Sherlock Holmes*. Sequeira, his wife and two children live in Sydney.

DENIS O. SMITH

A long-time enthusiast and scholar of the Sherlock Holmes stories, Denis Smith has written numerous Sherlockian pastiches, the first of which was *The Adventure of the Purple Hand*, published in 1982, and the most recent *The Adventure of the Brown Box*, which is included in this collection. These stories have appeared in various places, in magazines and anthologies, some under his own imprint of Diogenes Publications, and some in collections published by Calabash Press under the general title, *The Chronicles of Sherlock Holmes*. Born in Sheffield, Yorkshire, in 1948, of Anglo-Irish ancestry, Denis Smith has lived for many years in Norfolk, where he continues to write. Among his many interests are the history of London, Victorian and Edwardian railways and old maps, all of which contribute to the verisimilitude of his recreation of the world of Sherlock Holmes.

ALAN STOCKWELL

Alan Stockwell is a Yorkshireman who lives in Kent. Now retired, for over forty years he was a professional puppeteer travelling extensively throughout Britain and overseas. In 2000 he was awarded the M.B.E. for services to education in the north-east of England. He is the author of two books on puppet-making and is currently working on another about constructing puppets from matchboxes. *The Singular Adventures of Mr Sherlock Holmes* is his first work of fiction. Further information about the book can be found at www.mrsherlockholmes.co.uk. His current project is *Mr Dickens and Master Betty* in which the not-yet-famous author meets the 18th-century infant prodigy.

JUNE THOMSON

June Thomson, a former teacher, has written over twenty crime novels, many featuring her own detective, Inspector Jack Finch. June has not only published four collections of Holmes pastiches, *The Secret Notebooks of Sherlock Holmes*, *The Secret Chronicles of Sherlock Holmes*, *The Secret Files of Sherlock Holmes* and *The Secret Documents of Sherlock Holmes*, but she has also penned a biographical volume about the famous detective and his friend, *Holmes and Watson: A Study in Friendship*.

MARK VALENTINE

Mark Valentine is the author of two volumes of mystery stories featuring his aesthetical occult detective The Connoisseur, *In Violet Veils* (1999) and *Masques and Citadels* (2003), both from Tartarus Press. He also edits *Wormwood*, a paperback journal devoted to the literature of the fantastic. His biography of the Welsh mystic and supernatural fiction writer Arthur Machen was published by Seren in 1995.

THE GAME'S AFOOT

The Adventure of the Richmond Horror

DENIS O. SMITH

Part One: *A night at Hill House*

In publishing this series of memoirs, my constant aim, however imperfectly realised, has been to illustrate the remarkable mental qualities of my friend, Mhr Sherlock Holmes. In most of the cases he took up, his involvement was decisive: without it, it is likely that the problems would have remained unsolved, and the truth forever unknown. In a few cases, however, the part he played was less pronounced, and it is possible that the truth would eventually have come to light without his intervention. In the main I have passed over these cases when selecting those which were to be published. Yet among this group are some in which the facts of the matter are in themselves of sufficient interest to warrant publication, despite offering my friend few opportunities for the exercise of those gifts of observation and deduction which he possessed in so high a degree. Especially memorable among cases of this kind were the affair of the Purple Hand, and the Boldero Mystery. It is the latter case I now propose to recount. Regular readers of the Surrey County Observer will need little reminding of what that newspaper termed 'The Richmond Horror'. But the press accounts of the time were all very brief, and concentrated solely on the dramatic conclusion of the matter, to the exclusion of what had gone before; so that even those who are familiar with the case are unlikely to be aware of what lay behind those shocking events.

Our introduction to the matter came on a pleasant afternoon in the early spring of '84. Sherlock Holmes had received a letter from Farrow and Redfearn of Lincoln's Inn, the well-known firm of solicitors. He glanced over it, tossed it across to me and returned to the papers he had been studying before the letter's arrival had distracted him. I read the following:

> SIR, We beg to advise you as follows: that our client, Mr David Boldero, is desirous of learning the whereabouts of his elder

brother, Mr Simon Boldero; that the whereabouts of the latter having been unknown for some three months, and the circumstances being unusual, we have recommended that our client consult you, which he proposes to do at four o'clock this afternoon, when he will be able to apprise you of the details of the matter.

We remain, Sir, your obedient servants,

FARROW AND REDFEARN

'They have put a number of choice cases my way in the past,' remarked Holmes as I finished reading. 'Let us hope that it is not too troublesome a matter. I am somewhat preoccupied at present with this business of Archduke Dmitri's diamonds.'

'It does not sound a very desperate affair,' I remarked, aware of my friend's oft-stated rule that one case should not be allowed to intrude upon another. This was not from any fear that his mental capacities might be over-stretched, for, in truth, there was little doubt that, like a chess master giving an exhibition, he might successfully have handled half a dozen separate cases at once had he so wished. It was, rather, that his neat and logical mind preferred above all things an orderly, concentrated mode of thought. Yet it was also true of him that he rarely declined a case which had succeeded in capturing his interest, so that, despite his preference, this, of all his personal rules of work, was the one he most frequently set aside. As I waited for Holmes's client to arrive, I speculated idly as to the nature of his case, and wondered if it would provide any of those touches of the *outré* which so delighted my friend's intellect. The dry communication he had received from the solicitor did not appear to presage a case of any very great interest, I judged. But in this opinion, as it turned out, I was quite mistaken.

Mr David Boldero arrived on the dot of four. He was a tall, broad-shouldered and strongly-built young man, of about seven-and-twenty, with wavy black hair and a determined set to his strong, clean-shaven features.

'I see you are smokers,' said he, observing the wreaths of blue smoke which spiralled in the air above my companion's head. 'I will venture to fill my own pipe, then, if I may.'

'By all means,' responded Holmes, waving our visitor to a chair. 'Pray make yourself comfortable and let us know how we can help you. It is always a pleasure,' he added after a moment, 'to greet a member of the diplomatic corps, newly returned from overseas.'

Boldero looked up in surprise as he lit his pipe. 'Now, how on earth do you know that?' said he. 'I can hardly suppose that my return to England warranted a paragraph in the morning papers!'

'Your suit, Mr Boldero, whilst of excellent quality, is of a distinctively continental cut. The top button is a touch higher than English tailors are wont to place it. You have evidently purchased the suit abroad. The same, I might add, applies to your boots. Nor has your period abroad been merely a brief excursion, for your tobacco, too, is very characteristic of continental mixtures. Most English travellers, in my experience, take with them sufficient home-produced tobacco to see out their journey. You have clearly been abroad long enough to acquire a taste for the native variety. It is not Dutch and it is not French, but could possibly be Danish. You do not have the cut of a man of commerce, and the pallor of your skin precludes any prolonged exposure to the Mediterranean sun. I am therefore inclined to place you as an attaché at one of our embassies in the north of Europe.'

'Well I never!' cried our visitor, leaning back in his chair.

'To be precise,' said Holmes, 'you have been at the British embassy in Stockholm for over two years.'

Boldero's mouth fell open in astonishment.

'You have a small medallion on your watch-chain,' explained Holmes, 'which I observed as you leaned back in your chair. It is a decoration – the Order of St Margaret, I believe – which is conferred by the Court of Scandinavia on all foreign diplomats who have served there for a period of at least two years.'

'That is amazing!' cried Boldero.

'On the contrary, it is perfectly elementary,' said Holmes. 'Now, if we might hear the details of your problem? I know only that you wish to discover the whereabouts of your brother.'

'He has disappeared without trace, in the most mysterious circumstances,' returned our visitor, his features assuming a grave look. 'But there is more to the matter than that, Mr Holmes. Last night, so I believe, an attempt was made upon my life.'

'How very interesting! Pray, let us have the details!'

'My brother and I have seen little of each other in recent years. Circumstances have obliged each of us to pursue his own individual course through life. We were left very poorly off when our father died. There is great wealth elsewhere in the Boldero family, but little of it came our way. I was fortunate enough to secure a post in the diplomatic service some four years ago, but it has meant that I have spent much of that time abroad, after my posting to Stockholm. My brother, meanwhile, has been pursuing a career with a firm of solicitors. I last saw him three months ago, in January, on the occasion of my engagement. He attended the little celebration we had, and seemed at that time to be in excellent spirits.'

'He had no pressing financial concerns?'

'He has never been very well off, if that is what you mean. Neither of us has. But it did not appear to be causing him any particular anxiety. On the contrary, he seemed more cheery than I had seen him before.'

'His health?'

'First-rate.'

'He is not married?'

Our visitor shook his head. 'He lives alone in a little house just off Camberwell High Street. It was to there I went to look him up, when I returned to England last week. We have never corresponded with any great regularity, but during the last three months, he has not replied to any of my letters, and I wished to know why. If he was in difficulty of some kind, I wished to help him if I could. I have a key to the front door of his house, so I was able to let myself in. Inside, the apartment resembled the Marie Celeste: everything was in perfect order, the table in the dining-room neatly laid for a meal, but of my brother there was no sign. The only circumstance which gave indication that Simon had not simply stepped out of the house five minutes before my arrival was the large number of letters lying in a disordered heap upon the door-mat. All the letters I had sent in the previous three months were there, together with dozens of others. I quickly sifted through them, and established that Simon had not been in the house since the third week in January.'

'Your brother kept no domestic staff?'

'He lived very simply. A local woman came in twice a day to attend to cleaning and similar duties.'

'Did she have her own key?'

'No. My brother always admitted her himself in the morning before he left for town, and when she had finished her work she would lock the door with a spare key which she posted through the letter-box.'

'No doubt you have interviewed her?'

'I have tried to, but without success. It appears she left the area some time in February, and no-one there could tell me her present address. They did tell me, however, that she had been more annoyed than puzzled by my brother's disappearance. She presumed that he had simply gone away on business and forgotten to inform her of the fact, and he had left owing her a little money, according to the local sources.'

'You say you found the table laid for a meal,' interrupted Holmes. 'Could you tell, from the disposition of the cutlery and so on, what sort of meal this was likely to be?'

'I am afraid I did not notice,' returned Boldero, his features expressing surprise at the question.

'That is a pity,' remarked Holmes, shaking his head.

'I cannot see that the point is of any significance.'

'Nevertheless, it is. It might, for instance, have indicated whether your brother's housekeeper had expected him to return that day, or to stay away for the night. Were you able to establish more precisely the date of his disappearance?'

Boldero nodded. 'In his study was a copy of the Daily Telegraph, dated Thursday, January the seventeenth, which had clearly been read; and on his desk was a note he had written to remind himself to do certain jobs on Friday, January the eighteenth. Simon often left himself such aides-mémoire. When he had done the jobs in question, he would cross off the items on the list. None of the items on the note I found had been crossed off. I take it, then, that he was last in the house on the seventeenth.'

'Excellent!' cried Holmes. 'Your observation is commendable! Were everyone so thorough in their attention to detail, I should soon find myself without work!'

'I have the note here,' said Boldero, producing a folded sheet of paper from his pocket. He passed it across to Holmes, who studied it for a few moments, then handed it to me. The items listed were all of a domestic nature, and unexceptional: 'Baker – see again. Pay wine-merchant – inquire about sherry. Settle butcher's bill for the month.'

'I have spoken to all the people mentioned in the note,' Boldero continued. 'None of them could recall seeing Simon on the day in question, which confirms what I thought.'

'That may be interesting,' remarked Holmes in a thoughtful voice.

'I should hardly have called it "interesting",' responded Boldero in a tone of surprise; 'except that it indicates that my brother had the same mundane concerns as everyone else at the time of his disappearance.'

'That was not my meaning,' said Holmes. 'Pray continue. You have made inquiries, I take it, at your brother's professional chambers?'

'Indeed. There I learned that he had informed his colleagues he would be taking two weeks' leave of absence from the fourteenth of January. He had not said why he required this, but they understood that he was engaged upon some legal research. They could shed no light whatsoever on his prolonged disappearance, and had all the time been expecting to hear from him with an explanation. I subsequently made thorough inquiries at the police-station and at all the hospitals, in case Simon had met with an accident, but learned nothing. It appeared that my brother had simply disappeared off the face of the earth. Then Beatrice – that is to say, Miss Underwood, my fiancée – suggested that I try my cousin Silas, to see if he had any information on the matter. I thought it unlikely, as Silas is practically a hermit, going out little, and receiving visitors even less, and I was not aware that my brother had had anything to do with him for years; but in the absence of any other direction for my inquiries, I agreed to take myself off to Hill House, at Richmond-upon-Thames, which is where Silas lives.

'I perhaps ought to tell you a little about Cousin Silas, and about the family in general, so you will understand the situation. You may have heard of my great-grandfather, Samuel Boldero. He was one of the last of the great eighteenth-century merchants, and made a fortune in trade. Indeed, he was reputed at the time to be the second wealthiest commoner in the country. At his death, all his wealth passed equally to his two surviving sons, Daniel and Jonathan. Each of these two had, in turn, one son, Enoch and Silas, respectively. Enoch Boldero was my father.

'Unfortunately, my father and grandfather quarrelled and became estranged, and when my grandfather died, when I was an infant, it was found that he had virtually cut my father from his will altogether, and had left almost all he possessed to his nephew – his late brother's only son, and thus my father's cousin – Silas.

'Cousin Silas, as you will therefore appreciate, is very wealthy, having inherited the entire Boldero fortune, half from his own father, and half from his uncle, my grandfather. My brother and I hoped, without being at all avaricious, that a little, at least, of this enormous wealth might perhaps find its way to us, especially after my father's sadly premature death, which left us in some difficulty. By the time we had established my mother and my sister, Rachel, in a small house at Tunbridge Wells, near to my mother's relations, we were left with practically nothing. Simon was endeavouring to pursue a career in Law, and was attached to Nethercott and Cropley, a firm of solicitors in Holborn, but he was finding his lack of money a distinct handicap. Recalling that Silas had himself followed a similar career for a time in his younger years, Simon thought that his cousin might feel some sympathy for his position. He therefore appealed to Cousin Silas's generosity. Unfortunately, Silas does not have any. Every excuse one could conceive was brought in to explain why he was unable to help. The best he felt able to offer my brother was a small, inadequate loan, offered for an inadequate period of time, and at such an extortionate rate of interest that one could easily arrange a more favourable loan any day of the week in the City. Needless to say, Simon did not take up the offer. That was about four years ago, since which time – so far as I am aware – there has been no communication between them. I have myself seen Silas but once in that period. Last August I took Miss Underwood and her mother boating on the Thames, and knowing that our way would take us past Richmond, I proposed to Silas that we pay him a call. He received us into his house for an hour, but I cannot honestly say that he made us welcome. Miss Underwood formed a very poor impression of him, and the whole episode was an acute embarrassment to me. I had wanted her to meet Silas, as he is the senior member of the Boldero family; but my chief concern afterwards was whether, having seen what my relations were like, Miss Underwood would be permanently prejudiced against me.'

'Does your cousin have any family of his own?' Holmes interrupted.

Boldero shook his head. 'He never married,' he replied. 'He has always led a completely solitary life, and for the last twenty years has lived in almost total seclusion. His last appearance in public of which I am aware was about fifteen years ago, when he read his monograph on "The Dragon Lizards of China" to the Society for Snakes and Reptiles – or whatever the body is called. This society was formerly his chief interest in life, but about ten years ago, so I understand, there was a disagreement between Silas and the other members. He could not get his way over some matter, and resigned.'

'As I understand your account, then,' said Holmes, 'you and your brother are Silas's only kin, and will inherit whatever he has to leave when he dies.'

'That is correct, but our inheritance is by no means assured. Cousin Silas is quite likely to will all his money away, if not to the Society for Snakes and Reptiles, then to some similar body. I have certainly never founded my plans on any bounty I might receive from that direction!'

'From what you have told me, you are probably wise not to do so. Pray continue with your narrative.'

'I went down to Richmond yesterday afternoon, having notified Silas that I was coming for the night. Hill House is a strange, rambling old place, near the top of Richmond Hill. It is a dark and unattractive building, and has been made more so by the various additions and extensions which have been made to it over the years. It stands in its own very large grounds, which are entirely surrounded by a massive eight-foot-high brick wall. From the stout wooden gate, a gravel path runs dead straight for thirty yards or so to the front porch of the house, and this path is entirely enclosed, both above and at the sides, by a curious glass structure, something like a narrow, elongated greenhouse. This is not, as you might suppose, to protect visitors from the weather, but, rather, to prevent the denizens of Silas's garden from escaping; for his grounds are alive with all sorts of odd and unattractive creatures he has imported from the tropics: lizards, snakes, anteaters, and other things even less appealing. I have used the word "garden", but that is perhaps misleading. The grounds of Hill House are a complete wilderness, and must be the nearest thing to a jungle outside of the tropics. I shouldn't think that they have benefited from any human attention in forty years. I was taken there once as a small boy, by my father, and I can still recall the horrified fascination with which I regarded that tangle of luxuriant weeds and brambles, and the slimy creatures that slithered and crept about in the darkness beneath them. Now the place is even more overgrown than it was in those days, and the glass veranda over the path is covered with green mould and slime, so that practically nothing can be discerned through its murky panes.

'The daylight was beginning to fade as I arrived at the gate. I pushed it open, and was surprised to see a shabbily-dressed woman coming along the path, under the gloomy and shadowed glass tunnel. She was short and frail-looking, her garments were frayed and dirty, and she had a black shawl pulled tightly round her shoulders. Her head was down, and she did not see me until almost upon me. When she did, she started as if terrified, and the eyes she turned up to me had a disturbing look of fear in them. We passed in silence, but as we did so she suddenly shot out an arm from beneath her shawl, and plucked the sleeve of my coat. Startled, I stopped and turned to her.

' "Yes?" said I.

' "Don't go through that door," said she after a moment, in a low, cracked voice, nodding her head very slightly in the direction of the house.

' "Why, whatever do you mean?" I asked in surprise.

'For a moment she hesitated, then, mumbling something in which I caught only the word "regret", she pushed past me and hurried on to the gate. It was an unpleasant and unsettling incident, but I concluded that the poor woman was half-witted, and dismissed it from my mind.

'As I approached the front door of the house, I saw that it was slightly ajar. The hall within was in deep shadow, with no sign of anyone there. I knocked, and, pushing the door further open, stepped into the hall, calling out a greeting as I did so.

'The silent house returned no answer, but at that moment the front door behind me creaked slightly on its hinges. I turned, to find Cousin Silas in the act of closing it. He had evidently been standing in the shadows behind the door as I entered. Aware of his eccentric ways, I made no comment. I don't know if you are familiar with William Blake's somewhat whimsical painting of "the flea", but it has always seemed to me that anyone seeing Cousin Silas might well imagine that he had been the model for the picture. There is something shifty, stooping and watchful in his manner which could not be described as attractive. His facial expression habitually hovers somewhere between a sneer and a calculating smile, without quite being either; for in truth it appears scarcely like a human expression at all, resembling more that unpleasant reptilian grin you see on the faces of those creatures in whose company Silas has spent so much of his time. Were he not so bent and stooping, it may be that he would be quite tall. He certainly has broad shoulders and a powerful chest, and there must have been a time, in his youth, when his appearance was not unattractive. Now, however, both his appearance and his manner border upon the repulsive, and as I watched him close the front door I could well understand the effect he had had upon my fiancée. I waited, and he advanced towards me in his queer shuffling way, never quite lifting his feet fully from the ground. Then he gripped my arm, and thrust his face close to my own.

' "Well, my boy," said he, in a thin, reedy voice, "I don't have many visitors here. It's put me out a little, if I am to speak frankly, but I think you'll find I'm ready for you."

' "It is good of you to put me up at such short notice," I responded, and made to move away, but he held me back.

' "That person you met on the path is my charwoman," said he in a low voice, breathing in my face. "She's quite mad, you know. It's difficult to get servants out here."

' "Is it?" I asked in surprise.

' "Yes, it is," said he sharply. "She said something to you, I believe, as you passed. What was it, eh?"

' "Nothing intelligible."

' "But you replied to her. I saw you speak."

' "I tell you, I couldn't understand what she was talking about."

' "Not at all?" persisted Silas in a tone of disbelief.

' "I think she wondered if I had come to the right address."

' "Bah!" said he, stamping his foot on the floor in anger. "Interfering nuisance! I'll teach her to meddle in my affairs – you see if I don't! Still, that is something for me to consider later."

' "I take it you received my letter," said I, endeavouring to change the subject.

'For a long moment he did not reply, his hooded eyes flickering from side to side, as if he were considering whether he could deny having received the letter, and if he would gain anything thereby.

' "What if I did?" said he at length, in an unpleasant, argumentative tone.

' "I am anxious to discover Simon's whereabouts."

' "What is that to me, eh?"

' "I thought – as I mentioned in my letter – that he had perhaps written to you, or even visited you, before his disappearance."

' "Why should he do that?" retorted Silas quickly, in a suspicious tone.

' "I cannot imagine. But I can find no trace of him elsewhere."

' "Well, he didn't. I haven't seen him for years! Still," he continued in an unpleasantly unctuous tone, evidently fearing he had spoken too sharply, "we can consider the matter over dinner."

'He led me through the darkened house to the dining-room, where two places were laid for dinner. A single small candle in the centre of the table provided the only illumination. Silas must have sensed the despondency with which I viewed this dismal scene, for he chuckled.

' "No sense in wasting money on light we don't need," said he, laughing unpleasantly.

'There followed what I can only describe as the most wretched meal of my life, the central features of which were a miserable-looking joint of tough and highly-salted bacon, and a bottle of wine which tasted like vinegar, of which Silas informed me with great self-satisfaction he had been fortunate enough to purchase a whole case at "a quite remarkably low price". It quickly became clear that I should learn nothing from him concerning my brother, and I began to regret that I had ever gone to Hill House at all. His only suggestion was that Simon might have gone to Italy, but when I inquired why he should think so, he replied only that "people do go there sometimes, you know" and laughed unpleasantly at this feeble and inappropriate jest. As soon as the meal was ended, therefore, I began yawning ostentatiously. Silas reacted with alacrity to this cue, and offered to show me to my room. Taking the candle from the table, he led the way up the dirty, uncarpeted staircase and along a dusty, crooked corridor. Everywhere the smell of damp and rot rose from the bare floorboards. Presently he stopped and opened a door.

' "This is your room," said he, ushering me through the doorway.

'He lit the stump of a candle which stood on a small table beside the bed, and turned to go. As he was closing the door, however, he put his head back in.

' "There's water in the jug," said he, indicating a large, dirty-looking ewer which stood on a lopsided washstand at the side of the room. "If there's not enough, you'll find more through there," he added, nodding at a door in the shadows at the far side of the room.

'It was a dark and grim chamber in which to pass the night. Apart from the bed, table and washstand, the only furniture was a stained and rotten-looking chest of drawers. The stench of damp seemed even stronger in the bedroom than elsewhere in the house, and the wallpaper was hanging from the walls in sheets, yellowed and dirty, and dotted all over with the black marks of mould. I was glad to climb into bed and pull the covers over my head. For a while I lay awake, listening to the sounds of small creatures scurrying about beneath the floor, but at length I fell asleep. Before I did so, I vowed to myself that I would never spend another night in that wretched house.

'Some hours later, I awoke suddenly. A pounding headache seemed to split my head asunder, my throat was hot and parched, and I felt desperately thirsty. I struck a match and lit the candle, surprising a dozen large spiders on the wall above my head. Whether my thirst was the result of the salty meat I had eaten, or the foul wine, or something else, I had no idea. I knew only that I must have a drink of water. I climbed wearily from my bed, but found that, despite what Silas had told me, the jug was empty. Feeling a little annoyed at this, I took the candle across to the door he had indicated, and attempted to open it. I had presumed it would open inwards, as the other door did, but as I turned the doorknob it swung away from me, and, still half asleep, I stepped forward into the blackness beyond. Never in my life have such terror and confusion gripped my heart as at that moment. For in stepping from the rough wood of the bedroom floor, my bare foot had found nothing whatever, but had trodden on empty air. I think I must have cried out, but I cannot be certain, for my memory of that terrible moment is exceedingly confused. The step I had taken had created a forward momentum I could not stop, and in a split second I was plunging into the black void and had dropped the candle, which blew out almost at once. Scarcely conscious of my own actions, I somehow twisted round as I fell, stretching my arms out blindly and desperately. Abruptly, my right arm hit the door-frame, then the edge of the bedroom floor, which I gripped with all my might. I realise now that all this must have occupied the merest fraction of a second, but as I relive it now it draws out to great, horrific length.

'For a moment my fall was arrested, but it was only for the very briefest of moments, for the edge of the floor at the doorway was wet and slimy, and my fingers, which did not have a proper grip on anything, were slipping rapidly towards the edge. With a great effort I lunged upwards and forwards with my left hand, even as my right completely lost its grip. This time I was more successful. I had reached further into the room, past the slimy doorway, and my fingertips had found a narrow crack between two floorboards. I doubt it was a quarter of an inch wide, but it saved my life. Using this tiny finger-hold as a base, I managed to reach further with my right hand until that, too, had found a secure grip, and so, by slow degrees, I hauled myself to safety.

'For some time I lay on the floor of the bedroom, almost delirious, but presently I came to myself once more, and determined to see the nature of the dark pit into which I had so nearly plummeted. I crept carefully to the edge once more and peered over, but could make out nothing whatever in the darkness. As I crouched there, eyes straining, I became conscious of a foul, mephitic vapour which seemed to rise from the pit before me, smothering and choking me with its stench. I was turning my head away in disgust, when a slight noise from below made me stop. It was a soft noise, like the lapping of water, but with an odd and unpleasant heaviness about it. There followed a splashing sound, then what I can only describe as scratching noises, which were quite horrible to hear. For a moment, my heart seemed to stop beating, and the blood ran cold in my veins. There was something in the pit below me, something which was moving quietly about in the darkness.

'Scarcely daring to breathe, I drew back from the edge of that foul hole, dressed as quickly as I could in the darkness, and sat on the side of the bed to gather my thoughts. Then a slight noise set my jangled nerves on edge once more, and I quickly struck a match, but there was nothing to be seen save the dark open doorway, through which, I was convinced, Silas had intended that I should fall to my death. I could not rest while the door stood open like that, so, striking match after match to light my way, I leaned out into the void, managed to grip the panelling of the door, and pulled it shut.

'My supply of matches was by now almost exhausted. I had opened the curtains, but gained no more light, for the night was a dark one. Then it occurred to me that there might be a spare candle in the chest of drawers. I pulled each drawer out in turn, examining them by the light of the matches, but they were all quite empty. The top drawer was a very shallow one, and as I was pushing it back in, I could feel that there was something hampering it. I pulled it right out again and examined the recess behind it by the light of another match. It appeared there was some woollen article there. I reached in, freed it from the nail on which it was snagged, and pulled it out. To my utter amazement, I recognised it at once. It was a striped woollen muffler, belonging to my brother, Simon. I knew I could not be mistaken, for my sister, Rachel, had knitted it for him herself, and given it to him at Christmas. I had seen him wearing it in January, at the time of our engagement party. Clearly he had been at Hill House some time shortly after that, despite Silas's claim that he had not seen him for years, and had stayed in the very room in which I now stood.

'I was already extremely agitated and excited by my experiences, as you will imagine, but this latest discovery almost drove reason from my mind. I threw my few belongings into my bag, together with Simon's muffler, and crept from the house as quietly as I could, letting myself out of the front door. The first pale light of dawn was showing over the hill as I reached the road. Without pausing, or even considering what I was doing, I walked quickly down into Richmond and on to the railway station, caught an early train, and was back in town by seven o'clock. At nine I was at the door of Farrow and Redfearn's office, seeking their advice, and they, as you see, have sent me on to you.'

Sherlock Holmes had sat in silence, his eyes closed in concentration, throughout this strange narrative, and he remained so for several minutes longer.

'It is certainly a singular story that you tell,' said he at length, opening his eyes and reaching for his old clay pipe. 'It interests me greatly. Although one or two small points are not yet entirely clear to me, it seems undoubtedly a bad business.'

'I am convinced that Cousin Silas knows what has become of Simon,' cried Boldero. 'Otherwise, why should he lie about having seen him in January?'

'Why indeed?' said Holmes. 'You have not reported the matter to the police?'

'It was in my mind to do so as I walked through Richmond this morning, but there are difficulties.'

'The chief one being that you have no real evidence to substantiate your suspicions.'

'Precisely, Mr Holmes. I cannot prove that any of my story is true, not even, now that I have removed it, that Simon's muffler was ever at Hill House. Mr Farrow was of the opinion that the police would do nothing unless I could produce more telling evidence. He recommended that I seek your help at once.'

'I am honoured by his recommendation. What do you propose?'

'That you accompany me to Richmond, as my witness, and that we confront Silas with our suspicions. Beneath his shiftiness, he is mean-spirited and cowardly. I do not think he would dare lie so brazenly if you were there.'

Holmes did not reply at once, but sat for some time in silence, evidently considering the matter in all its aspects.

'I will certainly accompany you,' he responded at length; 'and Doctor Watson, too, if he will be so good. But it is necessary for us to prepare the ground a little before we confront your cousin, Mr Boldero. We must be armed with as much information as possible. I shall therefore spend the next twenty-four hours doing a little research into the matter. Be at the book-stall at Waterloo Station at three o'clock tomorrow afternoon, and we can travel down to Richmond together!'

*   *   *

'What a very odd affair!' I remarked when our visitor had left us.

'It is certainly somewhat recherché,' agreed Holmes. 'The curious arrangement of the door in the bedroom, which leads only to a bottomless pit, is quite unique in my experience. As a way of ridding oneself of unwanted guests it may have its merits, but it is hardly a feature which the builders of modern villas are likely to include in their brochures!'

'Can it all be true?' I wondered aloud. 'The black void into which he so nearly tumbled, the horrible noises he heard – they sound like the stuff of a disordered and terrifying nightmare!'

'Boldero himself is sufficiently convinced of their veracity to seek our advice on the matter,' responded my companion. 'We must see if we can bring a little light into the darkness tomorrow. You will accompany us?'

'I should certainly wish to,' I returned, 'if my presence would be of any use to you. The matter is so grotesque and puzzling that it seems to me quite beyond conjecture. The only hope of an explanation must be down there at Richmond, at Hill House.'

'And yet,' said Holmes after a moment, 'even there we may have difficulty in arriving at the truth. If – as appears to be the case – Silas Boldero has indeed murdered his cousin, Simon, and intended last night to take the brother's life also, we come up against the question of motive. What possible reason could Silas have for murdering his cousins in this way? He is, after all, the one with all the money. It would make more sense the other way round: if it had been Simon Boldero who had tried to murder Silas, in order to bring forward his inheritance a little.'

'Perhaps that is indeed what happened,' I suggested. 'David Boldero appears a pleasant and honest man, but we know nothing, really, of his brother, Simon. Perhaps Simon did try to murder Silas, and Silas killed him in self-defence. Then Silas, frightened, perhaps, that he would be accused of murder, hid the body, and decided to pretend that Simon had never been to see him at all.'

'It is possible,' conceded Holmes, 'but seems unlikely. You must remember that Silas had already made his plans to murder his cousin, David, last night – the highly salted meat, the jug with no water in it, the suggestion that more water could be found through the side-door – before David Boldero had expressed any suspicions at all. Why could he not simply deny having seen Simon, and leave it at that? He could not have known that David Boldero would find his brother's muffler, which is the only real evidence that Simon was ever at Hill House. Indeed, the muffler would probably not have been found at all had our client's rest not been disturbed so alarmingly. I sense, Watson, that we may be fishing in deeper waters than was at first apparent.'

Part Two: *A rainy afternoon*

When I descended to breakfast the following morning, I found that
Holmes had already gone out, without leaving any message. I took it
that he was pursuing his researches into the Boldero case, although
where he might begin such an investigation, I could not imagine.
Unable to make any sense of the matter, I endeavoured to dismiss it
from my mind; but the story of David Boldero's terrifying night at
Hill House had gripped my imagination, and returned unbidden to
my thoughts throughout the morning.

Just after one o'clock, a telegram arrived for me, which had been
sent from Richmond. I tore it open and read the following:

DELAYED. MEET RICHMOND STATION 3.45. S.H.

Evidently, Holmes's inquiries had taken him down to Richmond
already. Knowing my friend's amazing resources, I could not doubt
that he had made progress, and I looked forward eagerly to hearing
the results.

I met David Boldero at Waterloo Station as we had arranged, and
we travelled down to Richmond together. It wanted ten minutes to
the time Holmes had mentioned as our train pulled into the station,
but there was no sign of him there, so we waited by the main
entrance. It was a pleasant, sunny afternoon, with a light breeze
blowing. Fresh green leaves adorned the branches of the trees, and in
the air was the smell of spring.

After a few minutes, I observed a thin, disreputable-looking man
approaching slowly along the road. He was dressed in a tweed suit
with a bright red cravat round his neck, and carried a rolled-up
newspaper under his arm. Even from a distance I could see that he
was unshaven, and that his face was red and blotchy. I observed him
particularly because he was, so it seemed to me, keeping his own gaze
fixed steadily upon us.

'That man appears to want something of us,' remarked Boldero to
me as the stranger drew near. I was about to reply when the man
himself approached us and spoke.

'You are a little early, gentlemen,' came a clear and well-known
voice.

'Holmes!' I cried. 'I had no idea – '

'I judged it best to adopt this little disguise for my local researches,'
said he. 'I am sorry if I startled you, Watson. You were regarding

me so keenly as I approached, that I was convinced that you had recognised me. Now,' he continued in a brisker tone, 'let us be down to business. There is a hotel across the street where you can order a pot of tea while I bid adieu to Albert Taylor, footman out of position, and *bienvenu* once more to Sherlock Holmes, consulting detective!'

In ten minutes my friend had discarded his disguise and joined us in the parlour of the hotel, his appearance as neat and clean as ever.

'I have had enough indifferent tea already this afternoon,' said he with a shake of the head, as I made to pass him a cup. 'As Albert Taylor, I have made the acquaintance of Miss Mary Ingram, known locally as "Mad Mary", who is the woman Mr Boldero spoke to on his cousin's path, yesterday afternoon. I have consumed large quantities of tea with her, and, I believe, gained her confidence. She is a little unhinged, it is true, but not quite so much as is generally believed. She witnessed Simon Boldero's arrival at Hill House, one afternoon in January, but never saw him leave, although she was at the house early the following morning. She had been told by Silas to make a bed up for the visitor, but when she saw it the following day, it appeared not to have been slept in, and she assumed that Simon had simply decided against spending the night there.'

'But his muffler was in the bedroom,' said Boldero.

'Precisely,' said Holmes in a grave tone.

David Boldero put his head in his hands and groaned. Holmes reached out and put his hand on his shoulder.

'Have courage,' said he. 'I think we must accept now that your brother is dead, and that his death occurred at the hand of your cousin, Silas. It is our duty now to ensure that that unpleasant old man is brought to justice!'

'I shall wring the truth from him with my own hands!' cried Boldero in a suddenly impassioned voice, his eyes flashing with emotion.

'That may not be necessary,' responded Holmes calmly. 'There is now sufficient *prima facie* evidence, I believe, to lay the matter before the police. A slight snag is that Miss Ingram's somewhat eccentric manner is likely to mean that her testimony is given less credence by the authorities than it merits. Fortunately, my inquiries have brought to light one or two other points of interest.'

'I still wish to confront Silas myself,' said Boldero in a determined voice.

Holmes glanced at his watch. 'Come, then,' said he. 'Let us be off to Hill House. I can give you the details of my discoveries as we go.'

The breeze had freshened, and the clouds were piling up ominously as we left the hotel and made our way through the little town.

'There is a newsagent's shop on the way to Hill House,' said Holmes as we walked along, 'the window of which contains several interesting advertisements. Two of them, yellowing and faded, offer positions for hard-working servants in the establishment of Mr S. Boldero, one for a maid, the other for a male servant, duties unspecified. I inquired the details of the newsagent, representing myself as a footman seeking a post, and remarked that the advertisements appeared to have been in his window for some time. He acknowledged the truth of this observation.

' "Old Boldero's establishment is not such as appeals overmuch to the average domestic," said he, sucking on his pipe. "His advertisements have brought few enough replies, fewer still have ever taken up a position there, and none of them has ever stayed long enough to make it worth Boldero's while to remove the notices from my window. He's reduced now to relying on the services of 'Mad Mary', a local woman. She goes in to the house most days, but she won't stay there. She could tell you a thing or two about Hill House, I'd wager!"

'I took this as my cue, and inquired Mary's address, saying I should like to learn a little about Hill House before I applied for the position offered there. Thus it was that I came to make the acquaintance of that unusual lady, with the results I mentioned earlier. Here is the newsagent's,' he continued, as we approached a row of small shops.

We stopped by the window, and Holmes pointed out to us the advertisements he had mentioned.

'There is also this,' said he, directing our attention to a large piece of card towards the bottom of the window. The announcement on it ran as follows:

MISSING: THOMAS EVANS, some time footman to the Marquess of Glastonbury, butler to E. J. Archbould Esq. of Chelsea, and latterly butler to Mr S. Boldero of Hill House, Richmond Hill. Last seen on the morning of November 14th 1883, leaving his employment at Hill House. Will anyone having information as to the whereabouts of the said Thomas Evans please communicate with his sister, Miss Violet Evans, of Ferrier Street, Wandsworth.

'Who can say whether Mr Evans ever really left Hill House at all?' remarked Holmes in a thoughtful tone as I looked up from the notice. 'If Cousin Silas is the source of the information, I think we are justified in being sceptical of its accuracy.'

'The more we learn of it, the worse the matter becomes!' I cried.

Sherlock Holmes nodded his head gravely. 'The sooner Silas Boldero and the Old Bailey make acquaintance with each other, the better for all concerned!' said he. 'Come, let us make haste to Hill House!'

'But we still cannot say,' remarked David Boldero in a puzzled voice, as we walked briskly up the hill, 'why Silas should wish to take Simon's life, and attempt to take my own; nor, for that matter, why Simon went to visit him in the first place.'

'I am now able to shed a little light on those questions,' responded Holmes. 'You recall the aide-mémoire that your brother had written for himself, and which you showed us yesterday?'

'What of it?'

'One of the items on his list was "Baker – see again", in which the word "Baker" was begun with a capital letter. This might, of course, have been of no importance: the word "Baker" was the first word on the list, and there might have been no more significance to its capitalisation than that; but it did at least make it possible that the "Baker" referred to was not the man who supplied your brother's bread, but someone bearing the surname "Baker". Who this man might be, however – if he existed at all – there was no way of telling.'

'It all sounds a little unlikely to me,' remarked Boldero in a doubt-ful voice.

'No doubt; but you must remember that "the unlikely" falls, by its very definition, within the bounds of the possible.'

'But even if your supposition was correct, it seems a very trifling matter.'

'My work is built upon the observation of trifles,' said Holmes. 'Now, I had pondered last night what might have been your brother's purpose in calling upon your cousin, an unfriendly and miserly man, whom he had no reason to regard with affection, and every reason to detest. The only significant connection between the two men was their shared ancestry. Perhaps, then, I speculated, it was some family matter that had brought Simon down here to Richmond. This suggested to me your father and grandfather, which in turn suggested to me your grandfather's will, and I decided to see this document for myself. I therefore took myself down this morning to the Registry of Wills, and examined the copy of your grandfather's will which is deposited there.'

'I have seen it myself,' Boldero interrupted. 'It is very straight-forward. Save that it gives away my family's inheritance to our odious cousin, it is of little interest.'

'That rather depends on what one is looking for,' said Holmes. 'The will, I saw, had been drawn up by the firm of Valentine, Zelley and Knight, of Butler's Court, Cheapside, and witnessed by two of their clerks there. The appointed executor of the will was a junior partner in the firm. What do you suppose his name was?'

'I really have not the remotest idea,' replied Boldero.

' "Baker"!' I cried.

'Very good, Watson!' said my friend, smiling. 'You have the advantage, of course, of having witnessed "the unlikely" occur with surprising frequency in the course of my work! Yes, the exec-utor was a Mr R. S. Baker! You will imagine the satisfaction this discovery afforded me. But why, then, should Simon Bold-ero wish to see the executor of his grandfather's will, more than twenty years after that will was proved? It appeared from Simon's aide-mémoire that he had seen Baker at least once already, and intended to see him again on the Friday, having, as I believe, vis-ited his cousin Silas on the Thursday evening. Two such surprising appointments in the space of twenty-four hours must surely be related, I argued, and there must, therefore, be some connection between Baker and Silas Boldero. Upon consulting the Law Soc-iety records, I discovered that your cousin's own career as a solic-itor, which he abandoned many years ago, as you mentioned last night, was spent entirely with this same firm - Valentine, Zelley and Knight, and that he and this man, Baker, had been contem-poraries.'

'That is so, I believe,' remarked Boldero, 'but Silas cannot have interfered with my grandfather's will in any way, if that is the con-clusion to which your argument is leading, for he had already left the firm a year or two before my grandfather died.'

'Quite so,' responded Holmes, 'as I confirmed for myself from the records. He could not, therefore, have interfered personally with your grandfather's will. But he could, of course, have bribed another to do so, especially if that other was someone he had known well for nearly twenty years.'

Boldero stopped abruptly and turned to Holmes.

'Is such a thing conceivable?' said he.

'Betrayal of his client's implicit trust is the very worst crime a lawyer can commit,' said Holmes. 'Regrettably, however, it is not unknown. But come, we must make haste, for it looks as if we are in for a heavy downpour!'

I glanced up at the sky as we hurried on. The clouds had built up into a single, dark grey mass, and the wind was colder than before. After a moment, Holmes continued his account.

'I was quickly able to establish that Baker was still in practice, and with the same firm, so I called round at their chambers, late this morning. Baker is an elderly man, grey, wrinkled and distinguished in appearance, and his manner towards me was at first extremely supercilious.

' "I understand from this note on your card that you consider your business to be both urgent and personal," said he in a peevish tone, "but I do not know you."

' "You know, at least, the man I represent," I returned: "Mr Simon Boldero."

'At the mention of this name, the old man's face lost what little colour it possessed, his jaw sagged, and he appeared in an instant to have aged ten years.

' "I have been expecting him for some time," said he eventually, in a weak voice. "Has something prevented his coming in person?"

' "Indeed," said I; "but I am acting for him in the matter."

' "I have had a long and honourable career," said he, in a broken, defeated voice, "and had every hope of a respected retirement. But Mr Boldero found evidence of the one moral lapse of my life."

' "The business of his grandfather's will is a very serious matter indeed," said I in a grave voice. Of course, I knew practically nothing of the matter, but if you have ever played cards, you will know that it is sometimes possible to give the impression that your hand is stronger than it really is.

'Baker nodded his head sorrowfully. "And now what is to be done about it?" said he. "As you are probably aware, the will I executed after old Daniel Boldero's death was one he had made in a moment of stubborn anger, following a quarrel with his son, Enoch, who was Simon's father. He soon repented of it, however, and before a month had passed had made a fresh, more equitable will, by which all his property passed to Enoch, as he had originally intended."

' "That was the will that Silas Boldero bribed you to destroy," I ventured.

'Again he nodded. "I was not a wealthy man, and he offered me a thousand pounds if I would do it. Many men would have been tempted."

' "And many men would have resisted that temptation. So, you destroyed the will."

' "No, no!" he cried in surprise, eyeing me with suspicion. "Was that not made clear to you? I could not do it! All my professional training – everything I held dear – rebelled at the thought of destroying a legal document! Instead, I concealed it where no-one might find it, and, after Daniel Boldero's death, so far as the world knew, it had never existed. Of course, I have often regretted it bitterly, but what could I do?"

' "You could have told the truth." At this he fell silent, his head in his hands. "You must do exactly what Mr Simon Boldero proposed," I continued, feeling that my position was now a strong one. "It is your only chance."

' "Mr Boldero was, I must say, surprisingly magnanimous, considering all the circumstances," Baker remarked after a moment. "He said – bless his kindness! – that he would rather there was no scandal, for the sake of the family. I gave him the will, and he said he would take it down to confront Silas with it, and try to come to some arrangement with him. If Silas was amenable, then the whole matter could be dealt with privately, and the world need never know of it; but if Silas refused to meet Simon's terms, he would, he said, lay the matter before the authorities. This would, I need hardly add, mean ruin and disgrace for me. When Mr Boldero did not keep the appointment he had made with me, I feared the worst. But it seems, now that you are here, that everything will be all right."

' "I am afraid not," said I. "It has now become a capital matter. Simon Boldero has disappeared, and all the evidence suggests that he has been done to death by Silas." At this, the old man's lips turned white, and I feared he would have a seizure. I waited a moment before continuing. "As a party to the original conspiracy, and having seen Boldero recently and perhaps, for all anyone knows to the contrary, having deliberately sent him to his death at his cousin's house, you will of course be charged as an accomplice to this murder – "

' "No, no!" he cried feebly. "I knew nothing of this, as Heaven is my witness! Is there no way I can convince you?"

' "Unfortunately," said I, "if, as seems likely, Simon Boldero took the will down to Richmond with him, Silas will have destroyed it by now. There is therefore no evidence remaining that you were even repenting your earlier crime and assisting Simon."

' "Wait!" cried Baker, springing from his seat with an energy that surprised me. "At the time the original will was made, a copy was prepared, to be deposited at the Registrar's office; but, of course, I never sent it. It is still here now, in a trunk of my private papers in the lumber-room, upstairs. It will take me some time to find it, I am afraid, if you would not mind waiting."

' "I have more important business to attend to," said I. "You have my card. If that document does not reach the address upon the card by four o'clock tomorrow afternoon, then I can protect you no longer from the full force of the Criminal Law!"

'Baker seemed to shrink visibly as I spoke those last words. I declined the hand he held out to me, took my hat and left the chambers, feeling that I had done a good morning's work.'

'And so you have!' cried David Boldero in amazed admiration. 'I can scarcely believe what you have discovered! I shall forever bless the day that Farrow and Redfearn sent me to consult you!'

'Well, well,' said Holmes, clearly moved by his client's gratitude; 'it is largely a matter of experience, and I am a specialist. Once you have examined two hundred little problems, the two hundred and first does not present quite the same difficulties to your brain as the first one. But I have timed my account well! Here is Hill House, and we must deal now with Cousin Silas!'

'And here comes the rain,' said I, as the first icy drops fell upon us.

Boldero's face had set in a rigid mask of determination as we approached the house, and he made no remark as we pushed open the heavy wooden gate and entered the grounds. As we did so, the rain began to fall more heavily, making a soft drumming noise on the roof of the glass structure under which we made our way along the path. A movement off to the right caught my eye, and I peered through a murky pane of glass just in time to see some small dark creature slip swiftly beneath a bush.

For several minutes, our knocking at the front door produced no response, and as we waited on the step I caught the distant sound of raised voices from deep within the house. At length, someone approached the door, and there came a voice, thin and querulous, from the other side.

'Who is it, and what do you want?'

'It is your cousin, David,' Boldero called back, 'and I wish to speak to you again about Simon.'

'I've already told you I know nothing about him. Why can't you leave me in peace?'

'I know that Simon was here in January.'

'No he wasn't!'

'I found his muffler in the room I slept in.'

'If there was any muffler there, you put it there yourself!'

How long this exchange might have continued, it is hard to say, But Sherlock Holmes had clearly heard enough of it.

'If you do not open this door at once,' said he in a masterful tone, 'we shall put the matter in the hands of the police immediately.'

For a moment there was silence, then we heard the sound of a bolt being drawn, and the door was opened. The man who stood back to let us enter was one of the oddest human beings I have ever seen. He was somewhat over the middle height, but strangely hunched about the shoulders, so that his neck and head protruded forward like that of a tortoise. His chest and shoulders were very stocky, but the rest of him seemed to taper away almost to nothing, ending with a pair of very small feet.

'Come in, then, if you must,' said he in an impatient tone, waving his arms at us. As we did so, there came a terrific racket from somewhere upstairs, a woman's voice, shouting raucously, and a violent banging noise, as if someone were kicking at a door. 'It's only the maid,' said Silas irritably. 'She's probably got herself locked in the broom cupboard again. I'll deal with it in a minute.' He closed the front door behind us, and as he did so the noise upstairs subsided. 'Thank goodness for that,' said he in an unpleasant tone.

'Now,' he continued, addressing David Boldero, his head protruding forward as he did so. 'You wish to speak to me of your brother. It is true, I admit, that I saw him in January, but I had good reason for denying it, as you will understand shortly. The matter is more complex than you perhaps suppose. You had best all come this way, and I will explain everything.'

He opened a door at the right-hand side of the hall, and led us into a dusty, unfurnished room. A penetrating smell of damp filled the air, and plaster had fallen from the walls in chunks, and now lay in crumbling heaps upon the bare boards of the floor. As I closed the door behind us, I thought I heard the woman shouting again upstairs.

'You will excuse the slight disarray,' Silas remarked over his shoulder, as he led the way to a door at the far side of the room. 'This room is in need of a little redecoration. This will be the quickest way,' he continued, throwing open the door and passing through it.

We followed him along a narrow flagged corridor, which ran along the right-hand side of the house, and appeared to have been added at some time as a way of getting from the front of the building to the back without passing through the inside of the house. A row of dirty, smeared windows on our right looked out over the gardens, which were as Boldero had described them to us: a confused mass of overgrown shrubs and tangled creepers, upon which the rain was now falling steadily.

At the end of the corridor was another door, with a small rectangular pane of glass set in it, near the top. Silas Boldero glanced through this, then drew back a bolt and pulled the door open.

'Come on, come on!' he said impatiently. 'Let's get out of the cold!'

We filed through the narrow doorway after him, into a long, high-roofed conservatory, built on to the back of the house. The air in here was much warmer, very moist, and had an odd and unpleasant smell to it. I was the last to enter, and as I did so it was clear that our host was becoming very irritable.

'Hurry up!' he cried as I passed him at the doorway, and put his hand on my shoulder. 'Let's get this door closed!'

'Look out!' cried Holmes; but his warning came a fraction of a second too late, for at that instant I received a violent push in the middle of the back, lost my balance and stumbled into the others. In that moment of confusion, Silas Boldero slipped back through the doorway, slammed the door shut behind him, and shot the bolt home. A moment later we heard his rapid footsteps ringing on the flagstones of the corridor. Above us the rain drummed heavily on the glass roof of the conservatory, so that we had to shout to make ourselves heard.

'What the devil is going on?' cried Boldero in an angry tone.

'We have been tricked,' said Holmes, his keen eyes darting round the strange structure in which we found ourselves. It had been built against the wall of the house, so that on our left was a tall blank wall of brick. Incongruously placed high up in this wall, directly above where we stood, but with no way of reaching it, was an ordinary-looking door.

'That must be the door through which I fell last night,' said Boldero, following my gaze. From the house-wall, the roof of the conservatory sloped down steeply to a lower wall, on our right, which was composed entirely of glass panels. At the near end of this wall was a pair of doors of similar construction, which gave on to the garden. A quick examination showed that these doors were locked.

But though I quickly took in all these features of the building, it was the floor which principally arrested my attention. Where we stood it was composed of large square flagstones, moss-covered and slimy, which extended for about twenty feet. Beyond that, the floor sloped gently downwards, into what appeared to be a deep bathing pool, which extended for a further thirty or forty feet, to the far end of the building. The surface of the water was green-skimmed and unhealthy-looking, and covered with drifting vegetation and other debris. Even as I looked, however, I saw something moving there, a purposeful dark shape beneath the water.

'Holmes!' I cried, but he had already seen it, and his keen face was rigid with tension. Whatever it was, it was moving up the pool towards us, its swift, gliding motion sending little ripples out as it approached. Then, above the slime on the surface of the water, I saw the front of its snout, two large nostrils dilated to suck in air, and, some way behind, two large, evil eyes, fixed steadily upon us.

'My God!' cried Boldero in terror. 'What in Heaven's name is it?'

'It appears to be an African crocodile,' responded Holmes quietly, in a voice which was icy cold. 'The largest and most deadly reptile on earth. It is a monster of the species, too: it looks a good eighteen feet in length.'

As we watched, the creature slowed, and then stopped altogether and lay still in the water, barely ten feet from the edge of the pool, its unblinking eyes watching our every movement. Whether this quiet observation represented mere curiosity, or was the prelude to a sudden assault, it was impossible to tell.

Without turning his head, or taking his eyes from this awesome vision, Holmes reached into his pocket and drew out a pistol, which he passed to me, pressing it firmly into my hand. 'It may be utterly useless against such a beast, but we have nothing else,' said he softly. 'If it moves any closer, Watson, shoot to kill! Now, quickly, Boldero, help me! We must try to break down the doors!'

Behind us, on the flagstones, stood a low wooden bench. Holmes seized hold of one end; but Boldero had been struck rigid with fear at the sight of that terrible creature in the water, and did not move.

'Boldero!' cried Holmes again, in an urgent tone. 'For your life, man!'

At that moment there came a crash above us, as that singular door high up in the wall was flung open. Framed in the doorway stood Silas Boldero, and from his hand hung a large canvas sack. For a moment he looked down upon us in silence, a horrible sneering smile upon his face, then he laughed harshly, and drew from the sack what appeared to be a large piece of raw meat. With a careless movement of his arm, he flung it out into the air, and it fell with a splash in the shallow edge of the pool. The creature in the water made no discernible movement, and yet I had the disturbing impression that it had drifted very slightly nearer to where I stood.

The sudden appearance of his cousin had at least had the effect of breaking the spell of fear which had held David Boldero motionless. Now he quickly bent his strength to the wooden bench which Holmes was lifting, and the two of them charged with it at the garden doors of the conservatory. With a terrific crash of breaking glass and a splintering of wood, the lock gave way and the doors flew open, and the colder air of the garden rushed into the building. For a split second, as the doors were burst open, I had taken my eyes off the monster in the water, but now I saw to my horror that it was moving smoothly and swiftly forward, its long scaly tail thrashing the water behind it.

I raised the pistol, aimed between the creature's eyes, and fired. The bullet must have struck the top of its head and bounced harmlessly off the thick, armoured scales there, for it struck the brick wall with a ringing crack farther along the building.

'Watson!' came a shout from outside the shattered doors. 'Leave it! Fly for your life!' But I could not. The creature was too close. In a moment it would be on top of me. Like something from an evil nightmare it rose up out of the water before me, its huge red and grey mouth gaping open viciously, ready to crush me between its rows of colossal pointed teeth. I let off three shots in rapid succession as I backed away towards the door, at least two of which struck it in the throat. With a mighty splash, sending fountains of water up to the roof, it crashed down into the water; but its wicked eyes were still fixed upon me as I backed out into the garden, and turned to run.

Even as I did so, there came a cry of anger and a string of foul oaths from Silas Boldero. Glancing up, I saw that his face was contorted with rage, and he was stamping his foot in the doorway and shaking his fist at me, like a spoiled child whose plans have been thwarted. Behind him, in the gloom of the bedroom, there seemed some slight movement, and I thought I descried another, slighter figure, a woman clad in black; but I paid little heed, for I saw, too, that the crocodile was stirring once more. Clearly hurt by my shots, but not fatally so, it was beginning to rise out of the water once more.

I had turned away, but had not taken two paces, when the shouting and foul language gave way all at once to a long shriek of terror. I turned quickly to see Silas Boldero tumbling headlong into the conservatory, his arms waving wildly and uselessly in the air. He hit the hard floor with a heavy thud, and lay perfectly still. Up above, in the open doorway, the woman in black looked down. Whether he had simply lost his footing in his agitation and had slipped on the slimy edge of the doorway, or whether she had startled him, or struck him, or had even pushed him from the ledge deliberately, it was impossible to say. I had little time to consider the matter, however, for my attention at that moment was entirely directed at the crocodile. It was now out of the water, revealing its full gigantic length for the first time, and making its way towards the still figure of the recluse.

Holmes and Boldero were some way ahead of me, but had seen what had happened, and ran back to join me outside the conservatory. It was clear, even at that distance, that Silas Boldero's head and neck hung at a strange, unnatural angle, and that his eyes were wide open and unblinking.

'He's dead,' cried Boldero. 'We can do nothing for him now.'

Abruptly the crocodile lunged forward, hideous mouth agape, seized hold of the crumpled body on the floor, and made to drag it back into the water.

'Have you a round left, Watson?' said Holmes tersely.

I stepped forward, and from just outside the conservatory doorway, took careful aim and fired. The shot hit the monster in the side of the mouth, and he stopped and loosed his grip on his terrible bundle. Then, slowly, but with infinite menace, he turned his baleful eyes upon me.

'Quickly, Watson!' cried Holmes, tugging at my sleeve. 'We can do no more here!'

We turned and ran, and as we did so there came a terrific crashing noise from behind us. I looked back in trepidation, to see that the awesome creature was smashing his way through the remains of the conservatory doors as if they had been made of paper and card, and lumbering after us at a pace which both surprised and terrified me. Through the bushes we plunged, taking any route that seemed to offer a clear run, and dreading above all else running into a blind alley of vegetation, from which there would be no escape. Behind us without pause came the heavy padding of the monster, the constant crack and crash of broken branches as it forced its way through the undergrowth informing us that it was still upon our trail. All the time the rain lashed down remorselessly.

We must have run half-way round the grounds, in the direction of the road, when I saw Holmes stop, a little way ahead of me, and look in alarm at the path, and the glass structure which covered it. We could neither pass it nor penetrate it, and could not, therefore, reach the gate.

'The wall!' he cried abruptly, and set off towards a section of the high wall which appeared to have lost much of its mortar, and which might thus offer the possibility of handholds. But just in front of me, Boldero put his foot into some small creature's burrow, and fell to the ground, crying out with pain. In a second, Holmes was back, and had hold of his left arm. I took his right, and together we managed to get him to the foot of the wall. We could hear the crocodile close behind us now, smashing its way through the tangle of brambles near the wall.

In a trice Holmes had shinned up the wall, and was reaching down for Boldero's hand, while I stayed at the bottom to help him up. I was still standing flat-footed on the ground, as Boldero dragged himself on to the top of the wall, when with a deafening crash the monster burst through the last of the undergrowth, and thundered towards me.

'Your hand!' cried Holmes.

I thrust my arm up blindly, he seized it, and with quite extraordinary strength dragged me bodily up the wall. I swung my legs up on to the top as the creature charged, its colossal, dripping mouth just inches from my feet.

'You have saved my life!' I cried, panting with exhaustion.

'We have saved your foot, at any rate,' returned my friend in his customary dry manner.

'God's mercy!' cried Boldero suddenly, in a voice suffused with terror. 'It is climbing the wall!'

Indeed, incredible to see, it was raising itself up and clawing at the wall with its front feet, its fearsome snout almost reaching to the top of the wall, where we stood. As one, the three of us sprang down into the road, Boldero crying out with pain as he landed on his twisted ankle.

'It will not get over that,' said Holmes, eying the wall as he dusted off the knees of his trousers. 'Now we must make haste to notify the authorities of all that has occurred here.'

'The woman – ' I began.

'Oh, "Mad Mary" will be safe enough,' returned my friend. 'When she leaves the house she will do so by the covered pathway from the front door, where the creature cannot get at her.'

After a moment to recover our breath, we set off at a brisk walk down the hill, through the pouring rain, and half an hour later, having described our experiences to an amazed and incredulous police-inspector, we were sitting with a glass of brandy by the fire in the hotel. I was soaked to the skin, and my clothes had been torn in several places during our flight through the garden; but the closeness of our escape from death had made me almost lightheaded, so that such trivial matters seemed of no consequence. I believe the others were affected in the same way, for when Holmes spoke, there was a note of elation in his voice.

'Let me be the first to congratulate you upon at last coming into your inheritance!' said he, addressing David Boldero, who answered the remark with a rueful smile. 'The circumstances may not have been ideal, I grant you, but they have a certain memorable quality! I am sure that Miss Underwood will be interested to hear of your adventures!'

'Beatrice!' cried Boldero abruptly, clutching his head. 'I had quite forgotten! I am supposed to be dining with Beatrice and her parents this evening! I shall have to send a note to say I cannot come.'

'No, no! You must go!' insisted Holmes, laughing. 'This may be the one evening in your life when your late arrival for dinner will earn no disapproval! After all, it is not every prospective son-in-law who can honestly inform his fiancée's parents that he was delayed by an enraged crocodile!'

The Adventure of the Whitrow Inheritance

DAVID STUART DAVIES

I woke one morning in the February of 1889 to find London enveloped in the thickest fog of the winter. Pedestrians were glimpsed as mere phantoms slipping in and out of grey dense eddies, while ghostly unseen cabs clip-clopped eerily down Baker Street.

'Pickpockets' weather,' observed Holmes from the breakfast table, as I gazed out of our sitting-room window at the seething fog without.

'Even those villains may have difficulty seeing which pocket to pick in this stuff', I said, joining my friend.

He gave me wry grin. 'Fog is unpredictable and so is only of use to the petty criminal. No notable villain would rely on it and therefore it is bad for business. Not only does it hold up the important crime from being committed, but it prevents the client from reaching our door.'

As if providing an ironic counterpoint to Holmes's statement, the doorbell rang downstairs. 'And then again,' he continued with a sardonic lift of the eyebrow, 'I could be wrong'.

He was indeed wrong and within minutes we had a client sitting by our cheery fire, sharing a cup of hot coffee with us and regaling us with the problem that had brought him to our door. He was a smartly dressed youth, with dark good looks, a broad, open face and brown, sensitive eyes.

'My name is Matthew Whitrow,' he began in a clear but hesitant voice. 'I hold a position in the family firm of brewers. I live with my uncle Godfrey Whitrow. He is in essence my guardian until I reach the age of twenty-one in two months' time. My mother died in childbirth and my father was carried off by enteric fever while on a trip to India three years after I was born. My Uncle Godfrey, who was my father's partner in business – The Whitrow Brewery – took me in and brought me up as if I were his own. Oh, Mr Holmes, I shall be eternally grateful to him for his generosity and his kindness over the years. It has not been easy for him, running the business, educating his nephew and maintaining The Grange, his large house in Pinner.'

'Your uncle is not married?' asked Holmes.

The youth afforded himself a little smile. 'Good heavens, no. Uncle is a confirmed bachelor. I love him dearly but, I have to admit, he is somewhat frosty in his dealings with people, particularly women, whom he considers to be very much the weaker sex.'

My friend nodded with restrained enthusiasm and indicated that our visitor should resume his narrative.

'When I completed my education, I was given a position, a junior position, at the brewery with the understanding that eventually I should become a partner with Uncle Godfrey when I reached my twenty-first birthday. Those were the instructions left in my father's will.'

'And this birthday takes place in two months' time?' I said, checking my notes.

'Yes, on April the sixth.'

'So where lies your problem, Mr Whitrow?' asked Sherlock Holmes, leaning back in his chair and lighting a cigarette.

The young man's countenance darkened and bit his lip nervously. 'I have begun to fear for my life, Mr Holmes. Three times in as many days I have narrowly escaped death.'

'Really,' replied my friend languidly, but his eyes shone with interest. 'Pray give me the details.'

'On Monday a large section of masonry fell from the roof of our house as I was leaving. It crashed to the ground only a few feet away from me. Yesterday, on the way to the office, I was chased by a gang of roughs who, I am sure, would have killed me if I had not managed to give them the slip.'

'Why should they wish to do that?' I asked.

Our client gave a shrug of the shoulder. 'I have no idea.'

Holmes leaned forward and pointed a bony finger at our client. 'There is one other incident to relate. It concerns something which happened in the early hours of the morning, something which caused you to leave the house in a hurry – your shoes are unpolished, your tie is askew and you have cut yourself in four places while shaving – something more perilous than the other occurrences, something which has brought you in desperation to seek my help.'

'You are correct, Mr Holmes. A most frightening and damning incident.'

Holmes slumped back in his chair and waved his hand at the young man to indicate that he should continue.

'I am a light sleeper and some nights I can toss and turn until dawn without the benefit of sleep. But last night for some reason I slept deeply. It must have been the heavy dinner I'd eaten. Luckily, at around three in the morning some powerful instinct of survival prompted me to wake. If I had not done so, I would not be sitting here now. As soon as I gained consciousness, I began to choke. I quickly realised that the room was full of gas. I could hear the deadly hissing in the darkness. Someone had turned on the gas fire in the room without lighting it. The atmosphere was thick with poisonous fumes. With great effort I staggered from the bed hardly able to breathe. I tried to cry out but words failed me. As soon as I opened my mouth I began to suffocate on the foul vapour. I have no idea how I managed to summon up sufficient strength to reach the bedroom door and stumble into the corridor.'

'You had a very narrow escape indeed,' I remarked.

'What happened next?' enquired Holmes sharply.

'I fell to the floor, my head swimming from the effect of the fumes, but as I did so I noticed the door of my uncle's room close quickly as though someone had just entered at great speed.'

Holmes steepled his fingers. 'And what do you make of that, Mr Whitrow?'

He shook his head sadly. 'I dare not think. Some moments later, I was able to pull myself up into a sitting position and cry for help. Uncle Godfrey was at my side in an instant. I explained the situation as best I could and he clapped a handkerchief to his mouth and rushed into my room to turn the gas supply off. Thankfully, within an hour I was feeling more my old self again. Supported by my uncle, I had taken a walk in the grounds to fill my lungs with fresh air and then sipped a large brandy to warm me.'

'How did your uncle react to this incident?'

'That was a strange thing. He failed to see the seriousness of it. He thought that I had been careless and switched the fire on to warm my room while I read before retiring and that I had forgotten to light the gas.'

'Is that possible?'

'Certainly not.'

'Then how do you interpret the matter?'

Our client sat forward in his chair, his eyes wild with apprehension and fear. 'Someone is trying to kill me,' he said in a harsh whisper.

'Someone – who?' asked Holmes.

'I don't know.'

'For what reason?'

Again Matthew Whitrow shook his head.

'Come now, sir. The evidence you give shouts at us, giving us both culprit and motive.'

'That interpretation does not bear contemplation . . .'

'That your Uncle Godfrey has a need to get rid of you before you turn twenty-one when he, effectively, loses half of his fortune to you.'

'Not my uncle. Not the man who has been like a second father to me . . .'

'Have we any other candidates?'

Whitrow ran his fingers through his hair. 'Not that I know of.'

'Does your uncle know that you intended to seek my help?'

'I thought it best to keep my own counsel.'

'How very wise.'

Suddenly Holmes rose from his chair, walked to the window and gazed out at the coils of mist, which still pressed in on us from the cold grey world beyond the pane. 'There is more fog outside in the street than there is surrounding this affair, Mr Whitrow. Your story clearly implicates your uncle, but I appreciate that suspicions and accusations are useless without proof. I am somewhat intrigued by your case and I shall endeavour to blow away the foggy vapours that surround it and bring the clear light of truth to bear upon it. Call upon me early tomorrow evening and I should be in a position to bring this matter to a successful conclusion'.

With a hearty handshake and expressions of deep gratitude our visitor left. On his departure, Holmes threw himself down in his chair and bade me leave him alone for an hour while he ran his mind over the various elements of the case. From the density of the smoke that poured from his black clay pipe and the depths of the contractions on his brow I could see that the problem was not as simple as he had indicated to our client.

Just before noon he went out. 'I have a little errand at Somerset House in the Strand. Why don't you meet me at Simpson's at one for lunch, Watson?'

Holmes arrived promptly at one and we sat at a table by the window. The fog had lifted somewhat and through the net curtains we were able to glimpse the great tide of humanity pass up and down the

Strand outside. We ordered our food and then I prompted Holmes to explain his thoughts on the case.

'You seemed to suggest to young Whitrow that the matter was a simple one,' said I.

He grinned. 'It is – presented to me on a plate as it was. There was very little artifice in the story we were told.'

'Are you suggesting that Matthew Whitrow lied to us?'

'I am convinced that some of what he told us is not true. Let us consider this case from another angle. Why should Godfrey Whitrow take on the responsibility of bringing up his brother's child, look after him for nearly twenty years and then when he is but two months away from his twenty-first birthday try to arrange for his death?'

'For the reason you have already intimated: so that young Matthew does not inherit half the brewery fortune and the business.'

'But why wait so long? Surely there would have been far more opportune and less suspicious moments in the last twenty years. Why not carry out the murder then? Why wait until the last moment? No, it will not do. And consider also the three attempts on Matthew's life. Where is the consistency there? A piece of falling masonry, a murderous attack by thugs and death by asphyxiation. The diversity of these attempts on the young Whitrow's life indicates that they were not planned or at least organised by the same mind. And how would a respectable businessman know how to get in touch with a gang prepared to murder for money? Notice that none of these 'attempts' had witnesses. Certainly if there had been, scrupulous Matthew would have informed us. In essence, what we have is only one version of events. It is time to obtain another viewpoint. We shall visit Godfrey Whitrow at the brewery this afternoon'.

Godfrey Whitrow was a large, bald, red-faced man in his late fifties. In repose his face was crabbed and ill at ease and even his eyes seemed to flash with some kind of permanent irritation. However, in manner he was perfectly cordial to us when we were shown into his office at the Whitrow Brewery on the outskirts of Pinner later that afternoon.

'Take a seat, gentlemen. Would you care for a cup of tea?'

'No thank you, sir,' replied Holmes evenly. 'We are here on rather serious business.'

Whitrow glanced at my friend's card. 'I have heard of you, of course, Mr Holmes, and I have no doubt that your visit is in connection with the unfortunate incident that occurred at my home last night when my nephew was nearly asphyxiated.'

Holmes nodded. 'What is your view of the incident?'

'An unfortunate accident. Matthew is sometimes a careless boy and certainly he did appear to be somewhat preoccupied at dinner last evening. He hardly ate any of his food.'

'What do you make of the other incidents where he has narrowly escaped injury?' I asked.

Puzzlement registered itself on Whitrow's rubicund visage. 'What "other incidents"? I know of none'.

'The falling masonry, the gang of roughs?' I explained.

The brewer shook his head. 'I am afraid I do not know what you mean.'

'Your nephew is convinced that someone is trying to kill him.' said Holmes.

Whitrow gave a gasp of astonishment. 'Why, I have never heard anything so ridiculous. Why should anyone attempt to murder Matthew? What motive could they have?'

'Money. His inheritance possibly.'

'That is nonsense. I am the only one . . . ' Whitrow paused and his eyes widened in disbelief as the truth dawned on him. 'Good gracious, you mean he thinks that I wish him dead.' He shook his head in horror and mopped his brow with a large white handkerchief. 'Why, Mr Holmes, this would be comic if the implications were not so serious. I mean my nephew no harm whatsoever. I am happy for him to inherit his father's share . . . '

'I am a little rusty on some legal phrasing, Mr Whitrow, but I think I am right in saying that it would be more a transference than an inheritance, would it not?'

Whitrow stared open-mouthed at my friend. 'Great heavens,' he said softly, almost in a whisper. 'You know.'

'I know,' affirmed my friend.

An hour later we arrived at The Grange, Godfrey Whitrow's large house in the country, some five miles from the brewery. The manservant, Walker, admitted us. Holmes passed him a letter from his master, which instructed the servant to co-operate with our requests. Holmes asked to be shown to Matthew Whitrow's bedroom.

'The still waters of this case run very deep indeed, do they not, Watson?' observed Holmes once we were alone.

'Indeed,' I said, looking about me. It was a large chamber with a broad window, which overlooked the extensive garden. It was well furnished with a four-poster bed, a wardrobe, bookcases and a chest of drawers. Holmes began by examining the gas fire, the root of the mischief the previous night, and then the bookcases. 'These are new volumes and yet they are well-thumbed,' he observed holding up two volumes, each dealing with modern firearms. Opening the top drawer in the chest, Holmes gave a cry of delight. Slowly, with great theatricality, Holmes pulled out two pistols, a pair of Webley No 2s. 'Intriguing,' he muttered whipping out his lens and taking them to the window for a thorough examination.

'What do you make of the cartridges in this beauty?' he asked at length, passing me the lens and one of the guns.

It did not take me long to discover what he had found. 'They are blank cartridges.'

'And in this gun . . . ?' Holmes passed me the second revolver.

'These are real. What is it all about? Two identical guns, one with real bullets and one with blanks?'

'Not quite identical. Notice the little groove at the base of the handle of that one, the one with the real bullets.'

'Why yes. The mark has been scratched in.'

'So he will know which of these beauties can really kill.'

That night, as arranged, Holmes and I secreted ourselves in one of the guest bedrooms and waited for events to unfold. Just before eleven we were visited by Godfrey Whitrow.

'Matthew has retired for the night,' he told us in hushed tones. 'He made no mention of his visit to you or of any of those attacks made upon his person. However, throughout dinner he regaled me with tales that he has been hearing about a spate of local armed burglaries. Apparently someone in the next village was killed in his bed during such a raid. He is concerned for our safety. Walker sleeps in quarters in the stable block some way from the house and we have no other live-in servants. So he thought it prudent for us to have some means of self-defence and gave me this firearm to protect myself.' He pulled one of the Webley revolvers from his smoking jacket pocket. Holmes took it from him and examined the butt.

My friend gave me a knowing glance. 'No mark. Mr Whitrow, this gun is loaded with blanks.'

'What on earth is the boy up to?' the brewer asked, his head shaking in bewilderment.

'Murder,' replied my friend quietly. 'Now, sir, please make yourself comfortable here for tonight while my good friend Watson and I will move to your room until the last act of this dark drama is acted out. Whatever you hear, do not leave this room. Your life may depend on it.'

At a little after one in the morning we heard a crash from downstairs and a muffled cry for help: 'Uncle, for God sake's, help me.' This outburst was followed by a gunshot. 'The mischief has begun,' observed Holmes wryly and we ventured into the corridor and listened. The cry came again. The voice was that of Matthew Whitrow and it was emanating from the hallway. We sped along the landing but at the head of the stairs, Holmes held me back. 'Stay here, Watson, until I call you. If the lad sees two figures our game is up.'

With these words Sherlock Holmes moved halfway down the curving staircase, a lithe, shadowy figure in the darkened house. In a very close imitation of Godfrey Whitrow's voice he called out into the blackness below: 'Are you all right, Matthew? What is going on?'

'Help, Uncle, burglars!' came the response which was followed almost immediately by another gunshot. A bright flash illuminated the hallway where I glimpsed one darkened figure that appeared to be making his way to the door.

'Don't let him get away,' came Matthew Whitrow's disembodied voice once again.

Holmes fired his gun. The figure turned and aimed his pistol at my friend. There was a burst of orange flame and Holmes gave a sharp cry, pitched forward and tumbled down the stairs, landing in a heap at the bottom where he lay motionless.

'Uncle! My God, Uncle.' It was Matthew again and quickly he lit a lamp which filled the hallway with a dim amber light. It provided sufficient illumination to show that he was the only figure below. There had been no intruder.

On leaning over my friend with the mask of mock concern on his features, he staggered back in amazement. 'You,' he cried.

'Yes, me,' grinned Holmes, sitting up and aiming his pistol at the youth. 'Sorry to disappoint you but I am neither your uncle nor am I dead. However, this gun, unlike yours, is loaded with real bullets, so I advise you against any rash action.'

'I . . . I don't understand.'

'Watson, be so good as to rouse Mr Godfrey Whitrow and ask him to join us in the drawing-room.'

A short time later Godfrey and Matthew Whitrow sat opposite each other in the panelled drawing-room of The Grange, while Holmes explained the details of the case.

'You have a very scheming nephew here, Mr Whitrow. Scheming and unscrupulous. He has waited and bided his time to carry out his cold-hearted machinations until he was almost twenty-one, the age when he would inherit half the business and become a fully-fledged partner in the brewery. But, you see, half was not good enough for Master Matthew. He wanted it all. With you out of the way, he believed he would inherit everything and become a very rich man indeed. First of all he planned to have you arrested for attempted murder – of himself. A jail sentence would have put you out of his way for some time and then it would be very easy for him to eject you from the business.

'The first two attempts – the incident with the falling masonry and the murderous gang – were pure fiction, but the asphyxiation was real. It was self-inflicted and a compelling episode. The apparent veracity of the one attempt helped to give credence to the other two – or so he thought. He even attempted to strengthen the case against you by engaging the services of Sherlock Holmes, who was meant to accuse you of attempted murder. The facts as he revealed them when he came to see me could not fail to implicate you. But it was all too obvious, I am afraid. I suspect that he grew worried when I did not immediately arrange a warrant for your arrest and therefore he decided on another approach.

'He decided to fake a burglary where you would be shot. For this scheme he utilised two guns. He gave you the one with the blank cartridges so that if you managed to shoot the burglar – who was Matthew – no damage would be done. He reasoned that in the darkness of the hall with the excitement, the voices and the gunshots, you would not be able to see exactly how many figures there were there. Afterwards, he intended to say that you fired at the intruder, who then fired back, killing you. Matthew would then exchange the gun in your hand for the one with real bullets before the police arrived and dispose of the other one. It was a neat and bold plan . . . '

'And thanks to you, Mr Holmes, it failed.' Godfrey Whitrow shook his head sadly and turned to his nephew. 'But what remains a mystery is why you wanted, you needed, to do it. I cannot believe it was solely greed, Matthew. I came to look upon you as my own son and I thought you cared for and respected me.'

The young man sat up and sneered at his uncle. Passion raged in his flashing eyes. 'I was tired of being grateful and humble. Oh, how wonderful you were to take me in – the little orphan boy. How thankful I should be. But I was given no freedom, no choices. I had to do as you asked, you dictated. You arranged my whole life. I was robbed of any individuality. I determined to grab my freedom when I inherited half the business. And Holmes was right: half wasn't enough. I wanted it all – and with you out of the way I would have had it all.'

'That's where you are wrong,' interjected Holmes. 'Perhaps you should have done some research before you embarked on your treacherous scheme. After your visit to Baker Street, I determined to discover the exact nature of your father's will. It was a simple task. A visit to Somerset House on the Strand revealed a startling piece of information. The will certainly gives you half of the brewery business when you reach twenty-one, providing your father is deceased.'

'There is nothing new in what you are telling me,' snapped Matthew Whitrow.

'But your father is not dead . . . '

The boy's jaw dropped and the colour drained from his face. He shook his head in disbelief. 'Not dead . . . Don't be ridiculous . . . I don't . . . '

Godfrey Whitrow gave a heavy sigh. 'Mr Holmes is right, Matthew. When your father returned from India eighteen years ago he was not suffering from enteric fever as you have been led to believe, but brain fever. It was a cruel trick of Nature. He simply went mad. Within a month he turned from a sane rational human being to a raving imbecile. He could not be trusted alone and he was too dangerous, too volatile, to nurse at home. He had to be placed in an institution for his own safety as well as others'. He is still alive, residing in a lunatic asylum near the south coast. He does not know who he is and he does not recognise anyone. He cannot converse intelligently and cannot feed himself without help. But he is still alive. I visit him once a year out of a sense of duty and . . . indeed love, for he is my brother. I took it upon myself to protect you from this awful truth all these years. I intended to maintain this fiction by transferring half the business to you on your twenty-first birthday as though your father was dead. All my actions were designed to spare you the horrid truth.'

Matthew Whitrow listened open-mouthed to this confession and then buried his face in his hands, his whole body racked by deep sobs.

'I lost a brother,' said the brewer sadly, his eyes moistening also, 'and now it seems I've lost a son.'

We waited for the police to arrive to arrest Matthew Whitrow on the charge of attempted murder before leaving to catch an early train back to town.

'You know,' said I, as the train pulled out of Pinner station, 'I believe there will be reconciliation between uncle and the wayward nephew before too long. Now that the lad knows the truth about his father, I suspect it will bring him to his senses and cause him to appreciate the worth of Godfrey Whitrow.'

Holmes sat back in his seat and lit his pipe. 'You have a more sanguine view of events than I, Watson,' he said wearily. 'Matthew Whitrow has hated his uncle for a long, long time and now the lad has learned how he has been deceived over his father's death. This fact is certain to increase the boy's animosity.' My friend shook his head. 'No. I believe they are destined to be estranged permanently. As the poet has it: 'True hatred fuels tomorrow's fire.'

The Adventure of the Green Skull

MARK VALENTINE

I have mentioned before the three massive manuscript volumes that contain my notes on our cases for the year 1894. Circumstances now allow me to reveal the details of one of these, as weird and tragic a case as any we encountered. It was, I note, the beginning of November, and Holmes was on capital form, pleased to be back at the hub of matters in London after his long incognito wanderings in the East and elsewhere. There had been a high wind wailing outside our rooms and throughout the city, and Holmes was just beginning to become restless for some new matter to whet his keen mind upon. As was his habit, therefore, he was scouring the pages of The Times at breakfast, seeking evidence of anything untoward. Today his researches had an especial edge, for he had received word that Inspector Lestrade would call later, if convenient.

'Read that, Watson,' he said, passing the paper to me, and pointing to a brief paragraph.

Mr Josiah Walvis, 51, an overseer at the Bow-side match works, met an untimely end on Saturday evening when he fell from a high wall abutting the East India Wharf and cracked his skull. The cause of his sad accident has not been ascertained. It is understood that Mr Walvis had been entertaining friends at the Lamb and Flag public house before making his way home. Interviewed, his associates say the deceased was of his normal disposition upon departing, and was not excessively inebriated. It is considered possible Mr Walvis was contemplating a shorter route to his home but missed his footing. Two witnesses, a watchman and a street boy, aver that they saw the victim pursued some moments beforehand, but this cannot be better corroborated. The proprietor of the Bow match-works reports that Mr Walvis was a diligent and just employee who – well, etc, etc.

'There is the barest hint of promise in that, Watson: the pursuer, you know. But it is otherwise a drab affair. Yet it is all there is. Inventive evil appears to have quite vanished from London.'

Holmes sighed, and began to gather up the dottles for his morning pipe.

The visit of our colleague from Scotland Yard did not at first obviate his gloom. For it seemed Lestrade had indeed nothing better to offer.

'It's the Walvis business, Mr Holmes.'

'Oh, indeed? But that happened two days ago, Lestrade. The gales will have rushed all the evidence to the four corners. There is no point in coming to me now.'

'Well, it seems a straightforward case that is hardly worth your while. But one of the constables, a keen lad, saw something he didn't quite like.'

'Indeed?'

'Yes. Of course, an accident is quite the likeliest explanation. There was no robbery, and no other marks on the body but those caused by the fall. Yet, here is the thing. In the deceased's left hand, between the two middle fingers, protruding outwards, was a spent match.'

'Ah. That is singular.' I saw my friend's eyes gleam.

'Quite so. A drowning man may clutch at a straw, but – I say to myself – a falling man does not. He splays his fingers, so . . . '.

'Therefore, the match was placed there after the fall,' I interjected.

'Exactly, Doctor,' returned Lestrade. 'Now I am inclined to regard it as merely a macabre little joke on the part of the friends who found him. They all worked at the match factory, you know. They were pretty far gone in drink. So they put it there as if to say "You, Walvis, have struck your last match." I questioned them pretty fiercely about that, but they deny it. Half didn't notice it at all, the others say it must have blown there . . . '

'You have preserved the match, Lestrade?' Holmes demanded.

'I have, Mr Holmes, and – knowing your ways – have brought it with me.' Lestrade produced a twist of paper from his waistcoat pocket and handed it over.

Holmes inspected the exhibit carefully between thumb and forefinger, then handed it back.

'It tells us little. It is a Lyphant & Bray match – the people who have the Bow works. So it could well have come from his colleagues.

Or from almost anybody. It is a very popular brand. Yet, someone who has handled it may be an actor.'

We both looked suitably astonished, and Holmes favoured us with an explanation. 'It is very simple. I have studied the shape, size and composition of over forty types of lucifer or match – the matter complements my researches upon tobacco ash, you know. A combination of a certain ash and a certain match may help to mark a man. But not in this case. No ash, and a very common brand.'

'The theatrical connection?' I urged.

Holmes shrugged. 'Oh, merely that someone has left a small smudge of greasepaint upon the stick. Not you or your constable, I assume, Lestrade?'

'Indeed not.'

'Well, it does not get us very far. But what about this evidence of a pursuer, Inspector?'

Our visitor's face settled into a satisfied smirk.

'The witnesses are not very sound. An aged watchman, half deaf and almost wholly foolish. A street arab with a lively imagination.'

'And what do they say?'

'Well, Mr Holmes, I don't give it much credence. Indeed, I am trying what I can to suppress their little yarn. It doesn't take much to spread unreasoning terror abroad.'

There was a brittle silence, Lestrade savouring the matter that had really brought him to us, Holmes quiveringly alert.

'They say they saw Walvis chased down the street by a phantom. It wore a hooded cloak, but they caught a glimpse of its face – if you can call it that. It looked more like, they said, it looked more like – a green skull.'

Sherlock Holmes rose from his chair and rubbed his hands together. 'Come now,' he said, 'This sounds promising.'

The case may have caught my friend's imagination, because of its peculiarities, but for some days he made little progress. The scene, as he had anticipated, had been quite wiped clean by the wind and rain of the intervening days, and all the witnesses he interviewed stuck resolutely to the stories they had given the police, even the two who had seen the spectral pursuer. Lyphant & Bray would give nothing but a sound character to Walvis, conceding only that by some he might be regarded as somewhat stern in his duties. There was little more for Holmes to do, and he was succumbing again to his blue devils when, barely a week later, Mrs Hudson ushered in a new client. He was an angular, brisk young man, pale and peremptory in manner.

'Sit down, Mr Reynolds. This is my friend and associate, Dr Watson. What is your business with us?'

'I have read of you, Mr Holmes, from Dr Watson's accounts. I have observed that you see importance in matters others overlook.'

'And you think you have a similar matter?'

'I do. My employer, Mr Thomas Mostyn, died last night.'

'I see. The cause?'

'Heart failure.'

Holmes looked crestfallen.

'It is certain?'

'Yes. His medical man has treated him for years. He has long had indifferent health. I could see this for myself also.'

'Then why . . .'

'That was the *cause* of his death, Mr Holmes. I am concerned about the *occasion* of it.'

'There is something here that does not satisfy you?'

'A number of matters.'

Holmes tapped his fingers upon the arm of his chair.

'Pray proceed.'

'Mr Mostyn's face in death was distorted most disturbingly. It was a grimacing mask, exhibiting naked fear.'

I interrupted. 'Rictus, Mr Reynolds. It can give the most distressing effects.'

Our client turned to me. 'I understand. But there is rather more. Though in his nightgown and dressing-gown, as if prepared for bed, Mr Mostyn met his end in his study. Some matter had taken him there. And in death he was clutching between his middle fingers, pointing outwards – '

'A match.'

Mr Reynolds' face was a picture of astonishment. 'Great heavens, yes. How did you know?'

Holmes smiled. 'No matter. It was used?'

'Yes.'

'Well, perhaps he was about to enjoy a cigar before retiring. It is not uncommon.'

'Certainly not, Mr Holmes. My employer disapproved of smoking. It was the only matter of disagreement between us. If I wished to smoke, I had to do so clandestinely.'

'I see. He does not sound very companionable. Well, Mr Reynolds, let us have more of your story. You are his private secretary?'

'I am. I deal – I dealt – with nearly all his business and personal correspondence. He has many financial interests. I have been with him some seven years, since I successfully answered an advertisement he had placed upon his return from Guiana. He was reticent about his wealth, but that he had made a very great deal in the Americas was evident enough to me from his investments.'

'And had made enemies, no doubt?'

'I never heard of any. Indeed, all of his affairs appeared to me almost entirely untroubled, until – well, that is, until the particular incident that brings me to you. On Tuesday last week, I opened Mr Mostyn's correspondence as usual, and there was nothing out of the ordinary run of things, but one: an envelope that contained no letter, only a handful of matches. I could not imagine what the sender's purpose was, although sometimes the advertisement men do try the most foolish tricks to engage attention. I threw it in the basket. When I took in the rest of the day's post and went through it with my employer, we dealt with it all well enough, until – at the end – I mentioned the matches, light-heartedly. Quite a remarkable change came over his face. I had never seen him so agitated, except perhaps once when he felt he had been browbeaten by a hothead of a lawyer into some settlement he did not like – the one matter, as it happens, where he did not confide in me.'

'I see. The envelope arrived – what, eight days ago? Go on, Mr Reynolds. This may all be more germane than you know.'

'In his agitation, Mr Mostyn asked me exactly how many matches there were. I am afraid I laughed and said I did not know. He became vehement and told me to go and count them at once. I could scarcely believe the order, but I did as he bid.'

'And?'

'There were nine or ten.'

'Nine *or* ten, Mr Reynolds?'

'Ten, then. It seemed of no moment.'

'Do you have them?'

'Well, yes I do. But only because I found them in my employer's desk drawer, next to his appointments diary. I cannot imagine why he kept them.'

Our visitor handed them over and Holmes subjected them to scrutiny, separating three from the others.

Mr Reynolds regarded Holmes's actions quizzically, then resumed. 'A little later that day, Mr Mostyn gave me a most unusual instruction. He said that business compelled him to go abroad again and that it might be for some time. I was to realise as much as I could, and as quickly as I could, of his investments, so that within one week – he was most insistent upon that – within one week, he should be ready to leave.'

'He had never done such a thing before?'

'No. I was very much surprised. From what I knew of his business affairs, there was nothing of any consequence to call his attention overseas. But by requiring me to turn his holdings to cash so quickly, he forfeited a great deal of their value. I could not imagine what would impel him to that.'

'Is there anything more, Mr Reynolds?'

Our visitor hesitated.

'No.'

'Think back very carefully, sir. Over this recent period, has there been any matter whatever at all out of the ordinary?'

'Oh, only foolish talk from the boot-boy. He reads too much sensational literature.'

'Indeed? I find it has much to commend it. And what was his prattle? Spring-Heeled Jack? The Wild Boys of the Sewers?'

'Ha, very nearly so, Mr Holmes. He said he saw some figure skulking around the garden at night. He has an attic room that commands a view. He should have been asleep, but no doubt was reading his rubbish. He said he saw Death with a lantern. The maid, superstitious soul, says it had come for Mr Mostyn. I had to speak severely to both of them . . . Of course, there may have been an interloper, but scarcely in that form. Now, Mr Holmes, what is your advice?'

'I should like to visit the scene without delay, Mr Reynolds. And I am concerned for you, sir. You have had an unpleasant experience. Now there is no necessity for subterfuge, help yourself to one of these – a Macedonian – you will find it quite soothing – while we get ready. Now, where are my matches? You have some with you? Good, good. We shall not be long.'

Despite the tragedy that had taken place in No 4, Pavia Court, Mostyn's address, I relished our visit, for it was a pleasure to see Holmes prowling throughout the house and its modest grounds in his customary keen-eyed search for any clue that might bring substance to the shadows that had gathered here. I saw him crawling carefully around the garden at the rear, and its narrow entrance gate, examining the sash upon the study window that overlooked it on the ground floor, and walking up and down the small, blind street, itself off a very minor thoroughfare, that comprised the Court, in all these places picking up and examining any piece of unregarded flotsam. I heard him also in the pantry in animated conversation with Victor, the boot boy, comparing the merits of various thrilling pamphlets: and in the study, questioning Reynolds closely about his employer's business holdings.

For my part, I sought out Mostyn's doctor, Hawkins, on the pretext that I was a medical adviser to his insurance people. Although, as a matter of form, the district police had been called, they had relied upon his assurance that heart failure was responsible for the death. He conceded he had quite expected – and indeed hoped, since Mostyn paid well – that his patient would have survived some years longer, but it was still quite within the bounds of medical science that the condition had taken him earlier. Might – I suggested – some additional anxiety in his affairs, even some shock or other, have contributed? Dr Hawkins was affable: yes, of course, it very well might.

It was clear to me that Holmes had some definite line of enquiry in his sights, though I could not tell what. He was missing from our rooms for much of the time. I was a little taken aback when, shortly after our visit to Mostyn's home, Victor presented himself, somewhat wind-ruffled but evidently bursting with news.

'I did 'sactly as you said, Mr Holmes. I took a place in the bun shop opposite this inventor cove's place, Raffles, and watched and watched. I had to eat getting on for a dozen stickies before your mark came out, corst a terrible lot they did . . . '

Holmes threw him a coin. 'On, boy, on,' he urged.

'Well, thank you very much sir, anyways after you'd been to see him and he'd shut up shop that day, it was hours and hours after, he looks about him and sets off smartish. But I'm on his track like you told me . . . '

'You see, Watson, nobody ever pays attention to small boys loitering or getting up to mischief. It's what they do. A perfect disguise: behaving naturally. Well, where did the inventor Raffles go?'

'He went out Chelsea way, where all the artists and anarchists are sir, they're always up to plots in *The Black Paper*, 'sfact.'

'So they are, Victor. And who are they are in league with, eh?'

'That's what I was going to find out. He heads for a door in a yard off Blyth Street, and he's looking all around him, see: furtive, that's what they call it. But he doesn't see me. And he knocks and there's a wait and like a judas in the door opens, but I can't see much. And then – then the door opens just a crack, and he talks very excited like, and he gets let in. And he stays there not long, twenty minutes maybe.'

'See anything when the door opened?'

'You bet. Woundy – beg pardon sir – scary.'

'You're sure, Victor?'

'Blood honour, sir.'

'That's good enough for me.'

I looked from one to the other. 'Well?'

Holmes raised an eyebrow.

'He saw Death, Watson. Isn't that right? The thing that came to Mr Mostyn's garden?'

The youth nodded solemnly.

Holmes wasted no time. After swift directions from the boy, amply rewarded, we hailed a cab to the hidden, curious quarter he had indicated. In the neighbourhood, my friend enlisted another raga-muffin helper, a blind match-seller. A sovereign and a swift rehearsal of her role ensued. God knows she was battered enough looking, but she made her condition look even more distressing and knocked weakly and repeatedly at the door, imploring help. At the first the face behind the shutter ushered her away, but she swayed and cried and pleaded. The figure within went away a while, and then the door opened very slowly. We then abandoned all subtlety and flung our-selves at the crack. The child ran off. Meanwhile there was a harsh shout and a scurrying, and we burst in.

We were confronted by – a thing at bay. In one corner of the bare, meanly-furnished room, what stood there glowering at us was a figure wrapped around in cloaks from which emerged a hairless, shrunken, bony head, where such meagre flesh as there was had a vile, livid hue.

'I do not know who or what you are,' Sherlock Holmes said, 'but your business is at an end. I have evidence that will connect you with two deaths.'

The creature's eyes were filled with hatred, and cast wildly about for escape. Then they seemed to dim, and the skull sank down, before it looked up at us again.

'You have no evidence that would convince a court. Yet perhaps it is time to let things rest. And I believe you will not speak so harshly when you have heard my story.'

I gasped, and I could sense that even the icy Holmes was taken aback. For the voice was that of a gentlewoman, clear and well-modulated. She beckoned us to two rough chairs. We made introductions and looked at her enquiringly.

'My name is of no consequence. I was born in the colony of Guiana, where my mother succumbed at a young age to the foul waters. My father and a native nursemaid looked after me in my infancy, but he was taken, too, by some disease of the unhealthy conditions there. We had no close kin, but there was a distant cousin who had been once in the colony and had come to know my father before he returned to England. I found that I – and my father's wealth – were entrusted to this person, and I was shipped to a land I had never known as home. The next part of my story will hardly surprise you. This cousin and guardian, so called, claimed my father's business affairs were in disorder and it was all he could do to settle his debts, penurying himself in the process. I must be put to work. I was sent to the Lyphant & Bray match factory, and housed nearby in squalid lodgings. From then onwards – I was twelve, mark you – my life was one of unremitting drudgery and callousness, in the most terrible conditions. I saw my guardian infrequently and then, I am sure, he came only to ensure I was secure. The fact that I had been educated and prepared for a gentler place made matters worse. The taskmaster – Walvis – took a hatred of me. I believe he was in league with my guardian, for I saw them confer together when he came. My natural rebelliousness against the conditions meant this creature was able to taunt, scold, fine and beat me. There was not the slightest opportunity I might escape – I was kept under close watch and had no money anyway.'

'It is pitiable, Madam,' I conceded.

'It is the life of many of your fellow creatures. It would be mine still, had I not taken the one opportunity that came my way. You will recall of course the great match-girls' protest some five or six years ago? I am proud to confess I was one of the agitators. After much hardship, the proprietors permitted a tour of inspection of the factory by some eminent sympathisers – it was all well-managed, of course. But some of the more astute of them realised this, and deliberately looked for an opportunity to become detached from the party and learn the untutored truth. I told my story hurriedly to Mr Shardlow, the Radical, and he was much affected and promised to see me have justice. I know now that he confronted my guardian and wrung from him some settlement on my behalf – Mr Shardlow is a lawyer and a strong orator, of course. Since this release, I have done what I can for those left behind. The terrible yellow phosphorus that Lyphant & Bray use must be abolished: there are safer alternatives. That was my campaign. But it will be too late for me.'

'You have phossy-jaw, Madam? It is a bad business.'

'Exactly, Dr Watson. You may see the symptoms.'

I turned to Holmes. 'It affects those over-exposed to the noxious chemicals used in the match trade. It brings a green pallor, a sinking of the cheek bones, complete loss of hair, a shrinking of the flesh. It is incurable. But forgive me, madam – yours is an exceptionally severe case.'

'It is well advanced, Doctor. But also, since I cannot disguise its ravages, I decided to accentuate them, to render my appearance still more ghastly. For I had determined to confront my persecutors face to face with what they had done. With the cunning of theatrical make-up, I thought I could strike terror in their hearts and jolt them into some realisation of their evil. My craft was good. It worked somewhat better than I expected. Poor Walvis fled from me in mad panic and plunged to his doom. While – '

She hesitated.

'Mostyn,' supplied Holmes.

'Yes, I see you know everything. Mostyn was already full of fear from the little message I sent him.'

'The spent matches,' I put in.

'Yes, Doctor. You were my accomplice in those, of course.'

'I – why, I . . .'

'I read with great relish your account of the Five Orange Pips sent as a sinister warning. And so has half London, I should think. It gave me an idea.'

'So I see,' remarked Holmes, drily.

'Mostyn was an implacable opponent of the match reforms, and as a chief investor in Lyphant & Bray, was an obstacle to my plans. I had to chase him away. My guardian, I reasoned, would have heard of the strange death of his accomplice, the overseer Walvis. He would not be quite sure if it were the accident it seemed. He would hardly miss the significance of a packet of dead matches delivered to him. And a man less vilely cunning than he would reason that seven matches equals seven days. It was a fair warning. His face when I slid open the sash of his study and advanced upon him was dreadful to behold: yet not, you can see, so dreadful as what he had done to me.'

There was a silence.

'And now, gentlemen, what do you intend? You hardly have any case, you know. And it is all one to me. I cannot live much longer: but I would not harm my cause.'

Sherlock Holmes stared piercingly at her.

'There must be no more apparitions.'

'There will be none.'

'Then this matter is concluded. I am my own law, and you are not, as I judge, in breach of it.'

That the case had shaken Holmes I could tell from the brooding silence he observed on our way back to Baker Street in a cab. But once in our rooms again, and after he had played over Swettenham's sweetly melancholy violin sonata, he became somewhat restored.

'I shall be able to use this case in due course as an exemplar for my monograph on lucifers, matches and spills,' he observed. 'Here are the ones left on the dead men and sent in the envelope – all Lyphant & Bray – see the squared-off stalks and yellow reside at the head. Here are three that Reynolds cast in the waste basket after having several secret cigarettes – they are identical to the one he left here after smoking one of my Macedonians. They are from the Phoebus Match Co, a rounded stem and a more friable head. They led Mostyn to think he had ten days before Nemesis would strike: in fact, he had only a week.

'And here are those I found in Pavia Court. One at the top of the street, by the sign: struck to check it was the right street; one by the gate; one in the garden, for the dark lantern. These were my treasures. They are a very uncommon match indeed – Raphael's Hygienic. An experimental type, to see if some less deadly form of phosphor can be used in match manufacture, one that will do no harm to the poor creatures in the match manufactories. The lady of the skull, Watson, used Lyphant & Bray, the instruments of her oppression as a calling card on those she wished to harm, but in her everyday use she naturally patronised, and indeed part-funded, the safer design. I merely had to make known that I had connected the apparition to the Raphael workshop, and I felt sure the young inventor there would hurry to let her know and warn her off. In the morning, Watson, I shall visit to reassure him: and, after all we have heard, to place our order for matches always with him.'

The Case of the Gustafsson Stone

JUNE THOMSON

It was not long before my marriage that my old friend Sherlock Holmes was asked to inquire into a matter involving one of the crowned heads of Europe. It was of such delicacy that, although Holmes himself has referred to it obliquely in public on two occasions, I believe the time is not yet ripe for a full account of the case to be published, a decision with which Holmes heartily concurs.

I shall therefore place this record in my despatch box along with those other written accounts which, for various reasons, may never see the light of day even though I know from the many letters I have received that there is considerable curiosity among my readers to know the full details of the case, roused, I might add, by those two references I have already mentioned.

It was, I recall, a pleasant morning in early autumn when Holmes received a letter introducing him to the case. Considering the illustriousness of our correspondent, as we only later discovered, it was a curiously anonymous missive, bearing no coat of arms or other insignia to indicate the identity of the individual concerned, not even an address. However, the quality of the writing paper and envelope suggested it was someone of wealth and discernment.

Having read through the single sheet of paper and raised a quizzical eyebrow at its contents, Holmes passed the letter to me.

The handwriting was clear, educated and bold, the message short and to the point.

DEAR MR HOLMES [it read]. Having heard excellent reports of your skill as a private consulting agent, I beg your assistance in a case of great importance.

As I am in London for a limited period only, I should be exceedingly obliged if you could find the time to see me this morning at 11 am.

As the matter is of great delicacy, I trust I can rely on your discretion.

In contrast to the legibility of the letter itself, the signature was almost indecipherable but, on close scrutiny, appeared to be Erik von Lyngstrad.

'A German gentleman?' I suggested as I returned the letter to Holmes.

'Perhaps,' he conceded with a shrug. 'We shall find out in an hour.'

'So you intend to see him, despite the shortness of the notice?'

'I think so, Watson. No other client has presented himself. Besides, I am curious to find out what this matter of extreme delicacy involves.'

'An *affaire de coeur*?' I suggested.

Holmes burst out laughing.

'My dear Watson, you are an incurable romantic! But you may well be correct. Shall you stay and find out?'

'If I may,' I replied a little stiffly, for, to be frank, I was somewhat annoyed by his amusement at my expense. However, curiosity soon overcame any chagrin on my part and, taking the *Morning Post*, I sat down by one of the windows from where I could watch the street while glancing through the newspaper. Holmes had settled down with the *Times* and so we passed the next hour in companionable silence until the sound of a cab drawing up outside the house alerted both of us to the arrival of his client.

A few moments later, there came a ring at the front doorbell, footsteps were heard mounting the stairs, and the boy in buttons ushered in a tall, well-built gentleman with a noble, upright bearing and finely modelled head whose clipped moustache and beard gave him the air of a senior army officer.

There was a military air also in the brisk, authorative manner in which he shook hands with Holmes and myself and announced his name as Count Erik von Lyngstrad.

Here was a man, I felt, who was used to commanding others.

'May I introduce my colleague, Dr Watson?' Holmes continued. 'I should be much obliged, sir, if, with your permission, he remains during our interview.'

'Indeed! Indeed!' Count von Lyngstrad agreed, bowing in my direction with a little formal click of his heels which also suggested military training as well as a Continental background. His voice was deep and his English excellent, containing only a very faint foreign accent, the origin of which I could not quite place.

The formalities over, the three of us seated ourselves, Holmes in a chair set a little apart from his client's and in such a position that he had his back to the window, which afforded him a clear view of the count's features while leaving his own in shadow. His expression was curiously immobile, a facial rigidity I had noticed before when his mind was most engaged. But behind those lean features which had the inflexibility of a Red Indian Chief's, I knew his thoughts were working at speed like a steam locomotive under pressure.

Placing the tips of his fingers together, he leaned back in his chair.

'In your letter,' he began, 'you refer to a matter of extreme delicacy. Let me assure you on behalf of myself and Dr Watson that not a word of what you tell us will pass beyond these four walls.'

The count bowed his head in acknowledgement of Holmes's guarantee.

'Thank you, Mr Holmes,' he replied. 'It was partly because of your reputation for discretion that I have decided to consult you. Not on my own behalf,' he added hastily, 'but on the part of a very old and dear friend of mine.'

Holmes's features maintained the same grave, listening expression.

'I understand,' was all he said in reply. 'Pray continue, sir.'

Count von Lyngstrad hesitated as if not sure where to begin and then, after a moment's silence, he took up his account.

'About two months ago, this friend, whom I shall refer to as Herr Braun, was called to the bedside of an elderly and very sick uncle of his who wished to make a deathbed confession. It seems that six months earlier, the uncle, a gentleman of impeccable reputation, had taken a valuable jewel from among the family heirlooms and had used it as collateral to meet a debt of honour. The loan was only temporary and, within a month, the uncle was able to pay back the borrowed sum with interest and to retrieve the jewel, which he replaced in the family strong box. The crisis appeared to be over.

'However, when he had first handed over the heirloom to the moneylender, the uncle, whose instinct told him not to trust the man too implicitly, had marked the piece of jewellery with a tiny scratch which would be invisible to anyone not aware of its presence. On examining the jewel when it was returned to him, he found the scratch was not there and he realised he had been tricked. The heirloom was not the original gem but a copy.

'This discovery came as a final blow after a period of great distress, for it was a close member of his own family who had accumulated the large debt which the uncle had felt obliged to repay. In consequence, the uncle suffered a stroke which left him partly paralysed and bed-ridden. Fearing another stroke would kill him, the uncle sent for his nephew to confess the loss of the family heirloom, the nephew being the titular head of the family and therefore the guardian of all the family property.'

It was apparent that the count, who up to that moment had related the facts in a straightforward and unemotional manner, had now reached a point in his narrative which caused him personal concern.

Resuming his account again, he continued more hurriedly, 'As I have already said, all of this happened about two months ago. As soon as I learnt . . . '

The personal pronoun fell into the ensuing silence like a stone into a pool of still water. I was aware that I started up in my chair instantly alert, while Holmes, who has better control over his emotions than I, moved not a muscle but remained as motionless as a statue. As for the count, I observed a faint flush infusing his handsome features before, quickly recovering his composure, he said with a smile, 'Ah, gentlemen, I am afraid I have let the cat out of the bag, as you English so charmingly express it. I am, of course, the nephew in question.'

'And the uncle?' Holmes inquired, raising an eyebrow at his client who appeared about to continue his account.

The count smiled again.

'You are very quick, Mr Holmes. I had intended to pass over the uncle without further explanation. In fact, there was no relationship between myself and the elderly gentleman, except that between a master and an old and trusted servant. The man is now dead and I am anxious that his reputation should remain as unsullied as it was before all this tragic business concerning the family jewel. No one else knows about its loss and I would prefer that it remained a secret known only to us.'

'Of course,' Holmes agreed. 'Pray continue.'

'Very little remains to be told. As soon as I realised the jewel had been replaced by a fake by the moneylender, I made certain to find out all I could about him. His name is Baron Kleist.'

'Ah, Baron Kleist!' Holmes exclaimed as if the name were familiar to him. Rising to his feet, he went to a bookshelf in one of the chimney alcoves. Taking down his encyclopedia of reference, he carried it back to his chair where he quickly turned to the entries under the letter K and began to read out loud.

'Baron Kleist. Antecedents unknown although he claims descent from a cadet branch of the Hapsburgs. Immensely rich. Fortune derived mainly from dealing in currency, jewellery and *objets d'art* on an international scale. Also a moneylender and a blackmailer. It is rumoured he was responsible for the suicide of the Duchesse de Nantes and the Member of Parliament, William Pepper. Also suspected of forgery. Has no settled abode but moves freely between the major capitals.' Holmes closed the book with the comment, 'A notorious character of whom much is suspected but nothing proved. Unfortunately, I have never made his acquaintance but I understand he is at present in London. There was a small item two days ago in the *Morning Post*.'

'Then if you agree with my plans, Mr Holmes, you may soon have the pleasure of meeting the baron,' Count von Lyngstrad replied. 'I have made enquiries, and I am told he is at present staying at the Hotel Imperial in Piccadilly, and has been in contact with a certain American millionaire, Cornelius F. Bradbury, who is due to arrive in England in a week's time and who is a collector of rare items of jewellery, particularly those with an historic connection. It is my belief that the baron is intending to sell my family heirloom, which is in the form of a pendant, to Mr Bradbury and that he has come to London for this very purpose, bringing the jewel with him.

'This is where your services are called for. I have already had some inquiries made and I have no doubt that the pendant is kept in a small strong box which the baron always carries with him and which, I understand, he keeps in his bedroom, preferring not to entrust it to the hotel's safe. Your task will be to remove the real pendant and replace it with the fake one without the baron's knowledge. This way, the baron will suspect nothing, the fake jewel can be sold to the American collector and a scandal of international proportions will be averted. Moreover, if the baron should be aware of the substitution, he may seek his revenge and I have no wish to risk making such an enemy.'

'You are indeed wise,' Holmes said gravely. 'Should his enmity be aroused, Baron Kleist has the means to finance and organise an implacable vendetta which could include murder. It is rumoured that Petro Cecconi, a member of the powerful Mafia family, ran foul of the baron and was stabbed through the heart one evening as he left a restaurant in Rome although, at the time, the murder was attributed to a falling out between the Cecconi family and another Mafia gang, the Badaglio clan. I believe Baron Kleist travels everywhere with a bodyguard?'

'Two, in fact, Mr Holmes. My own inquiry agents tell me that one guard accompanies him wherever he goes, while the other, Igor, a Russian gangster, remains in the hotel suite to guard the strongbox should the baron leave the building for any reason. They are ostensibly manservants but both are armed and are, according to my informants, experts in the martial arts. I should add that my own agents are also staying at the Imperial in a suite of rooms, number twenty, adjoining the baron's at number twenty-four. If you take up the case, you will very likely meet them. One is named Oscar. He is a tall, fair-haired young man. The other, Nils, is short and dark and, being less conspicuous, is mostly engaged in shadowing Baron Kleist.

'I understand from Nils that the baron intends to go to the opera on Friday night with a young actress of his acquaintance and will afterwards dine with her at Claridge's hotel.'

'May I ask how your informant knows this?,' Holmes broke in to ask.

The count gave a smile.

'How very perspicacious of you, Mr Holmes!' he remarked approvingly. 'Besides being an expert in the art of shadowing, Nils can also lip-read. He managed to get close enough to the baron one afternoon at the hotel reception desk when he was making arrangements for two seats to be booked at Covent Garden for Friday evening and also for a table to be reserved, again for two, at Claridge's for later that same evening. As for the identity of the young actress, Nils has seen her in the baron's company on several occasions since his arrival in London. A few discreet inquiries on his part established her identity. Are there any more questions you would like to ask, Mr Holmes?'

'Not for the moment, Count von Lyngstrad/' Holmes replied. 'Pray continue.'

'As I was saying, it is unlikely the baron will return to the Imperial until the early hours of Saturday morning. It therefore seems an excellent opportunity for you to substitute the fake jewel for the real one. It will not be easy, Mr Holmes. You will have to find some means to get into the baron's bedroom past Igor, who will remain in the suite to guard the strong box. You will then have to open it and relock it once the substitution has been made, so that the baron's suspicions are not aroused.

'I should perhaps warn you at this stage that the strong box in which the jewel is kept is no ordinary container secured by a key. It has been specially made and is fitted with three separate locks, each requiring its own key, and is, I understand, kept in a leather grip which is itself locked and which is placed inside the wardrobe in the baron's bedroom.'

'Also locked, I assume?' Holmes asked with amusement.

'Almost certainly,' Count von Lyngstrad replied, smiling in return.

'May I ask why your agents are not themselves carrying out the substitution?' Holmes continued. 'From what you tell me, they seem highly professional.'

'At gathering information, yes. However, their skills do not extend as far as picking locks or slipping past bodyguards. That is why I have turned to you.

'How you carry out the substitution is entirely your decision. But however you contrive it, the reward will be substantial, I can assure you. And now for the jewel itself; or rather the baron's excellent copy of it, made I believe by Bieberbeck, the Viennese expert who supplies substitute jewellery for those members of the aristocracy who have been forced to sell the family heirlooms. It is said Princess Magdelena von Ullstein's famous tiara is one of Bieberbeck's copies.'

Reaching into his inner pocket, he took out a small jeweller's box covered in blue and gold tooled leather, which he set down on the table before opening it to reveal its contents lying on the white satin lining.

It was indeed a pendant, but to my untutored eye it seemed a crude object with nothing of either beauty or value about it, for it was merely an oval stone of a brownish-yellow colour, about an inch and a half in length, roughly engraved with the head of a bearded man with narrow, fierce-looking eyes and high cheekbones. The stone itself was enclosed in a broad gold frame bearing some strange, angular letters. There was a loop at the top of it to which was attached a chain made of coarse gold links so that, I supposed, it could be worn round the owner's neck like a locket.

It looked undoubtedly old but, apart from that, had no other merit at all, as far as I could see.

However, Holmes's response on seeing it was quite the opposite to mine.

I heard him draw in his breath in amazement, at the sound of which his client cast a keen glance in his direction. But my old friend had already regained control of his features and the face he presented expressed nothing more than a mild interest.

'I see,' he remarked noncommittally. 'Well, Count von Lyngstrad, I will do my best to arrange the substitution; but I can promise nothing.'

'I am staying at the Northumberland hotel, should you wish to contact me,' the count said. Rising to his feet, he held out his hand to each of us in turn.

'I am most grateful, gentlemen,' he added, giving the same court-eous little bow and click of his heels with which he had greeted us before leaving the room.

Hardly had the door closed behind him before Holmes let his true feelings find expression. Smiling broadly, he clapped me on the shoulder. 'My dear Watson, we have been honoured with an inquiry of some importance!' he exclaimed.

'Have we, Holmes?' I asked, casting a dubious eye at the pendant in its little box which the Count had left lying on the table. 'I cannot myself see the significance of the pendant. In fact, it does not look at all valuable to me.'

'No?' He sounded dumbfounded. 'Then let me ask you a question. Have you heard of the Alfred jewel?'

'I think so, Holmes. It is connected with King Alfred, I assume.'

'It is indeed. Now what value would you place on it?'

'I have no idea but as it is famous as well as very old, I suppose it must be worth a great deal of money.'

'It is priceless, my dear fellow – even though its intrinsic value is minimal, for it consists merely of some crystal and enamel plus a little gold. Its true value lies in its uniqueness as well as its age and its historical connection. A collector such as Cornelius Bradbury would be willing to pay a fortune to acquire it.'

Bending down, he picked up the pendant which the Count had left on the table and held it towards me on the palm of his hand.

'This is, of course, only a copy,' he continued, 'but were it the original it would, like the Alfred jewel, be priceless.'

After a pause in which he looked at me keenly, he added in a solemn tone, 'What you are looking at, my dear Watson, is the Gustafsson Stone.'

I could think of nothing to say in response and, after a moment's silence, Holmes remarked, 'I see you have not heard of it.'

'I am afraid not, Holmes,' I said humbly.

'Then let me enlighten you. The Gustafsson Stone is a sixth-century jewel which once belonged to Gustaf Gurfson, a Viking leader who is hardly known in England but is famous throughout Scandinavia as a national hero. The head etched into the stone, which by the way is amber, is supposed to be a portrait of him. You see these strange letters engraved on the gold frame? These are runes and are said to spell out his name. There is something else about the Gustafsson Stone which adds to its uniqueness. It is part of the crown jewels of the kingdom of Scandinavia.'

Holmes, who has a taste for the dramatic, paused again to give me the opportunity to respond appropriately to this startling statement and this time I was more prepared than on the earlier occasion.

'Good heavens, Holmes!' I exclaimed. 'Then Count von Lyngstrad must be the king of Scandinavia!'

'Precisely, Watson,' Holmes agreed coolly. 'I congratulate you on your powers of deduction. Count von Lyngstrad is indeed King Erik of Scandinavia. Now, having settled the matter of the real identity of our client, we must now turn our attention to a less easily solved aspect of it, namely: how are we going to contrive to exchange this copy of the Gustafsson Stone with the original without alerting the baron and his bodyguards? Have you any ideas, Watson?'

'I am afraid not, Holmes.'

'Neither have I. But they will come, Watson. They will come.'

With that, he rose from his chair and left the room. Returning shortly afterwards, he stretched himself out on the sofa and stared fixedly at the ceiling, his eyes hooded, as if inspiration were to be found up there upon its whitewashed surface.

Recognising the symptoms and realising that Holmes would be lost in whatever world he had drifted into through the needle of the syringe, I, too, rose and, quietly letting myself out of the house, hailed a cab and set off for my club and the consolation of a game of billiards.

2

By the time I had returned to our lodgings, Holmes had fully recovered and was overflowing with high spirits and impatience at my absence.

'Where on earth have you been, Watson?' he demanded. However, before I could reply, he had swept on. 'While you were away, I have devised the most brilliant scheme. So come along at once, there's a good fellow! Let us not waste any more time!'

'But where are we going, Holmes?' I asked as I hurried after him down the stairs.

'To inspect the lie of the land, of course!' he said dismissively over his shoulder, as if that should have been obvious.

Our destination, it seemed from the address he gave to the cab driver, was the Hotel Imperial, where Baron Kleist was staying, and I wanted to ask Holmes if he thought this was a wise decision but, having seen him before in this mood, I knew it was better to hold my tongue and simply follow where he led.

The Hotel Imperial, a large, white, porticoed edifice, its façade decorated with half pilasters and elaborate cornices, was situated in Piccadilly overlooking Green Park. A uniformed door-keeper saluted and held the doors open for us as if we were royalty, as we passed in to a magnificent entrance hall lined with mirrors and palm trees in huge brass pots. A grand staircase swept up in front of us to the upper floors.

However, we turned to the left into a large lounge furnished with small tables and tapestry-covered sofas and armchairs.

'Coffee, do you not agree, my dear fellow?' Holmes asked, seating himself on one of the sofas and, as he gave the order to a soft-footed waiter who had suddenly appeared before us as if conjured up out of the air, I lowered myself on to one of the armchairs.

'What are we doing here?' I asked in a low voice, hoping to encourage him by example into adopting a more discreet attitude, for he was glancing about him with obvious interest.

'As I have already told you, Watson. Like troops before battle we are carrying out a preliminary inspection of the enemy's position. And there is no need to whisper, my dear fellow. There is nothing more likely to draw attention to oneself than a furtive manner. And now,' he continued, lowering his voice a little to my great relief, as the waiter, having reappeared to serve our order, withdrew, 'I want you to glance about in a casual manner as you drink your coffee. For example, if you look over to your right, you will observe a dark-haired man reading the *Times* and, like us, taking a discreet interest in what is going on about him. You have observed him, Watson?'

'Yes, I have, Holmes,' I replied in an admiring tone; had Holmes not pointed the man out, I should have not noticed him at all, for there was nothing remarkable about him. Indeed, he was so ordinary in both his appearance and behaviour as to be virtually invisible.

'That, I believe, is none other than Nils, one of our client's agents who he mentioned was staying at the Hotel Imperial. The other, Oscar, the more conspicuous-looking of the two, is presumably keeping discreetly out of sight until his services are called for. And if you look over to the far side of the lounge, you will see a pair of double glass doors. These lead into the main restaurant from which, I believe, one can gain access to the famous Winter Garden at the back of the hotel, while on the far side of the reception desk are the doors leading into the Smoking Room, the Writing Room and the Ladies' Drawing-room. You look bemused, my dear fellow. Why is that?'

'I do not understand why all of this is necessary. You are, I assume, not thinking of making use of the Ladies' Drawing-room by any chance?'

'Not unless it is absolutely necessary,' Holmes replied solemnly and then, on catching sight of my expression, he gave a low chuckle. 'I am merely making sure of all the exits beforehand in case we need to make a run for it. I can assure you, my dear fellow, that the Ladies' Drawing-room will be my very last point of retreat.'

He broke off suddenly and, putting down his coffee cup, announced in a low voice which carried an undertone of excitement, 'I believe the situation is about to unfold, Watson. Our friend Nils is getting ready to make a move. No, no! Pray do not turn in his direction. You will give the game away. If you look to your left, you may watch the developments much more discreetly.'

With a nod of his head, he indicated the double glass doors on the other side of the room which led into the restaurant, one leaf of which had been left half open and which, like a mirror, reflected the opposite side of the coffee lounge and part of the foyer. Without needing to turn my head, I could see in its polished surface Nils, the Count's unobtrusive agent, in the act of folding up his copy of the *Times* and placing it under his arm, begin to rise to his feet.

'He has scented his prey,' Holmes remarked with a chuckle, leaning back in his chair. Although to any casual observer he was apparently quite uninterested in what might be happening behind him, I was aware that, even though his eyes were half-closed, he was watching with close attention the restaurant door and the events being reflected in it.

While he was speaking, the images had shifted. Nils was now fully upright and was examining a handful of small coins he had taken from his pocket as if searching for a suitable tip to leave by his coffee cup. At the same time, a man's figure advanced into the focus of the door's reflection.

He was a tall, well-built man in his mid-fifties, I estimated, and had apparently just descended the staircase which led to the upper floors.

'And there is the prey: Baron Kleist himself,' Holmes added, his eyes still hooded and his lips barely moving.

I sharpened my own focus on the new arrival, excited at being afforded my first glimpse of the man whose reputation as an international forger and blackmailer was notorious and whom Holmes was committed to outwitting on behalf of his royal client, the King of Scandinavia.

He carried his bulk and height with the confident air of a man whose wealth and status entitled him to the deference of others. His clothes also suggested money and social standing, for they were impeccably cut by the best tailors – English, I suspected – his morning coat fitting smoothly across his broad shoulders, his trousers of exactly the right length to the nearest fraction of an inch. His spats, too, were exquisite and his boots shone like black glass. But although the general effect was one of a wealthy gentleman-about-town, there were details about his appearance which failed to live up to this image. The gold watch and chain he was sporting was just a little too lavish; so, also, was the orchid in his buttonhole, while he handled his gold-topped cane with just a touch too much ostentatious flourish.

He was handsome in a rather florid manner, the colour in his broad, flat cheeks indicating self-indulgence and high living, a suggestion which was borne out by the small, well-padded mouth under his carefully trimmed moustachios. But it was his eyes which revealed his true nature. He had halted at the reception desk to speak to the clerk on duty who was bowing and smiling profusely in his anxiety to please. As he stood there, ignoring the man's obsequiousness, the baron turned his head to survey the foyer and the coffee lounge.

Even at a distance, I was aware of the quality of that scrutiny. It was hard, cold and implacable, like a snake's, and had the same fixed, bright, reptilian intelligence.

Here, I thought, was a clever, calculating man who would make a formidable opponent, and I felt a clutch of fear at my heart.

Involuntarily, I glanced across at Holmes, wondering if he, too, was aware of the Baron's dangerous potentiality.

He was still leaning back in his chair, his eyes half-closed, but he was now wearing a beatific smile as if the thought of the forthcoming mission to outwit the man was affording him pleasurable anticipation.

In the meantime, the reflections in the glass were shifting once more as the figures in the dumb-show changed their positions. As if anticipating the baron's next move, Nils was bending down over the coffee table to place some coins by his empty cup. At the same time, a third figure whom I had not been aware of until that moment stepped forward into the frame from his position a little distance from the reception desk. He was a young, stockily-built man, dressed all in black like a manservant, but it was immediately apparent that his role was not that of a conventional gentleman's gentleman. There was an air of menace about his movements and the manner in which he carried his hands loosely in front of him, half-formed into fists like a pugilist entering a boxing ring ready for the contest.

This newcomer, I realised, was one of the Baron's two bodyguards, the one who, as Count von Lyngstrad had remarked, followed him everywhere. He fell in a few yards behind the Baron who had turned away and was crossing the foyer towards the hotel entrance.

Hardly had the pair of them vanished out of sight than Nils made his own move. Strolling casually, as if he had all the time in the world, he too made his way towards the great swing doors which the uniformed commissionaire was holding open for him, disappearing in turn through them into the noise and bustle of Piccadilly.

Judging it was safe to turn my head, I glanced directly towards the foyer, empty now of both the Baron, his bodyguard and Nils, the King of Scandinavia's unobtrusive little agent, but not deserted, for there were plenty of other people arriving and leaving all the time, a situation which I was aware Holmes was watching with keen interest. Sitting alert and upright now in his chair, his eyes were following these comings and goings, particularly those of the new arrivals.

Suddenly, he announced in a low voice, 'Wait for me here, Watson. I shall not keep you long.'

With that, to my surprise, he rose and walked briskly across the room to the entrance hall where a middle-aged lady and gentleman, who had just entered the hotel through the swing doors, were about to mount the stairs. Giving them a slight bow as one might to acquaintances, he made some remark at which the lady smiled and the gentleman responded. Holmes then gestured to them to precede him and, as they began to mount the stairs, he fell in behind them.

For a few moments, I was deceived by this little charade, believing that Holmes had indeed met the couple before and that, for some reason known only to himself, he wished to accompany them up-stairs. Certainly the hotel staff present in the foyer, the clerks behind the desk, the doorkeeper, the pages standing about waiting to be summoned, were taken in by the ruse and raised no objection to Holmes's intrusion into the private upper floors, normally barred to non-residents unless they had first made themselves known to the management. Once again, I found myself full of admiration at my old friend's boldness and ingenuity which to my knowledge no other person possesses to quite the same degree.

As he promised, he returned within minutes and, as he seated himself again on the sofa, I congratulated him on his quickness of mind; at which he smiled, pleased with the compliment.

'One must always seize the moment, Watson, and, in my experience, if one waits long enough, the moment will always present itself.'

'And was the moment worth seizing?'

'Indeed it was, my dear fellow. I discovered two very important facts. Firstly, the baron's suite, number twenty-four, is on the second floor and, being an even number, must face the back of the building. Secondly, the locks on the doors are of a standard pattern and, should it be necessary, could be picked without too much difficulty. And speaking of pick-locks, it is time we paid a visit to an old friend of mine, Charlie Peak, a former screwsman, or burglar to you, Watson, and an expert in the field.'

'Former?' I inquired.

'He is seventy-four, too old, as he himself admits, for breaking into other people's property. We will now pay the bill and take a cab to Sydenham, where we shall sit at Charlie's feet,' Holmes replied, summoning the waiter.

3

To my astonishment, the cab set us down outside a neat red-brick villa with lace curtains at the windows and a brightly-polished brass knocker on the door, more the abode of a respectable bank clerk, I would have thought, than a retired burglar.

A trim little housemaid in a spotlessly white cap and apron showed us into a parlour where Charlie Peak sat comfortably ensconced in a large armchair among the domestic comforts of potted geraniums, buttoned velvet and family photographs.

He was a white-haired, pink-cheeked, cheerful-looking little man, his slippered feet resting on a stool and a walking stick propped up beside him.

'Mr 'Olmes!' he cried out in delight as we entered, holding out both his hands in welcome. 'You'll forgive me, I'm sure, for not gettin' up to greet you but the old pins ain't what they used to be.'

Having shaken hands vigorously with both of us, he waved us towards two chairs which we drew up on either side of him so that the three of us formed a triangle with Charlie Peak at its apex like a benevolent genius presiding at a feast.

After an exchange of tidings such as old friends indulge in after a long absence, Holmes came to the purpose of our visit.

'Now, Charlie,' said he. 'As well as to have the pleasure of seeing you again, I am here to seek your expert advice.'

'On locks, I suppose,' the old man replied with a twinkle.

'Of course.'

'What sort of locks? Door? Cupboard? Chest? Safe?'

'A metal container similar to a cash box in size, but very strong and fitted with, I believe, three separate locks, each requiring its own special key.'

Charlie Peak's face lit up.

'Ah, a Medici casket!' he exclaimed.

'You have heard of it?' Holmes asked eagerly.

'I've done better than that, Mr 'Olmes. I've 'eld one 'ere in these very 'ands. It was as beautiful an example of the locksmith's art as I've ever clapped eyes on. They're made by Signer Valori of Florence, a direct descendant, so 'e says, of Luigi Valori, the locksmith 'oo worked for the Medici family. 'E 'as a little shop in a side street be'ind that big church with the fancy black and white stonework . . . '

'The Cathedral of Santa Maria del Fiore?' Holmes suggested.

'Could be,' Charlie Peak replied, shrugging his shoulders. 'I didn't ask.'

'But you have met Signor Valori?'

'Indeed I 'ave. I'd heard of 'is special caskets and 'ow they're impossible to open unless you 'as the keys so, seein' as I made my livin' in those days by pickin' locks, I wanted to find out about 'em. So I went to 'is shop and talked to 'im about 'em.'

'How?' Holmes asked with genuine curiosity. 'Does Signor Valori speak English?'

Charlie Peak gave a wheezy laugh.

'No, Mr 'Olmes; no more'n I speak Eyetie. But when it comes to two men sittin' down to talk about a subject they're both in love with, if you follers me, they finds the means some'ow, whether it's using the'ands or drawin' little pictures or actin' it out. We managed it any'ow by one means or another. Signer Valori explained that he only makes them to order, usually for very rich people because they costs a great deal of money. In all 'is years, 'e's only ever made four. They're made of the strongest steel that no ordinary cracksman can cut through and, like you said, each is fitted with three locks, every one different and so crafted that even the most skilful screwsman can't get 'em open unless 'e knows the secret.'

'Secret?' Holmes demanded.

Charlie Peak winked and tapped the side of his nose.

''E wouldn't tell me, Mr 'Olmes, nor 'oo 'e's made 'em for, but as a very special favour to me, 'e showed me one 'e was workin' on. It was a beauty! Black-japanned, it was, with a brass bird let into the lid.'

Beside me, I felt Holmes's whole body become alert as if an electric charge had suddenly been passed through it. But his voice and manner remained matter-of-fact.

'What kind of bird?' he asked, as if only mildly interested.

'I wouldn't like to say, Mr 'Olmes. Apart from sparrers and pigeons, I can't tell one from t'other. All I can say is, it was a big bird with a bloomin' great beak and it was 'olding a leaf in its claws.'

'Oh, I see,' Holmes said, apparently losing interest. 'Pray continue, Charlie. You were describing the Medici casket Signor Valori showed you. Were you able to examine the locks?'

'I wasn't given the chance. I didn't 'ave it in my 'ands for more than a minute before Signer Valori took it off of me.'

'A pity!' my old friend murmured. It was quite obvious he was bitterly disappointed.

Charlie Peak watched him without speaking for a moment or two, his head on one side and his face alive with amusement. Then he said, 'But I can do better than tell you about them, Mr 'Olmes. I can show you! See that cabinet over there? Open the bottom drawer and you'll find a box. If you bring it to me, I'll let you see 'ow far I got in findin' out Signer Valori's little secret.'

Holmes did as he was requested and produced a plain deal box about ten inches square from the bottom drawer of the cabinet which he carried over to Charlie Peak. It was apparently heavy and, rather than place it on the old man's knees, he set it down on a small table which stood by Charlie's side.

'Open it up!' Charlie ordered. He was clearly enjoying the situation hugely.

Inside was a jumble of locks of various shapes and sizes, each one identified by a luggage label. Several of these locks which lay on top, as if of more recent construction, were joined together in pairs or, in some case, in threes. On the very top lay a small bundle about six inches long wrapped in black felt.

'Take that one out!' Charlie Peak instructed Holmes, pointing a gnarled index finger at one particular lock of the triple variety.

As Holmes lifted it out, its label dangled free and it was possible to see the inscription on it which read in capital letters: 'Medici Number Ten'.

'Number Ten?' Holmes murmured, raising an eyebrow.

'My tenth and last try at making a copy of the lock to the Medici casket. That's what all them locks are, Mr 'Olmes – copies or originals of every lock in the land that I'd be likely to run up against in a day's, or rather a night's, work. It took a lifetime to build up that collection and years to break the Medici combination. Give it 'ere, sir.'

Holmes silently obliged but I could tell from the look of admiration on his face and the almost reverent manner in which he handled the lock that he was deeply impressed by the old man's skill.

'And them picklocks,' Charlie added, pointing to the little felt bundle.

It contained, as we discovered when Charlie unrolled it, about a dozen slender steel rods of various widths and lengths.

'A superb set of "bettys",' Holmes remarked approvingly.

'I 'ad 'em specially made,' Charlie Peak replied, looking pleased at Holmes's compliment. 'Now, gentlemen, if you cares to gather close, I'll show you how to work the trick. And I'll tell you 'ow I found out about it.

'I didn't let on to Signer Valori that I was a screwsman. I let 'im think I was just an ordinary locksmith, sittin' like a little kid at the feet of an expert, oohin' and aahin' at 'is skill. 'E was flattered, just as I meant 'im to be. So, as a great 'onour, 'e gets out three little keys and opens up the casket for me. Now, I've got a good memory for the look of a key. It's part of my trade, like you with footprints, Mr 'Olmes. So as soon as I left the shop, I drew pictures of the keys and 'ad 'em made up as picklocks when I got 'ome. If you look 'ere, you'll see each one's marked at the end with their own sign. This one's got a little cross on it. That's the one you use to open the centre lock first.'

As he spoke, he inserted the narrow metal rod into the central aperture before continuing with his explanation.

'Then you twists it about to and fro until you 'ears the wards give way. But I don't need to tell you that, do I, sir? By all accounts you're an expert screwsman yourself. Now what follers is the first part of the trick. You leaves that "betty" in place and puts in the second, the one with the two little cuts on it, into the keyhole on the left. But don't take that "betty" or the first one out for it keeps them locks open. Then you moves on to the third keyhole. You get my meanin', Mr 'Olmes?'

'Indeed I do, Charlie,' Holmes said.

'Now watch this,' the old man continued, ' 'cos 'ere comes the best part of the trick. Once you've opened the third lock, the other two locks close. So you 'ave to go back to the first and second lock and open 'em again. Clever, ain't it?'

'Yes; but not as clever as you in working out the trick. I take my hat off to you, Charlie. That is expertise at its very best.'

The old man, his cheeks flushed an even brighter pink, looked pleased as well as embarrassed by the compliment.

'All in a day's work, Mr 'Olmes,' he said gruffly and, to cover up his self-consciousness, began to busy himself with replacing the set of "bettys" in the box, leaving aside the three he had used to open the Medici lock as well as the lock itself.

'If you like, you can borrer those,' he told Holmes.

'May I? Then I am eternally in your debt, Charlie. What can I do for you in return?'

'Nuffin' except to come and tell me if the trick worked for you, that's all.'

'I will certainly do that when I return the "bettys" and the lock,' Holmes assured him, putting these objects into his pocket before taking leave of his friend.

'A remarkable old fellow,' Holmes added when, having hailed a cab in Sydenham High Street, we drove back to our lodgings, a journey which he enlivened for me with accounts of the more colourful exploits of Charlie's career.

'I wish I had half his skill,' he concluded.

'But surely not his criminal record?' I asked dryly.

Holmes looked sideways at me and grinned broadly.

'*Touché*, Watson!' he declared. 'But I do sincerely believe that had my interests leaned towards committing crime rather than solving it, I could have been the most successful burglar in the business.'

Our little excursion had evidently stimulated my old friend into renewed action for hardly had we returned to Baker Street than he was off again, bustling out of the sitting-room and down the stairs, pausing only to call back at me, 'By the way, be a good fellow and make sure you have a pair of light boots with rubber soles and heels!'

'Why, Holmes?' I called back, much mystified.

But he had gone. All I heard in reply was the slam of the street door as he hurried out to whistle for a hansom.

He was back about an hour after my own return from my boot-maker's with the prescribed footwear, bearing the fruits of a shopping spree of his own which consisted of a small valise and a coil of strong cord which he placed inside the valise, together with a selection of implements from his burglar's kit. He had also bought, as I discovered later, the components of disguises for both of us.

'And you have the rubber-soled boots I recommended?' he asked me.

'Indeed, I have,' I assured him. 'But why should I need them?'

'You will find that out tomorrow night, my dear fellow, when Baron Kleist attends the opera and we shall scale the heights of the Hotel Imperial,' was his enigmatic reply.

Before I could question him further, he had disappeared inside his bedroom, taking Charlie Peak's picklocks and his copy of the Medici lock with him where, I assumed, he spent the next few hours practising opening the lock, a task which continued to occupy him for most of the following day as well.

4

We had decided to set out for the hotel at seven o'clock and before we left we put on our disguises, simple ones on this occasion although Holmes is an expert in changing his appearance and had, at various times, taken on the identity, among others, of an elderly Italian priest, a French workman and an old woman.

For himself, he had chosen a dark, waxed moustache which gave him the air of a stylish man-about-town. Mine was a brown wig *en brosse* and a pair of gold-rimmed spectacles. Thus disguised, we set off by cab for the Hotel Imperial where we were to make use of the suite of rooms adjacent to Baron Kleist's where Nils and Oscar, the king of Scandinavia's agents, were already installed.

Oscar, who opened the door to us, seemed already acquainted with Holmes and I assumed that part of Holmes's expedition on the previous day was to inspect the lie of the land, as he expressed it, from the closer quarters of the interior of the hotel suite. Oscar was a tall, very blond young man, too conspicuous to be seen in public, whose role seemed to be to keep watch on the baron's rooms. The small, dark agent, Nils, whom we had already seen the day before, sitting downstairs in the lounge, was not present. Presumably he was following the baron as he spent the evening with the actress at the opera and dining at Claridge's.

Oscar showed us into the drawing room of the suite and from there into an adjoining bedchamber, the master bedroom, I assumed, judging by the opulence of its furnishings, including a huge mahogany wardrobe which occupied almost the whole of one wall. Holmes examined the lock on its doors in an almost negligent manner.

'That will be easy enough to pick,' he remarked with a shrug. 'Now, I understand the servant's room where the baron's bodyguard will be keeping watch is next door to the baron's bedroom.'

'That is so, sir,' Oscar replied in almost perfect English. 'The one opens into the other. I can show you quite easily how the rooms are arranged, for this suite is like a mirror-image of the baron's.'

Opening a door in the far wall, he led us into a much smaller and more simply furnished bedroom containing a single bed where presumably an attendant valet or lady's maid would sleep.

Crossing to the window, Oscar raised the lower sash and then stood back to allow Holmes and me to inspect the route we would have to take in order to gain access to Baron Kleist's quarters.

It was the first time I had seen it and I confess my heart sank at the sight of it. It would be a dangerous approach indeed and I understood Holmes's remark about scaling the heights of the Hotel Imperial and also the need for rubber-soled boots. No other footwear would have given one the necessary purchase on the route Holmes apparently intended we should take.

Unlike the front of the hotel which was stuccoed, the rear façade was built of brick ornamented with stone cornices running horizontally across it, broadening out at regular intervals to form the sills of the windows which extended in tiers across the whole of the back of the building. Above each window was a triangular stone pediment which also jutted out a few inches from the brickwork, thus becoming part of a general geometric pattern of straight lines and angles.

The cornice was no more than three inches wide and the only visible handholds were those stone pediments above the windows. But, unlike the cornice, they were not continuous and between them there was a terrifyingly barren stretch of brickwork, offering no handholds whatsoever. Immediately below lay a sheer drop of two storeys, terminating in the glass and ironwork dome of the Winter Garden, for which the Hotel Imperial was famous. Lights shone up through the panes and I thought I could faintly discern the moving shapes of waiters and hear the sound of voices and violins rising up from among the potted palm trees.

If we fell, I thought, with a sudden rush of mingled terror and hysteria, we would crash spectacularly down among the wine glasses and the starched napery to the sound of a Viennese waltz. I dared not think of the injuries we might cause both to ourselves and to others, nor of the headlines in the morning newspapers.

Holmes seemed unperturbed by such considerations. He was calmly unpacking the small valise he had brought with him and distributing the picklocks and other burgling devices about his person, including a small jemmy should he need to force open the window of the baron's bedroom.

The blue and gold leather case containing the copy of the Gustafsson Stone was placed in his inside pocket which he then fastened with a large pin.

Catching my eye, he said with a smile, 'It would be a complete disaster if I dropped the whole object of our little excursion, would it not, my dear fellow?'

My mouth was so dry with fear at the thought of our 'little excursion' that I could only nod my head in agreement.

Lastly, Holmes took out the coil of strong rope and, passing one end round his waist and across his left shoulder, he handed the other to Oscar who tied it securely to the foot rail of the bed. Then he softly slid the lower sash of the window upwards and climbed nimbly over the sill.

It was several seconds before I dared approach the window to look out. When I did so, I had to force myself not to look down but to glance to the right where Holmes was balanced on the narrow cornice, his body pressed against the rear wall of the hotel and his arms spreadeagled as with one hand he supported himself by clinging to the stone architrave above the window while his other hand crept inch by inch across the brickwork, straining to reach the similar pediment above the adjoining window which I realised, from Oscar's account of the arrangement of the hotel rooms, was the bedchamber belonging to the baron's bodyguard, Igor.

For a few seconds, Holmes stood there motionless, his heels projecting over the edge of the cornice, his arms stretched out wide like a victim subjected to some hideous medieval torture. I thought he would never move. Then with a massive contortion of his shoulder muscles, which I could actually see taking place beneath the taut fabric of his coat, the fingers of his right hand touched and then tightened over the projecting border of the architrave above the adjacent window and, little by little, he was able to loosen the grip of his left hand and to inch his feet along the cornice ledge, the rope crawling along behind him.

Its presence should have been a comfort but watching as it slowly dragged its way from the bed, across the floor to the window and from there out into the night, it seemed far too flimsy to support Holmes's weight should he lose his balance.

After what seemed an eternity, Holmes reached the comparative safety of the adjacent window-sill where he stood for several long moments flexing his fingers which must have been aching with the strain of clutching the pediment. His face was pressed close to the glass and I had the impression that he was using this pause not just as a respite but as a chance to peer inside the room. Seconds later, his head turned in my direction and I saw him raise two fingers of his left hand to his lips as a warning gesture for silence. Then his head turned away and he again began the same laborious effort of stretching out for the architrave above the neighbouring window which offered the next handhold.

To take my mind off his perilous journey, I counted off the seconds under my breath and reached the total of two hundred and sixteen before Holmes arrived at his goal and once more was able to step off the narrow cornice and stand upright on the broader ledge of the window to the baron's room.

The window, thank God, was not fastened, a lucky chance which I fervently hoped could be taken as a good omen for the successful outcome of the whole enterprise. Within seconds, Holmes had slid the lower sash upwards and had disappeared over the sill into the room. Moments later, there came a slight tug on the rope indicating that he had untied it and, at the signal, Oscar and I drew the rope in hand over hand until the full length of it lay coiled up upon the floor.

I regarded it with the same horror as I might a poisonous snake, for the terrible truth had at last to be faced. It was now my turn to secure it over my shoulder and lower myself backwards out of the window.

I hung there for what seemed like an eternity, feeling with the toes of my rubber-soled boots for the cornice, which gave me some purchase on the stone, thank God. At the same time I was clutching desperately to the pediment above the window, as a drowning man might grasp at a lifebelt. Knowing that if I looked down I would lose my nerve completely, I kept my gaze fixed upwards straight into the face of Oscar who was standing at the open window looking down at me, ready to pay out the rope as soon as I began to inch my way along the ledge.

I think it was his expression which persuaded me to move. It was rigid with horror at my predicament as if it were a mirror reflecting what I imagined was the expression on my own face, and I realised I had two choices: either to scramble back ignominiously into the room or to follow after Holmes.

I chose the latter, more out of pride than courage. If Holmes could do it, then so could I. Indeed, I *had* to do it.

At that moment of decision, my right foot found the edge of the cornice although its narrowness struck me with terror. But I knew I was now committed and I took my first shuffling step sideways, my body pressed inwards towards the hotel's façade.

Bricks are familiar, commonplace objects. In London, or any town or city, one sees them everywhere and one assumes there is little more to find out about them other than their shape and colour. To see them less than an inch before one's nose was like a revelation. I saw in close-up their gritty surfaces with their coarse, open pores, and their colour, predominantly a reddish brown which was streaked in irregular patches with lighter and darker shades ranging from a dusky pink to a purplish black. I saw, too, the paler bands of mortar which bound them together, not smooth as they appear from a distance but pitted and scabbed. I also smelt them, a mingled odour of soot and damp cinders.

I was aware of nothing else about me, neither the rest of the hotel stretching up above me nor the lighted glass dome of the restaurant below.

As my feet crept painfully sideways, my right hand, as if attached to my feet, made the same slow, oblique progress across the wall, like a crab, feeling for the edge of the pediment above the next window, that of the room where Igor, Baron Kleist's bodyguard slept. My relief on reaching it and feeling my fingers grip the stonework is beyond description except that I knew then the emotion a mountaineer must experience when he successfully gains the summit of some dangerous, rocky cliff.

Seconds later, my shuffling feet had, so to speak, caught up with my hand and I was able to lift them slowly, one after the other, on to the broad safety of the window sill.

Like Holmes, I rested there for several moments, aware for the first time of the pain in the stretched muscles in my arms and the backs of my legs. I also copied the action I had seen Holmes make, pressing my face close to the glass, and saw what he must have seen which had induced him to signal for silence.

Although the curtains were drawn across the window, a pencil-thin gap between their edges allowed me a glimpse into the room beyond.

I could see little except for a strip of flower-patterned wallpaper and part of a cream-coloured bedspread together with the wooden foot-rail of a bed, similar to the one in the adjacent room to which Oscar had attached the rope. I could see no one, but something about the manner in which the cover was disarranged suggested that someone, Igor presumably, was either lying on it or had been recently. The sight of it made me strongly aware that, although absent, the baron's malign influence was still potent, a thought which spurred me to move on although I doubted if the occupant of the room could have heard anything above the sound of the orchestra below in the Winter Garden or the traffic passing by along Piccadilly.

The relief I had felt on reaching the first window was a mere tremor compared to the rush of emotion on my gaining the safety of the last.

Holmes had left the bottom sash open and was waiting inside the room to help me over the sill.

He said nothing for he rarely expressed his feelings but his face conveyed more clearly than words his own relief at my safe arrival. There was also both admiration and pride in his features as he took my hand in both of his and wrung it warmly, mouthing the words 'Well done, Watson!' as he did so. It was at moments like those that I felt closer to Holmes than to any other living person, my own dear wife excepted.

He had already scribbled down a note for my benefit which read: "Igor is in the next room. Keep *cave* for me."

He pointed to the far wall where a door connected the two rooms and I nodded in agreement to show I, too, was aware of Igor's presence before crossing silently to the door and kneeling down in front of it. Like a little window, the keyhole afforded me a wider view than the narrow gap between the curtains. I could see more of the bed and the legs of a man stretched out upon it. I could also smell the pungent odour of a Russian cigarette and hear the crisp rustle as the pages of a newspaper were turned over.

While I was thus occupied, Holmes himself had been busy for, by the time I glanced over my shoulder, the doors on the large wardrobe, the twin of the one in Oscar's bedroom, already stood open, although Holmes may have picked the lock before my arrival, and he was in the act of lifting out of it a leather valise, like a Glad-stone bag only smaller, from which he extracted a black-japanned metal box with a strong steel band going round it, in the centre of which were three small keyholes.

With most of my attention centred on keeping watch on the baron's bodyguard lying on the bed in the adjoining room, I was able to take only occasional quick glances at Holmes. By this means, I saw him carry the metal box to a dressing table with a mirror standing upon it, like the wardrobe an exact double of the one in Oscar's bedchamber, and, placing it carefully down on the surface, take from his pocket the three picklocks which Charlie Peak had given him.

The room was full of a heavy, dense silence which seemed palpable, as if an invisible fog had crept into the room, filling every corner and crevice. The only audible sounds were the tiny metallic clicks as Holmes manipulated the picklocks and, faraway, the distant sound of the Winter Garden orchestra which was now playing extracts from Gilbert & Sullivan.

It was evident that, despite the hours of practice Holmes had spent at our lodgings, opening the Medici casket was not easy. Each time I glanced hurriedly over my shoulder at his thin frame stooped over the task, his long fingers were busy delicately probing, his head strained forward in the effort to hear the faint sound of the wards yielding to his skilful manipulations. He was totally engrossed, deaf and blind to anything else going on about him.

And then suddenly, he gave a long, soft exhalation of breath and with it, the tension in the room fell away as if a great pressure had been released. The locks had at last given way.

The whole of my attention was now centred on Holmes. As I watched, he opened back the lid to look into the casket and then, reaching inside it, lifted out a little case covered in blue and gold leather, the exact replica of the one Holmes had in his pocket.

As he did so, I was aware of a new and unexpected sound which came, not from the room which we were occupying but from the adjoining chamber. It was an insignificant noise and had I not been kneeling with my head close to the door, it might have passed unnoticed for it was nothing more than the faint creak of a bed frame.

Immediately, I clapped my eye to the keyhole only to find to my consternation that my view through the tiny aperture had changed dramatically.

I could no longer see the outstretched legs of Baron Kleist's henchman. Instead, I saw the lower part of his torso, his garments strained upwards, an odd perspective until I realised the man was standing upright and was stretching his arms above his head as if loosening his muscles. The next second, I lost even this limited view of him as he stepped forward towards the door.

It is astonishing how quickly one's mind can work in moments of danger. Although I had only a few seconds in which to act, I knew instinctively what I had to do.

I gave a low whistle to attract Holmes's attention and, as he turned his head, I got up from my knees and jerked my thumb urgently towards Igor's room. At the same time, I stepped to the right where, once the door was opened, it would shield me from view for at least a few seconds as Igor crossed the threshold.

The next instant, the door was flung back and a huge man with the build and muscles of a prizefighter came into the room. His astonishment at the unexpected sight of a stranger standing by the dressing-table gave me a split-second's grace. So, too, did the additional few moments it took him to absorb and realise the significance of what he was seeing – the wardrobe doors gaping wide, the leather bag discarded on the floor and the Medici casket lying on the table, its lid opened back.

It was only then that he prepared to attack.

As he stepped into the room, I also made my first move. Flinging myself forwards from my hiding-place behind the door, I seized him round the legs from behind in a rugby tackle and, using my weight like a battering ram, slammed him face downwards on to the floor.

He collapsed with a grunt, dazed but not unconscious. As he struggled up on to his knees, Holmes, who had meanwhile strode towards us, delivered the *coup de grâce* with a powerful right uppercut at which the man fell forwards again, this time unconscious.

Rubbing his knuckles, Holmes gave me a rueful grin.

'It was, of course, very unsporting to hit a man when he was down but I am sure the Marquess of Queensberry would have forgiven me. Your fellow members of the Blackheath Rugby Club would certainly have applauded your tackle. It was superb, my dear fellow.'

However, while appreciating Holmes's compliment, I was aghast that my precipitate action might have not only ruined Holmes's plans but also those of the King of Scandinavia.

'What will you do now?' I asked anxiously. 'Once Igor regains consciousness, he will be sure to report to the baron and the cat will really be out of the bag.'

To my surprised relief, Holmes treated the matter with an off-hand air.

'It is of little concern,' said he, with a shrug. 'I doubt very much if Igor will tell Kleist anything. To do so would certainly mean in-stant dismissal. But should the baron be informed, his first concern

will be to examine the Medici casket which he will find securely locked and the Gustafsson stone safely inside it. It would not
cross his mind that it is the fake he himself so cleverly passed
off as the original. The King of Scandinavia, or rather to use
his preferred title, Count von Lyngstrad, only recognised it himself because of the secret mark his so-called uncle scratched on
it without the baron's knowledge. But if, by some unlikely chance,
he does suspect something, what can he do about it? Inform the
police? Hardly. It would mean admitting to fraud. Or would he
try to hunt us down and force us or the King of Scandinavia to
return the real jewel? Also unlikely for the same reason. As for
identifying us, that too is out of the question. Because of our
disguises any description of us by Igor or a member of the hotel
staff would be quite useless.

'Consider also another aspect of the situation: Baron Kleist's
arrangement to sell the Gustafsson Stone to Cornelius Bradbury,
the American collector, who is due to arrive in this country in a few
days' time. If Kleist admits the pendant is a fake then he will undoubtedly lose the sale.

'No, my dear fellow. We have no cause to fear any of these con-
tingencies. If the baron finds out about the substitution, he will keep
quiet about it. I know I would if I were in his shoes.'

'But Bradbury will be buying a fake!' I protested.

'Oh, Watson!' Holmes chided me, laughing heartily. 'The pendant
is part of the Scandinavian crown jewels! The man must know it was
obtained illegally. All I can say to that is *caveat emptor*, a very sensible
piece of advice to anyone buying an article of dubious origin. You
realise, of course,' he added, 'that because of this little *contretemps*,
there will be no need for us to leave by the window. We can go out
via the door like civilised human beings, a benefit for which I am
profoundly grateful.'

'And so am I,' I agreed wholeheartedly.

'By the way,' Holmes added a few moments later as he placed the
fake Gustafsson Stone in its leather box inside the Medici casket,
'have you noticed the emblem on the casket lid?'

In the general excitement of dealing with Igor, I had not given
particular attention to the box but now that Holmes had drawn it to
my notice, I saw that the decoration was in the form of an eagle,
inlaid in brass, its wings outspread and holding a single leaf in one
of its claws. The amused smile on Holmes's lips alerted me to its
significance.

'But is it not the same design which Charlie Peak described as being on the lid of the casket that Signer Valori was working on in Florence?'

'Exactly so, Watson! Which means we have here the very same casket bearing Kleist's personal emblem, appropriated, I might add, from the Hapsburg insignia of the imperial eagle. The bay leaf, a symbol of victory, of course, is Kleist's own personal touch. The vanity of the man is overweening! It gives me enormous satisfaction to have beaten him at his own game!'

With an air of well-deserved self-congratulation, Holmes placed the casket, now containing the fake Gustafsson jewel, inside the leather grip which he locked. That done, he closed and secured the wardrobe doors with a flourish.

Between us, we carried Igor's recumbent form into his bedroom where we laid it on his bed. After that, all that remained to be done was to tug on the rope to signal to Oscar to draw it in. Once it had slithered out of sight over the window sill, I closed the sash while Holmes made sure made sure everything else in the room was as we had found it.

As I lowered the window, I stood for a few seconds looking down on the lighted dome of the Winter Garden. Remembering my earlier image of crashing down on to the diners below, I allowed myself a small smile at the extravagance of my imagination.

We left immediately afterwards, pausing for a few seconds to make sure the corridor outside was empty, before Holmes locked the door behind us and we let ourselves in to the adjoining suite of rooms where Oscar was waiting anxiously, fearing for our safety when the rope returned with neither of us at the end of it.

Holmes gave him a brief account of our adventures, and then we left for Baker Street by cab, stopping briefly on the way so that my friend could send a telegram to our client, Count von Lyngstrad, alias the King of Scandinavia, announcing the success of our mission.

It read simply, but enigmatically to anyone ignorant of the facts:

YOUR FRIEND GUSTAF IS ON HIS WAY HOME STOP SUGGEST YOU MEET HIM TOMORROW AT 11AM STOP.

The following morning, precisely on the hour, our illustrious client, the King of Scandinavia, arrived at our lodgings and was shown upstairs to the sitting-room where, beaming delightedly, he offered both his hands to each of us in turn.

'Congratulations!' he exclaimed. 'It seemed an impossible task, but between the two of you, gentlemen, you have triumphed against all the odds. May I see the Gustafsson Stone?'

'Of course,' Holmes replied, indicating the table where the pendant was already laid out for inspection on a starched white napkin. The king seized it eagerly, holding it up by the chain towards the light and letting it revolve slowly so that he could examine it from every angle, all the time murmuring, 'Excellent! Excellent!'

Then turning to Holmes, he added, 'Tell me, for I am longing to know, how you managed to recover it.'

After Holmes had given a brief account of our adventure, to which the king listened with great seriousness, exclaiming out loud at the description of the dangerous route we had taken to enter the baron's room, my old friend concluded, 'I think we may assume that the matter is now concluded. If Baron Kleist learns of the substitution of the real jewel for the fake, he will keep silent for fear of losing the sale to the American millionaire.'

The king nodded in agreement and, returning the jewel to its leather case, he placed it in an inside pocket of his coat before again shaking hands with us and turning towards the door.

But the ceremony was not quite over. At the door, he turned back briefly to lay a large envelope on the white table napkin where the Gustafsson jewel had been displayed. Then, without a word, he bowed and left the room.

The envelope, which was fastened with an elaborate seal in red wax of the Scandinavian royal emblem of a crowned eagle, contained, as Holmes discovered when he opened it, a great number of English bank notes amounting to a fortune and a brief note which read:

> You will be committing *lèse majesté* if you do not accept this fee as well as my eternal thanks, both of which have been honourably and courageously earned.

It was signed Erik von Lyngstrad, the name by which he had first introduced himself.

'Well! well!' exclaimed Holmes.

He seemed uncharacteristically taken aback by the lavishness of the gift. Seconds later, however, he had recovered his usual *sang froid* and remarked, with a laugh, 'A truly king-sized fee, wouldn't you agree, my dear fellow, which could be the key to open our own Medici caskets.'

'I do not follow you, Holmes,' I replied, puzzled by the remark.

But he dismissed my question with an equally enigmatic reply. 'Money can buy many things, Watson; freedom, for example.'

I only understood his remark as it applied to himself some little while later when, not long before we set out together for a week on the Continent to escape from England while his arch-enemy, Professor Moriarty, was arrested, Holmes spoke of his longings to live in a 'quiet fashion', as he expressed it, and concentrate his attention on his chemical researches, an ambition which the investigation on behalf of the Royal Family of Scandinavia, together with the inquiry he had made for the French Republic, had made financially possible.

The relevance of the remark to my own affairs became clearer at a much later date, when Holmes had returned to England after an absence of three years following his apparent death at Moriartv's hand at the Reichenbach Falls.

In the meantime, my dear wife Mary had died, and on Holmes's return, I sold my practice in Kensington and moved back to share my former quarters in Baker Street with my old friend. A young doctor called Verner had, to my great astonishment, paid the high price I had asked rather hesitantly for the practice. I was later to discover that Verner was a distant relative of Holmes's and that it was Holmes himself who had found the money; at least part of which, I am sure, came from the fee paid to him by the King of Scandinavia'.

And so, as he had suggested, the fee did indeed serve as a golden key to open more than one Medici casket, so to speak, for that money enabled me to live comfortably in Baker Street and to enjoy with the greatest of pleasure the renewed companionship of my old and very dear friend, Sherlock Holmes.

The Disappearance of the Cutter Alicia

JOHN HALL

Towards the close of Mr Sherlock Holmes's professional career an investigation which I find recorded in my notebook under the heading of 'The Adventure of the Giant Leek', but which has no bearing at all on my present subject, took the two of us to Northumberland, a place which neither of us had visited before. The case which had originally taken us there was soon concluded satisfactorily, and for my part I looked forward to returning to London, for the spring was late that year, and the northern breezes with their hint of the sea, though indubitably bracing, were detrimental to the rheumatism which bothered me more with each passing year.

Holmes, however, seemed disinclined to hurry back. 'It was at this time of year,' he told me over breakfast, 'and not so very many miles away, that the cutter *Alicia* disappeared some ten or twelve years ago, in rather odd circumstances.'

'Ah, yes, I recall the case,' I said. 'Sailed into a small patch of mist, did she not, and never emerged?'

Holmes nodded. 'As you know, I was consulted, but could not think of any possible explanation. I did not visit the scene, since a search had been made by the local fishermen and coastguards, and it seemed to me that where local knowledge had failed, I could not hope to succeed. I confess I still cannot imagine what might have happened to the vessel.'

'But, now you are here, you would like to investigate more thoroughly?' I suggested with a smile.

'Well, frankly I would, although after this span of time the trail, if ever there was one, will have gone stone-cold. Are you in any great hurry to return home?'

'Not I,' I said. And it was true enough, for we could return any time, but such an opportunity might not present itself again. I knew that Holmes was bursting to look into the problem, and I too found my curiosity piqued by the proximity of the place where this curious disappearance had occurred.

When breakfast was over, then, we paid our bill, took our bags – we both travel light – and set off for the little fishing village, not many miles away, from whence the crew of the *Alicia* had been drawn. 'It was not a large crew,' Holmes told me thoughtfully, 'two men and a boy. The skipper was a man named Allinson, and the mate one Josiah Merritt. Allinson's son, young Toby, was acting as third hand. Allinson and his wife had but the one child, and then Merritt, who was only twenty or so, had recently become engaged to be married to the sister of Allinson's wife, and the wedding was set for a fortnight or so from the day the *Alicia* disappeared, so the tragedy was doubly and trebly poignant for that.'

'Indeed. It is said lightly that "worse things happen at sea", and I have no doubt that the deeps hold many a tragic secret, Holmes.'

'Now, Watson, you are, I know, an enthusiast for the sea stories of Mr Clark Russell, and you have done a bit of sailing yourself, I believe, quite apart from your passages to India and the like?'

'Oh, to be sure. Nothing like it, Holmes. Jigging in the rigging, and all the rest of it. A grand life, a man's life.'

'Well, then, in your expert opinion, why should a ship vanish from the surface of the sea?'

'By sinking,' said I immediately. 'Rough weather, a capsize, that sort of thing. All too common, I fear.'

'It was a calm day, no wind to speak of. As proved by the presence of that small patch of mist, which the wind would surely have dispersed.'

'Collision, then? Another ship?'

Holmes shook his head. 'There were no reports of another vessel missing. Visibility was good – '

'The mist?'

'Purely a localised patch. And, apart from the fact that no other vessel was missing, no other vessel was even seen in the vicinity.'

'There must have been some observer, though, Holmes, or the sighting of the *Alicia* going into the mist could never have been made?'

Holmes consulted his memorandum book. 'Ah, yes, Captain Mott is recorded as having reported seeing the vessel enter the mist patch. I have his address here, as well as his deposition, so I think we shall call upon him.'

'He might be at sea.'

'No, for he was already described as "retired" when the vessel vanished.'

I could not suppress a smile. 'You appear to have all the relevant facts quite at your fingertips, Holmes.'

'Well, I knew when we first set out from Baker Street that we should be in the locality, and so it would indeed have been remiss of me not to have looked up the details of so intriguing a case.'

We asked the way to Captain Mott's house, and made in that direction. As we walked, Holmes continued, 'No collision, and no wind to blow her violently off course. What else would there be to account for it?'

'A collision, but with some sunken object perhaps, rather than a ship? Or perhaps some floating object, that flotsam or jetsam the exact difference between which always seemed so important to one's schoolmasters?'

Holmes nodded. 'A logical surmise. But the water there is relatively shallow, and there was no trace of any sunken object, either before or after the disappearance of the *Alicia*, which indicates that she did not sink, for whatever reason. Nor was any debris found floating on the surface.'

'H'mm. It is a puzzle, Holmes.'

'Perhaps. But your expertise has narrowed it down considerably, has it not? There remain but two possibilities, surely.'

'Which are?'

'Well, one is that this singular patch of mist had some of the qualities or properties which might appeal to Monsieur Jules Verne, or Mr H. G. Wells, namely that in some supernatural fashion it caused the vessel to vanish utterly without trace.'

'Impossible, Holmes!'

He nodded. 'I quite agree.'

'And the other possibility?'

'Work it out for yourself, Watson.'

I thought a moment. 'You mean that the *Alicia* simply sailed out the other side of the mist, unobserved?'

'It is surely the only explanation which makes any sense?'

'But the testimony of this fellow, Captain Mott?'

'Ah, there you have me.' Holmes nodded at the little whitewashed cottage which stood at the end of the lane along which we walked. 'But we are almost there, and we can ask the man himself.'

We knocked at the blue-painted door, and after what seemed an age, it was opened by a man who might have served for the model of every salt-water captain that ever sailed between the pages of boys' adventure books. He was bearded, and had a patch over one eye, and more tattoos that any man is decently entitled to carry. He was very old, nearer eighty than seventy, so I could quite see that he had been retired ten years or so ago. He looked from one to the other of us, a question in his one unpatched eye.

Holmes introduced us, and said, 'It was really in connection with the curious disappearance of the *Alicia*, some time ago now, that we wished to speak to you.'

'Aye?'

'You recall the matter?'

'Indeed I do, sir.' The old fellow ushered us into his little parlour, all glass floats and lobster pots, and bade us sit down. 'Yes,' he said again, 'I remember it like it was yesterday, it being so strange and all.'

'Where were you when the *Alicia* sailed into the mist?' asked Holmes.

'Why, here, sir.' Captain Mott levered himself to his feet again with something of an effort, and took us to a door on the far side of the cottage, that is, the side which gave on to the sea. The cottage was at the very end of a tiny lane, and perched almost on the very edge of the cliffs. As a viewpoint, it could hardly be bettered. Captain Mott indicated a stand with a large telescope which pointed out to sea. 'Eyes none too good, these days,' he explained. 'Eye, I should say, for I've nobbut the one. Still, with the old spy-glass I reckon I can see as well as another.'

'I am certain you can,' said Holmes. 'And, that day, you saw the *Alicia* sail into a patch of mist?'

'Small patch, it were. Out there,' and he waved a hand in the general direction of the sea. 'By the shoals.'

'And then?'

'And then nothing. Never came out again, did she?'

'Did she not?'

'Well, I never seed her come out. And then she vanished, didn't she? Stands to reason, if she vanished, it must have been in that mist.'

'You say you did not see her leave the patch of mist,' said Holmes. 'No.'

'Ah, but did you look?'

Captain Mott frowned, and scratched his head. 'How d'you mean?'

'Well, had you the patch of mist under observation at all times? How long did you continue to look at it, after the *Alicia* had sailed into it?'

Another scratch of the head, more vigorous this time. 'Can't rightly say, sir.'

'Did you move the telescope to look for any other vessels, say, once the *Alicia* had gone from view?'

'Oh, aye.'

'So you were not actually observing the patch of mist the whole day?'

'Oh, not the whole day. But long enough.'

'What o'clock was it?'

'About dinner time, sir.'

'The evening?'

'No! Dinner time. Noon, near enough.'

'And you missed your luncheon, your dinner, I mean, that day?'

The old fellow grinned. 'Not me! I've a good appetite, better than many a young one.'

'Did you eat your dinner out here?'

'Not a bit of it.' Captain Mott's tone was scornful. 'I may be only an old sailing man, but I have my standards. I eats my dinner in the house, at the table.'

'So you left your vantage point for long enough to eat your meal.'

'Oh, aye.'

Holmes stood up. 'Well, thank you very much, sir. You have been most helpful.'

'A puzzle and all, isn't it? Her vanishing like that?'

'It is indeed.'

We took our leave of Captain Mott, and made our way down towards the little fishing village. 'Well, Watson?'

'Well, Holmes, despite the assurances of that delightful old fellow, it seems pretty clear that the *Alicia* might easily have sailed on unobserved. But none the less, that does not tell us what happened to her.'

'No, but it does enable us to eliminate one possibility, that of the supernatural, does it not? It gives us a course, as it were, by which to steer.'

'I trust there will be no more nautical metaphors in this case, Holmes?'

'It is said that the sea is in every Englishman's blood,' said Holmes didactically.

We arrived at the little village, and Holmes enquired if there might be a boat to hire. After one or two false starts, for the place was a fishing village rather than any recognised holiday spot, we found a young man who offered to take us out for the remainder of the day at a reasonable rate. 'Where exactly did you want to go?' he asked us.

'Ah,' said Holmes, 'that is something we have not settled. Where do boats go from here?'

'To the fishing grounds, of course,' answered our skipper with a certain degree of scorn in his voice. 'North-east, that is to say.'

'I see. Now, suppose you were to sail due east? That would bring you to France, would it?'

The skipper scratched his head. 'More like Holland or Belgium, sir,' he said at last.

'And south?'

'Oh, that would bring you to the nearest town of any size around here,' and he mentioned a name that was familiar to me.

'A holiday place, that, is it not?' I asked.

He nodded, and said, 'That's right, sir. Trippers, and the like,' and the scorn was palpable now.

'You sound as if it were not your favourite port of call!' I told him.

He laughed at this. 'We don't reckon much to that sort of thing round these parts, sir. We're a bit old-fashioned, you might say.'

'I see. Well, despite your lack of enthusiasm for the place, that is where we wish to go,' said Holmes.

As the skipper and mate began to make ready to sail, I took Holmes on one side and asked, 'Do you think that Allinson and Merritt really went to this town along the coast?'

'Well, they may have gone to Belgium or somewhere of course,' he answered, 'The *Alicia* was certainly capable of crossing that distance, and Allinson was a competent and experienced skipper. But quite frankly I cannot think that a couple of local fishermen, with no command of Dutch or French, would venture quite that far without good reason.'

'But their reason might have been excellent!' I pointed out.

'True, and they may indeed have gone in that direction. If that is so, then obviously we cannot hope to follow them. But I submit that this is the most logical course for them to have taken. There would be no language barriers, and the two men and one boy would easily be lost in the crowds of holidaymakers.'

'But the boat would not,' I told him. 'Even if they had evaded the eagle eye of the harbourmaster and simply left the boat there, it would not remain long undiscovered when once a search was instituted. True, the subsequent whereabouts of the crew might remain obscure, but the first part of the mystery, the supposed disappearance of the boat, would have been cleared up.'

'H'mm. That is quite correct,' said Holmes. 'Well, then, we must assume that they got rid of the boat somehow.'

'How?'

'That remains to be seen.' And he stared out to sea without further comment for a long while.

It was a pleasant enough day, and my earlier remarks to Holmes as to my enjoying sailing were quite truthful, so I composed my mind to a proper appreciation of the beauty of the sea, the skill of the crew, and the restful character of any sea voyage, however short and close to land. In short, I settled down on the foredeck and dozed off. I was woken a short time later by Holmes shaking me.

'Well?' I asked.

For answer, he pointed towards the land. I looked, and saw a little bay of sorts, with high craggy cliffs behind it and some treacherous looking rocks in the sea immediately before it. There was no sign of human habitation near, so this inaccessible little bay was completely deserted.

'Ever try to land there?' Holmes asked our skipper, pointing.

An emphatic shake of the head answered him. 'Not likely, sir! Too dangerous. See them rocks? There's nobody much goes there, no houses or anything close at hand, and no sort of beach that would appeal to the holidaymakers.'

'And yet it seems to me that there is something in the water there?' Holmes went on. I looked again, and could make out some planks, or something of the kind.

'Looks as if it might be a wreck of some sort,' I ventured.

'It does look that way, doesn't it, sir?' said the skipper, shielding his eyes with his hand and staring where Holmes pointed.

'Is there nothing marked on the charts?' asked Holmes.

'We don't usually bother with charts, sir. But in any event, it wouldn't be marked on the chart, not being so close to the shore.'

'I see.' Holmes thought a moment. 'The nearest habitation would be this town you mentioned, yes? And how far is that?'

'Just round the headland here, sir. No very great distance at all.'

'So that if I were to scramble up these cliffs and make my way inland, that would be the first place I should come to?'

'Beg pardon, sir,' the young mate put in, 'but the station's nearest.'

'Station?'

'Railway station, sir. Just over that hill, and a mile or so's walk,' and he pointed at the top of the cliffs. 'Station's not in the town, you see, but a couple of miles outside. They run a regular charabanc service backwards and forwards, in the season.'

'I see.' Holmes remained sunk in thought for the rest of the voyage, a matter of half an hour or so. When we had tied up in the harbour of the little town, Holmes paid our skipper the agreed amount, and told him that we should be making our own way from there. Waving a farewell, he led the way into the town, and set off along the road which led to the station.

'You really think this is where Allinson and Merritt came? And the lad?' I asked him.

'I think it is a distinct possibility.'

'So they beached the *Alicia* in that little cove place, sank her, then made their way over the cliffs and moorland to the station?'

Holmes nodded. 'It is surely more believable than that the vessel simply vanished into thin air, Watson. We shall ask at the station, though.' When we reached the little station, set among the hills, he consulted his memorandum book. 'Now, if they sailed in the direction which we took, and they took an hour to destroy the vessel as best they could, and if – too many "ifs", here, Watson! Still, let us try,' and he approached the station master with a question. Five minutes later, he returned, a satisfied look upon his face.

'Had any luck?' I asked.

'I think so,' said Holmes, and went on to tell me that if his estimates were correct, the men could have caught a train which would have taken them south, to a large manufacturing town in the south of Yorkshire.

'Suppose your estimates are wrong?' I asked him.

'That is a danger, of course. But there are other trains to other places,' he answered with a laugh. 'We cannot possibly hope to track them down at this distance in time. All we can hope to do is to demonstrate what they might have done.'

'Ah, but they might have done anything!'

'You have a most salutary outlook, Watson.' Holmes lit a cigar, and handed me his case.

'Why are we sitting on the platform, Holmes?' I ventured to ask.

'Because there is a train to the town I mentioned in thirty minutes, Watson. We can get a connection to London from there.'

'And suppose the men we are following – or we *think* we are following – did the same? Went on to London, I mean?'

'Oh, they may very well have done precisely that. In their place, you and I would probably head immediately for London. As I said, we cannot hope to track them down, or even follow their footsteps exactly. All we can hope is to show what may have happened.' But there was a curious note in Holmes's voice, and I knew that he hoped for the impossible.

We reached the grimy manufacturing town, and got out of the train into a sluggish rain. I shivered. 'Shall I look up our connection, Holmes?'

He did not answer, and I turned to him in some annoyance, to see his gaze riveted upon a large poster which decorated the wall nearest the spot where our train had halted. 'Rooms to let,' said the poster, and gave some details.

'Holmes?'

'That would have caught their eye, had they taken this train, would it not, Watson?'

'Perhaps so, Holmes, but it is a brand new poster!' I pointed out.

'Yes, but then there may be some record of what was here previously.'

I began to express my opinion of this optimistic theory, but Holmes did not bother to listen. Instead he went over to the poster, and examined it closely, returning a moment later with something like triumph in his eyes. 'That is interesting,' he told me. 'The old posters have simply been pasted over, and the address is the same, although the name of the proprietor has changed.' He glanced at his watch. 'Now, friend Watson, we could take a London train in some ten minutes, or we could follow this clue and take a later train. What do you say?'

'I say it's probably a complete waste of time, Holmes. But I know that you won't be happy unless we try, so let us find a cab, by all means.'

He shook my hand warmly, and led the way outside to the cab rank. A ride of no more than ten minutes brought us to the address which Holmes had given the cabbie, and we got down in front of a clean and cheerful detached house, standing back from the road in a spacious and trim garden.

'This is really a very long shot, Holmes,' I said as he led the way down the drive and rang the bell.

'I know it is, Watson, but – ah!' he said, as the door was opened by an attractive young woman, 'Mrs Blake, is it? We saw your poster at the railway station.'

Her face fell. 'I'm sorry, gentlemen, but I have no rooms free just at the moment. If you like, I can give you another address, a very nice place – '

'No, no,' said Holmes. 'It was not a room we were wanting. But I fear that you can scarcely be expected to help us in our investigation, for you cannot have been running this house ten years ago? You are too young, I fancy.'

'Thank you, sir! But I assure you that I was here ten years ago, and more. My Ma, mother, that is to say, had the place then, of course, but I helped her, in the kitchen and what have you. Then I met dear Joe, my husband, I mean, and we more or less took over the running of it, with Ma being ill. She died some four years ago now,' she added.

'Ah. I'm sorry to hear it,' said Holmes. 'Joe, you say? Joseph, that is?'

'No, sir, Josiah.'

'Ah, yes, Josiah Merritt, of course.'

She frowned. 'Blake, sir.'

'Of course, how silly of me.' Holmes glanced at me with something like triumph in his face. 'Tell me, would it be too much to ask for a word with Mr Blake? Is he in the house now?'

'He is, sir. If you'll wait in the parlour, I'll call him.' And, somewhat mystified, Mrs Blake went off into the back of the house.

'Well, Watson? We appear to be in luck, you see.'

'It may be a mere coincidence of given names, though. The surname is different, after all. And coincidence would be the right word, if it were – ' I stopped as the door opened, and Mrs Blake steered in a man of thirty-five or so. He was not unattractive, but had a worried expression upon his face.

'Mr Blake?' asked Holmes, in his silkiest tones. 'Do not alarm yourself, sir, it was merely a small point we wished to clear up.' He glanced at Mrs Blake. 'I wonder if you would be so very kind as to excuse us, madam? It is nothing serious, I promise you, that we wish to ask your husband.'

Looking even more mystified than ever, Mrs Blake muttered something about 'getting the veg on anyway', and left us.

'Now, Mr Josiah Blake,' said Holmes. 'Or should I say Josiah Merritt? I have here a photograph of you taken some twelve years ago, and you have changed remarkably little in the meantime.'

Blake, or Merritt, as I should call him, sat down heavily and buried his face in his hands. 'Did they send you?' he managed to ask at length.

'No-one has sent us, I assure you,' said Holmes gently. 'And no-one need ever know what is said in this room. But you left some questions unanswered when you vanished all those years ago.'

'And some grieving family,' I added.

Merritt's face changed at my words. 'Grieving family?' he cried. 'Why the devil d'you think we ran away in the first place, you great dunce?'

'I really have no idea, sir,' I told him stiffly. 'Perhaps if you were to explain the matter to us, without descending to personalities?'

'Allinson was the owner of a little fishing boat,' he told us, 'and I'd learned my sailing from my father, in a little village a few miles up the coast. Then when I was old enough, or thought I was, I set off to seek my fortune, as you might say, and walked down the coast. I met Allinson on the dockside, and we got to talking, and the upshot was that he offered me both a job going mate with him, and lodgings, for they had a spare room. It seemed ideal, and I moved my bits of gear in right away.

'Well, I soon worked out that something was wrong with the pair of them. Oh, Allinson was all right, you couldn't ask for a finer skipper or a better friend. And the lad, Toby, he was first-class too. It was the wife that was the cause of all the trouble, you see. She was the elder daughter of an old lady who lived a couple of doors away – the father had cleared out, he was nobody's fool! Well, the old lady had a tongue like the worst sort of fishwife, and the daughter wasn't far behind. She scolded poor old Allinson something terrible. And she drank. And when the daughter stopped, the mother came in and started! There was another daughter, a younger one, and – and don't ask me just how it happened, gentlemen, for I couldn't tell you, not to this day – but I found myself engaged to this other daughter, and the old lady set fair to running my life. Running it? Ruining it, more like.

'Well, you don't like talking of these things, but with being out at sea so much together, we couldn't rightly help mentioning it now and again. One day we were in the pub, and maybe we'd had one too many, you know how it is, and Allinson he's pretty well in tears. "You don't know the half of it, Joe", he tells me. "She drinks, and she hits the boy, and I'm sure there are other men. And what's more, her sister encourages it, and she's every bit as bad herself, if not worse," he goes on. Well, the wedding was only three or four weeks off, so you can imagine how that sounded to me! I got cold feet, and no mistake. "Tom", I say to him, "I'm scared, pal. What am I to do?" And he looks at me, and he says, "What gets to me is the boy. You and me, we're grown men, we ought to be able to handle it, but the boy's only young, delicate like, he takes it to heart. Tell you what," he says, half-joking, "we could run away to sea!" Well, I laughed a bit, and then I got serious. "Why not?" I says. "What", he says, "run away?" "Yes, why not, Tom?"

'Well, we talked it over a bit more, and then we went off home, and neither of us said anything more that night. But then next day, when we was out at sea, Tom looks at me, and he says, "We'd had a drop too much last night, hadn't we, Joe?" and I says, "Not too much, if you ask me. Just enough to make us see sense at last", and he looks at me and he says, "Yes. Shall we go through with it?" and I said, "Yes", and we started to make our plans.

'Tom, he didn't want to leave Toby behind, but at the same time he didn't want to grab the boy and take him off against his will, so to speak. So we decided that we'd let Toby have the last word – oh, you'll maybe say it was cowardly of us to leave it up to the lad, but you have to remember that it was a big step we were contemplating, gentlemen. We drew out our bits of money from the savings bank, and precious little it was, too, and we set off with the boy aboard as third hand. When we got fairly away from the shore, Tom asks his son, "Toby, my boy, how would you like to sail off to a new life?" and the boy, he says, "Australia, father?" him having always had a fancy to go there. Tom says, "Yes, Australia if you like, but it'd just be the two of us, or three if Joe wants to come as well", and the boy thinks a moment and then nods his head.'

'And that decided you?' asked Holmes.

'Yes, sir. We beached the boat in a little bay not far down the coast, broke her up, and set off on foot over the hills.'

'Were you not afraid the wreckage would be found?' Holmes put in.

Merritt shook his head. 'There wasn't much that would identify her. A brass plate with the name and registry number, and we threw that into the rocks, where it sank; and the name on the bows, and we broke off the bits of planking, smashed them up, and hid the bits in ditches and the like as we made our way to the station. Well, by the time we got here, we were ready for a night's sleep, as you can imagine, and we saw the placard with the address of this place at the station. Tom and Toby, they stayed the one night and then moved on. I had a postcard from them, from London. I don't know if they ever got to Australia. I hope so.'

'And you stayed here, of course?'

Merritt nodded. 'I met Violet, of course, that first night, and I was taken with her at once. And I could see she felt the same way about me. The old lady, Violet's mother I mean, was running the place then, but she was getting on, and not too well. She'd been looking for a handyman to do a few little repairs, so I offered to help out a bit, and one thing led to another.' He looked fro m one to another of us. 'Well, gentlemen, you've heard my story. What action do you propose to take?'

Holmes shook his head. 'You have committed no crime, of course,' he said. 'Watson?'

'I suppose there might be grounds for an action for breach of promise,' I said. Merritt looked horrified at this. 'But only if they catch up with you,' I added.

Merritt looked at me, his face changing. '"If"?' he asked.

Holmes laughed. 'I no longer handle domestic disappearances,' he said, 'unless there are outstanding features.' He stood up. 'Your secret is safe with us. I suggest you tell your wife that we were mistaken, and that it was another man we sought.' He shook Merritt's hand, and we made for the street.

'Not a bad day's work, Watson,' said Holmes as we walked along.

'A lucky day's work, Holmes.'

'Oh, I don't know. We followed the trail, and we were rewarded. A modicum of chance, I agree, but even had we not actually run into Merritt, we should none the less have demonstrated what might easily have happened.' He glanced at his watch. 'If we can find a cab, we can catch a London train in less than twenty minutes, and be back in Baker Street for dinner.'

The Adventure of the Forgetful Assassin

M. J. ELLIOTT

When leafing through my accounts of the adventures of Sherlock Holmes, I find details of no less than forty-seven cases which, even at this late date, seem unlikely ever to be released to the public. Several, including the curious matter of Colonel James Moriarty and the scandalous affair of the politician, the lighthouse and the trained cormorant, I am barred from relating by legal obstructions. Others are simply of too delicate a nature to be revealed for fear of causing embarrassment to any of the participants or their heirs. Indeed, it was only with the recent death of Miss Susan Cushing that I was released from my promise not to publish an account of her grotesque and unsettling experience.

There is but one case that I have withheld for the sake of my own feelings. However, recent remarks made by certain of those individuals who purport to be admirers of my writings have made it unavoidable. I refer to those enthusiasts who indulge in what I believe is referred to as 'the game'; namely, perpetuating the fantasy that the published extracts from the life of Sherlock Holmes are nothing more than an elaborate fiction concocted by my literary agent. In the past I have allowed such juvenilia to go unchecked, but I have been prompted to take action by a recent article in which it is alleged that a reference to my good friend Charles Thurston in one of my earlier reminiscences was intended as little more than a thinly-disguised advertisement for a firm of billiard-table manufacturers. It is only because I have no desire to see his memory sullied unnecessarily that I am at last relating the particulars concerning his demise, though there remains much about the affair that I have cause to regret – most of all, my passionate quarrel with Holmes over the pertinacity with which he conducted his enquiry. But the facts are always preferable to idle and grossly inaccurate speculation.

After so many years at Holmes's side I should, one imagines, be used to sudden incursion into our mundane existence by the tragic and dramatic, but of all our investigations, I find that I cannot describe the events of that day in the February of 1901 without what a more fanciful person might describe as a sense of dread. Finding that my fellow lodger's love of companionable silence had ceased to be companionable, I had decided to visit my club where, over a few more brandies than is perhaps advisable, I passed the time in the company of several old acquaintances, among them Julian Emery, Gideon Makepeace and Charles Thurston. So agreeable was the experience that I invited Thurston to return with me to Baker Street, where I could regale him with further tales of our many triumphs.

Beyond an initial handshake, Holmes paid no attention to Thurston or me, preferring instead to rearrange the items on his chemistry table. But a man of Holmes's stature and personality cannot be easily ignored, even when he works in silence. I suspect that Thurston may have grown uncomfortable in Holmes's presence, for he twice asked me to explain the solution to the Camberwell poisoning case.

'Once Holmes knew the victim had gone to bed within two hours of winding his watch,' I repeated, 'the case became as clear as crystal. A child could have worked it out.'

'Not your child, Watson!' he guffawed. I joined in, for I knew Thurston's good-natured ribbing of old.

Holmes cleared his throat loudly.

'You remember the Camberwell poisoning case, don't you, Holmes?'

Pretending that he had not been paying attention, the detective raised his head. 'Hm? I'm sorry, Watson, what were you saying?'

I felt certain that he was fully aware of the body of our conversation, but I nevertheless explained that I had been entertaining Thurston with the story of our most notable coup. 'Quite a pretty little problem, eh?'

'I prefer to think of it as an instructive exercise in logical deduction.'

Clearly sensing the coldness in Holmes's reply, Thurston rose from his chair and began to don his hat and coat. 'Well, either way, it was a rattling good yarn! And now I must be off, I'm afraid. Harley Street beckons. Mr Holmes?' He gave an informal salute, and received a nod of the head in return.

As we descended the stairs, I asked Thurston what he had meant when he mentioned Harley Street. 'Nothing serious, I hope?'

'Something very serious, Watters, old man – money! Half those medicos owe their gold cuff links to my advice. I say, I don't suppose you could talk Holmes into sinking a little capital into San Pedro tin?'

I laughed as I opened the door for him. 'I doubt that very much. I expect that he would say he has sufficient for his needs.'

'How very peculiar,' replied Thurston. ' "More" has always been *my* favourite amount! Well, good-day to you!'

As I returned to the sitting-room, I pondered whether I should refrain from commenting upon Holmes's apparent rudeness, but when I discovered him lounging in the chair so recently vacated by Thurston, I found I had to speak.

'Is it really too much to ask for a little common civility, Holmes?' I asked. 'This is my home as well as your workplace.'

Holmes's expression was one of innocent incomprehension. 'You are quite welcome to play host to whomever you wish – my dear Watters.'

Where I had taken Thurston's ragging in good humour, I was now profoundly irritated. I opened my mouth to speak, but whatever my reply would have been, it is now lost to my memory. For at that moment, the ghastliest cry I have ever heard reached us from the street below. In my capacity as a physician as well as that of assistant to Holmes, I fear that I have heard many screams of agony through the years. But this was all the more horrifying for the fact that I recognised the voice as that of Charles Thurston.

We rushed downstairs, and I flung open the door to be confronted by a mass of onlookers. I fought my way through the crowd, but it was far too late for any assistance; Thurston lay dead at the foot of our steps, blood spilling from a deep wound in his chest. I heard an aggravated grunt and realised that the gap in the wall of gawkers had closed behind me, and that Holmes was struggling to emerge. I looked about me in the faint hope that I might catch a glimpse of the party responsible for this terrible attack. To my amazement, my hopes were rewarded, for I observed a tall, thin young man clad in a long overcoat turn his back upon the spectacle and begin to depart. It was clear from the unnatural way he kept his right arm close to his side that he was attempting to hide something about his person. In an instant, I had risen and begun my pursuit. My quarry seemed at first confused, but realising that I was dogging his steps, he broke into a run. His long legs might have seen him halfway across Blandford Street had he not been hampered by the need to hold on to the murder weapon. My fury kept my own legs moving beyond the point where the pain of my old wound might ordinarily have forced me to stop. I wrestled the young man to the ground, placing sufficient pressure upon his arm that he was forced to drop the knife – it was a long thin blade, and seemed curiously familiar. But my anger was too great at that moment to permit me to take in all its details. My captive's bowler hat came off in the struggle, and grabbing a fistful of ginger hair, I pressed his face into the grime of the street. I dread to think what act my rage might have led me to perpetrate, had not Holmes arrived at that moment.

'Watson!' he cried. 'Watson, are you all right?'

At the sound of his voice, the spell was broken, and I felt in a rush all the agony I had blotted out in my desire to capture Thurston's killer.

'I'm quite all right, Holmes,' I gasped, though in truth I felt far from well. I attempted to rouse my prisoner, but he remained a dead weight upon the pavement. With Holmes's assistance, I was able to turn the fellow over. He was fully conscious: a man of about five and twenty years, with a narrow face and lank red hair. But in his blue eyes, I saw no comprehension whatsoever.

Despite Mrs Hudson's insistence that I remain at Baker Street and submit myself to her ministrations, I was insistent upon discovering all I could about this dazed madman who had murdered my friend. Inspector Lestrade, who had been placed in charge of the case, was, of course, only too glad of our assistance. So it was that we three were in a cell at the Bow Street station some hours later, as the prisoner began to stir from his curious waking slumber.

He stared at us in turn, before focusing upon his surroundings. 'What – what *is* this place?' he murmured. 'Where am I?'

'You're in the Bow Street cells,' Lestrade replied. 'Now, what's your name?'

The young man considered this for a moment. 'My name is Alexander Hydell. Have I been arrested for something?'

' "Something", he says! Only murder, my lad!'

It was not my place to participate in an interrogation, but I could not remain silent. 'Why did you kill Charles Thurston?' I asked, harshly.

'Who are you?' Hydell asked in reply.

'Never mind who he is, just answer his question,' Lestrade ordered.

'I've never heard of Charles Thurston.'

The inspector raised his arms to the heavens as though imploring the almighty for patience. 'Ah, the old sweet song! So you don't remember a thing about it? Don't remember stabbing Mr Charles Thurston, a respected member of the London business community, through the heart on the steps of number 221B Baker Street?'

Dark though it was, I was aware for the first time of some dawning realisation in the young man's features.

'No, I didn't – I mean, I remember killing – I'm not sure.'

'Fascinating,' said Holmes, the first word he had uttered since we had entered the cell.

'The knife we took off you looks like something a doctor might use,' said Lestrade. 'You don't look much like a doctor to me.'

'I'm not a doctor, I'm a shipping clerk,' Hydell protested. 'I told you, my name is Alexander Hydell, I live on Bolton Street and I've never heard of anyone called Thurston!'

'I'm not interested in your life story, I want to know where you got the knife!'

'I don't remember,' was the sulky reply. Hydell curled up into a ball and lay with his back to us. Lestrade simply sighed. I have never claimed to be a professional detective, but I fancy that after two decades' worth of investigations, I can tell when a person is concealing something. I saw it then, and I had no doubt that it was an admission of guilt.

When it became clear that we would learn nothing more from the killer, Holmes asked that he be allowed to examine the murder weapon. Lestrade led us to his office, a tiny room with a huge ledger upon the table, and a telephone projecting from the wall. He removed the knife gingerly from a drawer, and passed it to Holmes, knowing better than to remind my friend of the importance of handling evidence with care.

Holmes studied the long-bladed weapon minutely. 'Watson, this is more in your line, I think.' Observing my distracted manner, he added, 'If you feel up to it, that is.'

'It's quite all right, Holmes,' I told him. 'It's called a bistoury. It's a surgical instrument. Hasn't been sharpened in many years.' I refrained from observing that it had, however, been sharp enough to kill Charles Thurston.

'It's distressing when an implement meant to save lives is used to take them,' Holmes mused. 'The blade is the finest Sheffield steel, Thomas Firth and Sons, if I'm not mistaken. The engraving on the handle is specific to Featherstone's of Knightsbridge. This was therefore an order for a well-to-do customer – a former surgeon.'

'Why not a practising surgeon?' Lestrade asked.

Holmes shook his head. 'Why would the owner allow the tools of his trade to get into this condition unless he no longer practised surgery? It should be a simple enough matter for you to trace the owner, Lestrade.'

The necessity of this task eluded me; with Hydell in custody, I could not see how it mattered how he came by the knife. The Inspector voiced the same objection.

Holmes was unperturbed. 'Yes, but it would be interesting to discover, would it not, how the bistoury passed from the hands of a wealthy former surgeon to those of a working-class shipping clerk from Bolton Street? As you say, Inspector, the killer is behind bars. What harm could it do to satisfy my curiosity?'

Holmes's prediction was correct; the manager of Featherstone's, an efficient if somewhat aloof gentleman by the name of Davison, had no difficulty in identifying the owner of the bistoury.

'Ah yes,' he announced in strident tones. 'A somewhat out of the ordinary request. Usually, you know, we deal in fine cutlery. If any of you gentlemen are looking for a suitable purchase for a wedding or anniversary, might I suggest . . . ? No? Well, in any case, I think I can say with all modesty that we rose to the challenge on this occasion. Yes, Dr Saunders was most satisfied with his purchase.'

I found it hard to fathom as we stood in the elegantly-appointed Harley Street consulting rooms of Dr Felix Saunders, that the incident that set us on this erratic trail – the murder of Charles Thurston – had occurred only hours before.

Lestrade let out a whistle as he examined our opulent surroundings. 'Business must be good,' he observed, 'whatever business is.'

'His official title is "psychoanalyst",' Holmes replied, holding up the business card he had taken from the salver in the hallway. The Inspector held out his hand, clearly wishing to examine the card for himself, but Holmes, apparently failing to notice our colleague's action, placed it in his top pocket.

Overlooking the apparent slight, Lestrade said, 'So this fellow's an alienist, then, like that German doctor?'

A booming voice from the doorway caused us all to turn our heads. ' "That German doctor" is Moravian, and his name is Freud'.

Doctor Felix Saunders presented a gargantuan figure, his craggy and deeply seamed face and fierce eyes could not fail to hold the attention. His enormous beard was as grey as the flakes of cigar ash that spotted his waistcoat.

Holmes appeared unaffected by the entrance of our impressive host. 'Tell me, Dr Saunders, is the term "psychoanalyst" your own, or of Freud's devising?'

The doctor raised a quizzical eyebrow. 'You're unusually inquisitive for a policeman', said he. 'Does it really take three of you to return a missing instrument?

I could hardly fail to take note of the significance of this remark. 'A *surgical* instrument?' I enquired.

'I was not referring to a musical instrument,' Saunders replied, leaving me feeling somewhat foolish. 'I reported it missing some days ago. Dare I take it you've found it at last? What became of Sergeant Rance, by the way?'

Lestrade stepped forward and introduced himself. Saunders seemed unimpressed, as though a fly had attempted to disturb a deity. 'I'd like to ask you a few questions about Alexander Hydell,' the inspector continued.

A moment passed in silence, as though Saunders were considering how best to respond. 'Well, Inspector,' he said, 'I can spare you a few minutes before my next appointment. I hope you won't take it amiss if I don't ask you to be seated. Are these gentlemen also police officers? They seem a little old to be your underlings.'

Holmes smiled. 'We strive in our small way to support justice, Sir. My name is Sherlock Holmes; this is my colleague, Dr Watson.'

'Indeed? I always thought you were imaginary, Mr Holmes, like Father Christmas. Well, what is it that you wish to know about Hydell? I need hardly point out that I will most likely be bound by the rules of confidentiality governing my profession.'

'Hydell *is* your patient, then?' I asked.

'He is. What about him?'

'He murdered a man named Charles Thurston earlier today, using your stolen bistoury,' I replied, bluntly.

If I had expected some response akin to shock from Saunders, I was to be disappointed. 'Well, well,' was all he had to say.

'Were you acquainted with Mr Thurston?' Lestrade enquired.

Saunders gave a shrug of his massive shoulders. 'I doubt if there's a doctor on Harley Street who hasn't had dealings with Mr Thurston.' I recollected my friend's parting words as I saw him on to Baker Street: 'Half those medicos owe their gold cuff-links to my advice'. I looked to Holmes, wondering what he might make of the interview, but to my surprise, he seemed less interested in our impressive host than in the contents of his bookshelves.

'When did you report the theft of the knife?' asked the inspector.

'I would prefer it if you referred to the instrument by its correct name, Mr Lestrade; I reported the theft of the bistoury last Friday.'

'And did you see Mr Hydell on that day?'

'Last Wednesday, actually. But it was only by chance that I happened to notice the theft. When I changed fields six years ago, I cleaned my surgical instruments and put the case in that cabinet. I rarely have call to look in it these days. It was mere chance that I did so on Friday. And before you ask, no, I do not normally keep it locked. Doubtless that was naïve of me. You may rest assured that I have since taken the appropriate precautions.'

It struck me that Saunders' arrogant manner seemed entirely at odds with his chosen profession. I shuddered inwardly at the thought of spending even an hour in his company socially, let alone as a patient.

Holmes's attention returned, at last, to the matter at hand. 'From the little I have seen of Alexander Hydell,' he commented, 'he does not appear to be the sort of man who could meet your fees, Doctor. How, then, did he come to be your patient?'

'I don't- *didn't* charge Hydell for his treatment. He was referred by a colleague, Dr Reginald Ward. I have no truck, you see, with the modern preoccupation for leisure pursuits. I fill my remaining time treating those who cannot otherwise afford my somewhat expensive services.'

I began to think better of Saunders. Perhaps, I thought, I had allowed his apparent pomposity to blind me to his finer qualities.

'So, as a psycho . . . *analyst*,' Lestrade struggled with the term, 'you treat patients who are going round the twist. So tell me, Dr Saunders: how far round the twist was Hydell?'

'I find that a very vulgar and insensitive remark, Inspector,' the doctor grumbled, 'and I prefer not to answer questions regarding my patients.'

'And do your medical ethics stretch to a patient who is deceased?'

Saunders gave this point a moment's thought. 'That, of course, would be a different matter.'

'Well, in a very short space of time, your Mr Hydell will be hanged for murder.'

'Then come back when you've hanged him and we'll talk again.' I was quite taken aback by the callousness of Saunders' response. Perhaps I had, after all, been over-generous in assuming that he was possessed of an altruistic nature, unless he kept it uncommonly well-concealed.

'Really, gentlemen, I fail to see why you are wasting your time and, more importantly, mine. Clearly, Hydell stole the bistoury when I was out of the room, and then used it to kill Thurston for his own reasons.'

Holmes spoke up. 'Hydell's recollections of the incident are unusually vague. And unlike you, Doctor, he claims not to have known Mr Thurston.' Saunders would not be drawn on this point. He and the detective locked eyes.

'I wonder,' Holmes went on, apparently unaffected by the obvious tension, 'if you practise hypnosis on your patients? I notice several volumes about hypnotism on your bookcase, including one by Franz Mesmer himself. I envy you your collection.'

'Envy is the beginning of all true greatness, Mr Holmes. Am I to understand that you are of the opinion that Mr Hydell may have been instructed to kill Thurston under hypnosis?'

'Is it possible?'

'Not remotely,' Saunders replied, scornfully. 'Such notions exist only in the minds of authors of yellow-backed fiction.'

'Then what explanation do you have for Alexander Hydell's murderous attack upon a total stranger, Doctor? Or would that explanation breach medical ethics?'

With great care, Saunders removed a fat cigar from the box on his well-polished desk. 'Are you any of you, by chance, familiar with the condition known as *poriomania*?' he asked.

Although I have never treated a patient suffering from that malady, I did indeed recognise the term. I explained to my colleagues that *poriomania* is a cognitive function disorder in which the sufferer can behave in a certain way without having any recollection of his actions. Saunders seemed profoundly unimpressed by my display of medical knowledge.

'And did you diagnose Alexander Hydell as suffering from *poriomania*?' I asked.

'I did not, but I venture to suggest that it would explain his behaviour. He kills Charles Thurston during one of these blackouts; naturally his memories of the event would be hazy.'

I considered this. A diagnosis of *poriomania* might well account for Hydell's violent behaviour. It might even save him from the noose, although, to my shame, I had at that moment no real interest in seeing him escape retribution for Thurston's murder.

A ring of the doorbell brought the discussion to an end.

'My next patient, gentlemen,' Saunders observed. 'I take it you have nothing else?'

'I don't believe so, no,' Lestrade replied. 'Well, thank you for your time, Dr Saunders, and thank you for that suggestion about the *porio-* er . . . Thank you, Doctor.'

I was quite satisfied that matters should be left as they stood for the remainder of the day, and Lestrade expressed his opinion that we should consider our work done. If Alexander Hydell was indeed prone to a condition that caused him to act in a fashion he could not later recollect, then perhaps Dr Saunders could be persuaded to visit the young man in his cell and verify that diagnosis. Holmes, however, was quite insistent that we speak to Hydell at the earliest opportunity. Lestrade capitulated, but wishing to have nothing further to do with the matter, retreated to his minuscule office, leaving us to conduct the interrogation.

I was uneasy at the thought that Holmes might bring up the subject of Dr Saunders' methods during the discussion. I had little sympathy for Hydell's plight, but I felt that such an approach would hardly be ethical. I was particularly perturbed by Holmes's suggestion that Hydell might have been instructed to murder Thurston while under hypnosis.

'It is a fruitless line of enquiry,' I advised him, as the uniformed officer unlocked the cell door for us. 'A person cannot be made to perform an act that is contrary to their will or nature, especially murder.'

'A pity,' was all that Sherlock Holmes had to say before we entered.

Rocking back and forth on his cot, Alexander Hydell seemed more pathetic than before. He would not raise his head to meet my gaze. I was troubled to observe several clumps of reddish hair on the floor of the cell, as though he had torn them from his own scalp in frustration.

'You again,' he muttered, more to himself than for our benefit.

'Mr Hydell,' Holmes began, making no attempt to ease the man's misery, 'your own physician referred you to Dr Felix Saunders for treatment – why?'

Alexander Hydell let out a long sigh and stretched out on the cot. 'I've always found it difficult to keep a job, Mr Holmes,' he said, 'or my temper. There was a woman in my life. Lily. We were to be married. But my dark moods became too much for her. I thought if I could just find a cure for my anger, I might win her back'

'And what form did Dr Saunders' treatment take?'

'He was very interested in my dreams about my uncle,' Hydell replied, eventually. 'He and my father were brothers, partners in a successful glassware firm in Manchester. When I was very small,

Uncle Maurice forced his own brother out of the business. Dad took me with him to London to try and start a new life down here.'

'What had become of your mother?' I asked, unable to restrain my own curiosity.

'She died when I was a baby. My father was never able to rebuild his fortune, and he died a bitter and broken man. The Doctor seemed to think that might have been the start of it all. I really don't remember.'

'And in order to remedy this condition, did Dr Saunders ever place you in a hypnotic trance?' Holmes enquired. I cleared my throat loudly, but he chose to disregard my interruption.

'He . . . said it would help ease my nerves.' To my surprise, an unpleasant, almost vicious grin began to spread on the young prisoner's features.

'And what is so amusing?' I asked, unable to disguise my distaste.

'I was just thinking . . . it's funny. In all my dreams, my uncle always looks the same. Same clothes, same expression on his face. I haven't seen him since I was a boy, so I only know him from an old picture I keep in my rooms. Funny.'

Holmes's face flushed and darkened. His brows were drawn into two hard, black lines, while his eyes shone out from beneath them with a steely glitter. He placed his palm on my shoulder, indicating that it was time for us to leave. With his other hand, he knocked on the cell door. I heard the key turning on the other side.

'I'm sure we shall speak again, Mr Hydell,' was all Holmes said as we departed.

The prisoner gave no reply.

Silence reigned as we made our way back to Lestrade's office. The Inspector sat with feet propped up on his desk, reading *The Mystery of a Hansom Cab*. At our entrance, he made a futile attempt to hide the volume, but then relaxed upon discovering that we were not of the official force.

'Well, gentlemen,' he said with a sigh, 'did you get what you came for?'

I, for one, did not know how to answer this question, since I had not been entirely sure what we *had* come for; Holmes did not give a direct reply, choosing instead to answer Lestrade's question with a question of his own. 'Inspector, if you saw one man shoot another in public, would you then arrest the bullet?'

The policemen shot a baffled gaze in my direction. 'Do you know what he's on about, Doctor?'

I shook my head.

'Would it be fair to say,' Holmes continued, 'that I have, on occasion, been of some assistance to you in your investigations?'

'I'd say that was something of an understatement, Mr Holmes,' the policeman replied with disarming honesty.

'We might say that the slate had been wiped clean if you were to do something for me now. It is no small thing, you understand, but I feel certain that the results will prove worthwhile. Oh, Watson, would you be so good as to hail a cab for us? I shan't be more than a few minutes longer.'

I had long since grown accustomed to Holmes's intentionally mysterious nature – he was exceedingly loath to communicate his full plans until the instant of their fulfilment - but I felt certain that I was being sent out of earshot for fear that I might take objection to the request he was about to make. As I flagged down a cab, I felt my anger growing, but I was determined to prevent it from rising to the surface. To give voice to such strong emotions would be to create unnecessary discord, and though my nerves had long since settled following my Afghan experiences, I still retained an abhorrence of rows.

I resisted the temptation to question Holmes about the case on the journey back to Baker Street, but upon our arrival, I found I could no longer hold my tongue.

'Well, Holmes, do I take it your investigation is not at an end?' I asked.

'The faculty for deduction must be contagious,' he observed, lighting a cigarette. 'You are correct, Watson. Dr Felix Saunders knows a good deal more than he is telling.'

While I had been very far from impressed by Saunders' haughty manner, I saw nothing underhanded in his diagnosis.

Holmes threw himself into his armchair. 'I wish I could share your bland appraisal of the matter, old fellow. Like Da Vinci, however, I am a disciple of experience. Is it reasonable that Hydell should have been left alone in his consulting room long enough to be able to locate, steal and conceal the bistoury?'

'Holmes, you always say that once the impossible has been eliminated, whatever remains, however improbable, must be the truth. It may be improbable that Hydell should be left alone for a sufficient length of time, but it is hardly impossible. Surely Saunders' theory that Hydell suffers from *poriomania* explains his unorthodox behaviour.'

He sent up a great blue triumphant cloud from his cigarette. 'On the contrary, Watson, that is the one point where his story falls down. As I have had occasion to remind you before, there is nothing more deceptive than an obvious fact. The theft of the bistoury indicates premeditation. We must look for consistency. Where it is lacking, we must suspect deception.'

'So it is your contention that Saunders provided Hydell with the bistoury. But surely that defies logic, since he must have known that such an unusual weapon could easily be traced back to him. And why then report its theft to the police? '

'A cunning stoke, that. He *wished* the blade to be traced, in order that he might feed us the notion that Hydell committed the murder during a mental blackout – a story, I might add, that both you and the Inspector lapped up. For shame, Watson.'

My anger welled up once more, and this time I had no desire to restrain it. 'But the mighty Sherlock Holmes wasn't fooled for a minute!' I cried. 'You really are a thinking machine, aren't you? Utterly bereft of emotion! We're not dealing with one of your "exercises in logical deduction", Holmes! This concerns the death of my friend! Lestrade has the man who killed him under lock and key! Why can't you see the hurt your stubbornness is causing?'

For a moment, Holmes appeared on the brink of defending his position with the same vigour, but then his features softened. His clear, hard eyes were dimmed. 'Watson, I beg of you, just give me one more day to complete my enquiries. If after that, I cannot prove my suspicions, I'll drop the matter entirely.'

I considered his offer and the manner in which it had been given. 'Do I have your word, then?'

'As a gentleman. And, I hope, as your friend.'

Nothing more was said of the matter that evening, though I spent little enough of it in Holmes's company, before retiring to my room, exhausted. I was not surprised to discover upon rising that Holmes had already departed – indeed, I doubted that he had slept at all. Where such exertions as we had undergone the day before would induce torpor in any normal man, he seemed somehow to draw strength from them. I found a note affixed to our mantelpiece by a jack-knife. It read: 'Watson – we are too conspicuous together at present. We must take separate paths. S.H.' I took leave to doubt his stated justification for his actions. After the argument of the night before, it was obvious to me that Holmes wished to work undisturbed by the possibility of further confrontation. Deducing that he had no desire for me to 'take a separate path' in our present investigation, I spent the majority of my morning attempting to organise my notes of our recent cases. At lunchtime, Mrs Hudson announced the arrival of Inspector Lestrade. His face was flushed, and it was clear to me that he had some important information to relate. His expression became crestfallen upon discovering that Holmes had not yet returned.

'Our friend is a terrible timekeeper, Doctor,' he observed.

'He summoned you, then?'

'I received a telegram about an hour ago. There's nothing in it to tell me what he's up to, mind. He's inscrutable as a Chinaman when he chooses. If it weren't for the fact that he gets results, I swear . . . '

Lestrade was interrupted at that moment by Holmes's return. He was in high spirits, apparently oblivious of the violent dispute of the night before. His eyes were shining and his cheeks tinged with colour. Only at a crisis have I seen those battle-signals flying.

'Good afternoon, Inspector! Help yourself to a cigar, by all means.'

Lestrade gave a nod of acknowledgement as the detective dropped into his favourite chair with a noisy expression of relief.

'Ah, it's good to be off my feet after such a busy morning!'

'Are you ready to reveal what you have been up to, then?' I asked.

'No mystery, Watson. I've been busy in the financial district. After that, I paid a visit to the Bolton Street home of the incarcerated Mr Hydell. A few sovereigns in the palm of his grasping landlady, Mrs Ecclestone, afforded me entrance to his modest apartment.'

'And did you find what you were looking for, Mr Holmes?'

'I am delighted to say that my search was entirely in vain, Lestrade.' It was clearly pointless to ask Holmes to elucidate at this time. He would reveal the meaning behind his veiled reply when he saw fit. 'And now, you are obviously bursting with news. Let us have it.'

'I'm sorry to have to tell you, Mr Holmes, that your plans have gone awry.' From the satisfaction in Lestrade's tone, I suspected that he was not truly sorry at all.

'How so?' asked Holmes.

'I telephoned the Manchester police as you requested. They had no trouble locating Maurice Hydell and persuading him to come down to London on the double.' Now, at least, I knew the nature of the favour Holmes had asked of his Scotland Yard crony. 'The prisoner didn't seem to recognise him at first, but as soon as the uncle introduced himself – '

'Alexander Hydell attacked him,' Holmes concluded, sententiously.

Lestrade was crestfallen to discover that Holmes had been anticipating this outcome all along, but he was not to be put off. 'It took three of us to prise his hands off the old feller's neck. This proves his guilt beyond doubt, I'd say.'

Holmes laughed softly to himself. 'My dear Inspector, it proves just the opposite, I should say. And now, if neither of you gentlemen has any pressing business within the next hour, perhaps you might accompany me on a little excursion, at the end of which I expect to introduce you to the person responsible for the murder of Charles Thurston.'

'Really, gentlemen!' exclaimed Dr Saunders with exasperation. 'You must understand that I have a practice to run. You simply cannot monopolise my time like this.'

Lestrade offered his apologies and nothing more, for he had no more notion than I of what had brought us back to the psycho-analyst's opulent Harley Street consulting room.

'I fear that your patients will have to do without your treatment from now on,' Holmes replied, casually.

The doctor took his cigar from his lips and gazed sternly at my companion. 'Because you expect to arrest me, perhaps? Be sure of your facts, Mr Holmes. Be very sure.'

'Am I correct is saying, Doctor Saunders, that before you began a business association with Charles Thurston, your financial interests were dealt with by a Mr Foster Barrington?' The name Foster Barrington had a familiar ring to it, and I fancied that I might have seen it in Holmes's irregular index, under "F".

'I make no secret of the fact,' said Saunders. 'What of it?'

'Foster Barrington fled the country two years ago when certain improprieties in his business practices came to light. I suggest, Doctor, that you were in collusion with Barrington, and when you put your affairs in Thurston's hands, he discovered the illegalities and proceeded to blackmail you. I am most sorry, Watson, but I have no doubt that it is the truth.'

I was appalled at this suggestion, but Saunders' reaction was even more dramatic. His fierce face turned to a dusky red, his eyes glared, and the knotted, passionate veins started out in his forehead. 'Preposterous! Thurston was already a wealthy man and I was his paying client. Why on earth should he have wished to blackmail me?'

'Because, as I had occasion to overhear him say, "more" was his favourite amount.'

'A most astute and concise diagnosis, Mr Holmes.'

Holmes bowed his head in acknowledgement. 'In my years as a consulting detective I have gained some insight into human behaviour. You, for instance, strike me as a man who is nothing if not methodical and precise.'

Saunders bowed his own head in return.

'Why should it be, I wonder,' Holmes went on, 'that *your* fingerprints, as well as Hydell's, were on the bistoury when I examined it? Did you not tell us in this very room that you had cleaned your surgical instruments before putting them away?'

After the surprise of Holmes's initial accusation, the psychoanalyst was more guarded in his reactions. 'Forgive me, Mr Holmes, but since you have not taken my fingerprints for the purposes of making a comparison, I should have to say that you are lying.'

'They were on your business card, Doctor.' I recalled the careful manner in which Holmes had handled the card, and how he had prevented Lestrade from touching it. 'I ask again: how came your fingerprints on to the blade?'

Saunders gave a mighty shrug, and a large flake of ash dropped from his cigar and landed at his feet. 'I can only suggest, Holmes, that you have too high an estimate of my methodical and precise nature.'

'Please forgive me, but I would appreciate it if you would do me the honour of giving me my prefix, Doctor.' When Saunders said nothing, Holmes continued as though the moment had not occurred. 'I suggest that your fingerprints found their way on to the knife when, after placing him in a deep hypnotic trance, you handed it to Hydell in order to have him kill Thurston.'

I had been silent until that point, but I felt I could not allow the interview to continue without voicing an objection. 'Holmes, I'm sorry, but that can't be – one cannot be induced to kill if it is not in one's nature!'

The detective nodded, sagely. 'How right you are, my dear Watson. But murder *is* in Hydell's nature; at least in respect of one specific individual. Think.'

The answer came to me at the same moment it occurred to Lestrade. 'His uncle!' the Inspector cried.

'Their dramatic reunion in the cells proves as much. Through your "charity work", Doctor, you found your ideal subject in Hydell and exploited his murderous resentment in order to turn him into a – well, a living weapon. I fancy you did not even have to give the order to kill; you simply persuaded him to transpose the face of his uncle with that of Thurston and told him where to be on a particular day so that he might see his target. His hatred for his long-lost relative did the rest. No doubt Hydell followed Thurston and Dr Watson from their club before lying in wait at Baker Street. A poor choice of address from your point of view, Dr Saunders, but in his mesmerised state, the young man could hardly be expected to show much discernment.'

The bristles below Saunders nose quivered with amusement. 'Mr Holmes, what an interesting patient you would make, you really are quite the fantasist. What a pity you have no proof! Only surmise and wild conjecture!'

For a moment, Sherlock Holmes appeared defeated, for it was quite true that he had no further argument to make that might support his theory. Then, quite unexpectedly, he observed: 'A tidy office is indicative of a tidy mind, Doctor, and your consulting room is extremely tidy. Not an item out of place. Save for that book.'

As one man, we all three turned to examine Saunders' bookcase. All the volumes were arranged with great care save for one, a treatise on hypnotism by Mesmer, which was out of line with its neighbours. Clearly, the owner had referred to it quite recently. Before the doctor could object, Holmes removed the book from the shelf.

'May I open it?' Holmes asked.

'You may not,' Saunders replied, curtly.

'Why not?'

'I do not wish it.'

'You'll have to do as the Doctor says, Mr Holmes,' Lestrade informed him. 'The book is his property after all.'

Seeming to acquiesce, Holmes held the tome out at arms' length. As Saunders went to snatch it, however, he allowed it to fall from his grasp. As the book landed, two photographs slid from its pages. Holmes was quick to retrieve them. A sardonic smile broke through his ascetic gloom.

'What have we here?' he asked. 'My carelessness has resulted in a most important find. Of course, I recognise the gentleman in this photograph as the late Mr Charles Thurston, but the other is unknown to me. I wonder . . . Lestrade, could you identify this individual?'

As Lestrade studied the photograph, recognition began to dawn on his features. 'He's bald now, and fatter round the middle, but yes, I saw him only today . . . This is Alexander Hydell's Uncle Maurice.'

I began dimly to realise what my friend was hinting at. The idea was both incredible and appalling, and yet it might be possible.

'I failed to find the photograph in Hydell's rooms this morning,' Holmes explained. 'Tell me, Doctor, did you instruct him under hypnosis to bring it to you? You would prefer not to say? No matter, it will be quite clear to a jury that you used these pictures when instructing Hydell that whenever he saw *this* man, Thurston, the face he imagined he saw would be *this* face, his hated uncle. Of course, it would have to be the photograph your patient has kept since childhood. He might not recognise his uncle as he is today. It took him some moments to do so, in fact, when I arranged a family reunion earlier today.'

'Think you're clever, don't you, Holmes?' Saunders growled.

'As a matter of fact, Doctor,' Holmes replied, 'I do.'

There remains little more to tell. Saunders' bombastic nature proved no match for the relentless interrogation of a Scotland Yard official, and he soon confessed to the scheme Holmes had outlined. Maurice Hydell returned to his native Manchester, bruised and shaken but not badly harmed. His troubled nephew was removed to an asylum, and it pains me to say that after all this time I have taken no steps to enquire after his condition. A man of exceptional evil cruelly exploited his illness, that much I know. But I will always carry with me the memory of a tall, thin young man in a long overcoat, fleeing from the murder of a man I choose to remember as a friend.

The Long Man

RAFE McGREGOR

*A reminiscence of Roderick Langham, late of the Indian Army
and the Metropolitann Police Force*

It took me thirty-six hours to track the Macedonian to a village inn in
Sussex. My arrival late on a Friday night and my haggard countenance
both lent plausibility to my masquerade as a City stockbroker seeking
a tranquil weekend in the country. I was just in time to join the other
guests for supper, and our landlord – a *Signor* Rossi – introduced me
to all four of my fellow-lodgers, including Makedonski. I was seated
next to Edford, a cadaverous professor of European History at Brase-
nose College, Oxford. Without prompting, he confided that his true
passion was archaeology, the practice of which had brought him and
his two students to the South Downs. Hughes was a Welshman who
didn't look old enough to be at university, small, dark and surly.
Parker was tall, fair, and full of his own self-importance. Either Edford was gregarious by nature, or perhaps tired of the company of
younger men, for he spoke without respite.

Only he and I repaired to the parlour for brandy and cigars, the
others retiring upstairs. Rossi set a decanter of armagnac on the side
table, and asked if there were anything else we required, or if we
wanted the fire lit.

We both replied in the negative, but I asked, 'Do you have any cats
about the premises.'

'*No, no, Signore*. Not in the inn.'

'Thank you, a very good night to you.'

'*Buona notte.*'

'What's the matter, Langham, do they give you hay fever?' asked
Edford.

'No, I can't abide the creatures. Vermin.'

As our host retreated, Edford leaned closer to me and said in a con-
spiratorial tone, 'Did you know he's quite the red, our *Signor* Rossi?'

I was nonplussed, but didn't want to show it, so I merely said, 'Oh?'

'Absolutely. He was one of Garibaldi's Redshirts in the Austro-Sardinian War.'

'Really?'

'Yes. Rather curious, don't you think?'

I did, but feigned innocence. 'Is it?'

'Well, there he was fighting for a new Italy all those years ago, and now he's living abroad. It doesn't seem right for a nationalist to be an expatriate. It wouldn't surprise me if the fellow was an exile, on the run . . . '

It didn't take me long to realise that Edford was not only garrulous, but inquisitive to the extent of being rude. Naturally I was used to such interrogations, albeit with a far more sinister motive. I kept to the truth wherever possible and subtly turned the focus of the conversation back to his hobby of archaeology. I knew very little about the discipline – if indeed it could be called such – and was quite content in my ignorance, but Edford's impromptu lecture served a dual purpose: it facilitated my continued observation of the inn's entrance, and kept him from asking questions I didn't want to answer.

By a quarter past eleven, there was still no sign of Makedonski. I was considering turning in, but I knew I was too tired to sleep, and hadn't drunk nearly enough brandy to subdue my feverishness.

'I say, you don't fancy a walk up to the Wilmington Giant, do you? I suffer terribly from insomnia, so I always take some light exercise before going to bed. I stroll over every night to check on our dig and smoke a last pipe.'

'The Wilmington Giant?' I asked.

'Yes, the chalk figure carved into Windover Hill. I'm excavating at its feet, so to speak. It's only a mile away.'

I assented and we set out into a cool, crisp, June night, under a glimmering moon. I'd hoped the fresh air would sooth my frayed nerves, but its effect was quite the reverse. We took a winding course from the inn to Wilmington Street, and the undulating landscape was filled with shadows alien and ominous in shape. Edford waxed lyrical on the respective abilities of his two students, and his high-pitched voice exacerbated my agitation. I tried unsuccessfully to block out the sound.

' . . . I didn't mention that Parker is the eldest son of Sir Roger, Bart, of Melford Hall, did I? I try and avoid it, you see, because the fellow's rather too big for his boots as it is. He's a passable Classics student, hence his interest in the Roman remains we've unearthed. Hughes, on the other hand, is quite brilliant. He's one of my history students, but I suspect his real interest is my daughter, who is a bit of a hoyden, I'm afraid . . . '

My thoughts turned to my own family. I'd neglected them to the point where the distance between us seemed impossible to bridge. When my son, Albert, died of consumption, I hadn't shed a single tear. I don't know why, I just did not have it in me. Emma pleaded with me to take a rest from work. But there was always an excuse: the Fenians, the anti-czarists, the Jubilee Plot. Albert died four years ago, and I hadn't taken a single leave of absence since. It had taken an order from the assistant commissioner himself two days ago, and even then I'd followed it to the letter, ignoring the intent: *get out of London.*

I did: on the trail of the Macedonian.

As we entered Wilmington village, ruins loomed up ahead, behind a high stone wall.

'I say, do you know that it was very near here that the scientific study of archaeology began?' asked Edford.

I bit back a harsh reply, and tried to sound interested, 'No, I didn't.'

'Cissbury Knot. It was General Pitt-Rivers' first major dig – that's Wilmington Priory over there. The foundations are eleventh century, but the ruins are fourteenth. We'll cut along in front, next to the coppice. Now, I was saying about General Pitt-Rivers; he started . . . '

We turned onto a narrow footpath between the priory and a small, but dense wood. Moss and the tendrils of larger plants encroached on the path. The wall was covered with lichen and creeping ivy, their roots eating away at the stone, as if Nature was trying to reclaim the building and return the Earth to its primeval state. I glanced at the dank, fecund wood, and shuddered involuntarily.

Edford crooked his stick under his arm and enumerated on his fingertips, ' . . . One, stratigraphic excavation, meaning layer by layer; two, the significance of the small find and the plain artefact; three, the use of field notes, photography, and plan maps; four, the publication of results; and five, the cooperation of indigenous populations.'

'It sounds exactly like detective work,' I mused, darting another look at the eldritch trees.

'I say, Langham, what was that?'

I realised my blunder – my first ever – too late. 'I may as well tell you the truth. I'm a police detective, an inspector at Scotland Yard.'

'It's *Signor* Rossi, isn't it? I knew it! He's a socialist! Or a communist – no, an anarchist – he's an anarchist, isn't he?'

Although I usually err on the side of discretion, I thought it prudent to assuage at least a little of Edford's curiosity. 'I've no interest in Rossi, it's Makedonski I'm watching.'

'The Russian? Is he an anarchist?'

'He's Macedonian, and no, he's not an anarchist. It's more of a routine observation.'

He gave me an exaggerated wink, and pressed a finger to his lips, 'You can't fool me, Inspector, but don't concern yourself. I'm as loyal a subject as any; you may rest assured that no one shall learn your secret from me.'

It wasn't his politics, but his habitual chattering I feared. Despite my gaffe, I felt relieved when we passed the edge of the wood, out onto a sward. The feeling was short-lived, however, and I grew uneasy again as we approached a line of massive oaks. Edford pointed over the tops of the trees to a steep hill. In the moonlight I discerned the outline of a huge man in a sickly, sulphurous colour. I gasped, 'Is that him?'

'The Long Man, guardian of the South Downs. He is two hundred and thirty feet high, but he's faded away the last few millennia, so the local folk marked him out with bricks. Come along, I'll show you our dig.'

Edford strode in between the last two oaks, but I walked around instead, joining him at the foot of the hill. The row of trees extended away to our left. Immediately in front of them a curious garden consisting of alternating rectangular holes and semi-circular piles of loose earth had been dug. Very close to one of the oaks, a canvas sheet was secured to the ground with pegs.

'There you have it. Half a dozen separate excavations so far, and every one of them has yielded human remains.' He produced his pipe, and a tobacco pouch. 'But that one there,' he gestured towards the cover, 'is a rare find. A complete skeleton. We're taking our time with old Scipio, in order to keep his mortal remains intact . . .'

Edford's voice faded into the background as I looked from the giant to the trees and then back to the giant. A feeling of dread, or perhaps a wave of exhaustion, overwhelmed me – I saw a flash of movement on the periphery of my vision and spun towards the nearest oak, raising my penang-lawyer and reaching inside my coat.

'I say, old fellow, are you all right?'

'Oh, yes, quite. I saw something move – in the tree – it startled me, that's all.'

'Indeed. You do seem a little on edge. I'm not surprised with all those anarchists trying to kill Her Majesty. Now join me in a pipe and I'll tell you all about the Wilmington Giant . . . '

He proceeded to do exactly that, expounding his theory that the figure was originally a Wicker Man, used by the Druids to sacrifice captured Roman soldiers. It was horrible thought, made worse by the fact that there was much evidence to support it. I couldn't help feeling sorry for the Romans, even if they were invaders. When we returned to the inn, I knew I would dream of screaming, burning men – if I slept at all.

Makedonski and I breakfasted alone on Saturday. As soon as he was finished, he excused himself and returned to his room. I spent the rest of the morning smoking and reading the papers in the parlour. Makedonski didn't come down, but four visitors were sent up.

The first was a very large Russian, with a horribly scarred face, whom I recognised as Nevskaja. He and Makedonski had served under Karastoilov in Kresna in seventy-eight. I was surprised to see him, because we had no record of his being in the country. He did not stay long. The second visitor was obviously a sailor from his dress, gait, and speech. A merchant captain from Glasgow, I deduced. He left after a lengthy interview. I waited twenty minutes, and was about to rise when another two men arrived and asked for Makedonski. I picked my paper back up, and watched and listened as inconspicuously as I was able.

The man who addressed Rossi was about my own height, but much leaner, with a prominent nose and chin. His companion was shorter, with an athletic frame, and a slight limp. Rossi sent one of the boys up with the taller gentleman's card, and I was given time to refine my observations. The shorter man was a former Army officer; the handkerchief in his sleeve, his bearing, and his moustache bespoke as much. I was unable to determine his current employment without making my interest obvious, so I returned to his companion.

A cold chill ran down my spine: the man was scrutinising me – with a skill at least equal to my own. He knew I was watching him, and he knew that I knew I was being watched. His fingers were long and delicate, the hands stained with chemicals. His movements betrayed the controlled energy of a sportsman, but he was obviously a man of some intellect. His employment was also a mystery to me, but I decided he counted music and fencing among his interests. I wondered what he would make of my puffy eyes and weary mien.

The Chemist and the Soldier left a quarter of an hour later. I waited a further fifteen minutes, and when Makedonski had still not appeared, approached Rossi.

'*Buon pomeriggio, Signor* Langham. You have had a restful morning, I trust?'

'Yes, thank you, I have. I'd like my buggy, please, I'm driving out this afternoon.'

'*Si, Signore.*' He shouted for the stable boy, and gave the necessary orders.

'It was very quiet at breakfast. I thought you said you were full last night?' I asked casually.

'*Si, si,* we are. We have only six rooms, *Signore. Signor* Makedonski has taken two, one for a sitting-room. The other three rooms are taken by Professor Edford and the two young gentlemen. They leave very early in the morning, and I prepare them the cold luncheon. They are digging for the treasure in Wilmington.'

'Yes, we walked over last night.'

'And *Signor* Makedonski, I see why he has taken the two rooms. He has had four visitors already this morning.'

'Has he? I didn't notice.'

My buggy arrived and I thanked Rossi, tipped the boy, and set off for Newhaven. I'd decided that Makedonski was in Sussex for business rather than pleasure long before his meetings. The ship's captain could, of course, have travelled from anywhere, but the nearest ports were Newhaven and Shoreham. Newhaven's harbour was the smaller of the two – and the less likely – but I recalled seeing a barque docked there yesterday evening, when I'd hired the buggy. The *Lilian Younger* was still in the same place when I arrived, and I took a drive around the port before lunching at the Dolphin.

I was favoured with good fortune at the public house, for I found not only an ideal seat from which to observe the barque, but also a publican much given to gossip. For the price of my custom and a few compliments, I was told more than I wanted to know about life in Newhaven. Of interest, however, was the following: the Glaswegian sailor was Joseph Munro, captain of the *Lilian Younger*; the barque was due to set sail for Shanghai via Bremen and Le Havre tomorrow; and the crew were very reticent about their cargo, which hadn't arrived yet.

I supped mug after mug of ale, praying I would sleep peacefully later. Several sailors left and returned to the barque, but nothing out of the ordinary occurred until early evening, when a loafer shared some of his tobacco with the crewman on duty at the gangplank. I lifted my field-glass for a better look and noted that the man bore a faint resemblance to the Chemist. The deception would have fooled most, but I'd become something of an expert in the use of disguises myself during the Fenian bombings. The Chemist smoked and talked with the hand for about half an hour before sidling off in the direction of the high street. I added the likelihood that he had trained as an actor to my mental docket.

I was starting to feel drowsy from the alcohol. I considered following the Chemist, but decided against it and walked up Castle Hill, enjoying the sea breeze as I climbed past the new fort. I toured the summit, and found a vantage point from where I could maintain my vigil. My persistence was rewarded when, shortly after eight, Nevskaja – the Russian – boarded. An hour and a quarter later, with the sun setting, I reclaimed my buggy and returned to Alfriston.

I arrived to find Rossi waiting up for me. His night porter had reported for duty drunk, and Rossi had sent him home. He locked up behind me, told me he'd left a cold platter on the sideboard, and bade me goodnight. I was grateful for the supper, especially when I found it accompanied by another decanter of armagnac. I took the food and drink up to my room, and gave full reign to both my appetites. The last thing I remember was lying on the bed and looking at the clock.

It was an hour before midnight.

I woke with an unpleasant start, and an inexplicable fear. Something was wrong. I rubbed the sleep from my eyes and was immediately reminded of the Lushai Hills. Why the memory should come at such a time, I had no idea. I looked at the clock and cursed: it was already after nine. I cursed Rossi for not sending the maid up with my hot water, cursed myself for drinking half the brandy and bolting my door, and then Rossi again when I found my boots still filthy. I performed a hasty and perfunctory toilet, during which the combination of my unsteady hand and the cold water caused me to slice open my chin.

I stormed downstairs to find Rossi with a police constable. 'What the hell's going on?' I demanded.

'Scusi, Signor Langham, buon – '

'It's not *buon* anything. I've overslept, there was no hot water, and my boots haven't even been cleaned!'

'A million apologies, *Signore*, but your door was locked and the girl did not want to – '

'Excuse me, sir, would you be a guest at this inn?' said the constable.

'Of course I'm a bloody guest here,' I snapped.

'Now then, milord, I'll ask you to mind – '

I whipped out my warrant card, 'Chief Inspector Langham, Scotland Yard. State your business.'

He squinted at the card, took a few seconds to absorb the information, and saluted. 'My apologies, sir, I'm Constable Hampton, East Sussex Constabulary.' I nodded and he continued, 'One of Mr Rossi's lodgers were murdered last night, sir. Professor Edford. He were shot to death in Wilmington. Inspector Brown come down from Lewes. He sent me to – '

'Mr Rossi, my buggy – and quickly. Constable, pay attention. First, I want you to make sure that none of the other three guests leave the inn. Professor Edford has two of his students with him, Parker and Hughes.' Rossi opened his mouth, but I cut him off, 'There's also a foreign gentleman by the name of Makedonski. I'll be questioning all three of them when I get back. If any one of them does try to leave, you have my permission to take him into custody forthwith.'

'Mr Rossi just told me that Parker's already left, sir.'

'What?'

'*Si, si, Signore*. The boy from Wilmington came here first. I sent him for *Signor* Hampton and I went to get *Dottore* Roundtree myself. When I come back, *Signor* Parker had taken a carriage and gone.'

'If you ask me, you gentlemen from the police force should be looking for Parker. He bolted as soon as we heard about the professor.' Hughes had joined us.

'I do not require your advice, Mr Hughes, but I do require your evidence. Tell me what happened.'

'He was cool as anything at first, but then the boy came back and spoke to him. I was on my way to the kitchen to try and find somebody to brew the coffee. When I got back to the parlour, Parker was as white as a sheet. He mumbled something about leaving and dashed off to the stables.'

'Where's the body?' I asked Hampton.

'Where they was doing their digging, sir, under the Long Man.'

'You have your orders. I'll be back directly.'

I left my buggy outside the priory, and took the overgrown footpath. I had a sense of *déjà vu* and, even in the clear light of day, felt a minatory force emanating from the Sylvan demesne. I quickened my step, leaving the wood behind and crossing the sward. A uniformed policeman and three other men were standing at the foot of Windover Hill, a short distance from the last oak. As I came closer I saw Edford's body lying in the exact place where he and I had stood and smoked on Friday night. The Chemist, bent double, was scuttling round his corpse like an enormous insect. The image was repellent, and I averted my gaze.

I was able to determine the identities of all three of the men in civilian dress before I reached them: Inspector Brown, Dr Roundtree, and the Soldier, who I could now see was also a doctor. 'Inspector Brown? I'm Chief Inspector Langham, from Scotland Yard.'

'Good morning, sir. The Yard? That was quick.'

'I've been in Alfriston since Friday evening, at the Star Inn.'

'The Star! You knew – '

'I met him on Friday night. I've told your man Hampton to make sure the other lodgers await our return. Now perhaps you'll tell me who the gentleman examining the scene of the murder is, and what you know about the crime thus far.'

'Yes, sir. The energetic gentleman is Mr Sherlock Holmes. He and Dr Watson,' he indicated the Soldier, 'happened to be in Lewes, so I took the liberty of requesting their assistance. This is Dr Roundtree, from Alfriston.'

I acknowledged the doctors and asked Brown, 'Mr Sherlock Holmes of Baker Street?'

'Yes, sir. You've heard of him?'

'My colleague Inspector Gregson holds him in very high esteem.'

'Mr Holmes asked me and the doctors to keep back while he made his search. He's already recovered the bullet from one of the trees,' Brown unwrapped his pocket handkerchief, and showed me a flattened piece of lead.

'The projectile is complete,' said Watson. 'Quite remarkable when you consider it entered and exited the professor's skull before coming to rest in the tree trunk. My guess is point four-four-two calibre.'

'Army Medical Department?' I asked him.

'Yes, I served with the Berkshires,' he smiled.

I indicated his leg, 'Maiwand?'

'I had that misfortune. You are also an old campaigner; British Army or Indian?'

'Indian, the Sirmoor Rifles. If your appraisal of the bullet is correct then the weapon was very likely a Webley Royal Irish Constabulary Model. It's the most popular of the point four-four-two cartridge loaders.'

'Because it fires double-action,' said Watson.

'Precisely.'

'And I should think you are wearing the exact model on your person underneath your left arm, Chief Inspector Langham,' said Sherlock Holmes.

I was taken aback. I am never without the Webley, but it usually passes undetected because of my height, breadth of shoulder, and tailored coat. What disturbed me even more was that Holmes had been too far away to hear me introduce myself. His face was flushed, his brows drawn, and now that we were at close quarters, I could see a steely glitter in his eyes. 'You are most perceptive, sir.'

He turned to the inspector, 'Thank you, Brown, my researches here are complete. If you will be so good as to allow the doctors to examine the body?' Brown, Watson, and Roundtree left us. Holmes extended his hand. 'I am Sherlock Holmes, consulting detective by profession. I believe your business in Alfriston concerns Mr Nikulica Makedonski.'

My jaw dropped open as he took my hand in an iron grip. 'I . . . I see Gregson did not overestimate your skills.'

'Gregson? He is the smartest of the Yarders, although I confess I have not met all of the official force.'

'How do you know about Makedonski? And my own identity?'

'My brother is employed by the Home Office. He has alluded to a Chief Inspector Langham as the head of the Special Irish Branch upon several occasions, remarking that the man resembles his name.'

'My name?'

'Langham is derived from long, meaning tall. You are certainly a long man. Of late, Section D has turned its attention to Continental anarchists and it can hardly be coincidence that I saw you in the parlour of the inn where Makedonski, the Macedonian nationalist, has taken lodgings.'

'In that case, may I ask what you were doing visiting Makedonski and subsequently disguising yourself as a dockyard loafer in New-haven?'

He chuckled, 'A touch, Langham, an undeniable touch! I suggest that after we hear what the doctors have to say, we compare notes. I have no doubt each will supplement the other. In the meantime

I'll tell you one thing which may help you in the case – if you would care to hear it?'

I was disappointed that Holmes's energies had yielded only a single point. Nor had his knowledge of my identity and purpose seemed clever once explained. I wondered if Gregson hadn't embellished his tales of the criminal agent's prowess. 'Certainly, Mr Holmes.'

'The murderer is just under six feet high, blonde, wore badly worn boots of a size ten, and is an expert marksman. He was also no stranger to Edford, and arrived here some time after the professor.'

I was once again astonished. 'How could you possibly deduce all of that?'

'Excellent, Langham!' You have answered your own question: the science of deduction. I have applied my methods to the scene of the crime, but they are equally effective when put to other uses. In reading your own book of life, for example.'

'My book of life?'

'It is impossible to deceive one trained in observation and analysis. Thus I can say with confidence that you served with a Goorkha regiment in India, suffer from chronic sleeplessness, remonstrated with your landlord before leaving the Star, and have recently been engaged in the protection of the queen.'

'You do not need me to tell you that you are correct on all counts, Mr Holmes. As for your description of the murderer, Parker – the missing student – is five feet eleven inches in height, fair-haired, and wears a size ten boot. And I'm sure he's had plenty of opportunity to learn to shoot at Melford Hall.'

'He is missing? Well, well, let us see if the doctors can throw any fresh light upon this matter.'

Roundtree addressed me. 'Dr Watson and I are both of the opinion that Professor Edford was killed between ten and two o'clock of last night. Inspector Brown has confirmed that Edford was in the habit of taking exercise before he retired for the night.'

'He was,' I said to Holmes. 'He also suffered from insomnia.'

'Thank you, Doctor,' said Brown before turning to me. 'Will you be taking over the investigation, sir?'

'No, Brown, the case is yours, but I should like to satisfy myself that the assassination was not a political one.'

'Your assistance would be most welcome, sir.'

'Very good. If you and Dr Roundtree make the necessary arrangements here, perhaps Mr Holmes and Dr Watson will accompany me back to the Star?'

As I rode back with Holmes and Watson, I spoke plainly of my indiscretion on Friday night. It was possible that either Edford's loquaciousness or his curiosity had put Makedonski, or even Rossi, on their guard. While Makedonski and Rossi were short and dark, Nevskaja matched Holmes's description, and could have done the Macedonian's work for him. In return Holmes informed me that he had been engaged by Lloyds to investigate an insurance fraud, and believed the *Lilian Younger* of Panama to be the *Sophy Anderson* of Clydebank, reported lost with all hands off the coast of the Outer Hebrides three years ago.

On our return to the inn, we found Hampton in command, with Makedonski and Hughes awaiting us impatiently. Holmes went up to examine Edford's room, and I questioned Rossi.

'After you came back last night, *Signore*, I lock both doors. I leave the key to the back door on the peg, but I give *Signor* Edford the front door key because he say he want to go out for his walk before he goes to sleep. I hear him open and close the door half an hour before midnight, but I am asleep before he comes back. One of the maids says she hears a gentleman leaving by the back door at midnight. This morning, I find the back door is locked and the key is in place. The front door is also locked, but there is no key.'

'Did you or any of the servants hear anyone return in the night?'

'No, no, *Signore*.'

I joined Holmes and Watson upstairs. Until we discovered evidence to the contrary, it appeared that Edford had gone out for his usual ramble at half-past eleven. Makedonski, Parker, or Hughes had left the inn half an hour later. Had they left to follow the professor, or for another reason altogether?

'I have found nothing of interest,' said Holmes. 'I should like to speak with Makedonski.'

Makedonski was waiting in his sitting room. 'So, you are not Langham the stockbroker, you are Langham the secret policeman. Am I right?'

'I'm Chief Inspector Langham of Scotland Yard. You have already met Mr Holmes and Dr Watson, so I'll proceed with our business. What, exactly, are you doing in a country inn on the South Downs?'

Makedonski took a silver case from his inside pocket, removed a Turkish cigarette, and lit it with a match. He smiled as he exhaled. The acrid smell of the smoke reminded me of waking this morning.

'I did not kill Professor Edford. I came back to my room after supper, and I did not leave it until I went down to Rossi's excuse for breakfast this morning.'

'You haven't answered my question.'

He smiled again, full of contempt. 'I am taking the country air for my health.'

'No, you're not.'

'I think you will find that Mr Makedonski is organising an armed expedition,' said Holmes. 'When I asked you where the *Lilian Younger* was bound yesterday, what did you tell me?'

Makedonski said nothing and Holmes repeated the question. The Macedonian drew heavily on his cigarette, 'You remember as well as I do.'

'Yes, I do. Hong Kong via Bremen and Le Havre. And yet Captain Munro told his crew they are destined for Shanghai. You would do well to pay attention to detail. The barque is in fact bound for Macedonia, is it not?'

Makedonski shrugged. 'Have I committed any crime in this matter?'

'I believe you are innocent of the fact that the *Lilian Younger* is the *Sophy Anderson*. Did you leave your room at all last night?'

'No, I did not.'

'Did you hear anyone else leave?'

'No.'

'I very much doubt you had anything to do with Professor Edford's death. It would be extremely foolish to murder a hapless archaeologist while plotting another uprising, would it not?'

Makedonski said nothing.

'What are you doing in Alfriston?' I asked again.

'I am financing a trading expedition, Inspector. I was not aware of any subterfuge regarding the *Lilian Younger*. If you allow me to do so, my associate Mr Nevskaja – whom you will also have recognised yesterday – and I will sail from your shores tomorrow afternoon.' He tossed his cigarette end on to the floor. 'Never to return, I hope.'

'You will have to use another barque to transport your arms and ammunition,' I said.

'Quite so,' said Holmes. 'The *Lilian Younger* was impounded this morning and Captain Munro placed under arrest.'

The Macedonian swore between his teeth.

I asked Makedonski about the previous night, but his answers remained unchanged. I made a note of his London address, which I already knew, and informed him he was free to leave. Shortly after

Holmes and Watson left for Newhaven, Brown arrived and we commenced our interrogation of Hughes, *Signor* and *Signora* Rossi, and their staff – including the now sober night porter. It was a dull and disappointing process, which yielded nothing new. Makedonski left before we'd finished, and Hughes directly after. Brown returned to Wilmington to take charge of the local inquiries, and I found myself alone in the parlour.

I tried unsuccessfully to relax. Despite my first good night's sleep in weeks – no, months – my nerves were still in shreds. I was about to call for a brandy, but decided on a pot of coffee instead. It was probably yesterday's over-indulgence that left me feeling so wretched. Before I could summon him, Rossi appeared with a scruffy youth of about eleven.

'*Mi Scusi, Signore. Signor* Hampton has sent this boy to you.'

'Thank you, Mr Rossi. What's your name, lad?'

'Sid, sir.'

'Sit down, Sid. You've done a very responsible job today, well done.'

'Thank you, sir.'

'Where did you come from this morning?'

'The Priory House in Wilmington, sir. That's where I lives and works, isn't it?'

'You must have been up early this morning?'

'Yessir, I were.'

'And the master of the house sent you to fetch Constable Hampton and Doctor Roundtree?'

He nodded vigorously, 'Yessir – I mean nossir – it were the lady.'

'You came here first?'

'Yessir. I weren't too sure where to find Mr Hampton and I knows Mr Rossi is always up bright and early. Also, I had the telegram for Mr Parker.'

'You had a message for Mr Parker?' I asked.

'Yessir, I did. It was Mrs Wright as gave it me. Only I forgot. But then I remembered and after I found the doctor, I brought it back. I couldn't find Mr Rossi, but there was a gent in here. When I asked him if he knew where Mr Parker of Melford Hall was, he said it were him, so I gave him the telegram. Did I do right, sir?'

'Quite right. Did you see what was in the telegram?'

'No, sir.'

'Did the gentleman say anything to you?'

He shook his head, 'Nossir. He just said thank you and I hopped it back to the Priory.'

I tossed him a shilling, 'That's for your trouble, Sid, now off you go.'

He caught the coin, touched his cap, and disappeared.

Had Parker's flight been nothing to do with Edford? I wanted to think without interruption, so I asked the maid to bring the coffee up to my room. I considered Holmes's description of the murderer. Parker and Nevskaja were both possibilities, but Holmes had said that Edford knew his killer. That left only Parker. Either Parker or someone else, perhaps someone from Wilmington or even Oxford. Parker's sudden departure may have been because of the telegram. Similarly, the fact that someone had left the inn last night may also have had nothing to with Edford. Many a policeman has drawn an erroneous conclusion from mere coincidence.

And yet . . .

'Chief Inspector, are you in there!'

'Hold on, man!' I lay slumped in my chair while someone hammered at the door. 'Who is it?'

'Brown, sir. Mr Holmes would like to see us at Wilmington.'

It was half-past seven. I glanced at the mirror and was shocked by what I saw. My eyes had large, dark circles under them, my chin was caked in dried blood, and scores of yellow bristles had survived the cold blade. I was pale and drawn, in dire need of more rest.

I would take a holiday – but only after I'd solved Edford's murder.

'There you are, sir. Mr Holmes asked us to meet him at Windover Hill. I was going to suggest a walk, but you look all done in. We can take the trap – '

'No, let's walk.'

As we were leaving the inn, Rossi attracted my attention with a polite cough. '*Mi Scusi, Signore, Signor* Brown say that my front door key was found with the professor. I was hoping if I may have it back soon?'

'Brown?'

'I don't see any problem with that, sir, unless you've any objection?'

'No, of course not.'

'*Grazie infinite, Signore*. And once again, my apologies for this morning; the maid – '

'Don't worry about it,' I interrupted.

'And your boots, *Signore*, I sent the stable boy up to clean them at eleven o'clock last night. He says he did, but I have docked his pay . . . '

We left and I pressed Brown for news. Sir Roger Parker of Melford Hall had died yesterday. A courier was sent to Wilmington in
error, arriving late last night, and this was the news the boy had
delivered this morning. It didn't eliminate Parker as a suspect, but it
certainly explained his actions. We lapsed into silence as we walked
up Wilmington Street, and I considered Holmes's description of the
murderer again. Five foot ten or eleven inches tall, with fair hair, and
an experienced shootist. He may have used a Webley revolver, wore
much-used boots of a size ten . . .

Boots.

What had Rossi said about the stable boy?

The weather had taken a turn for the worse and the Long Man's
peculiar square head was shrouded in mist. Holmes and Watson
stood next to the end oak, motionless, like two prehistoric sentinels.
I remembered rubbing the sleep from my eyes this morning, and
I knew why I'd thought of Assam. My mind raced and my heart
pounded. Was Holmes always right? Not this time. This time he
was wrong, I knew it.

The murderer was over six feet, not under.

'Good evening, gentlemen,' he said. 'Before we discuss the results
of my investigation, I'd like to have a look at your revolver, Langham. You wouldn't object if I dry-fired it, would you? I should like
to test Watson's assertion of the superiority of the double-action
mechanism.'

I hesitated for a second, then withdrew the Webley, and offered it
to him butt-first.

'Thank you.' He broke open the breech, examined the cylinder, and
ejected the five rounds. He handed them to Watson and sniffed the
Webley. 'This revolver has been cleaned recently. Very recently.'

'You were wrong, Holmes,' I said.

'In which respect?' he closed the revolver.

'The murderer is over six feet tall, your own height actually.'

'You are quite correct. I deduced from the length of the man's
stride that he was less than six feet in height. In nine cases out of ten,
I should have been correct, but I did not take into account that the
gentleman in question is in very poor health, and that his weakness
reproduced the signs of a shorter man.'

I looked into his sharp, piercing eyes, exactly level with my own.

'Dr Watson is of the opinion that you were not aware of your
actions. I may have fallen into error over the height of the murderer,
but you could not have deceived me had you known. Therefore, you

did not know, and I can confirm the good doctor's diagnosis. None-theless, I took the precaution of disarming you.'

'Mr Holmes, this is outrageous! Chief Inspector Langham is a – '

'No, Brown, Holmes is right. I don't remember anything, but it must have been me. It could only have been me.'

'When did you reach that conclusion?' asked Holmes.

'As I walked over. My final memory of last night is an hour before midnight. This morning I woke late, and when I rubbed my eyes I was reminded of skirmishing in the Lushai Hills. Because my right hand smelled of gunpowder. After I – after I – found Edford, I must have returned to my room, bolted the door, and cleaned my revolver . . . '

'But not your hands,' said Holmes.

'No.'

Brown protested, 'But, sir! Doctor, surely this . . . '

'I have heard of similar cases,' said Watson. 'The alienists call it dementia. I'm afraid I noted the symptoms in the chief inspector as soon as we met.'

'I returned from Assam with my vision slightly impaired, an ague, and a hatred of cats. I was convinced there was something else too, but I had no idea . . . '

'I'm sorry Brown, Mr Holmes is right,' said Watson.

Brown sighed and said, 'Are you sure, sir?'

'Yes.' I looked up at the Long Man, his head in the clouds, 'And you'd better put the derbies on, just in case.'

Author's note: as with so many improbable tales, this one is based on historical fact. While Roderick Langham investigated his last case, the top thief-taker in the *Sûreté*, Inspector Robert Ledru, became the first recorded 'homicidal somnambulist', across the channel in Le Havre. Ledru had to solve the murder himself – which, to his credit, he did – and his schizophrenia was caused by syphilis rather than toxoplasmosis.

The Adventure of the Brown Box

DENIS O. SMITH

'Is it really possible, do you suppose,' said Sherlock Holmes to me one morning, as we took breakfast together, 'that a healthy and robust man may be so stricken with terror that he drops down dead?'

'Certainly it is,' I responded. 'There are numerous recorded instances. Of course, in many of them there were also other factors. If a man's heart is weak or diseased, for instance, the likelihood of such an event is increased. And if the fear arises suddenly, and comes as a terrific shock, that also increases the likelihood. Do you have a specific case in mind?'

'Indeed: that of Victor Furnival, of Wharncliffe Crescent, Norwood, who died suddenly on Tuesday. There was a brief mention of it in yesterday's papers.'

'I did not see the report,' I said. 'Was he in a situation of menace?'

'On the contrary, when the blow fell, he was seated at the breakfast table, as you and I are now, no doubt drinking tea and contemplating a boiled egg.'

'What, then? Why should the papers have reported that he died from fear?'

'It is not the papers that mention it. They give the cause of death as heart failure, and otherwise confine themselves to listing Mr Furnival's accomplishments. He was, it seems, a local councillor, a magistrate, and altogether a notable figure in the district; but I have this morning received a letter from the dead man's niece, Miss Agnes Montague, who has been acting as his housekeeper for the past eighteen months. She informs me that Mr Furnival was seated at the breakfast-table, opening his post, when he uttered what she describes as the most dreadful cry of terror she has ever heard. A moment later he was dead.'

'Then the shock he received must have come in the morning post.'

'That is, I agree, the logical inference. And something more than a steep bill from the gas company, to judge from the severity of it. Miss

Montague proposes to consult me this morning, so perhaps we shall learn a little more then. If she is as punctual as the urgency of her note suggests,' he added, glancing at his watch, 'she will be here in precisely seventeen minutes; so if you would ring for the maid to clear away the relics of our breakfast, I should be obliged.'

It was a dull morning in September, chilly and damp, and as I stood by the window for a moment, surveying the ceaseless flow of traffic in Baker Street, I was struck by the banality of the scene. It was certainly difficult to imagine anyone dying of terror in modern London, and I confess I rather doubted that Miss Montague's problem would be of much interest to Holmes, or would possess any of those *recherché* features which so delighted his eccentric taste.

His client arrived at the appointed time. She was a slim, dark-haired young lady of about five and twenty, a little below the medium size. She had a soft west country accent, and a quiet reserve in her manner which I had learnt to associate with those raised far from the brash clamour of London.

'I understand,' said Holmes, when his visitor was seated in the chair by the fire, 'that you wish to consult me in connection with the death of your uncle.'

'That is correct.'

'And yet I am not clear what it is you wish me to do. As I understand it, the cause of death was given as heart failure. In your letter you suggest that Mr Furnival's heart failed him as a result of fear. Do you have any reason for this supposition?'

'Mr Holmes, there can be no doubt. Mr Furnival cried out in the most terrible fear only moments before he died.'

'I do not doubt your conviction on the point, madam; but is it not possible that his cry was one of pain, occasioned by the heart seizure?'

Miss Montague shook her head. 'No, Mr Holmes,' said she in a firm tone. 'His cry was not one of pain, but of terror. There is a difference, which anyone hearing it would recognise at once. Even as I speak to you now, I can hear his last cry ringing in my ears, and it chills my very bones.'

'Very well,' said Holmes. 'Perhaps you could describe to us the circumstances, and what you suppose might have caused such fear in your uncle.' So saying, he leaned back in his chair, with his eyes closed, and his fingertips together, the very picture of motionless concentration.

'I will tell you what I can,' began his visitor. 'The difficulty is that I have known my uncle and his household for less than two years. I was born and raised at Swanage, in Dorset, where my parents ran a small hotel. Two years ago, my father died, and when the business was sold, I was obliged to look elsewhere to make my way in the world. Some three years previously, Mr Furnival had paid us a brief visit. He was a distant cousin of my father's, and thus not, strictly speaking, my uncle; but I have always addressed him as such. His visit to Swanage was the only previous occasion upon which we had met, for he lived in Norwood, in the suburbs of London, where he was, so I understood, an important and wealthy man. Now, despairing of finding a suitable occupation in Dorset, I wrote to him and asked if he would put me up while I sought employment in London. This he agreed to do, and I came up to London about twenty months ago.

'The household then included also Mr Furnival's widowed sister, Mrs Eardley. Her husband had died some years previously, upon which, having no children, she had gone to live with her brother in the West Indies, where he was resident at the time, and had subsequently returned with him to England. The household was a very regular and orderly one, and I soon learned that I should be required to fit in with its strict routines. Both brother and sister admired order and cleanliness above all else, and had a deep abhorrence of anything which fell short of this ideal. This inclination even extended to the garden of the property, for I subsequently learned from a neighbour that when Mr Furnival moved into the house, he had had most of the flowering plants cut back severely, so that little remains now but a strip of lawn and a row of small rose bushes. He also had the climbing plants – wisteria and so on - completely removed from the walls of the house, which are now perfectly bare of any such ornament.

'A few months after I took up residence in Norwood, Mr Furnival and his sister fell out. They were both very quarrelsome by nature, and had often exchanged sharp words, but on this occasion the rift was more severe, and shortly afterwards Mrs Eardley moved out, and went to live by herself in Peckham. Mr Furnival then asked me if I would act as housekeeper for him, which, having no other immediate prospects, I agreed to do. Since that time, Mrs Eardley has called round occasionally, but her visits have almost always concluded with the two of them quarrelling.

'It was not what I had intended when I came up to London,' Miss Montague continued after a moment of reflection, 'and I cannot pretend that the situation has been entirely congenial to me; for, even without his sister's provocation, my uncle was a severe and ill-tempered man. Our conversations were perfunctory and brief, and concerned only with household matters, for he had little interest in anything which was not of immediate personal relevance to him. Nor did he read much, except for newspapers, parliamentary reports and the like, which he would pore over for hours, in the hope, it seemed to me, of finding something with which he could quarrel. Save for this consuming passion for politics – Mr Furnival was of some celebrity locally in this field, and we often had his political colleagues for dinner, when they would squabble noisily all evening – my uncle had only one interest, and that an unusual one. He had developed a taste for exotic carvings and other curios from the most remote corners of the world, and had amassed quite a collection. No doubt his interest had begun during his time in the West Indies, where he spent over twenty years, but his collection had since grown to include objects from many different lands. One evening he showed me some of them.

' "To you, this may be simply a carved piece of wood," he said to me, as he held up some kind of oriental idol, which I must say struck me as perfectly hideous; "but the man who carved it has not simply shaped the wood, he has striven to impress part of his own soul into this object, in the hope of living on in it after his death, and gaining revenge on those that have done him down in life. In many parts of the world, you know, such an object is regarded as definitely holding a part of the man that made it – for good or evil." He laughed as he said this, in a hard, callous manner, which I found very unpleasant. "And this is an interesting little pot," he continued, holding up a small earthenware vessel, the size of a small coffee-cup, on the lid of which was a grotesque figure with its tongue out. "It is a death pot, from Central America. You put something in it belonging to your enemy – a lock of his hair, say – then bury it in the ground. Within one month, so they say, your enemy will die."

' "How horrible!" I cried; but Mr Furnival only laughed.

' "You are young and high-minded," said he, in a bitter, cynical tone. "When you are older, you will learn that a man has many enemies in the world, and must use what means he has to destroy them, and crush them beneath his feet."

'This conversation made a deep and disagreeable impression upon me. After it, I could not look upon my uncle's collection of curios without a shudder, and I began to long for the day when I might move away from this household.

'I come now to the events of Tuesday morning,' Miss Montague continued after a moment. 'It was in every respect an ordinary morning. The maid is away at the moment, so I took in my uncle's breakfast myself, then returned to the kitchen, leaving him opening the post, which had just been delivered.'

'Of what did the post consist that morning?' asked Holmes.

'Two letters, which I could see were simply tradesmen's bills, and a brown-paper parcel. I had been in the kitchen scarcely a minute, when I heard my uncle cry out – such a cry as I hope I shall never hear again in my life. I dropped what I was doing, and hurried back to the dining room, to find him sitting rigid with fear at the breakfast table, his eyes very wide, and his mouth hanging open, as if in terror.

' "What is it, Uncle?" I cried out, and hurried to his side; but even as I did so, he pitched forward onto the table and breathed his last.'

The young lady bit her lip, and shuddered at the memory.

'What was in the parcel?' asked Holmes after a moment.

'A wooden box,' replied Miss Montague, 'but a box such as I have never seen before. In shape it was like a cube, about five inches high, and the wood, which was ornately carved, was stained a very dark brown, and ornamented with little pieces of crystal. The lid, which was attached by brass hinges, was pierced in several places, forming a sort of open lattice-work within the carving.'

'Was anything in the box?' asked Holmes.

'No,' returned his visitor; 'nothing whatever. When I re-entered the dining room, and found my uncle on the point of death, the lid of the box was open. I could see that the interior was covered with thick black lacquer, so dense in its blackness, that as one looked into it, it was like looking into the very depths of evil; but it was perfectly empty. Mr Holmes, there is something sinister and unpleasant about that box, and I believe it was sent to my uncle deliberately to bring about his death. You may consider the suggestion ridiculous; but I am convinced it is the literal truth!'

I was surprised at Miss Montague's somewhat fanciful description of the old box her uncle had received, and expected Sherlock Holmes to display a certain impatience at her account. But when he spoke, it was in his usual placid tones.

'My dear Miss Montague,' said he; 'you need not fear ridicule for your convictions. I have frequently observed that the intuitions of those most closely involved in a case are generally nearer to the truth than the impersonal reports of the police or newspapers. However, a few more facts would be helpful. Do you have any reasons other than your own intuition, to believe that there is something malevolent about the box your uncle received?'

I was expecting our visitor to admit that she had not, and was therefore surprised when she nodded her head vigorously. 'Indeed I do,' cried she. 'My uncle's death is not the only misfortune which that evil box has caused. Yesterday – just one day after his death – it came very close to claiming a second victim!'

'Really?' said Holmes in surprise. 'How very interesting!'

'Yes, Mr Holmes! It was this second dreadful incident that led me to write to you yesterday afternoon. You have a reputation for divining the truth where others see only mystery. Mr Holmes, I pray that you can do so now, and destroy this evil!'

'Pray, let us have the facts of the second incident, then,' said Holmes.

'It was yesterday morning. I was making sure the house was in good order, for Mr Furnival's sister is coming today, when there came a knock at the door. I opened it to find a nautical-looking man standing there, a tall, middle-aged man with a grizzled beard, and a lined, weather-beaten face, clad in a black pea jacket and cap. He introduced himself as Captain Jex, and said he was an old friend of Mr Furnival's from the West Indies. He had been back in England only a few weeks, and had been hoping to see his old friend, but had not known his address, when he had chanced upon the notice of his death in that morning's paper. I conducted him upstairs, to see Mr Furnival's body and pay his last respects, and as we left my uncle's room, he appeared very much affected by the experience, so I offered him a cup of tea. He said that, while I made the tea, he would sit in silent contemplation in the room where my uncle had died, so I left him in the dining room and went to put the kettle on.

'It was scarcely five minutes later that I carried in a tray of tea things. Imagine my horror when I entered the room, to find my visitor lying stretched out, face down on the floor, unconscious. Quickly, I put down the tray and bent down to him.

' "Captain Jex! Captain Jex!" I cried. As I did so, he stirred slightly, lifted his head from the floor, and opened his eyes, but his features expressed confusion. "What has happened?" I asked.

' "I don't know," said he, rubbing his eyes. "I must have come over faint. I can't seem to remember."

'Even as he spoke, I saw that that horrid box was lying open on the floor beside him.

' "The box!" I cried. "Did you open it?"

' "Why, yes," said he, looking in puzzlement from me to the box and back again, as he stood up. "It happened to catch my eye, and I had picked it up to have a closer look at it when I began to feel faint. I can't remember any more. Why do you ask?"

' "My uncle had just opened that box when he had some kind of seizure, and died," I said.

' "Good God!" cried Captain Jex in alarm. "Let's get the thing closed, then!" With a quick stoop, he picked up the box from the floor, clapped the lid shut, and replaced it on the sideboard. You will understand, then, Mr Holmes, why I regard that box with such horror. Since that moment, I have not touched it. But if the box does have some evil power, it is but the means by which someone has attacked my uncle. Someone deliberately sent it to him, with malice in his heart. It is that person who is the source of the evil!'

'Does your uncle have any enemies?' asked Holmes.

Miss Montague shook her head. 'He has many political opponents, but I doubt that any of them would do anything so wicked as this,' said she. 'I do recall an odd incident about three weeks ago, however,' she added after a moment. 'My uncle had returned home in a state of great anxiety. He asked me if there had been any callers at the house that day, and I said that there had not.

' "What is it, Uncle?" said I. "Why do you ask?"

' "It is nothing," returned he, in an angry voice. "I thought I saw someone I knew, at the railway station, that is all. Forget that I asked." '

Sherlock Holmes sat for a moment in silence. 'I take it there was no letter in the parcel that contained the box,' said he at length.

'No, nor any label on the outside to indicate where it had come from.'

'Did you observe where the parcel had been posted?'

'Charing Cross Post Office.'

'Unfortunately, that is not very helpful,' said Holmes. 'So many parcels are received there that our chances of tracing any one of them are practically nil. Tell me, Miss Montague,' he added after a moment, 'did it seem to you that the parcel was damaged in any way when you received it?'

'Why, yes, it was,' returned his visitor in surprise. 'The brown paper on the top was torn in several places. I pointed this out to the postman, and he said that it had been in that condition when he had received it, and must therefore have been mishandled at one of the central sorting offices. As no real damage appeared to have been done to it, however, I gave it no further thought.'

Holmes nodded, and I could see from the little smile of satisfaction upon his face that he had already begun to formulate a theory. 'Did Captain Jex say where he was staying at present?' he asked his visitor.

'He mentioned that I might reach him at the Old Ship Inn at Greenwich,' replied she.

'Very well,' said Holmes. 'I shall look into the matter for you. Are you returning to Wharncliffe Crescent now?'

'Yes. Mrs Eardley is coming today, as I mentioned, and I wish to be there when she arrives.

Holmes nodded. 'I shall call at the house this afternoon, Miss Montague. Until then, you must put all thoughts of that wooden box out of your mind. Do not attempt to do anything with it. Indeed, you must not even enter the room which contains the box, and you must keep the door firmly closed. Do you understand?'

When his visitor had left us, I asked my friend why he was delaying his visit to Norwood until the afternoon.

'Because,' said he, 'I wish to go somewhere else first.'

'Where?'

'Greenwich. Do you wish to come?'

'Certainly. You think, then, that Captain Jex may be able to shed some light on the matter?'

' "Shedding light" scarcely does his position justice, Watson. Captain Jex is the pivot around which the whole of the case revolves. Surely that is apparent, if anything is! I doubt we shall get to the bottom of it unless we can lay our hands on him.'

I was surprised at Holmes's remark, and confess I could not understand his great interest in this man, Jex. But my friend would say no more, and I was left to ponder what might be in his mind. Forty minutes later, we boarded the Greenwich train at Charing Cross, and forty minutes after that, we were speaking to the manager of the Old Ship Inn. Our inquiries, however, were met with disappointment. The manager remembered Captain Jex very well, but informed us that he had paid his bill on Monday, the twentieth, and left that day.

'Did he leave a forwarding address?' asked Holmes, but the manager shook his head.

'He told me that if anyone came looking for him, I was to say that he had gone to stay with Captain McNeill; but he gave no address.'

'Well, well,' said Holmes in a philosophical tone, as we walked to the railway station, 'Captain Jex's disappearance is no more than I had expected; but we could not neglect the possibility of finding him still here, however slight the chance. Now we had best get down to Norwood without further delay. You will come?'

'Most certainly,' I said. I was keen to see what my friend might learn at Norwood. He appeared to have some very definite theory as to what lay behind the facts we had heard from Miss Montague. What this theory might be, I could not imagine, but knowing my friend's remarkable abilities as I did, I could not doubt that, like a ship following the Pole Star, his course was set unerringly for the solution of the mystery.

A ten-minute walk from Norwood Junction brought us to Wharn-cliffe Crescent, a pleasant tree-lined road of attractive modern villas, set back a little behind neat front gardens. As we turned the corner, however, my friend stopped. Some way ahead of us, a small knot of people was assembled on the pavement, and a uniformed police officer stood on duty.

'Halloa!' cried Holmes. 'This looks a bad business, Watson! Surely Miss Montague has not ignored the instructions I gave her?'

We hurried forward, and as we did so, a tall, burly man in a light raincoat and soft-brimmed hat emerged from the house in front of which the crowd was gathered, and I recognised Inspector Athelney Jones of Scotland Yard.

'Mr Holmes!' cried he in surprise, as we met him at the gate. 'I don't know how you got here so quickly, but, take it from me, you've wasted your time.'

'What has happened?' asked Holmes.

'Another death. Heart failure again, by the look of it. There's no reason for me to be here, really, but two deaths in three days sounded a little suspicious, so, as I happened to be at Norwood Police Station, I thought I'd best take a look. However there's nothing in it. It's obviously just some sort of family weakness, because, of course, the dead man and woman were related.'

I saw Holmes's face fall. 'Is it Miss Montague?' he asked.

'Oh, no, she's all right. She's just been relating to me what she told you earlier. It's Furnival's sister that's died. Come inside, and I'll show you. Ask these people to move along, will you, con-stable,' he said to the policeman at the gate. 'There's nothing to see here.'

We followed the inspector into the house, and found Miss Mont-ague in the drawing room with a middle-aged woman, introduced to us as Mrs Loveday, a neighbour. In a few words, Holmes's client described to us what had occurred.

'Mrs Eardley arrived soon after I returned home,' she began. 'She seemed in an irritable mood, and declared that the house looked untidy and could do with a good dusting, which was not true. "There's no point letting the house go to rack and ruin just because your uncle has died," she said, and began brushing and dusting noisily. Shortly afterwards, Mrs Loveday called, and, a little later, when she and I were talking in here, I heard Mrs Eardley open the dining-room door. I went out to speak to her. "That is the room in which Uncle died," I said. "I wish the door to remain closed." "Nonsense!" said she, and would not be contradicted, so I left her to do what she wished. For a few minutes, we heard her clattering about in there, then there came the most dreadful scream, like that of a soul in torment, followed by complete silence. We ran in there, and found Mrs Eardley stone dead on the floor, laid out full length, as Captain Jex had been. I at once looked for that horrible box, and saw that she had been doing something with it; for I had left it on the sideboard, firmly closed, and now it stood on the dining table, with its lid flung back. I immediately sent for the doctor, and when he had examined Mrs Eardley's body, we carried it upstairs to the spare bedroom. I have not touched the box, Mr Holmes, and the dining-room door has remained firmly closed again since Mrs Eardley's death.'

'You have acted correctly, Miss Montague. Now, I hope, we can bring this unfortunate business to a close. Have you a cardboard box in the house, big enough, say, to contain the wooden box?'

'I have a shoe-box, if that would suffice.'

'That would be ideal. If you could also provide me with a ball of twine, a pair of scissors and a long-handled broom, I should be obliged.'

Holmes and Miss Montague left the room, but were back again in a minute, with the items Holmes had mentioned; then he, Athelney Jones and I opened the dining-room door and entered that fatal room. It was a square room of modest size, with a window which overlooked the back garden. In the centre of the room was a table, to the left a sideboard, and, in an alcove by the fireplace, a large, heavy piece of furniture, consisting of a cupboard above, and drawers below. Upon the table stood the carved box, the arrival of which at this ordinary suburban house had begun the series of mysterious and dreadful events.

'I'm a busy man, Mr Holmes,' said Jones in a self-important tone, 'and I can't afford to waste any more time on this business. So, unless you can show me in the next two minutes that there is something of a criminal nature involved in it, I shall be off, and leave you and Miss Montague to deal with her precious box!'

'Very well,' returned Holmes in an affable tone. 'If you would stand over there with Dr Watson, I shall demonstrate the matter for you. He placed the items Miss Montague had given him on the table, then, taking the shoebox, from which he had removed the lid, and the broom, which he held by the brush end, he crouched on the floor, in front of the large cupboard.

For a moment, he peered into the dark recess beneath the cupboard, then, with a sudden movement, thrust the handle of the broom into the darkness. Jones glanced at me with a frown on his face, and it was clear that he thought that Holmes had taken leave of his senses. Next moment, his expression changed to one of horror, as, at a fearsome speed, there emerged from beneath the cupboard the most monstrous, repulsive spider I have ever seen in my life. It was at least the size of a man's hand, its black, hairy legs as thick as a man's fingers, and it ran at a terrifying speed along by the broom handle towards Holmes's hand. But, quick as it was, Holmes was quicker, and he clapped the shoebox over the top of it just before it reached him.

'For the love of Heaven!' cried Jones in a dry, cracked voice. 'What in God's name is *that*?'

'*Tarantula Nigra*,' returned Holmes, 'the Black Tarantula, the only one of the family whose bite is fatal to man – and a very striking specimen it is, too!' He spoke in the detached tones of the enthusiastic naturalist, but there was a suppressed tension and excitement in his manner which told me that even Holmes was not entirely immune from the horror which the sudden appearance of that fearsome beast had provoked in my own breast. 'Pass me the lid, Watson,' he continued, 'and let us see if we can slip it underneath the box.' In a moment, he had done as he said, then, in one swift movement, had turned the box right side up. 'Hold the lid down, Watson, while I wrap the twine round it. Hold it down firmly, old man,' he added quickly. '*Tarantula Nigra* is quite capable of pushing the lid off!'

His warning came not an instant too soon, for even as I put my hand to the top of the box, I felt it lift against my touch. With a thrill of horror, I pressed down hard, and in a minute Holmes had bound the box up securely with the twine. 'We'd better give the creature some air,' he remarked, as he poked half a dozen small holes in the top with the scissor. 'We don't want it to suffocate! Here you are,

Jones!' he continued, handing the box to the policeman. 'Here is your evidence of criminality! This deadly spider was, with deliberate intent, sent to Furnival in that wooden box. Its sudden frightening appearance at his breakfast table undoubtedly brought about his death. Whether it also bit him, we cannot say until his body is examined afresh, but it certainly bit his sister, Mrs Eardley, for I took the opportunity of examining her wrist a moment ago, and the mark is quite clear there.'

'The doctor didn't say anything about that,' said Jones.

'He didn't know what he was looking for, and the mark of the bite was under the cuff of her blouse.'

'How did you know that you would find this horrible thing here?' asked Jones. As he spoke, the spider evidently made some sudden movement inside the box, for he put it down hurriedly on the table, his face pale.

'It seemed more than likely,' returned Holmes. 'Miss Montague had stated that the box her uncle received had been empty, but as she was not in the room at the moment he opened it, it was always possible that it had contained something able to move of its own volition, which had made itself scarce as she entered the room following her uncle's cry of terror. If this were so, what could it be? The size of the box suggested a spider – although there were other possibilities – and this suggestion received some support from the fact that Furnival himself had spent over twenty years in the West Indies, where large spiders are not uncommon.

'I asked Miss Montague if the parcel containing the box had appeared damaged when it arrived. As a conjecture, this was something of a long shot, I admit; but I was gratified to find that it was correct. The paper on the top of the parcel had been ripped when it arrived at the house. This confirmed the theory yet further: for it seemed to me likely that the sender of the parcel had deliberately ripped the paper, in a way which would appear like accidental damage, in order to ensure that air reached the parcel's occupant during its transit through the post. Something else which was suggestive was that Miss Montague's uncle had had all the climbing plants removed from the walls of the house; for it is a fact that one of the reasons that some people do not like such plants is because their stems provide an avenue for spiders to enter the house via the bedroom windows. Taking all these points together, it seemed very likely that Furnival had a pathological dread of spiders, and that someone, aware of this fact, had deliberately sent him a particularly terrifying specimen. Whether Mrs Eardley suffered from the same aversion to spiders as her brother, we cannot say. She was certainly bitten by the creature, as the police surgeon will doubtless confirm in due course, and may have died from that cause, as the venom of *Tarantula Nigra* is very potent. In her case, it seems to have been her zeal to clean her brother's house which led to her death. She must have been poking with a brush beneath that cupboard much as I was, and the spider, considering itself to be under attack, would have sallied forth to repulse the attack, as you saw it do just now. Fortunately for me, I was expecting it; but Mrs Eardley was not.'

'You have certainly confirmed your theory, anyhow,' said Inspector Jones after a moment, eyeing the box on the table warily. 'But who the dickens could have done it?'

'I strongly suspect that Captain Jex, who called here yesterday, was the agent of these deaths.'

'What – the gentleman that had the fainting fit?'

'I think we may safely dismiss the fainting fit, Jones,' replied Holmes in a dry tone. 'It made sense to Miss Montague only because she was convinced that the box possessed some evil power, natural or supernatural. But if that is discounted as a possibility, as I had discounted it, then Jex's actions appear in a somewhat different light. Clearly he had been down on the floor for some purpose, and only pretended to have fainted when Miss Montague entered and found him there. What could that purpose be, but to find the spider? No doubt he had reasoned as I had done that the likeliest hiding place for the creature was in that dark recess under the cupboard. Spiders have their own fears and anxieties, you know, Jones, and finding itself in unfamiliar surroundings, it would naturally seek the darkest corner it could find. But if Jex was looking for the spider, then he must have known it was there, and how could he know of the spider's existence except if he himself had sent it?'

'He must be a cool customer,' remarked Jones, 'to return to the scene of his crime so soon. Why should he do so?'

'It may be,' replied Holmes, 'that he had intended only to frighten Furnival with the spider, and when he heard that Furnival had died, saw at once that if the spider were found it would put a noose round his neck. If, however, he could remove the spider, than that danger would be averted.'

'You may be right,' said Jones. 'Anyhow, we must get after the villain as quickly as possible.'

'Dr Watson and I have already made inquiries at the place he was staying last week,' said Holmes, and described our visit to Greenwich. 'He evidently left there on Monday, took the direct train to Charing Cross, where he posted his parcel, and then took himself off elsewhere. You may be able to trace him through his purchase of the box at a curio shop, or through Captain McNeill, the man whose name he mentioned at Greenwich; but I rather fancy that Captain Jex is a resourceful character, and not likely to sit about, waiting to be apprehended.'

'We shall see about that,' said Jones in a determined tone. 'If we haven't collared him by this time next week, then you may call me an idiot!'

This extravagant offer was politely overlooked, however, the next time Jones called in to see us at Baker Street. Three weeks had passed without any news, and I had concluded that Captain Jex had slipped through the net. But Jones began by stating that he had some new information about the fugitive.

'That is good news,' said Holmes.

'It's not so good as you suppose, Mr Holmes,' responded Jones in a gloomy tone. 'We have managed to trace him, but he is dead.'

'Ah! I see. When did it happen?'

'Twelve years ago.'

'What!' cried Holmes and I in astonishment.

Jones nodded his head. 'We are certain we have the right man. Captain Jex was murdered in 1874, on the island of St Anthony, in the West Indies, by a man called David McNeill.'

'What became of McNeill?' asked Holmes.

'There were evidently mitigating circumstances in the case, for he escaped the gallows; but he did ten years in a penal colony, and died shortly after his release.'

For some time we sat in silence, too dumbfounded by this information to speak.

'What on earth is the meaning of it all?' I asked at length.

'That is the question, Dr Watson,' said Athelney Jones in a tone of puzzlement. 'As to the answer, your guess is as good as mine.'

No further progress was made with the case, and it at length passed entirely from our thoughts, as new work took the place of old. In my own mind, I had long since consigned it to that list of cases which were unlikely ever to be cleared up satisfactorily, when, one morning, two years later, Holmes received a communication from Grindley and Leggatt, solicitors, of Gray's Inn. This consisted of a sealed foolscap document, with an accompanying letter explaining that the document had been deposited with them two years previously by a Mr David McNeill, with the instruction that in the event of his death, it was to be forwarded to Sherlock Holmes. McNeill's death, they informed us, had been reported within the last week. The enclosed document ran as follows:

> MY DEAR MR SHERLOCK HOLMES – I know of your reputation and am aware that you have taken an interest in the deaths of Victor Furnival and his sister, Mrs Eardley. I therefore venture to give you the following account, confident that you will recognise it for the truth that it is.
>
> When first I met Victor Furnival, he was the manager of a large sugar-cane plantation on the island of St Anthony in the West Indies, and had a reputation as a brutal and merciless overseer. I was master of a small tramp vessel at the time, sailing about the Caribbean, and happy enough with my lot. Sometimes, when we put in at Trianna Bay, which was the largest town on St Anthony, I would meet up with Furnival, and other Englishmen that were there, and we would drink and play cards, as men tend to do when they are far from home. It was a rough place, full of rough people, and with no pretensions to gentility; but even there, among such people, Furnival was known for his vicious tongue and his bullying, blustering manner.
>
> Among those with whom we sometimes played cards and passed the time was Captain Jex, who owned a small boat, and traded among the nearby islands. Occasionally, he picked up pearls from the local fishermen, which he sold to a dealer in Trianna Bay; but there was a persistent rumour that those he sold were the poorer ones, and that he was building up a secret cache of really fine pearls to pay for a life of ease when he finally gave up the sea. I had always doubted this rumour, but it was confirmed to me one day by the man himself. I was in Trianna Bay, and ran across Captain Jex down by the harbour. He told me that he had come to town to have his pearls valued by an expert from Jamaica who was staying there for a few days, and that the appraisal had been very favourable. Evidently pleased with himself, he showed me the pearls, as we sat in a bar by the harbour. From a small velvet pouch, he

tipped onto his hand a dozen of the most perfect and lustrous pearls I had ever seen. What they might be worth, I could not say, but I would guess that that they might set a man up for life. I motioned to him to put them away, for I saw that we were being observed by other men in the bar, men of the vilest antecedents, who would think nothing of slitting Jex's throat to get hold of his treasure.

Later that day, I was obliged to see Furnival on business, so I walked out to his house, which lay in an isolated spot, ten minutes from the town. As I approached the front door, I heard raised voices from within the house, which I recognised as those of Furnival and his sister, Mrs Eardley. She had come out from England to live with her brother the previous year, after her husband had died, and, to speak plainly, was generally disliked. She was a mean, grasping, shrewish woman, whose presence seemed to have made Furnival even more ill-tempered and disagreeable than before.

'You fool!' I heard her cry in a harsh tone. 'You must seize your chances! Or do you want to rot forever in this stinking place?'

I did not know what they were discussing, nor had any wish to know. I knocked on the door, was admitted by the servant, and heard no more. That evening, I attended Furnival's house again, for dinner. I had thought, from what he told me earlier, that there would be half a dozen of us there, but in the event the only other visitor was Captain Jex. The four of us played cards for a while after dinner; but I found Mrs Eardley's company so intolerable that I presently made some excuse and left, returning to my ship in the harbour.

In the middle of the night, I was roughly awakened by a party of soldiers from the nearby military garrison, and informed that I was being arrested for the murder of Captain Jex, who had been found beside the road with his head crushed in. I protested my innocence, but it did me no good, and I was sent to trial in Jamaica. I will not detail the court proceedings, a full account of which can be found in the Caribbean Law Reports, but note merely that the entire case against me was built on a series of lies by Furnival and his sister. In particular, they both stated that Captain Jex and I had quarrelled on the evening of his death, which was completely untrue, and that they had heard Jex cry out, a short time after he had left their house, and, upon going to investigate, had seen me running away, which was also completely untrue.

Of course, what had happened was clear to me, as was the meaning of the words I had overheard Mrs Eardley speak to her brother. Furnival and his sister had learnt of the pearls Jex was carrying, had plotted together to murder him to get their hands on them, and had planned to divert suspicion by putting the blame on to me. Had it been only the two of them testifying against me, I might yet have avoided a guilty verdict; but they had evidently bribed or threatened others, for a number of people I had never even seen before came forward to testify enthusiastically against me. The only thing that saved me from the hangman's noose was the question of the pearls. I, of course, did not have them, and nor could they be found anywhere else, as a result of which the prosecution scarcely mentioned them at all, even though they were the obvious motive for the crime. Instead, it was alleged that Jex and I had quarrelled over some other matter, and, inflamed by drink, had come to blows. This allowed the defence counsel to argue, from various incidental considerations, that, whatever had occurred, Jex had probably struck the first blow. This argument was accepted by the jury, and thus, although found guilty of causing Jex's death, I was spared the gallows, and sentenced instead to ten years' hard labour in the penal colony on Halifax Island.

There I passed a decade of my life, suffering for a crime I did not commit, and sustained only by a burning hatred of those whose lies had condemned me. Thus, when I was at last released to the world once more, a sick, broken man, I resolved that I would devote my last breath to hunting down Furnival and his sister. Shortly after my release, a clerk's error led to an incorrect report that I had died, but I did not trouble to correct the error. What did I care? I had no life, other than to seek justice for Jex, and revenge for myself. I learned that Furnival and his sister had returned to England several years earlier, and it was not long before I followed them there, assuming for my own satisfaction the name of Captain Jex, the man they had murdered. The meagre savings I had from before my imprisonment were just sufficient to pay for my passage, and keep me for a little while, and that, for me, was enough.

Once in England, it took me little time to track Furnival down, and I discovered that he was living as a respectable, highly regarded man of substance in south London. For some time I followed him about, until I knew his habits almost as well as my own. One day, at Norwood Station, our eyes met for a moment, but then the train I was on pulled away, and I do not think he recognised me. One thing I had remembered about Furnival was his deep loathing of spiders. I had therefore brought with me a large specimen of the Black Tarantula. At first, I was unsure how I might use it; but when I learnt of his interest in native curios, I at once thought of putting the spider in a carved box and sending it to him through the post.

The rest you know. I had not expected that the mere sight of the creature would bring about the death of my enemy, although I cannot say in all honesty that that outcome causes me any regret. When I learned what had occurred, I tried to recover the spider, but without success. I was immensely relieved when I read that you had captured it, for my greatest fear was that Furnival's niece, or some other innocent, would be harmed by it.

Now I am dying, and by the time you read these lines my tongue will be stilled forever, but I rejoice that some degree of justice has at last been meted out to the true murderers of Captain Jex. For the peace of your soul, pray that you never fall foul of anyone so vicious and callous as Victor Furnival and his sister.

CAPTAIN DAVID McNEILL

'What a dreadful business,' I remarked as we finished reading. 'But it illustrates, I suppose, that even the most banal suburban existence may conceal the strangest of secrets.'

'Indeed,' said Holmes. 'And it illustrates, also, Watson, the truth of the old maxim, that the darkest deeds cast the longest shadows.'

The Tragedy of Saxon's Gate

MATTHEW BOOTH

During my long and intimate acquaintance with Sherlock Holmes, I have witnessed some dramatic commencements to those investigations in which I was fortunate enough to play a part. I well recall the sudden and startling appearance of Dr Thorneycroft Huxtable in our rooms in Baker Street, which prompted our involvement in the mystery of the Priory School, and the punishment of the Duke of Holdernesse. There was also the distraught Alexander Holder, whose loss of the Beryl Coronet had caused him so much concern. Among all those vivid entrances, however, I cannot recall any which left such an impression on my mind as our introduction to Dr Moore Agar, of Harley Street. I have referred to the matter somewhere else in these recollections, but until now I have never set the matter down before the public, and I feel that the circumstances of the death of Elizabeth Merrison, and its tragic sequel, deserve their place in this series of memoirs.

It began one morning in the latter half of the year 1896. Holmes and I were seated at our breakfast table. His plate was untouched, and I had not seen a morsel of food pass his lips for two days. He was deeply engrossed in the dark mystery surrounding the Wyndham curse, and he was subjecting his iron constitution to constant hard work of the most exacting kind. I was attempting in vain to induce him to take some breakfast, when the front door bell was rung with such ferocity that we both of us stared in wonder. There was the sound of muffled voices as our landlady tried to calm down whoever it was who had intruded upon our peace. The voices were followed by frantic footsteps on our stairs, at which Holmes gave me a wry look.

'You may perhaps have to save your remonstrations till later, my dear Watson,' said he.

At that moment, the door to our sitting room was thrown open, and standing before us was a handsome, sturdy man of forty. His features were dignified, his hair a deep shade of luxuriant brown, and his square jaw free from whiskers. His bearing was impressive, but the look of horror and anxiety upon his proud face, and the disarray of his necktie, betrayed a recent distress.

'Mr Sherlock Holmes?' he gasped.

Holmes nodded in acknowledgement. 'My name, sir. This is my friend and associate, Dr Watson, before whom you may speak freely. Pray, draw near the fire and take a seat, and help yourself to some coffee.'

'Thank you, I can drink nothing,' said our visitor. 'I will however take the liberty of using your sofa. Thank you! Mr Holmes, my name is Agar, Dr Moore Agar.'

With this introduction, he sprang from the sofa and darted across the room to the window. Peering from behind the curtain, he stared down into the street. Having satisfied himself that there was nothing outside to trouble him, he fell against the bureau with a sigh of relief.

'Forgive me, gentlemen. You must think me mad, but I was afraid they might have followed me.' He glanced back through the window.

'Whoever might have followed you,' said Holmes, rising from the table and approaching our visitor, 'will surely see you if you continue to stare out of the window.'

Dr Agar nodded slowly, and moved across the room, settling himself in one of the armchairs which were placed on either side of the fireplace. 'You are quite right, of course, Mr Holmes. I am convinced that they are after me. I am certain that a man followed me from Oxford Street, and if I am right then they will be here in an instant!'

Holmes clapped his hands together impatiently. 'Come, come, Dr Agar! It is to be expected for a man in my position to have mystery in his cases, but to have riddles from the outset is really too much. Who has followed you and why?'

I handed the doctor, whose name I recognised as being one of the foremost nerve specialists in the country, a glass of brandy. Despite the hour, his wan face and shaking frame convinced me of his need of it. He accepted it graciously, swallowed it down, and sank back into his armchair.

'It is the police, Mr Holmes. They are after me for a crime of which I swear I am innocent. It is murder, Mr Holmes, as surely as I sit here before you. And if it were not enough that it is my own fiancée, my dear Lizzie, who has . . . ' He failed to say the word, but his implication was clear. 'If it were not bad enough, they say that I murdered her!'

Holmes glanced over at me with curiosity and amusement at the words. He sat down in his own chair, steepling his fingers and placing his elbows on his knees, and I saw in his eyes the familiar spark of excitement, which told me that he was keenly interested. He opened his mouth to speak, but his intention was cut short by a second, perhaps more violent, clang at the bell. There were heavy steps on the stairs, and a moment later the eager and alert figure of Stanley Hopkins stepped into the room.

Holmes rose to greet the Inspector with an affable smile on his face. 'My dear Hopkins, you are an early riser today. Watson, our little chamber seems to be at its most popular this morning.'

'Mr Holmes, I apologise for the intrusion and I trust you will appreciate my reasons,' said Hopkins. His eyes fell upon Moore Agar. 'I have, after all, my duty to perform.'

'I am innocent of the charge,' snarled the doctor.

'It is my duty to inform you,' said Hopkins solemnly, ignoring the protestation, 'that anything you say may be used against you. I arrest you in the Queen's name as having been concerned in the murder of Elizabeth Merrison last night.'

'Mr Holmes, please help me!'

'You will have your chance to speak in time, Agar,' said Stanley Hopkins authoritatively.

Holmes moved across the sitting room and intervened between the two men. His lips were compressed in thought and his brows drawn. 'What's all this about, Hopkins? I am not accustomed to having men arrested first thing in the morning in my sitting room.'

'Nothing more than a very commonplace little murder. Nothing to interest you, Mr Holmes. And I think I have my man right enough.'

Again, Agar raged in the air. 'You are wrong, damn you!'

'His protestations of innocence seem definite,' I felt obliged to say.

'When have you known a guilty man go quietly, Dr Watson?' replied Stanley Hopkins. 'He did it, and I know he did it, as sure as if I'd seen him. You have much to explain, Dr Agar, and much to answer for. When these gentlemen hear the facts, they, too, will be convinced of your guilt.'

'Then we shall have those facts,' said Sherlock Holmes in his most judicial tone.

Hopkins contemplated the matter for a second only, before taking out his notebook and sitting himself on the sofa. 'Well, since Dr Agar came here to consult you, Mr Holmes, perhaps I'd better let him do so.'

'A capital idea,' replied my companion. 'Proceed, Dr Agar.'

The doctor, accepting a cup of coffee from me, sipped it slowly whilst he gathered his thoughts. When he spoke, his voice was calmer, and his eyes remained fixed on Sherlock Holmes, as though any deviation from my friend's grey eyes might spell failure of the doctor's hope of salvation.

'My fiancée, Mr Holmes,' said he, 'is Elizabeth Merrison, the daughter of Stanislaus Merrison, the vineyard millionaire. You may know the name as being one of the most notable amongst wine merchants. His vintages are known across two continents, and he has recently secured a Royal appointment. Mr Merrison has two children: Elizabeth, and her elder brother Elias. The mother is dead; she died of heart failure three, four years ago. Since then the father and two children have lived together in the family mansion in Norwood.'

'Saxon's Gate,' I said. 'Built on the site of an ancient Saxon stronghold, I believe.'

'You are a mine of information, Watson,' said Holmes tersely. 'Continue, doctor.'

'I've known Elizabeth for almost ten years. I met her through her brother, Elias. We were at medical school together, he and I, and he invited me one year to stay at Saxon's Gate for a weekend. Our friendship flourished, and my love for his sister blossomed. When her mother died, I was there to comfort and care for her. She reciprocated my feelings, to my astonishment and joy.' He lowered his head, and his voice sank. 'We were to marry next spring. It's impossible to think I will never see her again.'

'How came you, Dr Agar, to be suspected of the murder of the woman you loved?' asked my companion.

Agar hissed his reply. 'It is inconceivable that I should be sitting here, manacled like an animal, while you gentlemen think such things!'

'If I may, Mr Holmes, the facts are these,' said the inspector. 'Two nights ago, the Merrisons held a dinner. The three of them, Agar here, and a man named Dennis Walcombe, an old friend of the family. From what I gather, Mr Walcombe was rather more friendly with Miss Merrison than anyone else.'

'The man is a snake!' spat Agar.

Holmes held up a restraining hand. 'Calm yourself, Doctor. That will not help you.'

'There was rather a heated argument at the dinner table about that very subject,' said Hopkins. 'According to the butler, Chambers, Dr Agar here accused Elizabeth and Walcombe of having an affair, before storming out of the house in great excitement. The following night – that is to say, last night, at about nine o'clock – Elizabeth Merrison died of morphine poisoning.'

Holmes looked across at me. I shook my head sadly, conveying to him the dreadful nature of the death which had befallen this tragic woman. He gave no reply to me, but turned his attention back to Stanley Hopkins. 'What is your evidence against Dr Agar? You will forgive me, doctor, for having to ask but it is of course the only way to assist you.'

'The evidence is overwhelming, though I admit circumstantial,' replied Hopkins. 'According to both Mr Merrison and his son, Agar has a terrible jealous streak. It is not the first time, is it, doctor, that you and Miss Merrison have had words about the subject of infidelity? And each time, upon resolving the issue, you have admitted to being in the wrong?'

'I shame myself to confess it,' said Agar.

Hopkins gave a pompous grin of satisfaction. 'Now there is this relationship between Miss Merrison and Walcombe, which is sufficient motive for a jealous man, don't you agree, Mr Holmes? By his own admission, a large quantity of morphine is missing from Agar's medical bag.'

'This is all true, Dr Agar?' asked Holmes.

'Every condemning word of it.'

'Do you have any alibi for last night?'

'Not a ghost of one, sir. I was at home.'

Holmes gave a brief nod of understanding. He leaned back in his chair, and his eyes drifted to the flickering flames in the grate. For several moments, we all four of us sat in silence. I knew Holmes well enough to recognise that despite his still exterior, his mind was racing with ideas and theories, sifting those facts which were vital from those which were incidental. With a sudden burst of energy, he sprang from his chair and darted into his bedroom. Upon his re-emergence, he had discarded his dressing gown for his frock coat, and I saw the recognisable glare of stimulation on his pale features.

'How far away is this house, Saxon's Gate, Hopkins?' asked he.

'No more than a twenty minute drive from Norwood station.'

'Excellent. Watson, your hat, coat, and a cab at once!'

Agar rose from his chair, the profound sense of despair which he had demonstrated slowly beginning to lift. 'Then you will help me?'

Holmes clapped him on the shoulder. 'The facts help you sufficiently, Dr Agar. For now, go with the police and remain in their custody. You will aid me more that way and I shall report to you once I have good news for you. By tomorrow I have no doubt you will be a free man.'

Such was my friend's confidence that Stanley Hopkins had no option other than to intervene. 'Mr Holmes, you go too far in making such promises! I have my noose squarely around this man's neck!'

'Then we shall have to find those few facts which will cut your rope, Hopkins, for while you waste your time badgering the doctor here, a murderer remains at liberty.'

The house was a short ride from the station, and although we were able to see its turrets from the road as we approached, the true magnitude of its splendour was not evident until we were at the lodge gates. The house stood back from the road and was surrounded by a high brick wall, in the centre of which were some wrought iron gates, at which stood a lonely constable. Beyond the gates, we made our way down a long winding path, which led to a magnificent structure of lichen-covered stone. Latticed windows illustrated the three storeys of the mansion, and a large oak panelled door signified the entrance. I knew well enough that the house had been built on an ancient Saxon stronghold, which had once been guarded by an impenetrable gateway, giving the house its name.

As we continued up the tree-lined avenue towards the house, Sherlock Holmes spoke in his most didactic tone.

'Really, Hopkins,' said he, 'I have high hopes for your career, but you must learn patience before rushing off to pursue the first conclusion which occurs to you. Examine every fact, test every link in your chain and only then take action.'

'I confess I think my case is almost complete.'

'Circumstantial evidence is a very tricky thing,' replied my companion. 'You see, Hopkins, you give this man Agar too little credit for his obvious intelligence. If he is guilty, why does he admit to the missing morphine? Again, would an intelligent man not concoct some form of alibi rather than meekly admit to none? Agar is no fool, he would not leave these details blank if he were a killer.'

'A man would have to be blind to murder his fiancée for a motive to which no less than four witnesses could testify,' I volunteered. 'The argument at dinner was bound to be mentioned.'

Hopkins shook his head gravely. 'An embittered man may not act rationally, Dr Watson.'

'Perhaps not,' replied Sherlock Holmes. 'But he would have foresight enough not to place his own neck in the noose. Your evidence seems to me to cut both ways, Hopkins.'

We had by this time reached the house, and Stanley Hopkins rapped on the huge oak door. After a matter of minutes, an elderly butler appeared in the doorway. He was a grey, bent old man but his eyes were as alive with fire as the young inspector's.

'Good afternoon, Chambers,' said the latter. 'You remember me? Inspector Hopkins. This is Mr Sherlock Holmes and his colleague, Dr Watson.'

'Come in, gentlemen,' replied the old servant. 'The master and Mr Elias are in the drawing room, with Mr Walcombe.'

'That is Dennis Walcombe, Mr Holmes, of whom you have heard. I asked everyone to remain behind for today. I thought it best until we had apprehended Agar.'

'Very right and proper, Hopkins,' said Holmes. Turning to the butler, he added, 'Now, my dear fellow, I wonder if you can assist me. Did Dr Agar come here yesterday, following the quarrel with the unfortunate mistress of the house?'

The old man nodded his head gravely. 'Oh, indeed, sir. To apologise, I fancy. Most upset he was. It was always the same whenever they would quarrel, the doctor and Miss Elizabeth.'

'What do you mean by it being always the same?'

'Dr Agar would always feel so guilty about causing a scene. Miss Elizabeth hated to argue in public, but the doctor sometimes couldn't control himself.'

'You see, Mr Holmes? He couldn't control himself,' said Hopkins with some excitement.

'Yes, but poison is a cold, calculating method of murder, Hopkins, not one likely to occur to a man in a rage. Now, Chambers, did you let Dr Agar into the house, yesterday?'

'I did, sir. At about six o'clock, sir, and then I let him out again at eight. There was a further heated argument I am afraid, sir.'

'Indeed?' Holmes appeared very interested by the fact.

'Yes, sir. It gave Miss Elizabeth a severe headache. The doctor and Mr Elias took her upstairs and to bed and Dr Agar gave her a sedative

I believe. Then there were words between him and Mr Elias, sir, and they used to be such good friends.'

Holmes nodded slowly. I could see from his eyes that he was much excited, but where he had discerned a clue in the dark business I could not fathom. 'And you showed Dr Agar out of the house at eight, after he and Mr Elias had put the poor woman to bed?'

The butler nodded.

'Did the doctor return?'

'No, sir.'

A thought had occurred to me. 'So, if Agar is guilty, he had to have administered the morphine when he prepared the sedative.'

'My thoughts exactly, Doctor,' said Hopkins with a satisfied nod of his head.

Sherlock Holmes, however, clicked his tongue with impatience. 'Dr Agar is not guilty. We now have definite proof. Into the house! Let us meet the family and Mr Walcombe.'

Chambers led us into a cheery sitting room, tastefully furnished in damask, with small vases of moss roses scattered around the space. A large fireplace was the centrepiece of the room, and before it stood three men. One was a small, wiry man with grizzled whiskers and a permanent scowl upon his face. To his right was a handsome, dark young man of thirty years of age or so. His eyes were alert and stared eagerly at us from under a swarthy brow. There was something about those eyes which so reminded me of the elderly gentleman next to him that the hereditary relationship could not be ignored. These two were, therefore, Elias Merrison and his father, of whom Agar had spoken, which could only mean that the fair-haired, suave man with them was Dennis Walcombe. His was an engaging face, but not so conventionally attractive as Elias Merrison. His expression was aloof, and there was a suggestion of arrogance about his pinched nose, and yet there was a definite air of command about his person.

As we entered, Stanislaus Merrison paced uneasily towards us, leaning in an ungainly manner on an old walking stick. 'Ah, Inspector Hopkins! I trust you have found that murdering dog Agar.' He spoke with a voice which betrayed both spirit and contempt.

Elias heaved a tired sigh. 'Father, please.'

'Your father's right, Elias.' Walcombe lit a cigarette, tossing his match into the fire with a melodramatic flourish. 'Poor Elizabeth would still be with us if it were not for that scoundrel. I could kill him myself for what he has done.'

Holmes gave a courteous bow. 'You are Mr Walcombe, I perceive?'

'I am, sir. And you are?'

'I am Sherlock Holmes and this is my associate, Dr Watson.' He turned to the dark-haired young man. 'This, then, must be Mr Elias Merrison.'

Elias gave a short nod of his head, before turning his gaze away from us.

Holmes paced the room, his keen eyes taking in every detail. 'You three were all present, I understand, at the dinner two nights ago, when Dr Agar and Miss Elizabeth exchanged words.'

'Yes. It was nothing new, I'm afraid. Agar is a little . . . hot-headed when it comes to ladies.' Elias stared down at his fingernails.

At his words, the old man struck his cane against the wooden floor. 'Better than being stubborn about them!'

'Father, not now!' roared the son. 'Lizzie's dead, for God's sake.'

'Yes!' came the bitter reply. 'Which is why I look to you to honour me more than ever. I have nothing left, Elias, nothing to make my remaining years peaceful other than you. Yet you still defy me. I am old, boy. Do I not deserve happiness?'

'And do not I? I cannot marry her, father!'

'You could have all the happiness you need!'

'I cannot marry her, for God's sake, how many times!' Elias held his hands to his head.

'You will do as I say, my lad, to preserve this family's name!' The old man's eyes blazed with scorn at his son, and for a moment there seemed to pass between them some form of understanding, an unshared agreement, to which none of us were to be privy. Finally, the father turned on his heel and approached my companion. 'Mr Holmes, do what you must. But your time is better spent elsewhere. The inspector has his man.'

As he walked past us, Hopkins held out his hand. 'Mr Merrison, may I speak with you, please? There are a number of points to clear up.'

'If you wish it, Inspector.'

The two men walked out, closing the large oak door behind them. For a moment the four of us who remained stood in silence. I found myself thinking of the old man, and the terrible loss he was suffering.

'Poor chap. He must be devastated,' I could not help but remark.

Elias' voice was low as he replied. 'His grief is twofold, Dr Watson. My father wants me to marry Lady Henrietta Forsythe, daughter of

Lord Falmouth. He has much influence in the House of Lords, as you may know.'

'You do not wish to enter into marriage?' asked Sherlock Holmes.

'I cannot. I have no cause to.'

Walcombe leaned against the fireplace, his cigarette hanging decadently from his fingertips. 'Lord knows why, Elias. After the latest disaster with your shares I'd have thought marriage to the girl was a safety valve.'

I stared hard at the man. 'Perhaps some people don't share your cynical view of marriage, Mr Walcombe.'

The glare he gave me in return was as stern as my own. 'The only person I could imagine marrying has been taken away from me, Dr Watson. Perhaps that gives me a right to cynicism.'

I said no more. Instead, I turned towards Sherlock Holmes who had paced towards the large window which looked out over the lawns. He was gazing across the expanse of green, his lips pursed, and his brows drawn tightly over his grey eyes. I could tell he was in the deepest thought.

'Marriage does not suit every man,' said he slowly. After the briefest of pauses, he threw a glance towards Merrison and Walcombe, his eyes darting from one to the other. 'But are you gentlemen convinced of Dr Agar's guilt?'

'Certainly,' replied Walcombe. 'I see no other explanation. The sooner he hangs the better.'

'Do you not believe it yourself, Mr Holmes?' asked Elias.

Holmes gave a genial smile, and waved the comment aside. 'Having a mind like mine is a curse, Mr Merrison, and I am forced to consider all possibilities before I accept the obvious.'

'That hardly answers his question,' sneered Walcombe.

My friend was not a man to allow such insolence to disturb him. He merely gazed back out of the window, and leaned against the shutters. 'When did Dr Agar realise the morphine was missing from his bag?'

'He mentioned something about it when we took Elizabeth to her room yesterday,' replied Elias. 'They had quarrelled again, I'm afraid, and I helped Agar take her upstairs.'

'And then you argued with Agar, too, I believe?'

Elias stiffened. 'I don't like seeing my sister upset, Mr Holmes, especially over something she is not guilty of.'

Holmes threw a glance at Mr Walcombe. 'Then there was nothing between you and Miss Merrison, sir?'

The young man walked over to my friend, his shoulders tensed, as though suddenly he found our presence intrusive. 'Not that I see it is any of your business, Mr Holmes, but no. Not in the sense you mean. There was good friendship on her part and, I confess it, deep love on mine. But friendship was enough for me.'

'A rare quality indeed in a young man,' replied Holmes, blithely.

Walcombe was leaning over Holmes now, his eyes fixed upon my companion's. For his part, Sherlock Holmes merely stared back placidly, without any sign of external or internal disturbance.

'Not a quality shared by Dr Moore Agar,' hissed Walcombe. 'Lizzie told me many things about their relationship, about his insecurity, his jealousy, her frustration with it. She trusted me, Mr Holmes.'

'Indeed,' replied Holmes. 'And with what else did she trust you, Mr Walcombe?'

There was a long pause whilst the two men locked themselves in a silent battle of will. I kept my eyes on Walcombe, confident in the expectation that Sherlock Holmes would not falter in his composure. As matters turned out, success did not come my companion's way, for Elias Merrison broke the silence with a sigh.

'She trusted him with too much I should think. She was fond of telling people secrets.'

Walcombe turned to face his friend. 'What an extraordinary thing to say, Elias. But, yes, I suppose it's true.'

Holmes crossed the room, coming between the two men, keeping his eyes upon Walcombe as he moved. 'And what other things did she tell you, sir? Besides any difficulties she may have had in her relationship with Moore Agar?'

'I would rather not say,' stated Walcombe, his eyes on Elias.

'I think you must.'

Elias threw his hands in the air and sank into an armchair. 'It's all right, Dennis, tell him. I suspected she might discuss it with someone.'

'Your own disagreement with your father over your marriage?' I asked.

'Lizzie was so eager to marry herself that she couldn't understand it,' replied Elias, with no small measure of sorrow in his voice.

Walcombe nodded. 'She couldn't fathom why anyone would want to turn their back on the feeling she had for Agar.'

'That must be hard for you to confess,' murmured Sherlock Holmes.

Walcombe nodded. 'She loved him far more than she could ever love me.'

For an instant, I felt for the young man whom I had initially treated with suspicion. I felt it took a brave soul to admit defeat in so important an issue as love.

'I'm sure you would never have made her choose between you both,' I remarked.

Walcombe gave me a small smile. 'I would never have made her choose. That, I fear, would be selfishness rather than love.'

'Perhaps there is a fine line to be drawn between the two,' I replied.

What may have been a reflective moment was violently interrupted by a cry of triumph from Sherlock Holmes. We all three turned to look at him, and I saw on his face that gleam of exaltation which victory would so often bring upon him. He was staring at me with suppressed excitement and when he spoke his voice seemed to fill the air surrounding us.

'Watson, you inspire me! You really are invaluable as a companion!' He paced to the door, and as he opened it, he turned back to face Elias and Walcombe. 'Thank you for your co-operation, gentlemen, but it is now time, I fear, for us to return to town. It is there that the solution to this problem lies, and a man's life is at stake!'

On the journey back to London, Sherlock Holmes would not speak a single word. It was a peculiarity of his mind that he was able to detach his thoughts from an investigation at will, not least when the solution was within his grasp. And so it was that he sat in the corner of our carriage, his head leaning back against the seat, talking at length on a variety of topics, including the influences of Paganini and the Buddhism of Ceylon. For myself, I barely listened to him, for I was endeavouring to find whatever clue it was he had identified which had led to his belief that the matter had been concluded satisfactorily. I had a suggestion in my mind of the guilty party, but it was only a vague outline, lacking any discernible contours. When I asked Holmes directly what the truth was, he responded only that he required a few missing links to have an entirely connected case.

Those missing links came to him in a series of investigations which he informed me would be conducted more swiftly without me. He directed me to Baker Street, and ordered that I wait for him there. Not more than two hours passed before he returned, his cheeks tinged with the fresh colour of success.

'The chain is complete, Watson,' said he. 'I have just dispatched a telegram to our quarry. A simple meal from Mrs Hudson and a quick pipe, and we shall see the truth of the matter standing upon our hearth rug before nightfall.'

Dinner was over and the table cleared before the strange business which had consumed us broke into our snug chamber. The fire crackled gently, and we two sat in silence. The clock had chimed eight before the soft tap at the door signalled the arrival of our visitor.

'There is our man, Watson,' whispered Holmes. 'Show him in.'

I opened the door, confident in my expectation of the face I was to meet. As the light of the room fell on the murderer's tormented expression, however, that confidence I had felt in my identification faded like a dying ember.

Holmes had risen from his chair and beckoned our visitor to enter. 'Sit down, sir. Help yourself to the brandy. You may need it.'

'I will attend to the brandy,' said I. As I poured it, I gazed again at the broken man who sat before our fire. I looked across at Sherlock Holmes. 'How did you know, Holmes? What gave you the clue?'

'For reasons I explained earlier, Watson,' he replied. 'I began this investigation with the belief that Moore Agar was innocent. Chambers the butler confirmed it for me the moment we arrived at Saxon's Gate.'

'How so?'

'Chambers stated that he showed Dr Agar out of the house at eight o'clock and that he did not return to the house that night. Now we know that Elizabeth died at nine o'clock, by which time Agar had been gone for precisely one hour. Does that not suggest anything to you?'

'I am in the dark,' I replied.

'Morphine poisoning is a terrible but fairly swift cause of death,' replied my companion. 'If Agar had administered it when he gave Elizabeth the sedative, she would have died at *eight* and not nine o'clock.'

'I entirely follow you.'

Holmes blew a smoke ring from his pipe, his eyes fixed upon his guest. 'There was a more telling clue, however.'

'Indeed?' I asked.

'The fact that there were neither signs nor mention of a break-in and that Chambers did not let Agar or anyone else back into the house.' Holmes walked over to our guest, who gulped his brandy in clear anxiety. 'Given those two facts, therefore, for Elizabeth to die at nine o'clock, the killer had to be *inside the house already*.'

'It's so simple,' I remarked.

Holmes paid no heed to me. His eyes and attention were reserved entirely for the man before him. 'My suspicions were, therefore, directed towards the household rather than to any external influence.'

I had another point of confusion. 'But given his feelings for her and her impending marriage, was Mr Walcombe not a more likely suspect?'

Holmes shook his head gravely. 'More likely possibly, but he was not in fact responsible. No, only Elias Merrison here could be the guilty party. You are guilty, are you not?'

'The fact I am here shows you that.' The young man drained his glass, which shook in his hands, the flames of the fire dancing across the crystal.

Sherlock Holmes seemed to fill the room with his lean frame as he peered over his quarry. 'My suspicions were directed to you from the first, Mr Merrison.'

The young man shook his head. 'I do not understand you.'

'When Dr Agar told me he was at medical school with you, it was no great leap of the imagination to assume that you would know precisely how much morphine to administer to kill. A man who is not medically trained might use a bullet or a knife, but a doctor favours his medicines when he turns to crime. He believes it makes him more than a common cut-throat.'

Merrison shook his head. 'I pretend to be nothing more than I am, Mr Holmes. Cut-throat, killer, slayer. Name it how you will.'

'How did you arrange it?' asked Holmes. 'When precisely did you steal the morphine from Agar?'

'It was the day he came to the house to apologise to Elizabeth after their quarrel. It was frighteningly simple to manage.' His voice faltered, and I noticed a tear form in his eye. I poured more brandy into his glass, for which he offered no thanks.

'Proceed,' commanded Sherlock Holmes.

Elias sipped some of the fiery liquid, but it barely seemed to calm him. 'She hadn't drunk the sedative Agar had prepared, so I merely replaced it with a poisoned mixture and left it by her bedside.'

'What was your reason?' I asked.

The question had a remarkable effect. Elias Merrison's shoulders began to rock, his entire frame shaking with emotion as the tears welled up in his eyes. For two minutes he seemed to sob without any control of himself. I looked across at Sherlock Holmes, who stood as impassive as justice itself.

'His proposed marriage to Lady Henrietta Forsythe, Watson,' said he. He turned to address Elias. 'Your sister had found out the reason why you could not honour your father's wish. Your violent protest-ations to the marriage indicated to me that there was some strong reason for your refusal.'

'Lizzie threatened to tell my father the truth.' Elias forced himself to meet my companion's gaze. 'Walcombe let it slip to you that I have lost heavily on the stock market. Had father found out the truth I would have been cut off without a penny.'

'And you could not support your current wife in those circum-stances.'

Never have I seen a man glare at Sherlock Holmes with such astonishment as Elias Merrison did that night. His eyes widened in horror, and his tear-stained cheeks paled in fright. 'You know?'

'You have a wife?' I whispered.

Holmes turned to face me. 'Why else would a man argue adam-antly that he could not marry into a brilliant match? Mark you, Watson, that Mr Merrison did not say he *would not* but that he *could not* marry. The inference was plain.'

I nodded my understanding. 'He simply was not able to enter into marriage.'

'Marriages, like deaths, are recorded. My independent enquiries this afternoon, Watson, were at the Registry.' He took out a copy of a marriage licence from his breast pocket. 'It was there that I saw this copy of the licence of marriage between Mr Elias Merrison and Miss Lucy Ketteridge.'

'Who is she?' I asked.

Elias rose from the settee. He stared into the flames, as though his soul itself was falling into them. 'She is a landlord's daughter in the East End. My father would never accept it.'

'And your talk with Walcombe, my dear Watson,' continued Holmes, 'about choosing between loved ones gave me the clue to the motive. Elizabeth was fond of telling secrets and Elias had to choose between her telling his secret or forfeiting her life. He had to decide between his sister or his wife.'

Elias, however, was shaking his head. He turned from the flames and looked my friend in the eyes. 'No, Mr Holmes. Not quite. Between my sister or my child.'

At this statement, it was Sherlock Holmes who seemed taken aback. For a moment, I saw his steel composure weaken, and the flickering of his eyelids betrayed to me his total astonishment at the guilty man's words. The embarrassment was only momentary, however, and before any who knew him only a little could detect the lapse, his stern countenance was replaced.

'Perhaps you should explain,' said he

'I have no money of my own, gentlemen,' said Elias, walking around the room with his hands wringing inside each other and his head sunk on his breast. 'I have only my allowance and my eventual inheritance. Without them, I cannot afford to feed or clothe my child or support Lucy as I should. Elizabeth was jeopardising that by threatening to tell my father of the life I have with them, of which he is totally ignorant.'

'She was your sister,' I said. 'To kill her is appalling.'

He looked over at me from the far side of the room. 'I hope, Dr Watson, that you can continue to live your life without making the sort of choice I had to make. I ask you, Mr Holmes, what choice would you have made? Destroy a sister or protect a son?'

'I pray I never have to make the choice.'

'I do not believe that men are born saintly or evil,' continued Merrison. 'Every child is born pure. I could not let my innocent son suffer when he has done nothing to suffer for. I acted illegally; but perhaps I also acted morally.'

'There must be a balance, Mr Merrison, between morality and legality,' said Sherlock Holmes. 'An illegal act must be punished. But for an innocent man to be punished for such an act is reprehensible, and defies every ideal a man in my position must stand for. There is Moore Agar to think of.'

'But my child!' protested Merrison.

'The truth must come out, Mr Merrison, and it must be the whole truth. This talk of morality and the law means nothing otherwise, for both rely upon the truth for their value.'

Merrison raced over to Sherlock Holmes, and sank to his knees, his hands clasped in suppliant prayer. 'Mr Holmes, you are a worthy man, a man of honour! Please, I beg you! Do not desert me in this dreadful hour!'

Holmes was impassive. 'You have taken one innocent life, Mr Merrison. I cannot allow you to take Agar's, too. Two lives for your child's is no balance, for it allows one life to be thought of as more valuable than those other two. We have not the power to judge that value, for it belongs to an intelligence far beyond ours. Watson, send word to Hopkins that there is work for him here.'

There is one final word of epilogue. Merrison said no more after Holmes's judgment had been given. When Hopkins arrived, the guilty man made no effort to avoid his fate. He gave neither Holmes nor me a further glance, but walked solemnly away from our chamber, which had seen so many strange experiences, and the door closed upon him. Holmes gave Hopkins a few brief words of explanation, and Agar's release was secured for the following morning.

Holmes and I spoke no more about the desperate moral question which we had been confronted with that night. Perhaps neither of us would wish to contemplate it too often. For an hour or so, Sherlock Holmes scraped on his violin, his eternal escape from the world, but the notes he produced were melancholic. Finally, he laid the instrument to one side and reached for the tobacco slipper.

'A final pipe, my dear Watson?'

'Of course.'

And so, we sat together on either side of the hearth, as we had done many times before, and smoked in silence. I felt an inclination to praise my companion on the extraordinary degree to which he had demonstrated his powers not only of detection but of wisdom. I did not do so. There was something in that gaunt face, hidden by the cloud of tobacco smoke, which told me that such congratulations would not be welcome. I did not ask what he was thinking of, but I didn't doubt that somewhere in his mind was the image of an innocent child, who would never see his father.

The Adventure of the Intermittent Jigsaw Puzzle

ALAN STOCKWELL

It was a cloudy spring day in the year 1890. Holmes was crouched over his microscope indulging in one of his interminable scientific experiments. I was idly flicking through a newspaper.

'You know, Holmes, we are very fortunate to live in such interesting and progressive times.' These thoughts were prompted by an article I was reading in the paper. 'The progress in scientific matters, manufacturing innovations and so on is increasing at a phenomenally rapid rate. It says here how much electricity is contributing to new inventions and talks about something called carbon arc welding where by means of an electric spark you can actually fuse two separate pieces of metal into one.'

'Indeed. I hear the Americans have invented a death chair worked by electricity to execute criminals,' said Holmes as he peered into his microscope.

'It says here that a man called Fink has invented a lens that fits on the eyeball and corrects deficiencies of vision. Amazing! The person can see clearly yet does not appear to wear spectacles or other artificial aids as the lenses are totally unobtrusive.'

'I fear we must defer further discussion on the nation's progression as it seems we have a visitor,' said Holmes as Mrs Hudson entered.

'A lady to see you, Mr Holmes,' she announced as she proffered a visiting card. Holmes glanced at it as he asked Mrs Hudson to show in his client.

The lady who entered was a fine specimen of womanhood of about thirty years of age. She was dressed very tastefully in the latest fashion and, unlike many of Holmes's female clients, was very much self-assured and self-composed.

'Do take that chair, Miss Dysart. I am Sherlock Holmes and this is my colleague Dr Watson. How may I help you?'

'Please take a look at this.' The lady handed a small flat piece of wood to Holmes, which he promptly examined with his lens.

'It appears to be the corner of a dissection. Obviously a photograph has been mounted on to a sheet of plywood and then divided up by means of a saw. See on the back, there are pencil markings to guide the track of the blade. What is remarkable about it?'

'It was put through my door several weeks ago. Since then, at intervals of one a week, I have received further pieces.' From out of a paper bag she tipped several more pieces.

Holmes spread out the pieces and eagerly scanned them. I immediately recognised that these were parts of one of the jigsaw puzzles that had gained in popularity in recent years. Another aspect of the progress in inventions. When I was a boy I learned my geography of the British Isles from a wooden map dissected into the counties. It was great fun to assemble the parts to form the complete country; it was a way of learning that was an unobtrusive pleasure. Since those days mechanisation has brought many kinds of automatic saws into use and I understand that these puzzles are now being cut with a treadle saw and as a result can be manufactured more cheaply than before. Today it is possible to make wooden puzzles from all kinds of pictures and photographs. What lay before us appeared to be something of a similar nature.

'Ten pieces. Do you recall in what order they were sent?' asked Holmes.

'The four corners were the first ones, although I cannot say precisely the sequence. There is no doubt as to the most recent. That is what has caused me to come to you. At first when these pieces began to appear I thought it was probably some kind of tease from my friend Penny – Penelope Boughton – as we often exchange trinkets and amusing trifles.'

'But you are sure these pieces are not from your friend?'

'I am positive. I have challenged her about them. She denies all knowledge of them.'

'I say,' I interrupted, 'perhaps it's one of those advertising stunts. You get one of these each week and when you finally put them all together it reads "Buy Wilson's Pork Sausages" or something of that sort.'

'Do you think so?' asked Miss Dysart eagerly.

'Ingenious suggestion, Watson. Perhaps you could have a career in persuasion. Judging by the way London is desecrated with advertising posters there must be a good living to be made out of it. However, I do not think you are right about this picture. See, although it is far from complete, if such a message were inscribed we would surely have small parts of letters visible on at least some of the pieces.'

'Well we do not know the size of the complete picture, Holmes. We only have a handful of pieces. Some of these puzzles can have a hundred pieces or more.'

'True, Watson, but as we are obviously looking at a photograph I think the likelihood is that we should expect the complete size to be one of the conventional photographic sizes such as plate or half-plate. Let us assume that we are looking at a half-plate, which is 6½" by 4½". So far we have ten pieces. There are the corners; if I place them apart at roughly those dimensions we can see that our ten pieces cover approximately half the area. I think, perhaps, we have roughly half the picture here and the perpetrator has deliberately sent alternate pieces so that none can be linked together.'

'Mr Holmes, this week this piece arrived. You will find that you can attach it to that one there.' Miss Dysart handed him the piece and indicated one on the table.

'Thank you, madam. Indeed you are correct.'

'If you look closely you will see why I am sure this is not a tease from a friend. I am positive no friend could be so cruel!' cried Miss Dysart.

Holmes examined the pair of linked pieces. 'It is now clearly a tombstone and I can just make out the name on the stone. Why – it is Rebecca Dysart. A relative perhaps?'

'Rebecca Dysart is my name, Mr Holmes.'

'But your card proclaims you to be Victoria Dysart.'

'I was named Rebecca Victoria Dysart. My mother and grand-mother were both called Rebecca and it was important to my mother that I was named so, too. I don't know why, but my father hated the name vehemently and insisted that I was called Victoria after Her Majesty. As my mother was called Rebecca while she was alive, it was natural to refer to me by my second name Victoria, to avoid confusion.'

'I see. So your mother is dead.'

'Yes, she died when I was twenty years old, eight years ago. You may have heard of Dulwich cream slipware? It is quite popular in some households. The pottery was founded by my maternal grand-father and as he had no sons to pass it on to he was very pleased when Mama met and married William Dysart. He took his son-in-law into the business and it proved a very wise thing to do because my father built up the business to a level my grandfather could only have dreamed about. By the time my father died some six months ago the firm employed a hundred men and exported to over two dozen different countries throughout the Empire.'

'So are you now the owner of that enterprise?' asked Holmes.

'I have one brother, Bertram, who manages the business. I have nothing to do with the running of the factory but I have shares in the company providing me with a very respectable income.'

'You are not married. Do you have your own establishment?'

'Yes. My father owned a house in Dulwich and I preferred to go on living there after his death. Although a little too big for a single lady, it is well placed in College Road with very pleasant neighbours. But, to be frank, gentlemen, I do not expect to remain a spinster all my life. The fact I have not married is not through a lack of suitors but a desire to remain with my father who missed my mother terribly.'

'Tell me, Miss Dysart, you say these pieces have come singly each week. Do they come through the post?'

'No. Each one has been wrapped in a twist of newspaper and pushed through the letter box at night.'

'At night, you say?'

'I presume so as they have been found on the mat in the morning and were certainly not there when the last of the staff went to bed.'

'Perhaps one of your staff is responsible,' I suggested.

'Of course I have thought of that but, whilst I cannot be certain, I do not think so. My lady's maid Sophie and I are very close and there is little that goes on in my household of which she is unaware.'

'Hum,' mused Holmes, 'are they always pushed through on the same night of the week?'

'No, the nights vary.'

'But always only one per week?'

'Yes.'

'We now have eleven pieces. If my assumption is correct, we are but half way through building up this complete picture. From now on I think we will find that the pieces all begin to interlink. That means we have some ten weeks or thereabouts before the full picture is revealed. At present I do not think I can do anything until we have more of the picture which I expect will reveal the purpose of subjecting you to this tortuous procedure. Take heart, Miss Dysart, the whole thing may be totally harmless, there may be no sinister purpose in it at all.'

'But the tombstone with my name on it? I am sure that is some sort of warning to me,' protested the lady, near to tears.

'It does appear to bode ill,' agreed Holmes, 'but it is too early, as yet, to establish any facts in the case. As my friend, Watson, will tell you, it is not possible to formulate theories until one has all the data in place. I beg you not to distress yourself, Miss Dysart. You have done the correct thing in coming to me; there is no better man in all London. Please accept my assurance that nothing will happen to harm you before the photograph is complete. Before then I expect to have solved your mystery. I need to keep the pieces here. It is imperative that you supply me with each piece new piece as it arrives. Is that understood?'

'Yes, Mr Holmes. And thank you. My mind is much relieved. I feared you would not take my problem seriously.'

The lady left us with a much lighter heart than on her arrival.

'Can you make anything of it, Holmes?' I asked.

'I am not sure, Watson. But I hope a little patience will reveal a little light.'

As forecast, over the following weeks the collection of jigsaw pieces increased at weekly intervals and Holmes devoted much study to the photograph as it was gradually assembled. Meanwhile, of course, he had other cases to occupy him but the jigsaw was left permanently on display on a side table and from time to time I often caught him staring at it. Eventually, when the picture was nearly complete, we were brought the expected weekly piece by Mr Bertram Dysart, the brother of our client.

'My sister has great faith in you, Mr Holmes,' said our visitor. 'For my part I think it is a lot of fuss about nothing.'

'What do you suppose is the purpose, Mr Dysart? Why should a person or persons unknown take this extraordinary procedure of delivering a dissected photograph piece by piece?'

'I've no idea, Mr Holmes. I agree it is most peculiar but I cannot see that there is much harm in it. Victoria seems to think it indicates that she is in great danger in some way.'

'I fear she may be right, Mr Dysart. I would not seek to disturb her unnecessarily though. I hope to get to the bottom of all this before any such danger manifests itself.'

'You alarm me, Mr Holmes. I had dismissed the whole affair as a harmless prank.'

'Perhaps it may turn out to be so, but to send a picture of a gravestone with a person's name on it that bears the same name as oneself is a little unsettling, would you not say?'

'I have brought the latest piece myself because I was apprehensive that Victoria was being encouraged by irresponsible persons but, having met you, I realise that you are in earnest.'

'I am in deadly earnest, Mr Dysart. May I have the piece you have brought?'

Holmes slotted the new piece in place. 'Ah, I think we are wanting but two more pieces and the picture will be complete. Have a look, Mr Dysart.'

'Good heavens, it is quite a pleasant scene. A country churchyard. I had the idea from Victoria that the picture would appear malevolent in some way.'

'Oh, no, not at all. It is, as you say, a pleasant vista; the sort of picture a visitor might take home as a reminder of a stay in the country. But look more closely at the area surrounding the missing pieces. You see, above the gravestone?'

'I see. There are some hands resting on top of the stone and what appears to be part of a coat.'

'There will be a man standing behind the stone. Not only are the hands resting on the stone, the position of the arms suggests he is almost embracing it. When we have the two remaining pieces the man will be displayed in his entirety.'

'But who is this man?' asked Dysart.

'There you have me, sir. I presume the whole process is intended to delay revealing who the sender is until the final moment.'

'You mean the sender of the pieces will be the man depicted in the picture?'

'That is possible. But the obvious conclusion is that the revelation of the man's face will be of the utmost significance to Miss Dysart. What that is we have yet to divine.'

Dysart was visibly shaken. 'I am glad I came to see you in person, Mr Holmes. No wonder my sister is so upset over this affair. It is most sinister. What do you propose to do?'

'Well, Mr Dysart, now you have brought the latest piece, thus completing the picture but for the centre, perhaps you would describe it to us?'

'What? Well – it is a photograph taken on a summer's day. The scene shows a country churchyard with a portion of the church on the left. On the right is a thatched cottage. There are some trees, then a vista of open country. The churchyard has tombstones dotted about, many of them ancient judging from their inclinations. There is a scythe leaning against the church wall and it looks as if the photograph were taken during mowing as most of the grass is still long but that around the stone in the centre - the focus of the picture – there it has been cleared. I think that is about all I could say about it.'

'Excellent, you have picked up all the points of importance. My intention is to find the churchyard shown here and pay it a visit.'

Both Dysart and myself gaped at Holmes.

'But Holmes,' I said, 'there are tens of thousands of churches in the country, how can you possibly find this particular one?'

'We have a few useful clues in the picture. It is, as you, Mr Dysart, rightly point out, situated in the countryside, therefore it is not in a town or city. Thus we can immediately eliminate half the churches in the country. Take a look at the section of building showing on the left of the picture.'

'I see it,' said Dysart eagerly, as we three pored over the photograph.

'Do you observe that there is no corner? The building is obviously round.'

'A round tower, you mean?' cried I.

'Just so. And note the construction of it.'

'It looks as though it is made from large pebbles. Certainly not stones or bricks.'

'Very observant of you, Mr Dysart. It is indeed a round tower constructed from flint stones. A type of building unique to one particular area of this country.'

'Norfolk!' I cried. 'I remember when we took our holiday there. You were very interested in the church architecture.'

'Correct, Watson. These towers appear on churches all over East Anglia, the majority in Norfolk and a lesser number in Suffolk.'

'Excellent, Holmes!' I cried.

'But there will be hundreds of churches in East Anglia,' protested Dysart.

'Yes, sir, there are approximately a thousand churches in Norfolk alone, but only one in ten of those have round flint towers. So you see, from the tens of thousands of churches in the country we have, by looking at this picture alone, narrowed our field down to one hundred.'

'Amazing!' said Dysart.

'Even so, Holmes,' I pointed out, 'one would still have to visit each parish to look at its church before finding this particular one.

Although possible it would take months whereas we have only two more weeks before the picture is completed.'

'Correct, Watson, but I think we can squeeze a little more juice from this scene. Pray take my lens and examine the thatched cottage on the right.' I did as I was requested. 'Well?'

'A thatched cottage, Holmes,' was all I could say, returning the lens.

'Thatched with reed, Watson. Most cottages are thatched with straw. Sometimes with heather, sometimes with reeds. It usually depends on the readily available material close at hand. Reed is very common in Norfolk, especially in fenland and estuary areas, as you should know from our foray there some years ago.'

'But as you say, it is commonplace, there will be many such areas spread about the county. It hardly narrows the field.'

'No, in itself it is not very useful, but it confirms my other deductions and will assist in my further ones.'

'I am dazzled,' said Dysart shaking his head.

'Permit me to dazzle you a little more, Mr Dysart. You have pointed out to us the vista of open country. Do you not observe an area of higher ground in the distance?'

'Yes I see that, but is that important?'

'The county of Norfolk is notoriously flat. I believe the highest point in the county is no more than 300 feet above sea level. Therefore such elevations as we see here are particularly prominent on contour maps. As you may know, towers are invariably built on the west end of a church, therefore we can tell that this hill or hillock is situated to the west of our location. Unfortunately, as camera lenses vary in their focal lengths, it is not possible to estimate the distance between hill and church in any way but tracing the general direction should be sufficient. With the aid of a detailed map I hope to pinpoint all the possibilities and visit each in turn. I shall be departing tomorrow and I have permitted myself a week to carry out the task. The situation will not become critical for a further week as we have two more pieces to arrive before the photograph is entire.'

Our visitor left reeling with wonder. I doubt if his everyday business of manufacturing and exporting cream slipware pottery often brought him into the compass of an analytical mind such as Holmes's.

'You will come with me, Watson?'

'Of course, Holmes, if you desire it.'

'We will cover the ground twice as fast if we divide our resources.'

Holmes had marked some six areas of high ground that he deduced conformed to the topography of the area we sought and methodically set out a system we were to follow. Taking the first area he made a sweep on the map eastwards of the high ground and noted the positions of the churches as depicted on the map. We then established our headquarters at the largest settlement within the sweep and divided the area in two sections from that base. Taking one section each we hired a boy with a pony and trap to take us from village to village, church to church, systematically covering our own area. We had lists of village names which we struck off when we had viewed the church. Essential to our campaign was to show, at every available opportunity, the copies of the photograph that Holmes had had made to locals in the areas we visited in the hope that somebody may recognise it. Each evening we returned to our base and exchanged our information which was marked off on the master plan.

Thus in that way we combed through the countryside. It was a succession of long, arduous, tiresome and frustrating days. Most often, on approaching the location of a church and immediately seeing from a distance that it had a square tower, I could cross it off my list at once. At others my heart would leap up as I discovered a round tower but on close inspection it was not the one we sought. It was a frustrating business as most of the churches were far from each other and the connections were via small winding country lanes. Most days I managed no more than six or seven churches. I presume Holmes found much the same conditions on his inspections.

Once we had exhausted the entire neighbourhood of one base we moved to the next designated area and started the whole process again. Had we the time available to us, I am certain we could have viewed every single church in Norfolk by these means. However, time was of the essence and even by stretching our allotted week to ten days, a rate of twelve churches a day crossed off the list meant we would only cover some one hundred and twenty churches out of the thousand or so available to us. I could only hope that Holmes's deductions were correct and that we would sooner, rather than later, find the one we sought.

It was on the fourth day when I had a stroke of luck. I had found a round-towered flint church which again, alas, had proved not to be the one we sought, but in the churchyard a man was digging a grave. He was the sexton, a man of well over fifty years of age. I showed him the photograph to enquire if he recognised the locale. He pondered a good while then said 'No, I do not recognise the place but that is a Swaffham scythe.' He explained that agricultural tools varied depending on the place where they were made, and what may appear to be two identical rakes will, on close inspection, reveal various differences unique to the maker. Apparently over the years these differences become part of the essential style of the tool and can be recognised on a regional basis.

'Now that scythe,' said he, 'is definitely from the Swaffham area. Take a look at the snaith. Snaiths always have a double curve but the Swaffham one is straighter than most and the beard on the chine is less cut away. Oh aye, that's definitely a Swaffham scythe.'

'So this church is in or near Swaffham?' I excitedly sought confirmation.

'Now, sir, I did not say that. I said the scythe was made in that vicinity.'

'But there is a very good chance that a scythe will be employed in the area where it was made?'

'Aye, sir, in the olden days you could be sure that a man bought all his tools locally. Why, see these spades? I've had them nigh on forty years and they was made by the village blacksmith that we had in those days. Him and the wood turner used to make spades between them. But now, with the railways come, you can buy spades from a catalogue and have them sent from Lord knows where. But you don't know what you're getting. I reckon a man needs to try the tools first. With a scythe especially. It should be made specially for your height. You would be a foolish man to buy a scythe without seeing if it fit you.'

I thought this information about the scythe pictured leaning against the church wall was a good omen and was eager to dash back to our headquarters to inform Holmes. But, of course, he would be still out in the field until much later so I decided to carry on with my planned day but secretly sure that I was looking in the wrong area entirely.

When we met up for our meal that night I could tell Holmes was flagging in spite of his efforts to conceal it.

'Well, Watson, the good thing about not finding our church is that our field of search is now much narrower,' he said with assumed cheerfulness.

'I think we should try Swaffham, Holmes,' I said.

'Swaffham, why? That is the last on the list. I did not draw up this list in an arbitrary manner, Watson, it is carefully selected with the order based on probability.'

I then explained about my encounter with the sexton.

'Excellent, Watson, it is the only clue we have gained. Do you think the man knew his business? He was not some country dotard?'

'I am sure he is right about the tool, Holmes. But whether it has remained in the same area that it was made is something nobody knows until we find it. But I think we should switch operations to Swaffham. Time is running out on us.'

'Very good, Watson. Swaffham it is. We move off in the morning.'

On the second day in the Swaffham area at the village of Thorpe St Napier I found the church and its graveyard with the elusive grave. The headstone read in its entirety Rebecca Dysart, born 1835 died 1863. There was no other writing. I sought out the vicar and made arrangements for Holmes to interview him the following day.

The Rev Artemis Johnstone immediately informed us that although he had not been the incumbent back in 1863, having arrived some years later, he had the parish record book to hand and hoped that he could be of some small assistance in whatever matter we sought his co-operation.

'Firstly, may we find the entry for the burial of Rebecca Dysart?' asked Holmes.

'I have already done so, Mr Holmes.' He opened the book at the necessary page. The entry told no more than the bald statement on the gravestone: 14th November 1863 Rebecca Dysart aged 28 years buried.

'Are there any more entries with the name Dysart?' asked Holmes.

'I do not know, Mr Holmes. It is certainly not a name known in this area. Please feel free to examine the book for yourself.'

Holmes ran his fingers backwards up the entries and eventually found what he sought.

'Here we are 14th June 1856 William Dysart bachelor aged 25 married Rebecca Howard spinster aged 21.'

'Ah, now that is very interesting, Mr Holmes. As no doubt you will have noticed, the name Howard is prominent in the records. The Howards are a long established local family. They claim to be related to the Dukes of Norfolk though I cannot say as to the truth of that. But there have been Howards in this parish for centuries.'

'Are there any elderly Howards living in the parish now?'

'Indeed. In the cottage next to the church is old Mrs Carr. She is the widow of Jabez Carr. The Carrs are another old Thorpe St Napier family. Before marriage Mrs Carr was a Howard; she may well have the information you require.'

We all made our way to the cottage and found Mrs Carr, a very ancient lady, but not too ancient to be highly suspicious of Holmes and his questions. It soon became clear, however, that it was not Holmes who was under suspicion but the Rev. Artemis Johnstone. She did not wish to reveal any family secrets before the vicar. However he, obviously accustomed to his parishioner's hostility, made an excuse and left. From then on, after getting Holmes's assurance that he would not say anything to the vicar, Mrs Carr was very free with her answers. As with many old people she kept straying from the point and we had to endure a series of side ramblings before Holmes could elicit the information that he sought. I will spare the reader the many diversions and paraphrase the gist of the story she had to tell.

Mrs Carr's mother and Rebecca Dysart's mother were cousins. Rebecca was a daughter in the more well-to-do branch of the Howard family. The future Mrs Carr was in the peasant branch. Rebecca Howard, renowned as a local beauty, had many admirers and was considered an excellent marriage prospect by the families of the district. One day from nowhere into the village rode William Dysart, a young man of stunning good looks and considerable charm. The hearts of local young ladies were thus set a-flutter, and, as he appeared to have wealth to go with his attributes, so the heads of their parents were also turned. Many a young lady set her cap at William Dysart but he chose Rebecca Howard. She was madly in love with him but her parents did not consider him a suitable match and Mr Howard refused permission to wed. The young couple defied him and were married in the village church. But they were shunned by the villagers because Mr Howard was a powerful man and nobody wanted to cross him.

Shortly after the marriage it transpired that Dysart owed money all over the place. But by then the young couple had left the village and no one knew where they had gone. Nothing more was heard from them until seven years later when Rebecca returned with a child. A son aged six. She was ill and destitute. The child was weak and sickly. Dysart had abandoned them both shortly after the child was born. He had married Rebecca on the assumption that he would be welcomed into the Howard family and that he would have a place of comfort and wealth and could not believe that all his roguish charm had failed. When the son was born he was sure the hearts of its grandparents would be melted but when the Dysarts visited in stealth they were turned away. Shortly after that Dysart finally realised that he had backed a loser and fled, leaving his wife and baby to fend for themselves. This they did for several years, though nobody knows where or in what manner. Obviously at the end of her tether, eventually Rebecca returned home hoping for some compassion but her parents were as obdurate as ever and she was again turned away. Scraping along on charity for a few months, she had eventually succumbed to death in the very room in which we were sitting.

Although the parish church had a special area where the Howards were buried, Mr Howard refused to have her buried there. In fact he tried to stop her being interred anywhere in the parish but the then vicar stood firm and she was buried as we had seen. An uncle, ashamed of his brother's behaviour, had provided the stone. The inscription was a compromise between the brothers' wishes.

'What happened to the boy?' asked Holmes.

'He was sent away to an orphanage somewhere. I don't know where. He was a thin puny sickly thing and so probably died there,' replied old Mrs Carr.

Back in our rooms Holmes took stock of the situation. 'When you write up this case, Watson, no doubt you will have me on my first sight of the photograph arrogantly proclaiming "it is obviously the church of St Such and Such situated in the village of Such and Such", without mentioning all the hours I have spent poring over maps in the library of the British Museum and the many tiresome hours we spent trotting all over East Anglia.'

'Fortunately we found the place in time. What would you have done if we had failed?' I queried.

'I should have had to rely entirely upon the plan we are now about to carry out. We must capture the man as he delivers the last piece. The last week starts tonight, so we must go over to Dulwich and make our preparations with Miss Dysart.'

That good lady was very relieved to see us. 'I am so pleased you have come, Mr Holmes. When I enquired, I was told that you had gone away.'

'Have there been any developments?'

'No. No. It is just that I am so afraid and feel so much more at ease when I know you are near to assist me.'

'Dr Watson and I will be here every night from now on until the last piece arrives which will be within the next seven days.'

'I am so relieved to hear you say that, Mr Holmes.'

'However, I think you may be in some personal danger. Is there somewhere away from here where you can stay?'

'I could go to my brother Bertram.'

'I think not. I am not certain of the malevolence of the man we seek. It could be that your brother too is in danger.'

'Heaven forbid!' cried the distressed woman. 'What creature is this? Why are we so persecuted?'

'All will become clear soon, Miss Dysart. But can you arrange to stay away?'

'Park Lane. My friend Miss Boughton resides in Park Lane.'

'Excellent. Pray make arrangements to move there at once and remain there until you hear from me.'

'But what will you do, Mr Holmes?'

'Dr Watson and I will stay here during the hours of darkness. These packages arrive during the night after the household has retired. When that hour approaches Dr Watson will be on watch, concealed outside the house. I shall be in your hall immediately behind the door.'

This was the first I had heard of this plan but of course I was willing to go along with the arrangements. However, a place of concealment was not easy to find. Miss Dysart's house stood without a front garden of any sort. There were a mere three steps from the pavement up to her front door. Fortunately, almost opposite, the house on the other side had a small hedge of laurel bushes and Holmes decreed that I should crouch there. An unexpected hitch, however, arose when he explained his part on the procedure.

'The door will be left unlocked. I shall be immediately behind it. When the package drops through the letter box I shall swiftly open the door and apprehend the man as Dr Watson approaches him from behind.'

'I'm afraid you will not be able to leave the door unlocked.'

'Why not pray?'

'Well, the policeman who does the night patrol checks all the doors in the street to ensure they are locked. If one were to be found unlocked he would rouse the household to ensure that they were safe and then have it locked.'

'Hum, I see. Is there a particular reason for this policeman's zeal?'

'It is since the burglary a year ago.'

'Burglary?'

'Yes. We were at dinner, entertaining friends, when there was a knock at the door. The servant who dealt with it came and told my father that there was a rough-looking man insisting on coming in although told that we were not at home. My father heard shouting as our staff grappled with the man in the hall and went out in person. It was awful, Mr Holmes. This tramp was trying to force his way in and my father was striking him. He knocked the man to the ground and was kicking him. I had to drag him off with the help of our guests. He was like a madman, shouting and cursing. I had never seen him so angry. The police were sent for and the tramp taken away. My father calmed down but he was never the same after. At the court hearing he accused the man of stealing a silver clock and an antique vase that were in the hall-way. But the poor man had never touched them at all. As far as I could tell nothing had been disturbed; the man had tried to come in and had been prevented and that was the extent of it. In the circumstances I think my father's brutal attack was most unwarranted. Two of our manservants were successful in controlling the intruder.'

'Most interesting, Miss Dysart. You say your father made accusations at the trial? Were you there?'

'Yes, I felt sorry for the poor man. My father behaved in a totally outrageous manner. He tried to get the man transported. When it was clear that such a punishment was far too extreme for the crime for which he was committed, my father put up everything he could to blacken the man's case.'

'We have not transported criminals for many years, Miss Dysart,' said Holmes.

'I do not know about that sort of thing but Father accused him again of stealing. He is a powerful man in our community, Mr Holmes, and his word carries a lot of weight, but the magistrate trying the case probed through the welter of accusations and, with my testimony, the charge was reduced to trespass by force. The man was only a poor tramp. No doubt he was merely knocking on doors begging but was simply too persistent in his importuning. Certainly, in the circumstances, my father's behaviour was totally extreme. Alas, from that time on his character seemed to alter. He was always a forceful man but now he seemed to have periods of great anger whenever some trivial thing annoyed him; then he would be plunged into gloomy morose periods. I think it likely that in the scuffle he received a blow to the head and this caused some disorder in his brain. Six months later he was dead.'

'A very strange affair. And what sentence did this tramp receive?'

'Twelve months in prison.'

'I see. Well, as regards the door, the matter is simply solved. I shall turn the key but leave it in the lock. The bolts will not be used. It will take but a second to turn the key – which is of little moment – as I shall be fully alert. I do not wish to complicate matters by confiding in your policeman.'

From 11 o'clock that night I was concealed behind the laurel bush. It was a dark night but fortunately there was a gas lamp situated not far from the house and a pale weak glimmer illuminated the doorway sufficiently. As house lights were dimmed and my eyes became accustomed to the dark, the patch of light seemed quite vivid enough to see when anyone approached the door. A few carriages passed by and an occasional pedestrian but once midnight had passed a complete absence of movement fell upon the street. It was rather cold and the position I was in was very cramping. My time in Afghanistan has taught me to withstand heat rather than cold and as the hours wore on I began to fervently wish for my comfortable bed.

At three in the morning I heard footsteps. Immediately I was alert, all my senses roused to their full abilities. A figure appeared out of the gloom and approached the door. I made ready to spring out as arranged but relaxed as I recognised the familiar shape of a London bobby. He tried the door quietly and satisfied went on his way. I heard him stop as he tried the next door then his footsteps resumed fading as he passed further down the road.

As the household arose Holmes opened the door and beckoned me in. 'Have some breakfast, Watson, the cook has kindly laid a table for us.' So, at an unaccustomed early hour, we partook of breakfast then returned to Baker Street.

The following two nights passed in an identical manner and I was becoming used to going to bed after having my breakfast! When Holmes caught up on his sleep I do not know.

On the fourth night I felt bound to remonstrate with Holmes. 'I say, Holmes, I think we should do this guarding turn and turn about. It's all very well for you sitting here in the warmth but I am outside in the bitter cold night after night.'

'My dear fellow, I am so sorry, how thoughtless of me. You are quite right. Tonight I shall condemn myself to the laurel bush and you must be in the hall. But please be alert as I am not, as yet, convinced that the packets are not being placed by someone who works inside the house.'

'You astonish me, Holmes!'

'We can rule out nothing, Watson, and this could well be our one and only chance of catching the villain.'

It was a much more comfortable billet sitting on a chair in the hall. I had a light, I had a book to read and my hand was within reach of the key. The hall being so comfortably warm, as the night wore on I found I was becoming a little drowsy. The book was not capturing my full attention and I am ashamed to confess that I slid into a doze. I woke with a jerk as the book made a noise falling to the floor. I noted with shamed alarm that by the hall clock I had probably been asleep for some forty minutes. But I would surely have been roused by Holmes shouting had the felon appeared and all was quiet and serene. I determined not to fall asleep again. I abandoned the book and thought to keep awake by trying to recall complete verses of poems and mathematical formulae. Then I saw it. On the floor in front of the very chair where I was sitting. A twist of newspaper. The thing had arrived whilst I was asleep!

But Holmes had not acted. He would have seen the man and pounced. Obviously the packet had been planted by somebody within the house. Possibly each night they had tried but Holmes, being constantly alert, had thwarted them. As soon as I took over and dropped off to sleep the coast was clear for them to silently put the packet in place. I opened the door and called softly. Holmes came across swiftly.

'What is it Watson?' I showed him the paper.

'But that is impossible!' he exclaimed. I had to confess that I had fallen asleep.

'I'm sorry, Holmes, I have let you down and failed miserably,' trying to allay his anger at my folly. 'But it proves that the papers are left by somebody in the house. That has narrowed the search down considerably.'

Holmes stalked into the sitting room and flung himself into a chair. He lit his pipe and closed his eyes. I thought it prudent not to say anything further and I took another chair some distance away and sat burning with embarrassment.

We remained thus until the cook arose and, as was her wont, made us breakfast. This we ate in silence. Then Holmes leaped up and said 'Our cab is here.' We had arranged for the same man to collect us each morning and return us to Baker Street.

'Baker Street as usual, sir?' asked the cabby.

'No, cabby, the police station,' said Holmes.

As we walked into the police station the sergeant on duty recognised Holmes immediately.

'Why, it's Mr Sherlock Holmes! This is a surprise and an honour. What brings you to our humble station so early in the day?'

'Good morning to you, sergeant,' said Holmes pleasantly. 'I think we have met before?'

'Indeed we have, sir. I was present at all that nastiness in Limehouse a couple or three years ago. Foster's the name.'

'I remember you well, Foster. I am pleased to see you thriving. I am conducting an enquiry in the neighbourhood and I wonder if you could tell me which constable was on patrol down College Road last night?'

'That was Constable Stead. He has gone off duty now.'

'Where can I find him?'

'I should think at this very moment he will be tending his vegetables, very proud of his garden is Arthur. I could send for him if you wish?'

'Pray do not trouble to do that. I would like to talk to him though; have you his address?'

'I'll write it down for you. It is not far away.' The sergeant pushed a slip of paper towards Holmes. 'I hope he is not in any sort of trouble?'

'Not at all, sergeant, just a query about a happening some time ago.'

We did, indeed, find the policeman in his little garden amongst a fine selection of vegetables.

'Good morning, Constable Stead,' said Holmes cheerily. 'I can see you truly have green fingers.'

' 'Tis good soil here, sir,' replied the bobby.

'Your sergeant gave me your address. I am Sherlock Holmes.'

'The famous detective?'

'This is my colleague Dr Watson.'

'Well, I don't know what to say. I'm really flattered having such well-known gentlemen in my little garden. I hope there is nothing wrong?'

'I have one or two questions if you could spare me the time from your magnificent tomato plants.'

'Certainly, sir. Anything I can do to help the law is my duty.'

'Last night you posted a tiny packet through the letterbox of a house in College Street. Is that correct?'

'Yes, sir, I did. I hope there was no harm in that?'

'It is not the first time you have done it; you have posted similar packets on numerous previous occasions.'

'I have, sir, I would think almost two dozen.'

'Are you aware of the contents of these packets?'

'Well, I presume they all contain a piece of jigsaw puzzle.'

'You presume? You do not know?'

'Perhaps I should explain, sir?'

'I think an explanation would be welcome, constable, as it is a rather singular thing for a policeman to do.'

'My brother asked me to do it.'

'Your brother?'

'Yes. Some month's ago he asked if Mr Dysart's house was on my beat; when I said it was, he asked if I could pop a little twist of paper through his door when next I was on the night shift. So I did.'

'Did you not ask what the twist of paper contained?'

'I did, sir, but George – my brother – said the less I knew about it the better. George is a decent chap and if he thought it was all right for me to deliver it then there would be no harm in it. That was good enough for me.'

'But then there were many more.'

'Yes, he kept them coming and, as I'd obliged him the first time, it seemed a bit churlish to start refusing such a simple request. After all, I have to try the door every night so it is hardly a chore to carry and post such a tiny thing.'

'Were you not curious about the contents?'

'I was, sir, yes. After I had delivered two or three I thought there may be something illegal in these packets so I opened one. When I saw it was a harmless piece of jigsaw my mind was set at rest.'

'I see.'

'Is there some harm in it sir?'

'No, no. It is just that this curious procedure has alarmed the lady of the house.'

'Oh, I did not intend any alarm, sir. Were the pieces not expected then?'

'Tell me: does your brother make these ingenious puzzles?'

'Oh no, sir, George couldn't do anything like that. No, my brother is a warder at Wormwood Scrubs prison.'

'Ah!' smiled Holmes in satisfaction. 'All now becomes clear. Thank you, my good man, you have provided the final piece in my own personal jigsaw puzzle.'

'I have, sir?' asked the baffled bobby.

'Many thanks, Stead, and best wishes for a bumper crop of tom-atoes.'

We had retained the cab and now Holmes instructed the cabby to take us to the offices of the local newspaper. I could not imagine the purpose of this and was getting quite dizzy with all this dashing from place to place. There he requested to look at the back issues of the Dulwich weekly newspaper.

'Here we are, Watson,' he whispered as he turned up a front page with the lurid headline Eminent Dulwich Man Defeats Burglar. Our case is complete. See the name of the so-called burglar?'

'Norfolk Howard,' I read in wonder.

'Come, Watson.'

Once again we leapt into the cab and this time we were whisked over to Wormwood Scrubs Gaol. Holmes changed manner entirely as he rapped on the forbidding door. A Judas door behind a grill opened and a bewhiskered face appeared.

'I'm so sorry to trouble you. I am from the Prisoners' Aid Society. We have been informed that Norfolk Howard is to be released today. Can you confirm that, please?'

The trapdoor snapped shut.

Holmes and I exchanged looks and wondered if that was a sign that the interview had been abruptly terminated. But after several minutes the little door opened again.

'No, not today. Tomorrow. Norfolk Howard is on the list to be released tomorrow.'

'Thank you, thank you, you are too kind,' said Holmes unctuously; and the cabby was at last instructed to return us to Baker Street. Finally we had a respite and I spent the day comatose before going to bed early.

The next day on coming down to breakfast, I found Holmes had already eaten.

'Good morning, Watson,' said he pleasantly. 'If you would like to be in at the dénouement of this tragic case pray make yourself ready to leave immediately.'

So after snatching a slice of toast and a gulp of coffee we once more took ourselves to Dulwich.

'What now, Holmes?' I asked.

'Yet again we are to wait patiently, Watson. But this time we will be in comfort and at leisure in Miss Dysart's sitting room. I visited her at her friend's house yesterday whilst you were catching up on your lost sleep. All arrangements have been made with her staff to treat us as if we were residents.'

And thus we spent the morning sitting at ease waiting, with Holmes never taking his eyes from the street outside. After some hours he hissed 'He's here, Watson, don't let him see you.'

Concealed by the window curtains I peered out and saw, loitering over the road, a thin badly-dressed man. He wandered up and down the far pavement, glancing at the house at frequent intervals.

'What do you think he will do, Holmes? Is he waiting for darkness?'

'I doubt if he will attempt to enter the house after the treatment he received the last time he tried it. No, I rather think he is waiting for someone to enter or leave the house.'

'Miss Dysart, you mean?'

'No, Watson, Mr Dysart.'

'But he's dead!' I protested.

'Indeed he is,' said Holmes. 'Perhaps it would be a kindness to inform his son of that fact. Come, Watson.'

We left the house together, putting into operation a plan that Holmes had pre-conceived. He turned left and walked one way – I turned right and walked the other. We both ignored the waiting man. Having gone some distance we both crossed the road and returned towards our quarry, timing it so that we arrived simultaneously at either side of him.

'Mr Norfolk Howard? Otherwise known as William Dysart, I believe?' said Holmes. 'Grab him, Watson!' The man tried to escape and run, but being enfeebled by a year of prison diet and a naturally weak constitution was easily overpowered as we marched him across the road and into the house.

'Now, Mr Dysart, I am Sherlock Holmes, a consulting detective retained by Miss Victoria Dysart. This is my colleague Dr Watson. I have to tell you that I know a great deal of your story. I also think you were loitering outside with the intent of killing, or seriously maiming, your father Mr William Dysart Senior.'

'Blast you, whoever you are! I have suffered enough through that accursed man! Now the minute I regain my freedom he sets his bully boys on to me!'

'Listen to me, Dysart. You cannot be avenged by killing your father. He is already dead.'

'Dead?' The poor man stared.

'He died some six months ago. You cannot now wreak your revenge.'

Dysart laughed a bitter laugh and drew out from his sleeve a vicious-looking knife which he tossed on the ground in front of us.

'That's it then. It has all come to an end at last.'

'I know your father deserted you and your mother many years ago. I know your mother died in poverty and destitution and is buried in the churchyard at Thorpe St Napier. I have visited the grave.'

'I don't know who you are to be so conversant with my history. Why should you know about me? I who know nobody and have only just returned to this country,' said Dysart in bewilderment.

'You were placed in an orphanage. What happened then?'

'I was only six years old when I was put in the orphanage. It was not a bad place; it was not a cruel existence like you read about in Oliver Twist – but miserable enough. When I was fourteen I was sent, with other boys, out to Canada. Indentured labourers they called us, but it was nothing but official slavery. We were all split up and dispersed over the prairies of Canada. Those poor pioneers were trying to make a living from taming the wild land and we lads were allocated to them. I suppose some boys were kindly treated but most were like me – cruelly abused, beaten and half-starved. If you ran away you were caught and sent back to the farm. It was a wretched existence – even our masters were in a desperate plight. Seven long years of that destroys a young man's spirit. But, by law, it all ended when you reached twenty-one years of age and you became a free man.

'Many lads never reached adulthood, and many spent the rest of their lives in that same wretched existence of abject poverty. But I had a bit of luck, the only luck I've ever had in my entire life, and got a job with a carpenter who taught me the trade. I had an aptitude for the craft and soon became very good, receiving decent wages for my work. I saved every penny I could as my sole desire was to return to England to find the villain who had killed my mother and destroyed me. I bought my passage back, sought out my mother's grave and had myself photographed mourning over it. Then I started searching for my father.

'Eventually I tracked him down to this house. I watched and waited outside. I watched him come and go. Although I had had it in my soul to kill him instantly on the spot, when I saw the respectable house, the honest area and decent normality of it all, I faltered in my purpose. Here was a man with children and a prosperous business – a pillar of the community. Perhaps he repented of his evil past, perhaps he had spent years in remorse? Perhaps he had even made extensive attempts to find his first-born son? I decided to approach him and make myself known to him. Then I would decide what to do.

'He had not changed one iota. As soon as he realised who I was he tried to kill me. He would have succeeded too if some people in the house had not dragged him off me. The best he could do was to have me banged up in jail under the pretence of attempting to rob him by force. In jail! In all the hard times of poverty and trial in my life I have never done anything to warrant being put in jail, and here was my own long-lost father doing it to me knowing that I was his own son who he had not seen since I was a little boy. And he got me put in jail simply because he was not able to kill me.'

The poor soul wept bitter tears.

I thought I knew my friend Sherlock Holmes very well after all those years together but his behaviour sometimes surprised me by differing markedly from what I had deduced to be his character. He was not a man who tolerated displays of emotion and I had often seen him exasperated by the tears of a woman, still more those of a man. He rang the bell and very soon our friend the cook appeared bearing a large tray with tea, hot buttered toast, scones and the like which Holmes had pre-arranged. She set this down and left. Holmes, taking up the tea kettle, poured tea and offered food.

'Come, my friend, do have a toasted tea cake. I always think it a mistake to confine tea to teatime,' he remarked while passing a plate.

Gradually Dysart came round and silently took tea with us.

'I am not clear who you gentlemen really are, but thank you for treating me with such kindness.'

'We represent your late father's daughter, Miss Victoria Rebecca Dysart.'

'Rebecca was my mother's name.'

'Indeed. And of course, that lady is your half-sister,' I pointed out.

'She was the lady who spoke up for me at the trial. She is a very nice lady.'

'Because of the death of your father, she received your pieces of jigsaw puzzle. As she did not understand the import she was distressed when a gravestone with her own name on it was revealed,' explained Holmes.

'Oh poor lady!' cried Dysart. 'I had no idea. How upset she must have been. What worry I have given an innocent creature!'

'How were you able to make the puzzle and send it out of the prison?' asked Holmes.

'The system of the jail is that groups of prisoners are permitted to manufacture items in workshops. They give training in certain skills such as basket weaving, tin ware manufacture and so on. By nature of my trade I was assigned to the carpentry workshop. In that workshop we made wooden toys and novelties. The best of them are sold in the shops. They are made in a top-class fashion. In fact I hear that there are complaints from manufacturers about unfair competition from prison-made goods. Of course I was under the eyes of strict warders but it was a joy to me to be doing something useful other than picking oakum and other mindless tasks as in the old days. Fortunately my sentence did not include hard labour like some of the poor wretches. One day the warden overseeing me asked if I could make him a dissected picture puzzle. I had never made one before but I had seen one and it is only a matter of careful cutting with a fret saw. I don't know why they have started calling them jigsaw puzzles as it is a fret you need, not a jig. Anyway I made one for the man and he was very pleased and it turned out he was the brother of the policeman who had arrested me. I then got the idea to turn my photograph into a similar puzzle and asked the warder if he could get his brother to deliver the pieces. He was an obliging chap and between us we worked out the way of doing it a week at a time so that, if he should be caught, one little piece of jigsaw would be a harmless trifle. You know, sir, we poor folk like to help each other. So it was done. Neither the warder nor his brother had any love for William Dysart after the way he had tried to murder me and then shift the blame.

I knew that my father would be fearful of what would happen when I emerged from my prison, so I taunted him with the picture. I knew he had never seen the gravestone of my mother and I wanted to put the fear of God into him. I had no idea the man had died. I did not foresee the prospect of somebody else receiving the pieces. Oh my poor sister! Does she know who I am?'

'No. She knows nothing. All she knows is that some unknown person is sending her a photograph with a gravestone bearing her name. She knows that the last piece will bear the perpetrator's face. I have intercepted it. I have it here.'

'She must not know, sir!' burst out Dysart. 'She will recognise me as the man her father sent to jail. She must not know who I really am!'

'Calm yourself, my dear sir, calm yourself. The matter is entirely in your hands. You must be aware that your father married again and had a son and a daughter. His second wife died some years ago. He built up the business inherited by his wife and that business is now being run very prosperously by his son Bertram who is, of course, your half-brother. If they knew you were their kinsman they might be prepared to share some of their wealth. I would think, after the vicissitudes of your life, that would be welcome.'

'No! I cannot appear from nowhere and thrust myself into these good people's ordered lives! A convict and ne'er-do-well. They would turn me away. I will ask for nothing.'

'You may call them good people, and so they are. But you must be aware that your father married while your mother was still alive. It was a bigamous marriage and was, therefore, illegal and not binding. You are your father's legitimate son, your half-brother and sister are, unknowingly, illegitimate.'

'I realise that. It makes no difference to me. I do not belong here. Now Dysart is dead my business is finished. I will return to Canada.'

'Have you the means?' asked Holmes.

'I can earn the fare. I am a good carpenter. I can make a living.'

'It would be no hardship for your kinsmen to supply you with a thousand pounds to take you back to Canada and set yourself up there.'

'Don't insult me, sir! I do not need paying off! I am an independent man. I do not need help from anybody!'

'I understand your feelings, sir, and find them commendable,' said Holmes. 'But you are not being "paid off", as you call it. Unless you, yourself, reveal the connection, your brother and sister will not even know who you are. Permit me to make a suggestion. I will ask them for a contribution to the Prisoners Aid Society – a charity which assists ex-prisoners. The Society will fund your passage to Canada. How will that suit?'

'Well,' said Dysart grudgingly, 'I can see no harm in that if that is what this Society does.'

'Very well, it shall be so!'

Holmes arranged for Dysart to return to Canada and he sailed from Liverpool in better style than he had arrived. He had been persuaded to accept money for clothing and other means to respectability. An account in the name of Norfolk Howard had been opened at the Bank of Ottawa and £500 had been deposited therein for emergency use. As far as I know, to this day it has never been touched.

The Adventure of the Christmas Bauble

JOHN HALL

Mr Sherlock Holmes looked up with a languid gaze from the depths of his armchair as the door opened and Inspector Lestrade came bustling into our little sitting room, shaking stray flakes of snow from his coat.

'Chilly outside, Lestrade?' I asked.

'Very seasonable, Doctor Watson, considering it is but a week to Christmas,' he answered.

'Sit down, then, and have some brandy and hot water. And a cigar.'

Lestrade found a peg for his hat and coat, and took the chair I had indicated. 'The right prescription, as always, Doctor.'

Holmes stirred again. 'Been Christmas shopping, Lestrade?' he asked, nodding at the parcels which the Inspector had brought with him.

Lestrade laughed. 'Hardly, Mr Holmes.'

'Ah! a case, then, and these are clues?'

'You have it, sir.' The Scotland Yarder leaned forward in his chair. 'You won't have heard anything as yet, but the matter will be in the papers in a day or so.' This thought seemed to bring him no comfort at all.

'Pray continue,' said my friend.

'The fact is, Mr Holmes, you may well be able to help me with this,' said Lestrade with a certain amount of reluctance.

Holmes sat up straight. 'From the beginning, Lestrade.'

Our visitor sipped his brandy. 'It's like this, Mr Holmes. A certain foreign noblewoman is in London at the moment, doing a little Christmas shopping on her own account. Now, she had a fancy to buy a diamond, but could not make up her mind whether it should be a ring, a pendant, or what have you. Accordingly, she summoned one of the better-known jewellers, made her predicament known to him, and asked what he might suggest. He in turn contacted one of the merchants from Hatton Garden, and the merchant handed the finest stone he had over to the jeweller, who took it along to the hotel where the lady is staying. This was a couple of days ago.'

'Have you a description of the stone?' asked Holmes.

Lestrade waved a hand impatiently. 'The jeweller showed the lady the diamond, together with some sketches he had made of possible settings.' He took some sheets of paper from his pocket book. 'These are the very sketches and that is the diamond shown in 'em, so you can see for yourselves what it's like without a lengthy description from me.'

'The scale?' asked Holmes.

'Life-size.'

Holmes, normally the most imperturbable of men, raised an eye-brow, and passed the sketches to me.

'Good Lord!' I said. 'It is the largest diamond I ever saw.' This was the literal truth. The stone was square-cut, almost an inch one way by three-quarters of an inch the other. 'I wonder who is paying for it. Must be some rich man, for in my experience ladies seldom pay for these trifles from their own funds.'

'The stone is certainly distinctive,' said Holmes. 'And the second point you raise is also an interesting one, Watson, though perhaps not strictly relevant just at the moment. But you had not finished your tale, Lestrade.'

'Not much to tell, for I think you have both guessed the rest, gentlemen. The lady made her choice, and the jeweller, his business done, took his leave and set off for his shop. He had scarcely set foot in the street when someone pushed against him, and he lost his footing. By the time he had realised what had happened, the man who had crashed into him was at the end of the street.'

'With the diamond, of course?' I asked.

'Just so, Doctor. And his pocket book and watch.'

'Ah!' Holmes leaned forward. 'Then it was not simply the diamond he was after?'

Lestrade shook his head. 'It appears that the theft was a spur of the moment affair, and the loss of the diamond was merely unfortunate.'

'Very unfortunate,' said Holmes dryly.

'Well, the jeweller gave chase as soon as he had recovered his wits. A constable saw him, asked what was amiss, and joined the chase. They found the watch and pocket book at the corner, the thief having evidently discarded them as being of lesser value than the stone. Now, when they turned the corner, all was normal, the street was quiet, or as quiet as it can be at this time of year, and there was certainly no sign of anyone running. The constable then asked the jeweller to describe the thief, but he was quite unable to do so, everything had happened so quickly that he had not seen the man clearly.'

'So they had no clue at all?' I asked.

Lestrade shook his head. 'Not at first, but then they had a bit of luck. There was another constable on his beat round the corner, and he had noticed a man running down the street. And he *had* recognised him!'

'Ah!'

'Yes, Mr Holmes. The man was a petty thief and pickpocket, name of Winter.'

'Appropriate for this weather,' I remarked.

'Be that as it may, Doctor, the second constable, knowing Winter for what he was, had taken particular note of him, and where he went. He'd gone into one of the big department stores.'

'Jarrod's, perhaps?' I asked.

'No,' said Holmes, nodding at Lestrade's parcels, 'Morton and Jason's. Their wrapping paper is quite distinctive.'

'Right again, Mr Holmes. The three of them went into the store, and found Winter right by the entrance, next to a Christmas display. He made no sort of fuss when they approached him, didn't run away, and offered no resistance when they arrested him. When taxed with the crime, he said he knew nothing about it.'

'And what explanation had he for the fact that the second constable had seen him running down the street?' asked Holmes.

'Ah, he said that he had seen the jeweller running towards him, and thought it was someone else, a man with whom Winter had quarrelled over a girl.' Lestrade sighed. 'I have some professional acquaintance with this man Winter, and that's just the sort of thing he would do. He's not very bright, and he had picked fights with his pals over girls and other trivial matters before today. Well, the constables took him in, and he was searched, but nothing was found on him. They gave him a stiff drink of castor oil . . . '

'Why on earth should they do that?' I interrupted.

'To see if he'd swallowed the diamond,' said Lestrade.

'Oh, I see.'

'And then – only then,' said Lestrade, with some warmth, 'did they think fit to inform me! Well, I told them what I thought, and then I ran straight round to Morton and Jason's to take a look at this Christmas display, where Winter had been arrested.'

'Believing that Winter had hidden the diamond somewhere in the display?' I asked.

'Just so, Doctor. Winter knew the police were hot on his trail, and of course he would want to get rid of the stone, so as not to be found with it on him. But more than that, he would want – if he possibly could – to hide it somewhere that he could find it again, rather than just chucking it away, like he did with the watch and pocket book, which were not so valuable.'

'Yes, I see. And did you find it?'

Lestrade shook his head. 'And before you say anything, Mr Holmes, I can tell you that I looked for it, good and proper!'

Holmes smiled. 'Would I venture upon any criticism? But, since you were unsuccessful, perhaps you could describe this "display" of which you speak?'

'It's the usual thing, sir. One of the counters has been dressed up with a little fir tree, tinsel, glass baubles, Christmas cards and decorations, and the like. All very glittery, if you know what I mean.'

'And thus ideal for concealing a glittering diamond?'

Lestrade nodded. 'So it seemed to me. A bit like that story about a stolen letter, you know the one.'

'Poe's "Purloined Letter", you mean?'

'That's it, Doctor. Anyway, that was the first thing that struck me, the display. The second thing was that on the other side of the aisle from that display was a little counter, with some Christmas puddings set out on it. And as soon as I saw those, I thought of that curious affair of the busts of Napoleon.'

'Ah! Where the thief had concealed a pearl in one of the busts?' said Holmes.

'Just so, Mr Holmes. I thought to myself, if I was a thief, and I wanted to hide a diamond, I might just stick it into one of them Christmas puddings!'

'There is a weighty objection to that, Lestrade,' I pointed out.

'You mean that the puddings might be sold, Doctor? Yes, I thought of that, too, but I told you that this fellow Winter is none too bright. It might not have occurred to him that the puddings would be sold. Anyway, I could not in all conscience neglect the possibility, so I made some enquiries. I found that there had been six puddings there when the store opened, and three remained when I got there, so three had indeed been sold during the morning.'

'Did they know who bought them?' asked Holmes.

'And when?' I added. 'How many were there when this fellow entered the store?'

Lestrade laughed. 'You know what these places are like at Christmas time, gentlemen. The world and his wife come to London for their shopping. All they could tell me for certain was that one of them had been sold to a Mrs Dunwoody, who has is a regular customer. I have the address here. And the three unsold puddings,' he added, with a nod towards his parcels.

'You have certainly considered every possibility,' said Holmes, with something approaching admiration in his voice. 'But this display, which had commanded your attention at first glance?'

'Ah, yes, the display. I was all for taking it apart then and there, but the store manager talked me out of it. Although I did station a man there to make sure that nobody touched it. Not that they should have, it was for show, and not for sale, but you know how people fiddle with things, can't keep their fingers off. Anyway, I went back when the store was about to close, and, when all the customers had left, I did insist on taking it to bits.'

'That must have made them happy at Morton and Jason's!' I observed.

'Well, they weren't best pleased, I'll grant you that,' said Lestrade with a grin. 'Particularly as I didn't find a solitary thing. The one and only bright spot seemed to me to be a box of Christmas crackers, five of them in a big box, labelled "extra de-luxe", which struck me as being suitably adapted for the concealment of small objects. I brought those with me as well,' and he gestured again at his parcels. 'I'll wager my pension that that's where the diamond is hidden, in the crackers! They weren't for sale, so he probably felt sure of finding them there when the fuss had blown over.'

'This Winter chap might have gone anywhere in the store, though,' I felt obliged to point out.

'Now there you're wrong, Doctor,' said Lestrade. 'The staff had noticed him loitering, as it were, by this display, and they said he hadn't moved from there before my chaps arrived and took him.'

'But if he were under observation the whole time, how could he hide the diamond anyway?' was my next question. 'And in my experience Christmas crackers are tightly sealed at the ends. It would take nimble fingers to undo them, hide something inside, and do them up again.'

Lestrade frowned, but answered readily enough. 'Well, the staff were not watching him particularly, of course, so he would have had the opportunity. And as for needing nimble fingers, Winter is a pick-pocket, so his living depends to some extent on the nimbleness of his fingers, the quickness of his hands. He could do it, you may be sure.'

'Well, that's true. Are we going to pull the crackers, then, and see if you are right?'

'I had thought it might be as well,' said Lestrade. 'I waited until the castor oil should have done its work, before coming round here.'

'And it has, and you found nothing?' asked Holmes.

'Nothing, sir. Or nothing that one would not expect,' said Lestrade with some distaste. 'Bad diet, some of these fellows.'

'I see. And Winter?'

'We had to let him go, with no evidence against him. Of course, had we found the stone, that would've been a different matter.'

'Well, let us see if we can find it now.'

'I thought we'd begin with the puddings,' said Lestrade with a grin. 'Not that I expect anything from them.' He produced three Christmas puddings of the medium size, and placed them on the table cloth.

Holmes brought a cake knife, and we proceeded to dissect the puddings, each in turn, but found nothing more than three silver charms, which Holmes suggested we might give to Mrs Hudson, and three silver sixpences, which Lestrade pocketed absent-mindedly.

'Incidentally,' said Holmes, glancing at his own diamond ring, 'I wonder just what chemical changes might be produced by steaming a diamond inside a suet pudding?'

'Holmes,' I told him, 'do not even think of such a thing! What would the King of Holland have to say if you treated his present in so cavalier a fashion?'

'Perhaps you are right,' said Holmes with some disappointment. He gathered up the table cloth with the great mound of crumbs, and threw it into a corner of the room. 'Now, Lestrade, the puddings concealed nothing, just as you thought, so let us try the Christmas crackers!'

Lestrade set a large box, containing five fat Christmas crackers, on the table. 'I'll bet anything you like the stone is in one of these. Doctor, will you assist me to do the honours?'

'Oh, a paper hat!' said I, as the cracker came apart with a loud 'pop', and the contents spilled out. 'And a charm, and a motto or riddle of some kind. Listen to this: "An unsuccessful fisherman enquired of a luckier fellow angler what was the fly he used. 'It's not the fly,' the other replied, 'but the driver!'" Rather good, don't you think?'

The others looked blank. 'The point is, you see,' I explained, 'that the implement matters less than the man employing it. Oh, well, please yourselves! Another cracker, Lestrade?'

We pulled all five crackers, to discover five paper hats, sundry mottoes and jokes, and assorted small presents – a tiny comb, which I appropriated for my moustache; a folding magnifying glass, which I handed to Holmes; a tiny pair of silver handcuffs, which Lestrade rather dismally said he would wear on his watch chain as a memento of an unsuccessful case; a fan, which we proposed should be given to Mrs Hudson; and finally a tiny penknife, which seemed suitable for Billy, the pageboy.

Holmes picked up one of the mottoes. '"A lady at an exceedingly tiresome party asked her neighbour, 'Why do people attend these dull affairs?' The other replied, 'Well, I am here because I am the hostess!'" Rather appropriate, don't you think?' and he gave a wan smile at our lacklustre countenances.

Lestrade stood up. 'It's me that's casting a blight on the proceedings,' he mumbled. 'I could've sworn I'd read it right. Sorry for wasting your morning, gents, and I'll be on my way.'

Holmes waved the Scotland Yard man back to his seat. 'Stay a moment, Lestrade. You are sure this Winter would not simply throw the diamond away, so that it was not found on him?'

'He may, of course,' Lestrade answered doubtfully, 'but I'd have said he had just enough wit to try to conceal it where he could find it again.'

Holmes stood up. 'I think perhaps I should like to see the display at Morton and Jason's.'

'Yes,' I said, 'and there's always the Christmas pudding that was sold to Mrs Dunwoody, or whatever her name is.'

'Oh, blow the Christmas pudding!' said Lestrade.

Holmes raised a hand. 'It may just be worth a look,' he said. 'You have the address, you say?'

'Yes, sir, and it is on the way to the store, so we might call in there first, if you are wanting to take a look at the problem.'

'I have nothing else on hand just at the moment,' said Holmes.

We set off to walk, for there were few cabs about and such as there were moved slowly thanks to the snow, which was now falling steadily. Lestrade took us to a fashionable street, and consulted his notebook. 'Here we are, number thirty-five,' he said, ringing the bell.

We were shown into a drawing room furnished with considerable good taste, and a moment later Mrs Dunwoody, a handsome woman not yet forty years old, joined us. 'Gentlemen, how may I help the police? And Mr Sherlock Holmes, whose name is, naturally, not unknown to me.'

'It is curious matter,' said Holmes with a laugh. 'But may I ask if you recently bought a Christmas pudding from Morton and Jason's?'

'Why, yes. It was sent round two days ago. But why on earth . . . '

'Oh, it is not very serious,' said Holmes in an offhand tone. 'The pudding was a display item only, and should not have been sold. If you are agreeable, I shall take it away now, and have another of the same sort sent round.'

'Of course. But – could the manager not have sent someone? It seems rather odd, a Scotland Yard inspector, Mr Sherlock Holmes . . . '

Holmes smiled confidentially. 'You know how it is at Christmas, madam. How busy people are, especially the big stores.'

This did not seem to convince Mrs Dunwoody absolutely – and indeed I cannot think of many people whom it would convince – but she did not pursue the matter, but merely called out, 'Freddie!'

A young boy, some eleven or twelve years of age, appeared from nowhere, and Mrs Dunwoody told him, 'Freddie, take these gentlemen to see cook, would you?'

'Cook, Mama?' The boy seemed more than puzzled at the request.

'Yes. Run along, there's a good boy.'

We followed Master Freddie to the kitchen, where he said, 'Cook, there are some gentlemen to see you.' Having delivered this news, Freddie seemed disinclined to leave, but loitered by the kitchen door, evidently eager to see what might happen next.

'Madam,' said Holmes, 'I am Sherlock Holmes, and this is Inspector Lestrade, of Scotland Yard.'

This information had a predictable effect upon the cook, a motherly creature of ample proportions, and it was some time before we could calm her down sufficiently for Holmes to continue, 'I understand you have recently had delivered a Christmas pudding from Morton and Jason's?'

Now, when Holmes asked this question, I could have sworn that Master Freddie was unsettled, for he seemed to me to give a guilty start. However, I could see Freddie only out of the corner of my eye, and when I turned for a better look, he had vanished.

The cook looked as surprised as her mistress had been by Holmes's query, but replied, 'Yes, Mr Holmes, and it's in the cupboard there.'

'May we see it?'

The cook shrugged her broad shoulders, but opened the cupboard. 'There – well, bless me!'

'Well?'

'Well, sir, it's gone! Stolen!'

'Stolen?' Lestrade shot a significant glance at Holmes and me. 'Are you sure?'

'I'm sure it's gone, Inspector, and I'm sure nobody in this house has eaten it! It was there yesterday afternoon, I'll swear to that.'

'And this morning?'

'That I couldn't say, sir, for I never looked in that cupboard today, until just now. But yesterday afternoon, the pudding was in that cupboard, and now it's gone.'

'Well, Lestrade,' I began, 'it rather looks as if you were wrong, and the puddings . . . '

'And, begging your pardon, sir,' the cook interrupted, 'but it's a very strange thing that pudding going like that. The thing is, Mrs Trumbull, her that's cook at number forty-two, across the way, she was telling me only last night that one of her Christmas puddings was stolen as well, day before yesterday!'

'Good Lord!' I said.

'Thank you, madam,' said Holmes' And he raced up the stairs, out into the street, and across the road. 'Ah, forty-two.' He pulled eagerly at the bell.

Again we were shown into a fashionable drawing room, and again the lady of the house, about the same age as Mrs Dunwoody, received us. Holmes spun his yarn once more, and the maid showed us to the kitchen, where the cook told us, with many appeals to the deity of cooks to demonstrate that she spoke the truth and nothing but, that, although it was rankly impossible, nevertheless a Christmas pudding had vanished from its rightful place in a cupboard.

'Tell me,' asked Holmes, 'was the pudding from Morton and Jason's, by any chance?'

The cook snorted. 'Not a bit of it, sir! It was one of my own, made three months back.'

Holmes had evidently not expected this. 'I see.' He glanced at the ceiling, thought for a moment, and then asked, 'Is there perhaps a young man in the house? Has the family a son, about eleven or twelve?'

'Why, yes, sir, Master Bertie.'

'Thank you.' Holmes led us back upstairs, sought out the lady of the house, and requested an interview with her son. The lady seemed somewhat taken aback, but made no difficulty about summoning the lad.

'If we might see the boy alone?' murmured Holmes. 'I assure you he will come to no harm.' When the boy's mother had left, he asked, 'Now, young Bertie, what is all this nonsense about the Christmas puddings?'

The boy started. 'Has Freddie said anything?'

'Not he, but his behaviour did rather lead me to suspect that he knew something of the matter. Were the two of you in it together, then? And what became of the puddings?'

'And why?' I added.

Bertie looked down at his boots. 'We were reading *A Christmas Carol*, you see, sir.'

Holmes frowned. 'I do not quite follow.'

'Well,' said Bertie, 'we got to thinking how much better off we are than some of the poor children you see in the streets. We decided to do something about it, so we each took a Christmas pudding to give to them.'

'Ah, I see! Very laudable. And did you actually give the puddings to these poor children?'

'Yes, sir. We sent them to the East End Mission to Underprivileged Children.'

'I see. Well, I am sure you meant well, and I shall not tell your parents. Although you may wish to do so – I am sure they will quite understand your motives.' Holmes shook the boy's hand, and we took our leave.

'Well, Holmes? What now?' I asked when we were out in the street again.

Holmes looked at his watch. 'It is the luncheon hour,' he said, 'and I expect Morton and Jason's will be full of customers just now. Your man is still on duty at the display, Lestrade? Yes? So it is quite safe. In that case, I suggest we visit this East End Mission to Underprivileged Children.'

We found a cab, and drove through the streets, thick with snow by this time, to the East End, and soon found the charitable organisation we sought. It was run by a middle-aged clergyman, a Mr Butterworth, who showed no surprise when Holmes asked if any well-wishers had donated Christmas puddings.

'Several, sir,' replied Mr Butterworth with a sigh. 'It seems to strike our benefactors as appropriate. One does not, of course, wish to appear ungrateful, but one could do so much more good with hard cash.' He opened a cupboard, and waved a hand to indicate some two dozen Christmas puddings stacked inside.

'Ah, but any from Morton and Jason's?' asked Holmes, rummaging through the pile. He found no less than four with the imprint of the fashionable store, and surprised Mr Butterworth by offering to buy all four for twice their commercial value. The transaction concluded, Holmes proceeded to attack the puddings systematically with his pocket knife, but without revealing anything that should not be found in any self-respecting Christmas pudding.

'I fear your Christmas puddings are a red herring, Lestrade,' said Holmes with a laugh, as we set off back to the West End. 'Let us hope that all is not entirely lost, though.' Lestrade did not answer, but his face told its own story.

We arrived at Morton and Jason's, where Lestrade said he would leave us. 'It'll only make me even more downcast to go in there again, gents,' he said.

'Well, at least join us this evening at Baker Street for dinner,' Holmes told him, and Lestrade promised that he would.

'Now, Watson, let us see this famous display.'

'Holmes, the store is full of customers. You can hardly dismantle the display now, so we really should return later.'

'Watson, I do not propose to dismantle anything, I propose merely to look, to imagine what a criminal who is being pursued might do, and to act accordingly.'

'And what shall I do?'

'Oh, take a look round for yourself, and tell me anything that occurs to you.'

I followed him inside, and nodded a greeting to Lestrade's man, whom I recognised. Holmes stared intently at the display counter, the usual assemblage of glass baubles, carved wooden reindeer, and the like. I could not imagine what he hoped to see, and he did not even touch any of the items. I wandered further into the store, not knowing quite what I was supposed to be doing there. What if Winter really were innocent, if in truth he had thought that it was some personal enemy who was chasing him?

Again, if Winter were guilty, he may well simply have thrown the diamond away, rather than risk its being found on him. The thief, whoever he may have been, had, after all, discarded the watch and pocket book, and those must themselves had been quite valuable, since their owner was a fashionable jeweller.

I stared at the floor. Presumably that was swept once, perhaps twice, a day, and the theft had been two or three days ago, so there was nothing there. I glanced up, and stopped in my tracks, for in front of me, at no great distance from where Holmes stood, still and silent as any statue, I saw a counter covered with dress jewellery, rings, necklaces, bracelets, all glittering in the light from the chandeliers overhead.

This was surely more like it? Where better to hide a tree than in the forest? And this counter was at no distance from the entrance, so Winter could easily have taken a couple of steps forward, unseen by the staff, dropped the diamond amongst the items here, then darted back to the display where he was arrested. I rummaged amongst the treasures on the counter, for so long that the salesman enquired, 'Was there anything in particular, sir?'

'Looking for a diamond, about so big,' I answered.

He raised an eyebrow, but Morton and Jason's staff are too well trained to comment on the humours of their customers.

I continued my search, but found nothing of interest apart from a gentleman's amethyst ring, which fitted me perfectly, and looked rather fine on my finger. I caught the salesman's eye, and he shook his head ever so delicately.

'No?'

'One could possibly get away with it if one were an Archbishop, but not otherwise, I fear, sir. I could show you a plain signet, perhaps?'

I moved on. I am fond of people, and shops, and the warmth of a crowd, and the Christmas mood was strong here. I bought a meer-schaum calabash, all the rage at that time, for Holmes, and a purple dressing gown with abundant gold frogging, to replace the old and frayed disgrace he habitually affected.

Next I spent some time studying a display of the latest fashions in ladies' night wear from Paris, and wondering if my motives would be misunderstood if I were to treat Mrs Hudson to one of the more conservative of them. By the time I had concluded that they would, and rather regretfully walked away from the display without pur-chasing anything, I was surprised to see that the clock on the wall showed the hour to be considerably later than I should have thought.

I hastened back to where I had left Holmes, to find him waiting rather impatiently with a parcel under his arm.

'Been shopping?' I asked him.

'I thought a small decoration might not be out of place. And you?'

'Oh, bits and pieces, Holmes.'

We returned to Baker Street, where Holmes went off to his room. I passed the afternoon reading, or looking out of the window at the scene in the street. It had stopped snowing by this time, and the traffic was busier than it had been earlier, so the crisp white was turning to a yellow slush. This seemed to me a metaphor of life itself, and I sighed, my festive mood giving way to the thought that another year was fast slipping away. Holmes emerged, clutching his parcel, and I cheered up somewhat.

'Now,' said Holmes, tearing the paper, 'where to put it to best effect?' He held up his purchase for my inspection, and I saw it was a sort of idealised Christmas scene painted on a wooden panel perhaps one foot by eighteen inches, a landscape with a cottage and a frosting of glittering sequins, or something of the sort, reindeer, and a jolly tin plate Father Christmas with round belly and jovial countenance. I recognised it as having been amongst the display at the store.

'Never known you take particular notice of that sort of ornament, Holmes,' I said.

'Ah, Christmas comes but once a year, Watson. It may perhaps bring a smile to Lestrade's face.' He set the thing upon the table, and rearranged a knife and fork more to his liking. 'I have asked Mrs Hudson to provide something a little special for our feast. And perhaps a little treat from our modest cellar? I shall leave the choice to you, my boy.'

'Delighted, Holmes!' And off I went to find a suitable bottle or two.

Lestrade arrived soon after, and sat down heavily at the table.

Holmes waved a hand at his ornament. 'You saw this?' he asked Lestrade.

'Very nice, I'm sure.' Then Lestrade sat up. He looked at me; and I looked at Lestrade. We both know that Holmes does not as a rule make any great display of sentiment. Whatever he does, there is some reason for it, and usually a good reason. Lestrade stared hard at the ornament.

'The frosting, as one may call it, rather resembles diamond chippings, does it not?' asked Holmes.

'It does indeed,' said Lestrade with a frown. 'But you're not suggesting – what? – that Winter somehow ground the diamond up and stuck it on here, are you? Why, he wouldn't have had time, and they'd have seen him do anything of that sort.'

'And besides,' I added, 'the diamond would be valueless if it were ground up. I agree that it looks like diamond chippings, but it can't be.'

Holmes laughed. 'No, no. The notion is preposterous, is it not? This is merely chips of glass, or bits of silver foil, or something of that sort. But it does glitter, in a manner that reminds one immediately of diamonds. Of course, one then immediately rejects the idea, knowing it to be merely dross, and one turns one's attention elsewhere. Which is a pity. A classic case of misdirection.'

'So the diamond is here?' I asked.

'Oh, yes.' Holmes picked up a knife. 'You are forgetting your childhood, Watson. Who brings Christmas presents, except Santa Claus?' and with the tip of the knife he levered the little rotund Father Christmas away from the wood backing, allowing the square diamond concealed behind the tin plate figure to fall on to the table cloth, where it glittered in the light from the candles.

Lestrade clapped his hands. 'Well done, Mr Holmes!'

'Holmes,' I said, 'it was indeed well done, but it was surely a bold guess? You cannot tell me that you knew for certain the diamond would be there?'

'On the contrary, Doctor, I knew before ever I brought that ornament into this house that it held the diamond.'

I considered his remark. 'And when you first saw the ornament in the store?'

'Ah, then I confess I did not know. Although it seemed likely. As I say, it was a classic case of misdirection, and it immediately struck me that it might be such. Naturally, I verified that theory by examining the ornament in the store, before I brought it here for this little drama. A rather neat piece of work, though, don't you think?'

I took a scrap of paper from my waistcoat pocket. 'Here is one motto I did not read. "Why is a vain man like the Cyclops? Answer: Because they both have one big 'I'!" Rather good, don't you think?'

Holmes threw back his head and laughed. 'You must allow me my moment of triumph.'

'Yes, Doctor,' said Lestrade. 'It was a good job, no doubt of that.'

'You are right,' I said, filling Holmes's glass. 'And what of this fellow, Winter?'

'Oh, I shall not pursue that line, not now that we've got the stone back,' said Lestrade. 'It is Christmas, after all. No, I'll go along to the store tomorrow, and make a big fuss about telling my man not to bother keeping watch any longer. Winter is sure to be loitering somewhere handy. He'll think that we've abandoned the search in there, and try to recover the ornament, and the diamond, himself. I'd like to see his face when he finds it's gone! That'll be a heavier punishment than any beak could dish out, you may be sure!' He raised his glass. 'Mr Holmes, Dr Watson, as someone once said – a Merry Christmas and God bless us all, each and every one!'

The Return of the Sussex Vampire

CHRISTOPHER SEQUEIRA

Although Sherlock Holmes often revealed the varying patterns of circumstance between one event and another in the composition of a crime, his own role in his cases normally remained constant: he was the catalyst who brought about the resolution. I can think of only two exceptions to this, and the first, the Tabram affair and its horrific revelations, deviated from that design in such a profound fashion as to rewrite criminal history (and almost end my own life); but my record of that case must remain unpublished for legal reasons. The other investigation is one that I can now put before my readers, with the additional information that it was a case in which it also turned out that both Holmes and I had actually inspired the crime.

In the year 1926, in my retirement, I had chosen to turn my mind to problems quite apart from the medical and investigative matters that had filled my days during Victoria's reign. My interest in social issues such as the suffragette cause and the Indian independence movement amply occupied my time; although these activities also caused me to be suspended from two of my clubs, and were certainly the root cause of my omission from the invitation list for the reunion dinner for the Fifth Northumberland Fusiliers, in '20. But, as my daughter reminded me on my seventy-fourth birthday, I had already tired of celebrating my time in Afghanistan, or I would never have sold my daguerreotype of the Iron Amir, Abdur Rahman.

I had, in similar fashion, lost contact with many longstanding acquaintances. My fellow practitioner and one-time confidant, Arthur Conan Doyle, could not hide his confusion and disappointment when I described my conversion to atheism. So, too, old Stamford, and Thurston, who had taken up shared quarters, rarely invited me to chalk up the billiard cue because they had rumours aplenty to contend with, without the eccentric John H. Watson visiting and attracting attention. My sons always smiled at my reports of my social endeavours, however, and their own children's antics would always lift my spirits in these often lonely times. The comfort of family did much to improve my moods when poorly-concealed public whispers about me losing my grip on reality reached me. I say 'poorly concealed' with a sense of irony, because, although I suffered from terrible gout and a small amount of rheumatism, my hearing was still nigh perfect.

In this existence, the constant agitation of controversy too often kept me from remembering that the man I regarded as greatest friend, wisest counsel, and most abominable fellow lodger, was deeply missed. In 1919, shameful as it is to recount, an ancient priest lent me a steady shoulder as I wept at the funeral of Holmes's brother Mycroft. My tears were not for the brilliant Mycroft, and not even out of sadness that the rotund genius had no mourner other than me in attendance. Rather, I had wept like a child when I realised that my best friend would not make the journey and appear that day. For, if he did not feel the need to bid farewell to his brother, then that inhuman calculating engine might easily end his own days without ever feeling the need to brave London again, and never renew our friendship.

However, I did have leave from Holmes to put many of his cases into print as I saw fit – and I still did so occasionally – often when a principal malefactor had passed from harm's way, whether by dropping through the trap of a gallows or passing away in their sleep. However, I still knew not what to do about my notes from the Beefsteak Room Horror, the Nikola Formulae, or the incredible affair of the fourth stain. Nevertheless, the bundle of manuscripts approved-for-publication was still sizeable, so I continued to release them, often feverishly awaiting a note in the post from Holmes, and always disappointed when such did not arrive.

Residing in this strange, reflective realm I was astounded therefore to answer the door at an unusually early hour one day only to find Sherlock Holmes himself sipping from the milk bottle that had been delivered to my house. The lean figure was more stooped than when I had last seen it, but even at seventy-two there was a surety, a liveliness, that would have made me envious were we in Baker Street in '91 about to run down Moriarty.

'Watson, do forgive me, I have not drunk or eaten since yesterday. I know that you do not take milk yourself, and that you have not married again – yet – but hairs on your doormat advertise the fact that you now keep a Persian cat. That feline, I am sure, will not mind my drinking from the bottle before it has its breakfast,' he said.

'Holmes,' I said, 'you opened that milk on purpose. So that you might expound on my personal situation and show me that your ability to uncover every aspect of my domestic life is intact. By God, it's good to see you, man.'

He laughed. 'Bravo, old fellow. You at least are slower of step but proportionately fleeter of mind. I doubt I can say the same for myself.'

My eagerness to invite my old friend in was hampered by the questions that were on my lips simply at the sight of him – and the most obvious question.

'It's a case, isn't it, Holmes?' I asked.

'Indeed, Watson, and you will be intrigued to know that we are travelling in the direction of the place I now call home. The impending case is in Eridge, in Sussex, not altogether removed from my cottage on the Downs. We go to Tunwell Castle, and a most unusual situation. We can make the train if you don't dawdle.'

* * *

So, soon it was that I sat facing the aquiline features of my friend and his diabolical rate of tobacco consumption aboard a South-bound train.

'You remember the case you entitled "The Adventure of the Sussex Vampire", where Big Bob Ferguson's infant boy was being bitten in the throat, supposedly attacked by his own wife, Maria, until I discerned that Maria was in fact only sucking poison from a bloody wound inflicted upon the poor child?'

'My Lord, but that was years ago. Bob, the dear fellow, has since passed away. Yes, the culprit turned out to be little Jacky, Bob's other son; an invalid child, twisted with jealousy. Bram Stoker was sorely disappointed when I recounted the tale to him some years ago.'

'An accurate summary; indeed, no supernatural blood-drinker was involved,' laughed Holmes, 'so you should find it intriguing to hear that claims have been made that the Sussex Vampire stalks again! The family we go to assist are distant relatives – wealthy ones – of the late Mr Robert Ferguson, and they seem to believe that the "hushed-up" case from years ago was some sort of genuine vampiric curse – which has now been visited upon them.'

'Ridiculous,' I retorted. 'My own account of the matter was published not long ago – surely that should dispel such idiocy?'

'Watson, Watson, we are about to encounter a family in a state of crisis, and such an environment permits every form of hysterical contamination imaginable. So we fly to meet Josiah Ferguson, uncle of the late Robert, and it is through the pleadings of Bob's wife Maria that we do so.'

My friend continued, 'Maria Ferguson wrote to my solicitors, who forwarded her letter to me. Her tale was that her late husband was never close to his Uncle Josiah, but many was the time Bob had said that he was proud of the family history and its reputation for benevolence within its ancestral seat. The local people had been grateful for charity and support from the owners of Tunwell Castle more than once, and Josiah had also been an employer of many in his businesses.'

'Josiah is a widower, with two daughters, neither of whom is married, although both are now near forty, and Maria Ferguson had met the family on three or four occasions over the years, finding the women to be quiet and level-headed. Maria had last seen them at her husband's funeral four years ago.'

'Now, Watson,' Holmes said, with that perverse delight he took at human frailty, 'there comes the drama, for Maria Ferguson's letter to me was followed immediately by a terse note from Josiah Ferguson himself. This man is in trouble, yet he does not appreciate Maria's appeal to me. Why? Perhaps he believes the old whispers about Maria; many a rumour escaped that house and maligned that family, and remember, Watson, the *Strand Magazine* only saw fit to print your record of the matter two years ago, far too late to counter suspicions held for so many years.'

I understood his reasoning and nodded. 'So, Josiah might believe his family is being attacked by a family curse – an actual Sussex Vampire?'

Holmes grinned and sprang up like a child's Jack-in-the-Box as our train pulled in at our destination. 'We shall soon have an opportunity of testing that very notion.'

Holmes and I clambered down from the carriage, and I was pleased to find that my gout was virtually non-existent that day. As we left the platform Holmes spied what could only be the driver Josiah Ferguson has assigned us, a man leaning against a shiny automobile in dark chauffeur's livery, wearing tinted glasses. This individual introduced himself as Wentworth, and helped us into the vehicle, and soon enough we were speeding away.

Wentworth proved inscrutable to the point of rudeness, for when Holmes cheerily posed a few questions the man actually grunted, and replied brusquely, 'Couldn't say, sir.' I was about to rebuke the man when Holmes pulled my sleeve and winked – clearly my friend's patience was superior to mine.

It was not to Tunwell Castle that we were first taken but to the squat, brick housings of the Ferguson Ironworks. Here we were escorted past the din and heat-flashes of foundry furnaces to a suite of offices, and taken into the presence of Josiah Ferguson. With Ferguson was another man who was dressed in a minister's clothing and introduced to us as the Reverend Hilliard. Sporting two large tufts of grey hair on either side of his head separated by a shining pate, Josiah Ferguson had obviously once been a strong man, and still retained an authoritative eye and brow. But while his handshake was crisp, I detected that fondness for the grape had weakened him; his protruding belly and veined nose were plain enough.

'I shall be frank, gentlemen. I was originally completely against my late nephew's wife's suggestion that you be consulted in this horrible matter, because it is exceedingly personal, affecting my family, my daughters. But my eldest girl, Bessie, thinks highly of Maria and is desperate for an answer to our problem. I love my daughters dearly and as I have failed utterly to safeguard them against the – the threat we face, I must admit defeat.'

Ferguson then looked at Holmes as if he would attack him, and slammed his fist on the table. I jumped, but Holmes seemed prepared.

'God in Heaven, man, I am at my wits' end. Please, please do not fail me!'

Holmes laid his hand gently on Ferguson's sleeve, and spoke almost in a whisper; the effect was instantly pacifying.

'Mr Ferguson, you believe that your family is being preyed upon by some sort of evil force, akin to that which plagued your nephew. You believe the Sussex Vampire has returned, do you not?'

Never have I seen such relief manifest itself in a man's face – and then be swept away so suddenly by a mask of imperiousness. Here was a man who was often a victim of his feelings, yet who also knew how to cloak himself in the emotions he thought would provoke the results he most sought. He reminded me of my long-dead brother, Henry, and Henry's incredible mastery of deceit and manipulation, fuelled by drink and vice.

'I know, of course, there never was a vampire in Bob's household,' said Josiah. 'This is why this matter is a double infamy; my daughters are attacked, and old family ills are dredged up as well!

'Young Jacky grew up to be a fine, stable adult, Mr Holmes, because of your advice to his father to send him to sea, I was told. He and the little brother he had wronged later became the staunchest of companions, and are now both thriving in the mining business in northern America; very prosperous fellows. So, your name means much, despite my desire to keep outsiders from becoming involved in my troubles, for you removed a shadow from my family. And now, now, I don't know what to think! Is someone hoaxing me somehow, mocking me with the family's darkest days? Or is it even stranger? Is there some real, dark blight that marks the Ferguson line? I must get the dreadful tale off my chest!'

'One evening about two months ago,' Josiah Ferguson began, 'I had retired and been asleep for perhaps two hours when a scream awoke me. I dashed into the corridor perhaps less than a minute later to find my Bessie, in her nightclothes, standing outside her room and clutching at her throat, and sobbing and shaking. Her sister Jennifer, and my manservant Mawes, soon joined us on the landing as Bessie began to calm herself and revealed her throat was badly bruised by severe finger marks. Bessie claimed that she had awoken to find a man dressed in dark clothing, with his face partially obscured by a large hood, choking her whilst she lay in bed. Then, she claimed, he tried to bite her on the neck. He was strong, but as she struggled, her shifting weight somehow managed to slip her right out from under the monster and she ran from the room.'

'We searched the house and found nothing, certainly no signs of forced entry. The local doctor was summoned and examined Bessie, and his view was that she was telling the truth.'

'For the next two weeks we slept with doors locked, and I kept a loaded pistol at my bedside. Nothing happened until, as I say, two weeks later.'

'I count as one of my friends the Reverend James Hilliard. He was to join me on a cross-country ramble at dawn, so I had invited him to Tunwell to spend the night. The Reverend is immensely fond of my library and was up late enjoying its treasures when he heard a frightful cry – a female voice. He dashed to the source of the sound, the second-floor corridor.'

The minister finally spoke. His doughy white face was weathered, but with none of the weaknesses of his friend's.

'Mr Holmes, and Dr Watson, I reached the landing and the corridor and immediately looked towards the right, to the women's quarters.'

'I swear that what I tell you now is true. Jennifer was crouching on the floor, batting her arms about in defensive gestures, speechless, only whimpering. The object of her fear stood right in front of her.'

'It was a man dressed head to foot in black, not a speck of colour about him anywhere. He wore a huge, black, hooded cloak. At my appearance he snapped his head in my direction. I saw a face that was chalk-white, with dark, pronounced eyebrows – sir, I do not jest, they pointed upwards, quite abnormal they seemed. The eyes were sunk into blackened hollows, also very distinct, unnatural. They looked at me with vicious anger, and the creature literally hissed at me, and then ran down the corridor.'

'I pursued it, watching in astonishment as the thing exited the hall through the French windows at the corridor's end, proceeded out into the night and the balcony that was beyond the glass doors, and then this being jumped up on to the stone railing of the balcony. Gentlemen, there is nothing but a sheer drop of perhaps thirty feet below, on to a stone courtyard. If a man jumped or fell he would break a leg, at least. The intruder was trapped, or so I thought . . .

' . . . until he flung his cloak out behind himself and, as the Lord is my witness, he leapt into the darkness – a suicide leap. I heard a strange sound like a roaring bellow of laughter or rage. I reached the balcony and looked out, then down.'

'He was gone. In the moonlight I could see clearly for miles about. There was no one.'

Holmes was tapping his pipe against his knee, a sure sign that he was bored.

'I would be correct in saying that you organised a search of the grounds and the vicinity, for signs of an injured or dead man in black, and that you found nothing?' said Holmes.

Ferguson looked at Holmes sharply.

'You mock me, sir? You have made your own inquiries with the local police, I see?'

Holmes coughed. 'No, I have not. Mr Ferguson, if you had found something or someone you would not have retained me. I can only be here because this . . . assailant has not been found, and because you fear a further assault.'

Josiah rubbed the sides of his face with his hands, and looked to the Reverend Hilliard for support. The minister nodded and gave a weak grin.

'You are correct, sir, forgive me,' said Ferguson. 'I believe your judgement is sound while you can both see that mine is quite unsettled. Let us not waste more time. Let us go to Tunwell, immediately.'

The strange driver, Wentworth, appeared again, and we were escorted to the rear of the large industrial premises to the motor car. As we passed back through the furnace area and its glowing red fires, Ferguson muttered.

'I have been a champion of industry here for years – providing employment for the local folk, giving them an income. But this business – some of the anonymous letters I have received – abominable! Disgraceful! The envy, I never realised the envy and the hatred some have for me, simply for being born into position and responsibility.'

I offered words of support, but Holmes himself ignored Ferguson's remarks and pretended that he could not find a match for his pipe. The drive to Tunwell was pleasant, the scenery serene. We passed a few other motor vehicles, several horses and townsfolk. At one stage a high-headed horse with wildly colourful bridle and saddle rolled past, ridden by a white-shirted jockey, and Wentworth scowled and muttered as he passed it.

'I didn't quite catch that, Wentworth', said Holmes. 'That fellow is not a friend of yours, I take it?'

Our driver for once became quite voluble.

'Trouble, is what he is, pure trouble, though I never set eyes on him, before. They's French entertainers, like a circus, wit' clowns, dancin' horses an' all, not afar from here, but they's bringin' thieves with 'em, and worse. I was once set upon by their likes in a tavern, and they set on me pretending one man was alone, then four of them appearing and trying it on with me.'

I nodded. 'Cowards. Lucky you escaped such thugs.'

Wentworth grinned, an unpleasant thing. 'I didn't say I escaped, sir, I stood my ground and fought. And they near killed me. But near doesn't win it, sir, it doesn't, and I won, I did.'

Wentworth's disturbing delight in violence was forgotten as we approached Tunwell Castle. It was a splendid structure, a castle three storeys in height, square in configuration but with circular, tower-like structures at each corner. Ivy heavily festooned most of the walls and the façade presented a great arched doorway facing on to well-kept grounds. Most of the top of the walls and towers displayed traditional crenellation and I could see a balcony at one side of the building that I suspected matched that in the story we had been told.

Arriving in front of the massive doorway via a smooth driveway we alighted, and Holmes instantly set to work, announcing briskly to Josiah Ferguson that his work must begin with a personal interview with the two ladies of the house.

Bessie, the elder of the Ferguson women, was a shock to behold. Auburn-haired, plump, she could not conceal the dark circles around her red eyes, and periodically a trembling took hold of her hands. She sat with her sister, Jennifer, who seemed like the older though we knew this not to be true. Jennifer squeezed her sister's hand often when Bessie seemed to lapse in concentration or will.

'It's just as Father has told you,' said Bessie, 'I awoke and the creature was virtually on top of me, his hands shaking my throat. I barely had time to open my eyes and realise what was occurring when he knelt, his evil, white face to my neck. I could not believe what he was going to do.'

'So, he almost had a chance to bite you, but you threw him off,' said Holmes. 'Is that correct? Please, I need every detail, no matter how awkward for you, if I am to deal with this attacker.'

Bessie looked at Holmes, stifled a sob, and then breathed in and out deeply before she continued.

'Yes, Mr Holmes, I understand your methods. But it is as I say. He held me down by the throat, I screamed, and he moved to bite my neck, I am sure I saw his mouth open. I tried to rise and somehow I slipped free and that was it, I had one foot on the floor and I ran as I have never run.'

'I reached the door of the room and flung it open. He grabbed me again, and pushed me down. As I lay there wondering what to do next he stood snarling at me, ready to pounce on me again at any minute.'

'Then Father's feet pounded down the corridor. I looked up – and the fiend was gone – probably to the balcony down the hall – the same one he jumped from two weeks later – I can think of nowhere else he could go.'

Holmes and I both examined Bessie's neck, but there was little that could be discerned from old bruises. It was Jennifer we turned our attention to now.

The younger woman seemed far more in control of her emotions, was very protective of her sister, and seemed unconcerned with her own recent bout with an intruder to the house. Her presentation of the facts was quite restrained, even perfunctory. Everything that the minister had told us was confirmed. She also explained that the attack on her had begun exactly as Bessie's had – she was asleep then awoken by the feeling of being throttled, grasped tightly round the neck.

Holmes interjected. 'Why was your room unlocked? Surely the entire house was on its guard?'

Jennifer glanced at him with ill-concealed indignity, and I felt ashamed of my friend's blunt manner.

'Mr Holmes, it does not make me proud to say I thought the danger had passed. With the added presence of the minister, here, I also thought the house safer.'

Holmes leant forward. 'Safer, in what way?' he said.

Jennifer flushed. 'I thought if there was some sort of devilish influence, the presence of a man of the cloth would dispel it, I suppose. Yet I was wrong.'

Holmes raised his eyebrows. 'Of course, I forget for a moment the climate of this event – the family vampire. So the thing attacked you, and, I deduce, actually damaged your throat more severely than your sister's?'

Jennifer put her hand to the very high collar she wore and unceremoniously, even defiantly, pulled it down and turned her head so we might see all. Holmes and I made a close inspection.

Two jagged marks, such as might be made by a canine or other animal bite, were plainly visible on the poor woman's neck, on either side of which were large bruises.

'If you think I am imagining things, if you think I am a silly, distressed woman, perhaps you might reconsider your assumptions now.' she said, with undisguised bitterness.

Holmes clicked his tongue. 'Your opinion, Doctor?' he said to me.

'I can't be certain so long after the event, but the flesh was torn, and the marks are consistent with a bite mark – and the spacing with that of human teeth. It was not a deep bite, though, that is correct?' I said, turning to Jennifer.

The woman scowled and covered her throat. 'There was some bleeding but it was not profuse.' she said.

Holmes was kinder to her now. 'But horrible in any case, dear lady, quite horrible. Well, I have heard enough. Let us examine this balcony.'

Holmes and I were shown the balcony that had served as the intruder's egress point, and although my friend crawled and sniffed all about it in his manner of years past, he seemed dissatisfied. I noticed that he pocketed neither chips of stone, nor fragments of cloth or fibre. Finally he looked out across the open expanse of green countryside that could be seen beyond the courtyard below, across the gentle hills that led to the township not far away. He gestured.

'Watson, this view is inspiring, and that is what is troubling me. How can such a pleasant vista figure in this dark case of nocturnal predations?'

I was truly at a loss, my friend was rambling – losing himself in poetry, and I said so.

Holmes smiled. 'Yes, I am being needlessly picturesque. What I should say is everyone has looked out in this direction for a solution to this outrage, when they should be looking *here* instead.' and with that emphasis he turned back to the building and pointed up to the wall above us.

The view was sheer stone wall ascending many feet to where the roof commenced.

'I'm sorry, Holmes, but that's still not much help. Unless our vampire really can fly, I see no way to climb to that roof and escape.'

'Of course, Watson, but you would agree that if he could fly, and flew off in that direction, that is from the roof and back, then those looking for signs of him by looking outwards from the balcony would not see him?'

'Not see him flying away? Of course not, but that is absurd, Holmes.'

'Quite so, my friend, you have put it nicely. Please, wait here.' And with a jaunty step Holmes strolled back to Ferguson. I remained at the balcony and soon saw the two of them below me, looking over the courtyard, but Holmes – despite leaning over a patch of flooring while Ferguson studied what he was doing – did not actually appear to find anything. The two then re-entered the house and I soon joined them in a sitting room. Holmes advised Ferguson that he wished to speak to all the serving staff. Ferguson laughed at the notion that they would be of any help, pointing out they were not even present when any attacks took place. He also made it quite clear he thought them not intellectually equipped to speak much beyond their official duties.

Nevertheless Holmes insisted and had all servants brought into the room, in the presence of both Ferguson and his daughters. Altogether there were an elderly woman housekeeper, Mrs. Hastings; a young maid, Sarah; the odd driver, Wentworth; and the man-servant, Mawes. Holmes asked them all what they knew of the attacks, but he was strangely unspecific, and, not surprisingly, as a

consequence he received answers that to me seemed largely unhelp-
ful. He then asked them all if they liked working at Tunwell and I
noticed that they all answered affirmatively, but with nervousness,
with the exception of Wentworth, who snickered as he sarcastically
described his post as 'a right treat'. I thought he was quite antagon-
istic towards Holmes.

The servants were dismissed and Holmes declined Ferguson's
offer to stay at Tunwell before returning to London on the morrow.
Holmes said he needed time to review the facts he had gathered
and ponder them, and his mind worked best removed from the locale
of the inquiry. Before we left, Ferguson took us aside from his
daughters and made a quiet but passionate appeal.

'Mr Holmes, you have heard the accounts, you have examined the
building. I consider myself a hard-headed man, some even call me
uncompromising, but my mind is reeling. The original vampire that
plagued my nephew was nothing of the kind, so the menace to my
family must also be a fraud, and yet the impossible has happened!
No one could have avoided terrible injury after a leap from that
balcony, and yet this fiend not only did, but he remains out there, at
liberty! Mr Holmes, I think I will go mad if we cannot ensure this . . .
if this evil cannot be barred from my house. I beg you, please, lift
this cloud from my life!'

It was a moving speech, and the desperation seemed genuine.
Holmes was steely-eyed as he responded, and Ferguson seemed to
gain some comfort from that.

'Mr Ferguson, I can promise you one thing. To all intents and
purposes I regard your enemy, the hostile force behind this, as every
bit the resurrection of the horror that tested your late nephew and his
family. What is happening now is only occurring because the original
evil happened. I do not like it when the dragons I slay rise up, so you
have my word that I shall not be content until this house is safe again.'
Holmes waved a farewell and we left the Castle, and I morbidly
wondered if Holmes and I, at our advanced ages, had any chance of
finding a flying, befanged demon, let alone laying one to rest.

*   *   *

Wentworth delivered us to the local inn, where we found clean,
warm rooms, and I was given a task, even as Holmes disappeared,
explaining he would be gone until morning.

My job was simple enough, one I imagined I would have undertaken anyway. It was to spend the afternoon, and then the evening

after I dined, chatting to the local customers, and asking what they thought of Tunwell and its inhabitants. I was not disappointed.

It seemed that talk of the vampire was rife in the township – many were convinced that the family was cursed, and being preyed upon by some sort of evil influence. Ferguson was not liked too well, also. Talk of his harshness to his workers at the foundry was mentioned, and I sensed people would have been even more scathing were they not being guarded in their words, guarded because of fear.

I finally settled into bed full of thoughts of ancient curses and fanged demons, but, interestingly enough, not at all troubled by this. I realised that I was enjoying the welcome return of the feelings of stimulation an investigation has on the senses and the mind; it had been many years since Holmes and I had worked together.

My reveries were interrupted by Holmes's sudden reappearance. It was after midnight and my friend was shaking me awake, an action that reminded me that there were some aspects of our investigations that I had never enjoyed.

Soon I was in a tiny automobile he had somehow secured in the town and we were driving back to Tunwell in the chill of the night. I relayed to him what my inquiries had yielded.

'Ah, my friend, it is like the old days, is it not? The truth lies, waiting to be discovered, all around us. I have enquired after the Fergusons in the town, and my researches were just as fruitful as yours, if revealing in a different way, for I was able to provide enough of a hint to those I questioned to reassure them that Ferguson would not hear what they said.

'The fellow is hated by many. You saw the disregard he has for his servants? Well, it was no surprise to me to learn that there have been several occasions where he has been accused of molesting his female employees, and then trying to cover his indiscretions with bribes to the mistreated girls, or their families. One agency in the town refuses to send him domestic staff any more.'

'So what is going on at Tunwell?' I said 'Surely, good Lord . . . you're not saying he's attacking his own daughters?' I was horror-struck, but had heard of worse things in my three-quarters of a century. I suddenly felt tired, as the evil of man to his fellow loomed larger than the intellectual concerns of solving the case.

'No, I believe the Sussex Vampire that preys upon that house is a genuine threat, not contrived by Tunwell's owners. In a few hours, it is my hope we shall end the predator's activities forever.'

We had reached a spot on the road about twenty minutes walk from Tunwell, where an empty, broken haycart had long rested beside the road. Holmes pulled the automobile alongside and then behind this cart. When we walked away from the vehicle I realised no one passing would see the conveyance in the dark, even though the moon was bright.

We struck out on foot for Tunwell, cutting across an expanse of grassy paddock. I was now starting to truly feel my age, and was grateful the journey was a short one. Reaching the grounds we exercised more stealth. We approached from the side, through the very courtyard below the balcony Holmes had examined so carefully. He produced a key which he explained with a whisper he had palmed from Ferguson earlier that day when he was pretending to seek clues here. We entered, and found that the house was not in complete darkness; a huge candlestick burned near the foot of the stairs and its illumination allowed us easy ascent up the stairs to the first-floor corridor, that same corridor leading to the family members' rooms and the large balcony at the end of the hallway. However, Holmes silently led me by the elbow back, away from the family rooms to the opposite end of the corridor. We stood in the darkness there, and I realised that while we had an excellent view of the hall and the huge glass doors that let out to the balcony we would have been invisible to anyone looking in the opposite direction towards us.

I began to dread what awaited us, because I knew that here, now, was a situation where I could no longer pretend I was not an old man. Already my leg was beginning to throb from my ancient war wound, and I was becoming fatigued. I knew I could not stand here for hours, keeping a vigil of the type Holmes and I had made so many times in those years when Baker Street was our shared address. I felt a pang of sadness and the futile frustration of the no-longer-young. I lowered my head and gritted my teeth in anger.

It was a galvanising miracle then to feel Holmes's gloved hand on my shoulder and hear his voice whisper in my ear: 'There.' I looked up and scarce believed my eyes. A figure was in the act of stepping down from the balcony railing and into the balcony itself, a hooded, caped figure. It turned and pushed the glass door inwards, carefully, silently, and advanced down the hall.

There was no doubt that the thing indeed had an almost glowing white face and demonic brows that slanted savagely. It paused at the door to one of the rooms and held out a key, inserted it, then turned it, with extreme care. Then it gave the door a little push and watched it swing inwards.

'That's quite enough,' said Holmes, and he stepped forward and into the moonlit hall. He had a revolver extended in his hand.

There was an angry snort from the being in black, and then events unfolded with explosive suddenness. Holmes had begun to move forward, with me right at his heels, when a door was flung open and Bessie appeared. Blocking the pathway between the intruder and Holmes's pistol she began to scream, jumping up and down. The intruder turned and headed for the point at which he had entered the house, but Ferguson burst from his room, a pistol in hand. He yelled an epithet and pointed the weapon directly at the creature.

The black-cloaked figure was too fast. It slammed a fist into Ferguson's arm and the gun flew away. A second swift blow rocked his head back and he hit the wall behind him before smashing to the floor. The figure in black moved to the balcony, stood on the railing and seemed to flail about with its arms. I heard a strange noise, like a rasping roar. Holmes and I reached the balcony seconds later, and we saw the man in black's feet rise up from the railing, rise up and continue to rise, defying gravity. My jaw hung open but Holmes seemed unshaken. He grabbed the man's legs and it took me seconds again to realise he had snapped a pair of handcuffs around the creature's ankles and was holding on to them for dear life!

I looked up and I understood. I grabbed the madly kicking legs of the cloaked attacker. He began to descend, to fall back down, with his feet were returning to the balcony. Finally, I jumped and threw all my weight upon him, and the man crashed down into the balcony, crying out in pain.

Above him, a huge, hot-air balloon floated, its massive, round canvas painted solid black, a black rope ladder hanging from it still, but that ladder no longer in the assailant's grasp.

*   *   *

Our captured Sussex Vampire refused to answer a single question while we held him under armed watch in the sitting room of Tunwell Castle. His face was covered in theatrical make-up, to provide a grotesque, devilish–looking visage, but even when this was forcibly removed with a cold sponge, none of the Fergusons recognised him. A search of his pockets revealed a nasty-looking weapon: a brass clip fashioned to resemble human teeth. Holmes pointed out to Jennifer that this was what she had been 'bitten' with, not the man's own teeth, and Jennifer nodded, even as she studied the wicked device.

Finally, two hours after the man was snared, the police arrived and with them was Ferguson's driver, Wentworth, who smiled a great deal more than usual. He had a small armful of items that he handed over to Holmes, who in turn dumped most of them in front of the mysterious vampire, with the exception of one crumpled, old magazine, which Holmes flipped through and then handed to me.

'Watson, I'm sure you recall this little effort,' said Holmes. 'A taut little narrative, indeed.'

I blinked in surprise for the old booklet was nothing less than a 1924 copy of the *Strand Magazine*, containing my account of 'The Adventure of the Sussex Vampire'.

'This,' said Holmes 'was the seed of the idea for the campaign of revenge of Walter Jacard, the man we now see before us. Mr Jacard has been a successful hot-air balloonist in France for some years, and tours Europe with different entertainment troupes. But recently he formulated his own itinerary, just so he could be placed near Tunwell, for Mr Jacard had business to settle with the Ferguson family.'

'You damned filth, coming into my house,' rasped Ferguson, who had been recovering from his fall, sitting in a chair. 'I'll see you hanged for – '

'Enough!' said Jacard, turning like a lion and even in restraints appearing agile and ready enough to spring at the old man. 'Enough, you pig!'

Holmes's voice calmed the situation, and produced as great a shock in Jacard as it did in Ferguson.

'Mr Jacard, I understand your anger. A matter of honour, was it not? A woman preyed upon by this man, a woman in his employ at one time?'

Jacard nodded, tears welled in his eyes. Ferguson looked at Holmes and saw only cold contempt, and he hung his head.

'She was my wife, and she carried a deep sorrow. It was a long time before she revealed what he had done to her. But that was not the worst,' said Jacard.

He turned to the two daughters of Ferguson Ferguson. 'They knew! They saw! But they cared not. Although my Beatrice was a woman, she was inferior to them, because she was a servant. They considered her to be some sort of animal, to be used, and to be thrown out if she displeased them.'

The police constable nodded at Holmes. 'This one's given me more than I need, sir. All right, come along, you can make your complaints in front of a magistrate,' he barked at Jacard.

Jacard stood, haughty. 'With pleasure. I shall fully recount my wife's fate at this foul beast's hands. It will not spare me much in an English court, but it will ensure every man woman and child knows what this family is like.'

The constable looked annoyed, but not for long. Jennifer sprung to her feet, cold fury on her face.

'Let him go, let him go! He is a liar and we will not allow him to poison the town with his lies in a court room. Just get him away from here!'

The constable spoke 'But, Miss Ferguson . . . '

'No,' she said. 'There will be no charges laid, is that not so, Father?'

Ferguson could not speak, his head hung on his breast like that of a broken doll. He could only weakly nod.

* * *

'There were two elements to this crime.' said Holmes as we sat in the tiny railway station tea-room awaiting my train to London. 'Firstly a familiarity with the family's private affairs and the layout of the house, possibly duplicate keys, too, so I immediately made inquiries about recently departed servants. In this regard Wentworth was a veritable catalogue of information – but only after he was suitably recompensed and could talk unseen. He met me in the town as I asked him to and gave me much data.'

'In the town I inquired with agencies and former serving staff and I also found a poster advertising Jacard's hot air balloon exhibitions as part of the travelling entertainment troupe. I took on the persona of an out-of-county entrepreneur who was interested in engaging the troupe, and was able to speak to Jacard himself, and immediately knew I had my man, for as I engaged him in banter about his balloons he showed me a special gas burner he used to provide extra lift for his conveyance, and I knew the sound this device made was the rasping roar that had been heard at Tunwell.'

'I confess, Watson, I then decided to try and push our friend to strike again tonight. I made an offer to him that was generous in the extreme, but only provided he could disassemble his show here and head to London tomorrow. This would give him one last opportunity to attack his hated quarry, and I thought him bold enough to take it.'

'The motive had to have been personal to have inspired such a protracted revenge, and as Jacard was a strong, forceful male I knew the pathetic Ferguson could never have harmed him without immediate direct rebuke. A female victim, then, and what more likely a victim than a servant, one who either already was, or had since, become important to Jacard?

The attitude of the Ferguson women to serving staff fitted my hypothesis perfectly; surely this was why they were being attacked, because they were complicit, perhaps considered more guilty than he; for they would not even protect one of their own sex.'

'And our own adventure, Watson, that only made international publication a couple of years ago – this was the inspiration for Jacard's revenge! I'm inclined to think there may be more, perhaps Jacard's wife knew of the tale, perhaps the publication prompted her to reveal to her husband what had befallen her in the household connected to the late Robert Ferguson's – I cannot be sure. But it is undeniable; your writing was the spur to this man's plan. Ironic, is it not?'

I shook my head. I felt ancient. 'I am so sorry, Holmes. I never imagined I might inspire a crime, it is a miserable reunion for us, I suppose.'

Holmes looked at me with a shocked expression, and then he grabbed my arms. 'My dear fellow, no, no, no!

'I meant no criticism of you, not at all! Jacard was astute, Ferguson would never have been successfully prosecuted for his crimes, money and power have protected him. No, Jacard was in fact a man who was inspired to try and right a wrong by committing another wrong, but look at what our balloonist did – he was a showman – he terrified the family, but he did not balloon into Tunwell and blow their brains out in their sleep with a pistol! No, no, if you – and I – inspired something, it is a crime I can easily live with.'

I struggled to find words – I managed a weak 'Thank you'.

Holmes smiled.

'All these years I have chided you for embroidering my cases for publication, but what I have realised is that I should have been thanking you for capturing an audience – which I hear numbers in the millions, internationally. Yes, I do read your press!'

'This audience sees that my investigations are motivated by the need for seeing justice done, the innocent aided and the guilty exposed through diligent inquiry. That was the real merit of the original Sussex Vampire case, and I must shamefully admit, that was not a viewpoint I was able to understand fully when we solved it all those years ago.'

The train had pulled into the station. Holmes walked with me to it, and carried my bag, as my leg was paining me greatly.

'If Sherlock Holmes was ever an example to his fellows, it was because you showed the world the human dimension of my cases, and the worthiness of protecting the innocent and bringing the perpetrator to book. I mocked you in years past for changing the focus of my cases from exercises in ratiocination to dramatic episodes.

'I was wrong to do so, completely wrong. It has taken me too many decades, old fellow, but I must thank you for that.'

I made a fumbling goodbye; I cannot even remember what I said. Holmes seemed to understand that his words had caused me to become quite overcome.

I boarded the train, and waved to Holmes. I saw the lean figure turn and stride off, as purposefully as when we were much younger men.

Then a swirl of steam obliterated his image, and when it cleared I could no longer see him.

The Adventure of the Hanging Tyrant

M. J. ELLIOTT

1. *A letter from a client*

I believe I can say with all honesty that, following a period of several years during which he was believed dead by all but two people, nowhere was the surprise and disbelief resulting from the return of Mr Sherlock Holmes to public life felt more powerfully than in my own household. After the death of my beloved wife, I had dedicated my life and, save for a few hours a week spent at my club, all of my time to my medical practice. To the extent that any man who has lost that which made his life meaningful can be said to be happy, I believe I can claim that I was happy. Or, at the very least, I was not unhappy, which doubtless amounts to the same thing.

But in the spring of the year 1894, I was astonished to discover that my friend Sherlock Holmes was not dead, but alive and well and standing before me in the study of my Kensington home, having evaded the clutches of his arch-nemesis, the late Professor Moriarty. Now, some months later, I stood alone in that same study contemplating the wallpaper for which I had never truly cared but to which had voiced no objection when my dear wife Mary had selected it. 'The bright colours will cheer your patients, James,' she had said. In truth, there was nothing else left in the room to contemplate, all of my possessions being stored currently in the furniture van waiting at my front door. I am no longer certain exactly how I reached my decision, but I had chosen to throw in my lot with Holmes once more and return to the Baker Street address which had been my home for many years during my bachelor days. Was I mad to hope that I would again be swept up in the hectic adventures that had been such an essential part of my existence for the best part of a decade? To my knowledge, Holmes had already turned down one potential and influential client just a few weeks earlier. I was by no means completely comfortable with this change of direction in my life, but I made it simply for the sake of doing *something*. I might just as easily have boarded a vessel bound for Australia or attempted to rejoin my old regiment. Holmes's reappearance in my life had filled me not with a sense of relief but one of total confusion. My wife was dead and my best friend, whom I had believed dead, was alive. The situation was the cause of many contradictory emotions, none of which I would have dreamed of burdening Holmes with and none of which, I am pleased to say, I can recall accurately today.

A fist rapped politely on the open door behind me.

'I shan't be much longer,' said I, over my shoulder. 'I am almost ready to go.'

'I am delighted to hear you say so,' a well-known voice replied. 'There is not a moment to be lost, Watson. We are expected in Pangbourne by noon. If we hurry, we can just make the next train from Paddington.'

I turned to discover Sherlock Holmes waiting in the doorway, clad in his long grey travelling coat, and effecting what I might almost describe as a warm smile.

'Holmes!' I cried. And then, after I had taken in his last remark: 'To Pangbourne, now? But what about my furniture?'

'It will, I am certain, be waiting for you at Baker Street upon our return. Your hat and boots, old friend, and don't dilly-dally!'

We were barely in time for the Berkshire-bound train and we had only just settled down in our carriage before I began to feel overcome by weariness. I had experienced an unaccountably restless night and I intended to shut my eyes for only a short time. How much of our journey had elapsed before I was suddenly snapped back to wakefulness by Holmes's abrupt tone I could not say.

'Watson! Remember I said that there might be some danger involved. I trust that you are carrying your service revolver?'

'Sorry, Holmes,' said I, attempting to stifle a yawn with the back of my hand. 'It is presently on its way to Baker Street with the rest of my possessions. I had no idea we would be drawn into a case so soon.'

'Ah, well, it may be that our correspondent overestimates the threat against her.'

'Threat? Holmes, you seem to be developing an appalling habit of starting a story from the middle. You forget that I have no knowledge of any of this.'

Without replying, Holmes extracted a folded sheet of writing-paper from his jacket pocket and held it out to me.

'From your – from *our* client?'

'A most provocative letter, Watson. Kindly refresh my memory as to its contents.'

Holmes's remarkable faculty for storing the smallest details (despite his claims to the contrary) made this exercise entirely unnecessary, but he always seemed to derive some satisfaction from hearing his correspondence read aloud, so I obliged gladly. The letter was addressed 'Field House, Pangbourne', and ran thus:

> DEAR MR HOLMES – *I have recently had a most troubling experience and am uncertain to whom I should turn for advice and assistance. The newspapers have been full of your astonishing return from the dead, and I am all too aware from your good friend Dr Watson's stories that you are possessed of both great intelligence and great wisdom . . .*

'My blushes, Watson!' Holmes interrupted.

The letter went on:

> *. . . Please forgive my reticence in providing details and my unwillingness to call upon you in London. If there is any danger to be faced, I should not wish the servants to confront it on my behalf.*
>
> *I should be most grateful if you would call upon me at noon tomorrow. Please arrange for Dr Watson to accompany you. I cannot guarantee that you will be granted admittance in his absence.*
>
> *Yours faithfully,*
> MRS FRANCES CARTNER

I found the content of the letter intriguing, not least because my presence seemed so important to the writer. Was she unwell, perhaps, and in need of the services of a doctor? I put the matter to Holmes.

'It is certainly very puzzling,' he replied, 'and we cannot know the answer until we have spoken to our client. Yes, I have decided to accept her case even though doing so breaks the rule I enforced with such fierceness only a fortnight ago. However, the matter is simply too intriguing and the lady is clearly in need of my – what was it? – great intelligence and great wisdom. We can, at any rate, form a few conclusions about her circumstances and personality from her letter. She is clearly a woman of strong character, and she was once quite wealthy, but has had to make some quite severe adjustments to her lifestyle, no doubt following the death of her husband. How unfortunate to be both widowed *and* childless.'

'And to think that a while ago you were concerned that your abilities were failing you! The writer's strong character I can see from the content of her letter, but as for her failing fortunes, I confess I did not read anything that indicated such a condition. She writes that she keeps servants.'

'Until recently, Watson, you had servants also, and very attentive servants at that.'

I had no idea how Holmes reached such a conclusion. I had found Megan even more insolent and lazy than Mary Jane Kelly, and I had been only too pleased to give her notice.

'My reasoning is based upon the letter itself, not its subject matter. The paper is of the very best quality, but there is a tear on the left side, just below the fold. That tear did not occur after writing, for the lady has taken pains to avoid it; the line beginning "great wisdom" is deliberately out of true. Now, why should an affluent writer not simply use a sheet that is not torn? On its own, this is merely suggestive, but observe that the ink, again of the finest sort, has run out early in the final paragraph. The replacement ink is of a cheap variety, common to most hotels. You will recall that during the von Lammerain blackmail case, I made a special study of the history and manufacture of ink. I have not yet written a monograph upon the subject, but I intend to do so when time permits. The combination of factors can lead only to the conclusion that our correspondent is using her final sheet of expensive paper and her final bottle of expensive ink to summon us. We should feel flattered therefore.'

'That is perfectly sound reasoning,' I confessed, 'but I do not see how you can tell that the lady is widowed. She signs herself "Mrs Cartner", after all.'

'Then why does she not turn to her husband in this time of peril, Watson? Why write to us? Why does her husband not send her away and out of danger? It will not do.'

'He might be elsewhere – perhaps his business requires that he travel.'

'A fair objection, Watson. It is good to see that you are keeping up. But was there ever a husband who would allow his employment to keep him from his wife's side if he believed her in danger? Again I ask, where is the husband, if not dead?'

'Divorced!' I announced, triumphantly. 'The husband wants nothing more to do with her, and so she must face this burden, whatever it is, alone.'

'You paint a vivid picture, doctor. I might add, in favour of your objection, that a lady might continue to use her married name after her divorce. Congratulations, old friend. It appears that your sleep has done your intellectual capacities some good.'

I felt a keen pleasure at these complimentary words, such as I had not experienced for many a year.

'Then you agree with my conclusions, Holmes?'

'Not in the slightest, you are wholly incorrect.'

'Oh.'

'But you have certainly grasped the method, to consider all probable explanations before determining the only possible conclusion. But you remain too timid in your inferences. If this woman is divorced as you suggest, surely she must have secured some sort of financial settlement from her former husband. Why is she now reduced to writing to complete strangers on torn paper with inferior ink?'

I slumped back in my seat, defeated. After nearly fifteen years of acquaintance, on and off, I ought to have learned not to question my friend's logic. But I suppose that I should never appreciate the wonder of his gifts were I to accept it all with no objection. His ingenious observations had, however, caused me some disappointment in my own abilities; I had wished to surprise Holmes with a display of deductive reason regarding the letter writer, but had been unable to contribute anything of worth. As I mulled this over, a thought sprang to mind.

'Wait, Holmes!' I said. 'You say that this woman is childless – I believe that I can see your reasoning, in that she would surely send her children away rather than see them at risk, and that such a caring mother could not bear to be separated from her offspring.'

Holmes merely nodded in reply.

'But might not the writer be an elderly woman, whose children have grown up and left home? I know what you are about to say, that they would surely wish to protect their mother as any husband would his wife, but what if she had only daughters and no sons? Surely, she would not place them in a perilous situation.'

Holmes gave a slight groan, as though in some discomfort.

'It was my understanding, doctor, that you have attempted to keep up the good work during my time away from London, is that not so?'

'Largely for my private satisfaction, but in my own small way, yes,' I replied, modestly.

'Then it disappoints me to learn that you have not studied my writings on the science of detection. You recall the puzzle at Reigate?'

'The matter involving the local squire?'

'*Squires*, Watson. Your inability to recall such pertinent details no doubt explains your failure to recollect my familiarity with the study of handwriting. A woman's age can be ascertained as tolerably as a man's, and this is a woman who, while no longer in the first flush of youth, is very far from the bath chair. There is passion in her *D*s and vigour in her *T*s. In the past three years I have extended my studies to include numerous languages and alphabets, and I believe that my monograph upon the subject is due for some revising. I may wish you to take notes when the time is propitious, Watson.'

And with that, he closed his eyes and remained motionless until our arrival. I attempted to return to my earlier slumber, but found myself completely unable to relax, wondering as I did whether the mystery that was about to be placed before us would afford me an opportunity to prove to Holmes that my skills had improved to such a degree over the last three years that I could claim without affectation to be his equal as a detective.

2. The strange story of Basil Valentine

From Sherlock Holmes's description of Mrs Cartner's failing re-sources, I had expected to find the lady residing in the sort of homely cottage that Mary and I had often discussed when planning my eventual retirement from medicine. Instead, we discovered Field House to be quite a large affair that in former times would no doubt have been considered almost grand. As we alighted from our wagon-ette, it became clear that the building was in a poor state of repair. A climbing plant of some variety – now completely dead – covered much of the front of the house. I considered this, and was suddenly aware of a flurry of movement behind one of the windows.

'I observe it also, Watson,' said Holmes, before I had the opport-unity to remark upon it. 'Be on your guard. I must confess, I am beginning to experience some apprehension about asking you to accompany me here.'

'And had I not, who knows what might have happened to you?' I replied as we made our way slowly to the front door, the pebbles crunching beneath our shoes with each step.

'You forget Watson, that I have already been dead. The experience is quite liberating.'

Holmes rapped on the door with a confidence I must confess I did not feel also. A moment later it opened a few inches, sufficient for me to observe the shape of a man blocking our entrance. I could ascertain no further details other than that he was of a stocky build and in height an inch or two shorter than me.

'Who are you gentlemen, and what is the meaning of this call?' he growled.

'Not the welcome I was expecting, Watson,' the detective remarked, deliberately ignoring the menace implicit in the man's tone. Given the unpredictable nature of his own recent caller, I should have imagined that Holmes might have thought better of this offhand approach.

From within the house, I heard a cultured female voice say: 'That will do, Peter. You are Sherlock Holmes I presume?'

Holmes removed his travelling cap. 'I am, ma'am. And this is my associate, Dr Watson.'

Unable to see the speaker, and feeling somewhat foolish, I followed Holmes's lead in removing my hat. Clearly, we were being inspected, but for what purpose I could not imagine.

'You are not unlike your pictures, Mr Holmes.

'And you have a moustache, doctor, as you appear in the illustrations,' the voice continued.

I was somewhat nonplussed by this strange observation.

'Mrs Cartner,' said Holmes taking a step forward, 'I am sure that you summoned us here for a more serious purpose than to discuss our likenesses. May we be allowed to enter and discuss your problem at leisure?'

There was a moment's wait, during which, I supposed, the lady of the house must have indicated to her man, Peter, that we be allowed to pass him. It struck me as I entered that although it was early afternoon on a pleasant spring day outside the house, in the hallway it felt and appeared closer to early evening. An unmistakable musty odour reached my nostrils. As my eyes roamed the walls in search of traces of damp on the wallpaper, Peter, the formidable manservant, came into my view. His grizzled features and muscular frame could hardly have been considered a pleasant subject for close inspection at the best of times and it was clear that nothing I could say would budge the man if he did not wish to be budged. I craned my neck in an attempt to see our troubled letter-writer positioned behind him. It must have been evident from my reaction that I was quite surprised by what I found.

'Are you unwell, Doctor Watson?' the lady asked.

I have heard many women on several continents described as 'handsome', but the phrase never seemed appropriate when – many years later – I was to compare them all to Mrs Francis Cartner. She was, I imagined, not quite forty, nearly as tall as I, dark-haired and blessed with a pleasing regularity of feature. The true individuality of her beauty, however, must surely have been her piercing blue eyes. I must admit that I was quite distracted by them, and a moment passed in silence before I realised that she had spoken to me.

'I am . . . quite well, Mrs Cartner. That is – '

'I fear that Watson is not a good traveller and our rather frantic journey here has quite unsettled his nerves,' Holmes interjected. I agreed that this might well be the case and Mrs Cartner insisted that I be allowed to sit and gather my wits. Taking our outer clothing with some apparent resentment, Peter led us into a sitting room made surprisingly cheerful by the bright sunlight beaming in from a large picture window. I noted the unusually grand and expensive items of furniture on display, quite at odds with the general state of the property. We were invited to sit and Peter was instructed to have the maid bring tea.

'By any chance, would it be possible to request coffee?' I asked, hesitantly. 'I know that it is not quite the time, but I have not had . . . '

A barely perceptible crease at each corner of her small but sensitive mouth was the only indication that I had embarrassed our host in some way.

'I am sorry to say that we have none, doctor, nor any strong liquor. In the last year, I have been forced to make some rather drastic economies.'

'It is really of no matter,' I assured her hurriedly. 'It was merely a whim.'

'Following the death of my husband,' she went on, seeming not to hear my last remark, 'I was horrified to learn that the solicitor responsible for managing his financial affairs, a Mr Ronald Sawyer, had misappropriated that income and – when the situation became known – absconded with much of it. My husband was the founder of the Haydock Tobacco Company, and had amassed a considerable sum in a very short time. When we married, he had already sold his interests in the firm and was content to live off his early profits for the remainder of his life. A life that was too prove all too short, gentlemen, for last February he succumbed to a family illness and it became clear that, although not poor, I had been robbed of much of the hard-earned money Francis would have wished me to have. I need hardly say that if I were asked to choose between wealth and having my husband restored to me, I should wish to have Francis always at my side.'

For a terrible moment, I recalled the wording of her letter and feared that Mrs Cartner was of the opinion that Holmes actually *had* returned from the dead and was on the brink of requesting that he retrieve her husband from the afterlife.

'But I am reconciled to the fact that I will not see him again, just as I am reconciled to the fact that the man who stole those funds will never be brought to justice. Mr Sawyer was last heard of in Ceylon, I have been informed. I am a realist and I sought thereafter to tailor my life to my ability to pay my way. I have been forced to sell what valuables I could bear to part with – a Greuze painting brought a very good price from a scholar who professed to being something of a collector.'

Holmes raised an inquisitive eyebrow.

'The final degradation for me was when it became clear that I could no longer maintain our family home and its large staff. I gave notice to the majority of the servants, put the sale of the house in the hands of an agent more trustworthy than Mr Sawyer, and moved the remainder of my belongings – all that you see around you, gentlemen – into one of my husband's smaller properties, which he kept for letting purposes only, although I now know that what little profit arose from both houses did not go into my husband's account with Silvester's.' This brave speech was made without any discernible emotion on the part of the speaker. I was much impressed with the determination and strength of character she displayed in the face of such a devastating alteration to her circumstances, to say nothing of her commendable frankness.

'I hope that you will forgive the behaviour of my manservant, Peter, upon your arrival. He is fiercely protective of me and I believe that he would remain in my service even if I were unable to pay his wages, a day I fear may come sooner rather than later.'

Holmes leaned forward in his chair. 'And does Peter have good reason to be protective, madam? You state that you believe yourself in danger. From whom?'

'I . . . I have only seen one of them at close quarters,' she replied, with the first trace of hesitancy, 'the man who calls himself Basil Valentine.'

'Basil, did you say?' Holmes asked. 'The name is oddly familiar to me. But please relate to me the nature of your meeting with this Mr Valentine.'

Mrs Cartner folded her hands in her lap; a dignified act of self-composure, I thought. 'He wrote to me on the fifth. I regret to say that I did not retain the letter, which merely stated that the writer intended to call upon me with some information he believed would be to my advantage. Some odd presentiment, however, led me to put his business card in a safe place. It is on the table before you.'

'A model client, Holmes,' I noted.

'It is a great pity that the letter has been disposed of – it might have been quite instructive,' Holmes responded, somewhat grumpily. Without bothering to ask whether he might be permitted to examine it, he snatched up the card and scrutinised it. I wondered whether he might employ his high-powered lens upon the task, but he seemed not to find much that interested him in the card.

'There is little here that is of any use. The card reads: "Basil Valentine, Professor of Arcane Antiquities, University of Wittenberg", an institution renowned for its unconventional ex-students. I do not suppose that, if we were to make enquiries, the University would ever have heard of a person purporting to hold such a vaguely defined position. Any scoundrel with an ounce of ingenuity could arrange for the printing of such a card. I have done so myself.'

I took the card from his fingers and studied it intently, hoping to spot some feature that my friend may have missed. 'Holmes, there is a thumb-mark on the reverse of this card,' I remarked

'Probably the printer's,' Holmes replied, without bothering to see my discovery for himself. 'I have yet to investigate a case in which the identification of such a mark has had any bearing on its solution.'

'I have done a great deal of reading on the subject over the last few years, and I understand that every fingerprint is unique and cannot be duplicated.'

'I have heard something of the kind; I remain unconvinced.'

Feeling somewhat embarrassed by his dismissal of this clue, I replaced the card on the table. Looking into our client's clear blue eyes, I gave her what I hoped would appear to be a smile of reassurance. I was glad to note that the gesture was returned.

Appearing not to notice, Holmes resumed his questioning. 'You permitted Mr Valentine to call?'

'His letter did not offer me the opportunity to give my permission or to withhold it, Mr Holmes; it simply stated that he would arrive the next day. Impertinent it undoubtedly was, but I imagined – foolishly, as I now realise – that he might know of a way in which my fortunes might somehow be improved. Not, of course, that money is the most important thing of which I have been deprived of late. If I had not been at such a low ebb at the time the letter arrived, I might well have refused. I wonder how differently events might have transpired if I had done so.'

The lady began to drift into a melancholy mood once more. I could not, of course, blame her for that. More than once during that period in my life I had found myself descending into a gloomy state without any apparent cause. I had learned that work was the best antidote to sorrow, but Mrs Cartner could not, of course, avail herself of that solution.

'Please relate the details of Mr Valentine's visit,' Holmes said, sharply, breaking into our host's thoughts. 'And try to include as much detail, however irrelevant you may consider it.' He leaned back in his seat and pressed his long fingers together, but – in deference to our client – his eyes remained open and keen.

'I have to say that I consider everything about the man to be irrelevant. When he arrived, one week ago tomorrow, it was apparent to me that he was scarcely the sort of gentleman who could have been a professor of any subject. I wondered whether he wore such a large moustache – your own, doctor, would be called modest by comparison – in order to hide his true appearance or his true age, for he could not have been older than twenty-five. To add to his improbable appearance, his taste in clothes might, I imagine, have been better suited to a comedian of the music hall stage. The checks on his jacket were overstated to the point of vulgarity.'

I was reminded by this remark of our old friend Sir Henry Baskerville. 'Might he not,' I suggested, 'have been a Canadian or an American? Both nationalities' choice of attire is often less restrained than our own.'

She shook her head gently, a most captivating gesture. 'No, Dr Watson, I am certain that he was an Englishman. Unless, of course, he was an exceptional actor, and the improbability of his story makes me doubt that.'

'And what was that story?' Holmes prompted.

'He related it to me in this very room. I was seated in this same chair, but Mr Valentine could not be persuaded to sit. Instead he paced the floor, walking up to the window and back again several times. I did not think such agitation particularly strange, since by this point I had ascertained that there was nothing about the man that was not strange.

' "I suppose that the name Edward Kelley is unfamiliar to you, dear lady?" he asked.

' "I do not believe that I have ever met anyone of that name," I replied.

'He guffawed in a manner I considered more appropriate to the smoking room. "No indeed!" he barked. "It is not likely that you should, for he lived and died some centuries before you were born! Kelley, also known as Talbot, was the son of a humble baker, but he became one of England's greatest alchemists, and I know what you are thinking about *that*!"

'In truth, I doubted very much that Mr Valentine knew what I was thinking at that moment.

' "Alchemy, my dear lady, is commonly thought by an ignorant public to be the act of turning lead into gold, which any person with a jot of intelligence will tell you is impossible. In fact, alchemists, as the name suggests, experimented with all manner of chemicals for many purposes, the majority of them a good deal more practical than the accumulation of shiny metals. I think it is safe to say that we would have no doctors today were it not for the pioneering work of these alchemists – why, we might still be sticking leeches on one another!"

'I began to fear that my it was my visitor's intention to attempt to sell me something, and I pondered how best he might be ejected from Field House before the interview took a disagreeable turn.

' "Exactly two hundred and twenty one years ago, Kelley is believed to have been in this area and to have purchased, along with an alchemical tract entitled *The Book of St Dunstan*, a vial of red powder said to possess remarkable properties. Of course, in books and letters of the time, these properties were described as either magical in nature or else possessing the power of the Almighty, but in these enlightened times one may see past the ignorance of a former age and understand this powder to be an extraordinary medicinal compound. Kelley buried the vial in an unknown location and no more of it is known to exist, but if it were ever to be unearthed, it could be analysed by one of our prominent scientists, and hopefully duplicated. It might prove invaluable in aiding patients to recover from surgical procedures. My own dear brother was injured so badly during the war in Afghanistan that his leg was amputated and the fellow died three days later from the shock. If the doctors had had access to Kelley's extraordinary red powder . . . well, dear John might still be with us today."

'I need hardly tell you, gentlemen, that I believed not one word of this preposterous yarn, including the details of this unfortunate brother. I decided that it was time to get to the crux of the matter.

' "This might be a very pretty story to a collector of fairy tales, Mr Valentine," said I, "but in what way am I affected by it?"

' "It is no fairy tale, dear lady, I assure you. I will not bore you with the details of my researches, but I can promise you that the story of the red powder and its value to medical science is quite true. There was little enough of it when Kelley first discovered it, so there may only have been a few grains remaining when he finally hid it away. The last seven years of my life have been devoted to locating the spot where that vial was buried. Having followed certain hints found in Eckermann's *Alchemy and Britannic History*, I can now say with tolerable confidence that that spot is somewhere on the grounds upon which Field House presently stands. I propose – with your permission, of course – to conduct an archaeological dig on your property. With the assistance of my fellow scholars, I estimate that the endeavour should take no more than a week. To prevent your experiencing any inconvenience during this time, I have arranged for you to spend the week at one of the hotels on Northumberland Avenue in London. I recommend that you dismiss your servants for that same period; I can see no reason for their staying on when the lady of the house is not in residence."

'I had felt it only polite to allow this Mr Valentine to speak his piece but I had begun to weary of his tomfoolery.

' "Mr Valentine," I said, firmly, "thank you for the time you have taken to call upon me with your interesting request, but I regret to inform you that it holds no attraction for me whatsoever. I wish Field House and its environs to remain undisturbed."

'To my surprise, he did not seem at all disappointed by this setback. "I can see that it would be useless to ask you to reconsider, madam," he said, "but I cannot stress the importance of this matter sufficiently, not only to the public at large, but to yourself in particular."

' "But I am quite well, Mr Valentine," I responded.

' "And I pray that you remain so. Your refusal makes me very sad. Very sad indeed."

'Feeling somewhat unnerved by his remarks, I rang for Peter, who escorted the gentleman off the property. It was as I heard the door close behind him that I was struck by a sudden realisation – he had not been striding to the window and back out of some sort of nervous agitation, as I had thought. *Rather, he had been watching for a confederate waiting outside the house.'*

'You say someone? Might it not have been some*thing*?' Holmes queried.

'No, Mr Holmes, for I was just in time to see the two of them together by the beech tree.'

Holmes rose and strode to the window. I followed, not wishing to appear uninterested, and hoping to observe something of significance. But, apart from confirming that Mrs Cartner could indeed have watched two men in conversation under the large beech tree just outside the gate, I could see nothing.

'Unfortunately, the other man remained in the shade and I could see little of him, save that he was about a head shorter than Mr Valentine, who was himself not a tall man. His hair was black, I believe, but I could not swear to it. They spoke for about two minutes, my visitor frequently gesticulating and glancing at the front of the house. Standing at the window as I was, I do not know how he could have failed to see me.'

'A singular occurrence, to be sure,' Holmes observed, returning to his chair. I waited a moment longer, on the off chance that a clue might suddenly present itself to me, but disappointed, I resumed my seat also.

'You do not strike me, Mrs Cartner, as the sort of person who would allow themselves to be frightened by such an incident,' said Holmes. 'What has happened since then?'

'Your confidence in my nerve is gratifying, Mr Holmes, but I must confess that for some reason I had the idea of contacting you immediately after my meeting with Mr Valentine. However, it seemed such a trivial matter that I immediately put the idea out of my head. The next afternoon, I was visiting a sick neighbour, when the fellow called again. He came to the kitchen door claiming to be a representative of a London auctioneers. From the description given by the maid it could only have been Basil Valentine. He claimed that he had been summoned to value several items of property. Obviously, the rogues had discovered the details of my situation, not it that would have been difficult for them to do so. The girl had no instructions from me in this regard and thought it peculiar that anyone calling upon the lady of the house should knock at the servant's entrance. Growing impatient with her uncertainty, Mr Valentine then produced a sovereign from his pocket.

'"Look here, my girl," he said, "this money is yours if you will allow me half an hour without interruption inside the house. When I leave, you may have the same amount again."

'Frightened, the maid called for Peter the footman, at which point Valentine fled, scrambling over the hedge and disappearing. He has not called again, but I have been aware of figures prowling about the outskirts of my property at various times of the day. In one instance, I was alarmed by a sudden crash and discovered that the stone sundial in the garden had been tipped over, presumably by accident. I was more or less certain at that moment that I would engage you on this matter, but Peter's experience two nights ago decided me on this course of action. Perhaps you would care to hear it from his own lips.'

Before she had a chance to ring for the intimidating servant, the girl entered the sitting room with our tea. I felt a twinge of unease at the remembrance of my earlier *faux pas*. Mrs Cartner asked the maid to summon Peter, and less than a minute after her departure the fellow was standing over us, appearing no less fearsome than he had upon our arrival. I wondered whether, with his military bearing, he had seen service at some point. However, following Holmes's some-what shoddy treatment of my deductive capabilities that morning, I decided against asking his opinion.

'With the events of the last few days,' Peter began, 'I have been reluctant to leave the mistress alone at home.'

'However, I insisted,' Mrs Cartner interrupted. 'Peter has been on the alert for intruders for some days now, and I was quite adamant that he take a well-deserved respite. It was not an easy matter to persuade him, however, and he eventually agreed on the condition that he would not be away from the house for more than an hour. Please continue, Peter.'

'I spent that hour in the local hostelry, *The Dutch Masters*. I was sitting alone when that blighter slid into the chair next to me. I should have had him by his collar and marched him to the police station that very moment, but the scoundrel had the gift of the patter all right and he started up before I even realised he was there.'

'"You would probably like to see me up to my neck in the river," he says, "and I can't say that I blame you. This whole business has been shockingly badly managed, and I promise you that that was not my idea. I don't take pleasure in distressing – uh, pardon me, ma'am – childless widows. That is why I am putting a stop to it here and now, and to do that I need your help, sir."

' "If that's the case," I asks, "then why the devil – pardon me, ma'am – do you need my help and why the – what makes you suppose that I would be willing to help you?"

' "I don't see that your employer need be troubled at all, Mr Tierney, is it? All I ask of you is that tomorrow you deliver a note into her hands that will draw her away from Field House for a short time. Then you and the rest of the staff may enjoy a pleasant lunchtime in this establishment, and when you return to your duties, everything will be as it was before, so far as you can tell. Mrs Cartner will never see or hear from me again. How do you like the sound of that, eh?"

'Well, I've met plenty of fancy talkers in my time and I never trusted a one of them. I made a grab for the rascal's coat, but he was just a little too fast for me, and he was out of his chair and through the door of the pub before I'd even got up. Ten years ago, or even five, I'd have caught up with him, right enough.'

'Peter did not wish to upset me with an account of the incident,' Mrs Cartner added, 'but I swear that I can always tell when something is troubling him and I soon coaxed the whole story out of him. He has a charming lack of affectation in that regard. Thank you, Peter, that will be all for now. After he told me the tale, I finally put pen to paper, as I had meant to do for some time. Forgive me, Dr Watson, if my insistence that you accompany Mr Holmes caused you any inconvenience.'

I shook my head vigorously.

'But by this stage I was so excessively nervous that I imagined these people, whoever they are, might be capable of intercepting my letters. If a risk existed that they could do so and send impersonators in your stead, I thought that if I were adamant that you both come they would be less likely to find suitable doubles at short notice. Hence my relief upon seeing, doctor, that you are just as you are depicted in the *Strand* Magazine, moustache and all.'

'To return to the matter of your peculiar persecution', said Holmes, 'you say that you have often been aware of these intruders during the day, Mrs Cartner. Has there ever been any sign of them at night?'

'Why, no.'

Holmes eyes glistened and I recognised the look of satisfaction he wore when he was on the right scent. 'Then if I have your permission, and if Dr Watson has finished his tea, we will examine the grounds. Please make a start without me, Watson, I wish to have a brief word with Peter.'

3. *I theorise*

I was alone in the garden for several minutes. The day remained fair and the heat of the late afternoon sun tingled on my neck most pleasurably. It would have been quite easy to forget for a moment that I was patrolling the grounds of a house under siege. The charming and personable Mrs Frances Cartner was relying on us, and I did not intend to see her disappointed. With this intention in mind, I got down on all fours and began examining the grass minutely.

'Watson, your ungainly pose will almost certainly have obliterated any traces upon that spot.' I looked up to see Holmes, his stick in one hand, his other outstretched. 'Let me help you up. I wished to discuss a few matters with Peter and he is presently dispatching telegrams on my behalf. We must hold off any invasion together until he returns. His employer was quite effusive in her apologies regarding the quality of her stationery. If you are quite satisfied that there is nothing to be learned here, shall we continue?'

As we made our way around the grounds, I was occasionally aware of our client watching us from the house.

'You have an admirer, I think, Watson. A very attractive woman, is she not?'

'Is she?' I said, languidly. 'I did not observe.'

'Oh, come, Watson! Your indifference surprises me. After all, I am indebted to you for the fact that I now acknowledge a pretty face when I see one.'

'I am very pleased to hear you say so, Holmes.'

'Yes, I freely admit that it was foolish of me not to allow for the importance of physical attractiveness as a factor in the commission of a crime. I have been involved in several investigations over the years where a problem may hinge on an individual's weakness for a beautiful woman. You will recall, Watson, the Adventure of the Unpowdered Nose.'

'Should I ever decide to write it up, I'm sure I shall choose a better title than that,' I responded, testily.

My irrition was not due solely to Holmes's manner but also to his apparent lack of interest in the problem at hand. On more than one instance I had seen him lie flat upon his face, searching for evidence, but now – despite the trust placed in us both by an anxious and gracious lady – he did little more than poke at the untended grass with his stick.

'I count at least three persons so far,' he said, at last, 'none of them the manservant Peter, whose left foot is at least a size larger than his right. Does it strike you as peculiar, Watson, that a man should manage to knock over a heavy stone sundial in broad daylight?'

'Perhaps he thought he had been observed and simply panicked,' I suggested.

'Watson, your dogged refusal to eliminate even the impossible is a continual source of astonishment to me.'

This last jibe was, I felt, quite the wrong side of too much and I took my companion to task. 'Holmes, all morning you have derided my attempts to put into practice your theories on the science of deduction, theories upon which I might say I have expanded considerably over the passing years.'

Holmes raised a quizzical eyebrow.

'For instance,' I continued, 'I have formed my own opinion regarding our client's unnerving experience and I venture to suggest that my theory fits the facts as we know them.'

Holmes slumped back against the nearest tree. 'Pray enlighten me, doctor.' I was pleased to note that I did not detect even a trace of mockery in his tone.

'It seems to me evident that this story of the red powder buried somewhere in the vicinity is nothing more than a flimsy concoction of Valentine's, intended to mask some sinister purpose.'

'I am certainly in agreement with you on that point, Watson, but there is at least some historical basis for the story of Edward Kelley, although he lived considerably earlier than Valentine claims. Many properties, including the bestowing of the ability to commune with the angels, have been ascribed to the fabled red powder – which he came by in Wales, by the way, not Berkshire. I am unaware of any work by Eckermann suggesting that it might be located in these parts. Indeed, I do not believe Kelley ever visited this area in his life.'

'As I say, merely a ruse in order to gain entry to Field House, a motive made clear by the later unsuccessful attempts. Incidentally, Holmes, I *am* quite aware that Edward Kelley was a real person, in fact I am certain that our adversary's scant research into the subject suggested his own *alias* to him - Basilius Valentinus was a sixteenth century Benedictine who published a treatise on alchemy. No doubt that is why you thought his name familiar. You need not appear so astonished, Holmes, you are not the only person with access to the reading room of the British Museum, you know.'

In truth, although I had been quite offhand about the matter, I was extremely satisfied at the effect my words had upon Holmes, who – after a moment or two of uncertainty – emitted a sharp bark of a laugh.

'You do well to chide me, Watson! Our client's agreeable nature seems to have had a remarkable effect on your cognitive abilities – I would go so far as to say that you positively scintillate this morning. Very well then, what do you suppose was the reason for our Mr Valentine's error regarding the time in which Kelley lived?'

'Oh, that! Simply a mistake on the blackguard's part, I imagine. I ascribe no importance to it whatsoever.'

Holmes smiled a tight-lipped smile. 'I see. Please continue, Watson. What do you suggest is the sinister purpose for which Valentine and his associates wish access to Mrs Cartner's home?'

'Evidently, there is something hidden in that house which is of great value to them and which Mrs Cartner does not realise she even possesses.'

'And what might that item be, pray?'

'Ah, there I am at a loss, I am afraid. I am loath to theorise without data, you see . . .'

'Watson, does it occur to you that we are witnessing a curious parallelism of events? A visitor presents an improbable scenario; when rejected he resorts to menacing promises of disastrous consequences . . .'

I frowned as Holmes described the sequence of events. Put that way, they did seem curiously familiar.

'The missing papers of ex-President Murillo!' I gasped. Holmes merely nodded. 'But how is it that a matter on which you are consulted mere weeks ago should play a part in our present investigation? Surely that is more than coincidence!'

'I admit that there are some features of this case that are not yet clear to me, but I hope to have them clarified by tomorrow. In the meantime, Watson, you are doing so well that I think it would be nothing short of criminal to rob you of the credit for discovering the missing memoirs and I therefore put you in charge of the investigation from this point on and place myself entirely at your disposal. Your instructions will be followed to the letter. Now, where do you propose we begin our search?'

4. *An influential visitor*

I had first learned of the Murillo matter some two weeks earlier, when I was still in residence at my Kensington practice. Although I had long since abandoned the habit of sleeping late, as I had done so often when still a bachelor and in most respects carefree, one Saturday morning in May I somehow failed to rise at my usual hour. Donning an unnecessarily thick dressing-gown for the time of year, I wandered the house, eventually entering my study where I discovered Sherlock Holmes seated at my writing desk, skimming through a draft copy of my account of the involvement of Professor Moriarty in the outrages known to the public as the Jack the Ripper crimes. Although the full facts of the matter may never be known, some readers – Inspector Tobias Gregson among them – will be aware that it was on a balcony high above the streets of London that Holmes was able to remove a plague-spot from the Whitechapel area.

'You will never be allowed to publish this, you know,' said Holmes, holding one of the pages aloft while still poring over another. 'Too many reputations, including that of an innocent woman, would be damaged.'

I stepped over to the desk, removed the paper from my visitor's hand and replaced it in its proper order in the pile on the desk. 'I had already reached that conclusion,' I replied, 'after receiving a strongly-worded letter from the brother of Professor Moriarty.'

'Which one?'

'James.'

'Ah. Forgive the hour, Watson, but I was re-acquainting myself with the mud stains of the Kensington area and decided to drop in. I told your maid not to wake you on my account.'

In the weeks following his dramatic return, Holmes had made a habit of appearing unannounced at my door. It was often so in the past, of course, although I can recall only one occasion – during his investigation of the supposed murder of Colonel Barclay in '88 – when he stayed under my roof overnight. But now, for some unaccountable reason, his visits filled me with dread. I dared not say anything of the sort to Holmes, of course, and if he had deduced it from my unconscious actions he did not say so. I could only hope that my unease would abate once I found myself back at Baker Street.

'And how goes the sale of your practice?' Holmes asked at last.

I lowered myself into the chair usually reserved for patients and noticed for the first time how uncomfortable it was. 'Surprisingly well, in fact,' I replied, 'Dr Verner has expressed no opposition to the sum I have requested, although I confess it seems to me far too high.'

'Then you should raise it. I am certain the doctor's capital is as good as his name.'

I considered Holmes's curious recommendation as the maid entered, bearing a tray of coffee things. I hastily rearranged my dressing gown as she placed the tray on the desk beside Holmes.

'Why, thank you, Megan,' said Holmes, charmingly. Although I never knew him to have close relationships with females, he appeared to exude a certain allure when he chose. 'And perhaps a cup for the doctor?'

The maid curtsied and left the room, not to be seen again for the remainder of the morning.

'It's a strange thing,' I remarked as Holmes poured his cup of coffee and I pondered the furnishings, 'but my practice has been all that I have existed for during these past few years, but in a matter of weeks I shall be abandoning it utterly.'

'I am very glad of it,' Holmes said, after taking a tentative sip. 'I did not rise from the dead, so to speak, in order to resume a solitary existence.'

I did not pursue the point, but Holmes's remark addressed a problem that had been troubling me of late; why, having returned to London to orchestrate the capture of Colonel Sebastian Moran, had he elected to remain? More than once had he told me that he considered that his career would be over following the arrest and execution of Professor Moriarty. But the so-called Napoleon of Crime had been dead these three years, and yet here was Sherlock Holmes, back in his Baker Street lodgings of old and on the brink of resuming his career as a consulting detective. Looking back, I imagine that I shied away from the subject out of a fear that he might simply vanish again, leaving my life in even greater chaos. Instead, I asked whether he had yet accepted any cases.

'I regret to say that the level of public interest has been somewhat disappointing. The natural cynicism of the Londoner, I suspect, leads him to believe that reports of my return to life have been greatly exaggerated. However, I have hopes, my boy. Why, only yesterday, I turned away a representative of the San Pedro government. You recall San Pedro, I trust?'

'I should say that I do, and with good reason. Who could forget the brutal crimes committed by Henderson, alias ex-president Murillo, "The Tiger of San Pedro", at Wisteria Lodge? The country is doing so well without him, I hear, that I am considering making a small investment in its future.'

'You interest me exceedingly, Watson, please tell me more. Oh, before you proceed, I should inform you that the phrase "The Tiger of San Pedro" has fallen out of favour in his home country, where the preferred term is now, I understand, "The Hanging Tyrant".

I continued, 'I have been advised by a chap at my club that there is money to be made from the San Pedro tin mining industry. He assures me that with sufficient backing from the state as well as a few discriminating investors, San Pedro could become the largest manufacturer of tin in the western world.'

'Excellent, Watson. I'll make you my handy guide to the stock market should the need arise. But will the profits from your sale of the practice not be sufficient for your simple wants?'

'One must have money in order to make money, Holmes,' I informed him, perhaps a little more brusquely than was necessary. 'The first rule of commerce.'

'I consider myself instructed. But Mr Santini – that was my visitor's name – called upon me regarding a matter of greater moment than the tin mining business.'

'And yet you say you sent him away?'

'I distrusted him from the start. This is excellent coffee, by the way, old fellow.' He drained his cup and replaced it on the saucer.

'I am delighted to hear it. Was it some deduction you made based on his appearance that caused you to distrust him?'

'That was just the point, Watson. For the very first time in my career, I have met a man about whom I could reach no conclusions whatsoever. His clothes were neat enough and expensive enough, but there were no identifying features about them, no traces of the wearer's individuality. This Santini was a study in practised anonymity. There is no doubt, however, that he is exactly what he says he is, an agent of the San Pedro government, but I regret to say that I was able to ascertain this fact only by communicating with my brother Mycroft at his Whitehall office. I certainly hope that my talent for observation and inference has not deserted me during my travels; the day may yet come when I am forced to go through a client's pockets in order to form any conclusions about him.'

'Never, Holmes,' I reassured him.

'You are kind to say so, Watson. For much of the interview, Santini alternated between an ingratiating cherubic grin and an aspect of funereal seriousness that I must admit I found almost comical. It was with the former expression that he sang my praises.

' "Mr Holmes," he began, "may I say what a sincere pleasure it is to shake hands with the man who defied the Hanging Tyrant himself, Don Juan Murillo."

' "My part in the affair was a very small one, Mr Santini, and I cannot say that I was at all satisfied with the outcome," I replied.

' "But all has worked out for the best. Indeed, I am proud to say that I was one of the crowd who cheered so enthusiastically that glorious day when the brown and yellow flag of the old San Pedro was taken down from the palace roof and replaced with the green and white flag of the new, democratic San Pedro. An inspiring day, Mr Holmes. Like so many, I believed that following Murillo's death – no doubt the result of a falling-out with his confederates – my homeland would be forever free of his tyranny."

' "But something has happened to change all that," I suggested.

' "I have received certain disquieting information from San Pedro that could put at risk all that we struggled so hard and for so long to achieve." As he spoke, Watson, the benevolence all but disappeared from Santini's face, and he adopted an air of excessive solemnity in his attempt to convey to me the seriousness of the situation. "It seems that, during his time in your country, the Hanging Tyrant dictated his memoirs to his secretary Lopez, the man you knew as Lucas."

' "I knew him not at all, Mr Santini. I am sorry to say that both Lopez and his master escaped not only my clutches, but also those of the very capable Inspector Baynes." '

Holmes broke off from his reminiscence and turned to face me. 'By the way, Watson, do you know anything of Murillo's death?'

I felt somewhat ashamed at this unexpected question, like a disobedient schoolboy, for in all the uproar following Holmes's return to London, I had completely forgotten to tell him what I had learned of the outcome of our adventure. I began to feel even more physical discomfort than before as I explained: 'Inspector Baynes wrote to me about it,' I replied. 'It happened in Madrid, about six months after you . . . about six months after. Murillo and Lopez were both discovered stabbed in their rooms at the Hotel Escurial. Definitely *not* the result of a falling out, Baynes says. Knowing your high regard for the fellow's gifts, I feel certain that you would have agreed with his conclusions.'

Holmes mulled over this new information for a short while before reacting. 'A most unsatisfactory ending for your readers, Watson.'

'I may make a few changes if I ever decide to write it up.' He gave me his most disapproving gaze, which he usually reserved for discussions concerning my literary ventures. 'You said yourself that I would not be able to relate the affair in my usual style.'

'Did I? Hm. I do not recall. How is Baynes, by the way?'

'I regret to say that he has not been as successful in his career as you predicted. He is working in Sheffield at the moment, I believe, but he still has hopes of one day receiving his transfer to Scotland Yard.'

Holmes shook his head, regretfully. 'He will not get it. The Yard is fearful of his imagination and intelligence. It is their way, and I am saddened to learn that it has not altered these last three years. But to return to my story, I pressed Santini for details regarding these memoirs of which he spoke.

' "It is understood that within this valuable document, which has yet to be located, the cursed Murillo has named several members of the current government who are loyal to his cause."

' "And you wish me to trace it for you?" I began to rummage in my dressing gown for my black clay pipe as I spoke, for I was beginning to lose my enthusiasm for this interview. "I have been away from polite society for several years, Mr Santini, but it seems to me that this is hardly a matter of the greatest moment – "

' "*But it is!*" he cried. And I must confess, Watson that so taken aback was I by the unexpected ferocity of his interruption that I dropped the pipe, which then rolled beneath my chair. "The future of San Pedro rests on the recovery of the – of those papers." As suddenly as it had arrived, the storm subsided and he returned to his beatific persona of a few moments earlier. He brushed an imaginary speck of dirt from his trousers and resumed in a calmer tone. "Should any of these men choose to follow his path, San Pedro could once again find herself under the thrall of a second Murillo. As long as they hold positions of power and influence, they are a threat to democracy. They have no place in our government or in our country, to say nothing of this life and the next. I hope I make my position clear, Mr Holmes?"

' "Abundantly, Mr Santini," I replied, hoping that my sense of unease could not be detected in my speech. I decided that it would make a poor impression were I to attempt to retrieve my pipe at that moment. "But surely the . . . friends of democracy had an agent within the Murillo household. Could not she tell you where the papers are to be found?"

' "Regrettably, *Signora* Durando entered the employment of Mr Henderson – as he was then known – after the notes had been dictated. She dared not pursue the matter, for her position as governess was a tenuous one at best. It took a great deal of persuasion to induce Miss Stoper to place a governess of limited accomplishments with such an affluent family."

'I did not say so at that moment, of course, but it occurred to me that the accomplishments of the woman we knew as Miss Burnett were truly remarkable in areas other than the purely educational. Not only did she operate as a spy in an enemy's territory, she also planned and played a part in two assassination attempts, the latter successful. I think that, knowing what we do now, we may place the responsibility for the deaths of Murillo and Lopez squarely at her door.'

'I think that she would even feel gratified were she to hear you say so,' I suggested.

'Phaedrus puts it best, I think – *Saepe intereunt aliis meditantes necem.*'

'I believe the Chinese have a similar saying about digging two graves,' I offered, not wishing to be left behind.

Holmes chuckled. 'I see we still have much to teach one another, Watson. That is very good. Well, Santini went on to clarify the situation for me.

' "I have been assured by the associates of Miss Burnett," he said, "that these treasured papers were not stored at High Gable or anywhere in the vicinity. They have been quite thorough on this point. However, there is a limit to how far they can operate effectively in a country not their own, and, despite their zeal, they lack the skill of the seasoned investigator. All that is required of you, Mr Holmes, is to trace Murillo's movements in England in the period before he was identified under his alias of Henderson, and then to clarify where the manuscript is hidden. You will then advise me of the fact, and I shall make appropriate arrangements for its recovery. I would also appreciate a detailed accounting of your expenses."

' "You go too fast, sir," I interjected, raising my hand in a placating gesture. "This is a matter in which – to employ the term favoured by an associate – the old hound is the best. I am hardly the most suitable agent to act on your behalf in this business. There are few of the opportunities for logical deduction that I require in order to hold my attention."

'Santini appeared more aghast than infuriated by my refusal. "But, Mr Holmes. I assumed that as a friend of democracy – "

' "As a friend of democracy, sir, I advise you to seek assistance elsewhere. Here in London we have lots of Government detectives and lots of private ones. I even understand that I am no longer the only unofficial consulting detective. Indeed, you might do a good deal worse than to employ a young man named Frederick Darnay, who has studied my methods quite closely. I am certain that he would be better suited to the task. Who knows, he might even provide you with a detailed accounting of his expenses. Now, if you will excuse me, before your arrival I was in the process of organising my files, which, I am sorry to say, have got quite out of order in my absence. Good-day to you, sir."

'I am uncertain whether or not I am acting rashly, Watson, but we must all make sacrifices for our art, and that is mine.'

'And it sounded so promising!' I groaned.

'Bah! The mere show of detective work. Where are the features of uniqueness upon which I pride myself?'

'But have you not said yourself that some of your most interesting cases have arisen from the observation of trifles?'

My irrational annoyance at Holmes's cavalier attitude must have been evident either in my manner, for his reply was in the calm and measured tone one might employ with a fractious child. 'I am not retained by the San Pedro secret police to supply their deficiencies, Watson. For all its implications of international intrigue, this is so transparent an affair even a Scotland Yard official could clear it up. I would be happy to pour you the remainder of the coffee, Watson, but I am afraid that it has gone cold in the pot. There is only one small mystery provided by the encounter, and that is why Mr Santini should presume to lie to me.'

'To lie?'

'I found his story of the Hanging Tyrant's memoirs improbable on two counts. I may be out of touch with modern political practice, but it seems peculiar to me that the discovery of the existence of a list of potential traitors made in San Pedro should not lead in due course to their exposure.'

I considered the likelihood of this. 'Caesar's assassins perished after Mark Antony's speech,' I offered.

'A daring metaphor, Watson! But there is another reason for supposing Santini's claim to be a fabrication. When he became agitated at my lack of interest – a response that, I am sorry to say, I appear to provoke in others – I am certain that he came perilously close to disclosing the true nature of his mission. I have a very strong rule about permitting mystery at only one end of my cases; I would not break it for the Prime Minister and I see no reason to break it now.'

I shrugged wearily, and rose to replace the coffee things on the tray in the hope that the maid might discover them and return them to the kitchen. Holmes glanced up at what he must have assumed was a sorrowful mien.

'Do not despair, old fellow,' he said. 'I should be very surprised if we do not hear from our mysterious Mr Santini again.'

'What makes you say that, Holmes?' I asked.

'The unsettling nature of his departure. After my somewhat brusque refusal of his request, he rose slowly from his chair like an invalid. He trembled, and the action changed from one of premature frailty to barely repressed rage. He retrieved his cane, turned and held it out before him like a weapon, ramrod straight, with the iron ferrule only inches from my nose.

' "You have made a terrible mistake this day, Mr Holmes," he said, his voice quivering with fury. "You have held many lives in your hands and you have abandoned them all."

'I saw no reason to prolong the interview by responding and thereby inflaming his passions further. He left without saying another word, and I retrieved my pipe at my leisure. It seems to me that I have been threatened in those rooms many times over the years, but I promise you, Watson, that it is only through Santini's obscure words that I have experienced a genuine sense of menace. I cannot believe that too much time will pass before we discover their meaning.'

5. An unexpected development

In the course of my long and fruitful association with Mr Sherlock Holmes, I have seen rediscovered many valuable items which were believed to be lost forever. I was not, however, under the impression that the search for the missing papers of ex-President Murillo would be a simple one. Although not an enormous dwelling, Field House was certainly a sizeable property containing many rooms. A thorough search of all of them might last well into the next morning. In addition to this, I was all too aware that Holmes had chosen that moment to place his reliance on my abilities. I felt considerable pride at the thought that he believed me capable of uncovering the hiding place of these documents, and I did not wish to disillusion him by failing to locate it.

Our first port of call was the library, where I began to examine with great care the titles on the shelves. After a few minutes of silence, I became aware that Holmes, still standing in the doorway, was growing impatient.

'May I ask the point of this exercise, Watson?'

'We both know, Holmes, that secret passages are the stuff of romantic fiction. However, we have discovered more than one hidden room in our time. I need hardly remind you of the supposed murder of Mr John Douglas, I suppose? Or of the terrifying experience of Miss Grace Farrington? Or even of the horrifying incident at Arnsworth?'

'The point is well made, Watson,' Holmes snapped. 'But what has this to do with our client's choice of reading matter?'

'Well, I hoped that I might find a history of Field House here, describing the inclusion of some concealed chamber during construction.'

'And have you?'

'No.'

'Of course, in certain examples of romantic fiction, a particular book on a shelf is often merely a lever that opens a door hidden behind the bookcase.'

I reflected on this for a moment. It was certainly improbable, but by no means impossible. Of course, the way to find the correct book would surely be to identify an appropriate title. Not *The Future of the Argentine*, surely, nor *Mirror of Society*. My eyes ran across volumes including *The Clue of Crimson* and *Sport in the Rockies*, no doubt purchased by the late Mr Cartner.

'It is worth adding in this particular instance,' Holmes observed, 'that if this bookcase *were* a hidden door, it would lead only into the sitting room, which is directly behind that wall.'

I sighed, before setting my shoulders straight and adopting a determined air. 'Then I suggest we begin a room-by-room search of the premises. We will start upstairs and work our way down.'

As I had feared, the task went on for many hours, with Holmes unwilling to offer any suggestions of his own or to search without instruction. A grateful Mrs Cartner kept us provided with refreshments, but I was becoming more and more dispirited and concerned that our client's faith in us would begin to wane.

It was growing dim, and I was slumped against a wall with fatigue and frustration, when a thought suddenly struck me.

'Holmes,' I said. 'We have been fools.'

'Have we? Do go on, Watson.'

'Why have Valentine and his allies waited until this moment to approach Mrs Cartner?'

'An excellent question, Watson. One that no doubt strikes at the very heart of the matter.'

'I suggest that whatever these persons desire, the lady unknowingly brought here with her. It was not in the house prior to her arrival, rather it is secreted somewhere about the expensive furniture in the sitting room. No doubt that is why Valentine posed as an auctioneer upon his second visit, so that he might study these items.'

Holmes made no reply, from which I gathered that he was quietly impressed with my display of logic.

'There's not a moment to lose, Holmes!' I cried, feeling a sudden resurgence of my original enthusiasm. 'The game's afoot!'

The thrill of the hunt had quite revived me, and I now understood what it meant to Holmes to be hot on the scent.

But, alas, it proved not to be so. Despite a quite thorough examination of all the items in the sitting room – performed under the watchful eye of Peter, who was determined to see that none of his mistress's property was in any way marked or damaged – the papers were not unearthed. I was quite disconsolate, unable to see where my deductions had been at fault. To make matters worse, Mrs Cartner – who by this stage insisted that I refer to her as Violet – had been present at what I hoped would be my triumphant moment. She hid her disappointment skilfully, which only made my shame greater. Holmes was of little help, suggesting only that he and I should retreat to a nearby inn for the night and approach the problem afresh in the morning.

'Contrary to Dr Watson's exercises in romantic fiction, matters are not always quite so easily worked out,' he advised our client. Violet Cartner nodded in reply and wished us both a restful night.

I was extremely glad that Holmes could not be persuaded to remain in Field House for I do not think I could have continued to look into the lady's eyes, imagining that I could see in them intense disillusionment.

As we sat over a meal at *The Dutch Masters*, Holmes seemed suddenly to become aware of my gloomy disposition.

'Do not be so downhearted, old friend. I am certain that events will reach a satisfactory conclusion in time for me to make my appointment in Bedfordshire tomorrow. Now that we are on the case, Valentine and his compatriots can have no more interest in Field House. We will have ample time to clear this business up.'

The night I spent in my room at the hostelry was, if anything, worse than the last night spent under my own roof in Kensington. Had it really only been a day ago? So much had gone amiss in that time. I had wished to prove to Sherlock Holmes that my contribution to our partnership might be a valuable one, but instead there had been some flaw in my chain of reasoning, and try as I might, I could not identify it. In the early hours, I had quite made up my mind that I would inform Holmes that I would not, after all, be joining him at Baker Street. It was clear to me, at least, that I had nothing of any worth to offer in the business of criminal detection and that it would only be a matter of time before Holmes began to weary of my bungling.

At what point during these cogitations I eventually fell asleep, I am unsure, but it was light when a persistent rapping on the door awaked me.

'Watson, stir yourself! There is a trap waiting to take us to Field House. This is a matter of some urgency!'

'Holmes, is that you?' I was somewhat disoriented, expecting to awake either in my own home or at Baker Street and instead finding myself in an entirely unfamiliar room. 'What is wrong?'

'I have made a critical miscalculation, Watson. A murder has been committed in the night.'

6. A singular reunion

'Fool that I am! I felt certain that there would be no danger, tonight of all nights! What can it mean?'

These words Holmes uttered to himself, appearing to ignore my presence altogether. Thus far on our journey, Holmes had not so much as looked in my direction, preferring instead to stare straight ahead, appearing more than ever like some dark bird of prey, as though contemplating a point just beyond the horizon.

'Holmes, you still have yet to tell me who has been murdered. Is Violet safe?'

'Mrs Cartner is perfectly well, although somewhat distressed, I imagine. It was from the lady that our message originated. Why did they enter Field House at all? What was the need?'

'Then it is Peter, the footman, who is the victim. He disturbed an intruder and paid for it with his life.' Even as I spoke these words, I found them hard to believe; surely few opponents could have bested Peter in a struggle.

'Nor is it Peter.'

With a stab of guilt, I realised that I had never learned the name of Mrs Cartner's maid, for surely it must be she who lay dead. Poor child, how old could she be?

'Nineteen, I should estimate,' said Holmes, breaking in upon my thoughts. 'No, it is not the maid. The body we are to inspect upon our arrival is that of Mr Basil Valentine.'

As we alighted from the trap a representative of the local police met us. Sergeant Patchett wore a Chinese Gordon moustache that succeeded only in exaggerating his inflated features. Upon seeing us, his cheeks turned pink and he chuckled, as though amused by some private joke.

'Well, by Jove!' he cried, with a cheerfulness inappropriate to the situation. 'When Mrs Cartner said it was you, I swore it couldn't be true, but it's you, right enough. Who'd have thought – Sherlock Holmes! And I thought you were just a character in a book, and a dead character at that! I expect to dine out on this for many years to come. And you must be Dr Watson, a pleasure, sir. To think, you're neither of you figments of some feller's imagination – what a laugh!'

We exchanged uncomfortable formalities as briefly as possible, for I was anxious to examine the body and to lend support to Mrs Cartner, for whom the whole affair must have been a terrible shock.

'The lady has been telling me something of the business, Mr Holmes,' said the sergeant, reining his jollity in at last, it appeared. 'It all seems very queer to me, I must say, although I'm sure you solved it in an instant, just by lookin' at the butler's bootlaces! Haw, haw!'

'Well, I could not foresee this development, sergeant. I suppose we will never know for certain whether the regret Valentine expressed to Peter over the matter was genuine or not. Rascal though he undoubtedly was, he surely did not deserve this fate, for I do not believe he ever intended harm to the occupants of Field House. Shall we enter?'

As we passed the sitting room I observed our client being comforted by an elderly lady whom I did not recognise, but assumed to be a neighbour. For a moment, I thought of joining them. After all, we were here at the lady's request and it would not only be courteous, but also compassionate. Mary, surely, would have expected nothing less from me. I came to my senses, however, upon recollecting that our previous attempt to assist Mrs Cartner had gone very badly awry, and my incorrect assumptions coupled with Holmes's misplaced certainty that she had seen the last of Basil Valentine had led in some way to these tragic circumstances. Surely I could accomplish more at the scene of the crime. Holmes's masterful cry of 'Watson!' decided me in the matter. The sergeant led us upstairs, bestowing upon us as he did his opinions of Holmes's former cases as though they were nothing more than works of fiction.

'I'm bursting to know how you got out of that dreadful chasm,' he said, 'but whatever you do, don't tell me. I shall enjoy the surprise when I read about it. Body's just along here, gentlemen.'

The weak ray of sunlight emanating from the window at the end of the passage stopped just short of the dark figure sprawled before of us. An hour or so earlier, and he might have been discovered only if one happened to trip over his inert form. Although laid on his chest, Valentine's head was twisted to one side; clearly, Peter had not needed to move the body in order to recognise him from their encounter days before in the bar room of *The Dutch Masters*. He had been a young man, by my estimation not quite thirty. In profile, I recognised the expression I have seen all too often when examining those to whom death has come suddenly: utter disbelief that life had chosen that particular moment in which to cease.

'I'm sure you won't consider it a slight, Mr Holmes,' said the voluble policeman, 'but as soon as I heard this strange story from Mrs Cartner's lips, I instructed the constable to send a wire to Scotland Yard. Perhaps we'll have Inspector Lestrade on the case with us as well.'

'Inspector Lestrade has duties elsewhere at the moment,' Holmes responded, flatly.

'I am certain, however, that the three of us will be able to arrange matters to Mrs Cartner's satisfaction.' I added, feeling an unnecessary resentment toward the officer.

'I'm sure we will, doctor,' Patchett replied, with some hesitation. 'First person to find the dead man was the footman, feller by the name of Peter Tierney. 'Least, I think that's what his name is, I could be wrong.'

The dark clothing worn by Valentine I recognised as the sort favoured by the many burglars and cracksmen I had encountered over the many years of my Baker Street residence. Not black, which Holmes informs is easily detectable even in darkness, but a deep shade of blue. I could tell immediately from the position of the limbs that the man had suffered convulsions in his final moments. As I crouched to get a closer look at the body, the reason became plain.

'A knife has been inserted in the back of the neck, just below the skull. The blade probably pierced the brain. In fact . . . ' Gently, with my fingers I probed the wound.

'Careful, doctor,' said the sergeant, warily.

'It's quite all right,' I assured him. 'Yes, a small piece of the blade broke off upon extraction – no doubt chipped against the skull. Here you are, sergeant. Find a knife with a missing tip to match this fragment and you have your murderer.'

'Excellent, Watson,' said Holmes, without emotion. 'But this fellow still has one more secret to give up. Do we have your permission to turn the body over, sergeant?'

Sergeant Patchett, who appeared to be perspiring freely, nodded slowly. With Holmes's assistance, I rolled the corpse onto its back.

'Good Lord!' I exclaimed, the moment his full face became visible.

'You recognise him also, Watson?'

'I understood from the butler that this chap's name is Basil Valentine,' the sergeant offered.

'He is familiar both to Watson and to myself as Oswald Crawshay, a most adept criminal from a family of blackguards. We encountered him in '87, when he was performing as neat a piece of larceny as I have ever seen under the *alias* Hugo Fitch. His uncle – at whose knee he no doubt learned his formidable housebreaking skills – was suspected of the theft of the Melrose necklace, a problem I was never able to resolve to my complete satisfaction. Crawshay has been used and discarded by the men behind this scheme in the cruellest manner imaginable. His murder is a final, desperate gambit and the cards are in their favour. Sergeant, I leave you in charge of the body. Watson, there is nothing more to be learned here and we have an appointment to keep elsewhere.'

He leapt to his feet and took the stairs at such a pace that he was already out of sight as I rose to follow. Standing at the head of the stairs and looking down into the damp-infested hallway, I could see him no longer, but I fancied that I heard his voice emanating from the sitting room. No doubt he was apprising the unfortunate lady of how matters stood at present. Leaving the local officer appearing somewhat ill at ease, I descended and rejoined my colleague.

'Mrs Cartner,' Holmes was saying as I entered, 'I feel confident in assuring you that this entire ghastly experience will shortly be over for you. I can assure you that you are in no danger and I expect to be able to provide you with a full explanation of events by this evening.

For the moment, however, Dr Watson and I have urgent business in Bedfordshire.'

She appeared somewhat startled at this announcement. 'Bedford-shire? But that is where – '

'I know full well what is to be found in Bedfordshire, I assure you, madam. I will contact you again in due course.'

Mrs Cartner cast aside the consoling hand of her neighbour and rose from her chair. I imagined that she doubtless wore the same seriousness of expression when ejecting the late Crawshay from her premises. 'Mr Holmes, a man lies dead in my home, the victim of an act of violence. After all that has taken place here in the past week, I assure you that I have no intention of remaining here simply to await enlightenment by post.' The elderly lady opened her mouth to speak but managed only to draw breath before our client resumed. 'Mrs Lomar has been very kind in calling upon me so soon after rising from her sick bed, but you have my word, gentlemen, that I will not be satisfied until I witness the arrest of the person responsible for this horrible crime.'

Once again, the depth of this young lady's character and integrity astonished me. I am not entirely certain, but I might even have murmured 'hear, hear' under my breath. Then, remembering my manners, I gave a nod of acknowledgement to Mrs Lomar, who to my knowledge remained entirely silent during the entire discussion.

Holmes bowed his head. 'Very well, Mrs Cartner. You are in the right and I in the wrong. I agree that you have a significant stake in the outcome of this affair, and I will see that you have justice. I regret to say that you must abandon the social niceties, and take your leave of Mrs Lomar this instant, if we are to make the next train to Bedfordshire.'

An observer unacquainted with the details of our situation might – had he looked in upon us three in that railway carriage – mistakenly have believed that we had not been introduced to one another prev-iously and so now feared to strike up conversation. In truth, each of us had our own reasons for remaining silent.

Holmes insisted upon humming an unfamiliar tune, the work of a foreign composer named LaFosse, as he later informed me. Clearly he did not wish to speak of what might await us at our destination and I knew him well enough to realise that it would be pointless to attempt to draw him out upon the subject.

Mrs Cartner had become troubled at Holmes's mention of Bed-fordshire and could not be drawn into conversation either. Evidently, there existed some personal association with this area, although I could not imagine what it might be, and she was clearly attempting determine the significance of this connection.

For my part, I feared to speak, lest I embarrass myself further. I had been guilty of misplaced pride in imagining that I had arrived at the correct solution, but I no longer had any understanding of recent events, let alone whether there indeed existed a link between the plottings of the late Oswald Crawshay and the missing memoirs of the Hanging Tyrant, Don Juan Murillo of San Pedro. I had faced similar discomfiture in the past and I was certain that my relationship with Holmes would survive my current disgrace – indeed, I had begun to suspect that he had been aware of the truth from the very beginning and had wished only to amuse himself by placing the case in my hands and observing how far I strayed from the truth. But Violet Cartner had shown faith in me, and I could not discard the notion that her faith had been destroyed utterly by my inaction. I felt the urge to speak to her, but I was unsure as to what might be appropriate for me to say under the circumstances.

After an almost unendurable period of silence, I had composed my thoughts sufficiently and summoned up the nerve to speak, but as I turned to address her I saw that, no doubt overcome by the strain of recent events, she had fallen asleep. I saw no need to disturb her, and what little remained of the journey passed in almost total silence, save for Holmes's incessant humming.

We were pulling into the station when Mrs Cartner was jolted awake by my friend leaping to his feet, exclaiming: 'And here he is, waiting for us! Hello again, Mr Santini!'

7. Sherlock Holmes explains

'I must confess that I did not expect to hear from you ever again, Mr Holmes.' Santini was exactly as Holmes had described him several weeks earlier, excessively polite, immaculately dressed and apparently benign. Now, sitting opposite me in a cab bound for the nearby village of Marsden Lacey, he wore a guarded expression on his childlike features. Clearly, he had no idea what Holmes had arranged for us. I wondered whether I wore the same expression.

'First of all, may I say, Mr Santini, that I hope I am not encroaching upon the territory of a fellow investigator by contacting you in this manner.'

Santini waggled a gloved hand. 'By no means, Mr Holmes. My countrymen have continued their investigations following our . . . consultation, but regrettably, we are no closer to recovering the manuscript.'

'Is this the manuscript of which Dr Watson was telling me?' asked Mrs Cartner, the first time she had spoken since our introduction to the apparently genial foreigner.

With uncharacteristic rudeness, Holmes ignored the question. 'I must add that I know the true nature of the item – or perhaps I should say *items* – you seek.'

There was no joy in Santini's smile. 'I knew I had picked the right man when I approached you, Mr Holmes. Very well, so you know. And you know also that it changes nothing. In fact, it makes the hunt more important. Do I take it that we expect to make the recovery in this town of Marsden Lacey?'

'You may. And may I take it that you observed the precautions I suggested and have not been followed this time?'

Santini nodded. 'I still cannot believe I could ever have been so foolish. I am a slave to my arrogance, and now a man is dead, and the responsibility is mine!'

'There is one last matter to be agreed. Whatever fee you were intending to pay me I wish to be given instead to this lady, minus our expenses, which have not been inconsiderable – train fare and accommodation at a peculiarly-named inn, and payments to my colleague, Mr Darnay, for his overnight vigil on my behalf. Is that acceptable?'

The gentleman responded that it was. He appeared a little surprised but otherwise satisfied at the limited payment he would have to make.

I, however, was far from satisfied, being more in the dark than ever. Who was this fellow Darnay, what had been the nature of his vigil, and why did his name sound so familiar? 'Holmes,' I said, 'is it too much to ask that you begin to explain yourself? Have you identified the person behind this tangled web of events?'

'I have. In fact, that person is at this moment present in this coach. Please, Mr Santini, Mrs Cartner, do not glower at one another. I do not refer to either one of you but to my good friend Dr Watson. Incidentally, Watson, I apologise for any remarks of an unfavourable nature I might have made in the past concerning your accounts of my doings. But for them, this fascinating problem might never have been conceived.'

I was, for a moment, dumbstruck. Then, aware that my companions were considering me in a new light, possibly as some sort of master criminal, I spat out: 'But in what way has all this to do with me?'

'If my investigations were not public knowledge thanks to your arrangement with the editors of *The Strand* magazine, it would have been exceedingly difficult for Crawshay, *alias* Valentine, to persuade Mrs Cartner to employ my services.'

'This is the man you say has been killed, Mr Holmes?' asked Santini.

'Please, Mr Santini, do not interrupt a lady. Mrs Cartner, you were about to speak.'

'I was about to point out, Mr Holmes, that Mr Valentine did *not* persuade me to contact you. He never even mentioned your name.' I recognised the serious demeanour the lady had exhibited when remonstrating with my friend a few short hours earlier.

'No madam, he did not. But you told us that you had the notion to write to me after his original visit to your home. His deliberately improbable story was, of course, a blind. But his true purpose lay in the deliberate inaccuracies, which included references to "Baker" – my address – and a brother named John who had been wounded in Afghanistan, clearly intended to suggest my friend and colleague Dr John H. Watson. He all but told you to seek my guidance, Mrs Cartner.'

'Coincidence, surely?' I protested.

'You remember, Watson, my asking whether you considered Valentine's dating error of any significance? How many years ago did he claim Kelley obtained the miraculous red powder?'

I racked my brains. I began to see dimly what he was hinting at. 'Two hundred and twenty one!' I exclaimed.

'Precisely. Valentine planted a highly ingenious trail, intended to direct you to my very door, Mrs Cartner. Were he still alive, I should congratulate him on a commendably subtle approach, intended to appeal to a part of your mind you did not even know existed.'

'I believe that I have read something of the matter in a medical journal: a German doctor writing about what he referred to as the *un*conscious.'

Holmes smiled condescendingly. 'There is very little that gets past Watson,' he advised our fellow passengers.

'But for heaven's sake, Holmes, why should he wish you to become involved?' I persisted.

'Dear me, things are getting a little confusing, are they not? Perhaps it would be best if I recounted the events in their proper order.

Some two weeks ago, Mr Santini requested my assistance in a matter of location and recovery. Unbeknownst to him, however, his adversaries were keeping watch and had followed him to my Baker Street rooms. They too, you see, were in pursuit of the same goal for a quite different purpose. When it was realised that Santini was – as far as they were aware – employing the services of a renowned consulting detective, they decided to take whatever action they could to delay me for as long as possible. They were quite far along with their own enquiries, and had already ascertained that what they were looking for had been hidden in a property owned by the late Mr Francis Cartner for letting purposes, and unoccupied since his death. That property is to be found in the town of Marsden Lacey in the county of Bedfordshire.'

'The other house,' Mrs Cartner almost gasped.

'Of course, these persons could not know that I had in fact refused Mr Santini's case. Believing that I was engaged to act on his behalf, it seemed to them only a matter of time before I followed the trail to Bedfordshire. Wishing to throw me off the scent, the criminals formulated a desperate plan. They obtained the assistance of a gifted criminal practitioner named Oswald Crawshay who – in the guise of Basil Valentine, Professor of Arcane Antiquities – proceeded to relate to Mrs Cartner a tale even more improbable than your own, Mr Santini.'

Santini shifted uneasily in his seat.

'It was immediately obvious to me that the sole purpose of his implausible story was to convince me that these villains expected to find their objective hidden somewhere in Field House, and not in the second property, which I am advised by your valet Peter, is known as Croftlands. The further acts of annoyance you experienced were intended merely to encourage you to bring me into the affair, hence the pantomime with the deliberately overturned sundial, Watson. All these intrusions occurred during the day so that we might be put off our guard at night, when they had already decided Valentine was to be murdered. My one regret in this case is that I did not foresee that element of their plan. You see, once I had arrived on the scene they had no further use for him. They wished only to delay me, to have me waste as much time as possible at Field House, thus providing them with more time to search Croftlands. The killing of Valentine was simply another element, calculated to confound and impede. Please forgive our elaborate charade yesterday, madam, but it seemed most likely that we were being watched – as proved to be the case – so it was necessary that we made a show of it for at least a day. Dr Watson, knowing that my heart was not really in the enterprise, generously offered to direct our elaborate performance.'

I might have congratulated Holmes for as brilliant a display of logical deduction as I had ever seen had I not been infuriated by his casual maltreatment. I felt aggrieved, and was on the brink of saying so.

'Congratulations, doctor,' said Violet, warmly. 'You had me quite fooled.'

I smiled foolishly, aware that Mrs Cartner was now considering me with something close to admiration.

'And all this time,' said Santini, excitedly, 'Hector Miras and his confederates have been free to locate the – '

'Hector Miras, eh?' Holmes interrupted. 'Former Ambassador for the government of Don Juan Murillo and, my brother advises me, missing since the coup. I had a suspicion he might be behind all this. To allay your fears, Mr Santini, as well as instructing Mrs Cartner's manservant to issue a telegram to Scotland Yard requesting the presence of Inspector Lestrade and several local constables at Croftlands when we arrived, I also contacted one Frederick Darnay, a promising student of my methods. He has been watching Croftlands all this time and would have contacted me the instant anything of note occurred. You would have done well to engage him as I advised you. And now I see that we are close to our destination. Mrs Cartner, I must insist that – halloa, what the blazes is going on?'

Holmes leaned far out of the cab window, and I feared that he would fall beneath its wheels. I could see nothing from the opposite window, and my attempts to adjust my position in the hope of getting a better view were hampered by Santini pulling on my coat-tails in a frantic effort to make me give up my place. I attempted to swat him away with my free hand, and I can only imagine what Mrs Cartner's opinion of this spectacle must have been. There was certainly some commotion up ahead, but the cries of anger I heard made no sense to me whatsoever.

Mercifully, the cab halted at that moment, and Holmes wasted no time in jumping out and haring off. I extricated myself from Santini's grasp, advised our fair client to remain where she was for safety's sake, and followed in my friend's wake. As I alighted, I narrowly avoided being run over by a carriage heading in the opposite direction. I flattened myself against our cab, and, as the other vehicle passed, I was aware of its occupants apparently hurling themselves against the windowless walls and cursing in some foreign language.

It was not until the carriage had passed that I observed the metal bars on the door and a pair of small hands attempting determinedly to pull them loose.

Turning, I had very little time to take in the details of Croftlands, save to note that in size and shape it might almost have been a mirror image of Field House; the ivy clinging to the front of this building seemed a touch more alive than that attached to its twin, and rows of large and ill-kept conifers fronted the gardens. My attention was swiftly focused upon the heated argument taking place in the drive-way between Sherlock Holmes and a stout police official I had no difficulty in recognising immediately.

'Inspector Bradstreet!' I cried. 'You are the very last man I expected to see.'

Bradstreet was visibly irritated by my friend's reaction to the arrest he had clearly just made. 'Dr Watson,' he said, 'I hope that you too are not going to take me to task over my actions today also. In thirty-two years on the Force I have never heard such a thing, to allow an act of burglary to go unpunished.'

A young bespectacled man, slightly built and sporting a brown Derby, approached, his hands outstretched in an apologetic pose. He could be none other than Holmes's protégée, Frederick Darnay, 'I couldn't stop him, Mr Holmes,' he said. 'I told him your instructions, I told them all . . . '

'A fine business, when some young pup thinks that he can order a Scotland Yard inspector around. In thirty-two years on the force I never heard such a thing, doctor.'

'You need not reproach yourself, Darnay, you have done everything that was asked of you,' Holmes responded, ignoring Bradstreet's outburst. 'Now go home and get some rest. I specifically asked for Lestrade's assistance on this case. At least he knows how to take instruction. Where in Heaven's name is he?'

'In Pangbourne,' Bradstreet replied. 'He got word of a murder there early this morning. Asked me to take over here.'

'Confound the man!' Holmes cursed.

It seemed to me preposterous that we should be engaged in a fierce quarrel in such pleasant surroundings, with the warm sun beating down upon us as it had the day before. I shook my head in bewilderment, and realised that Santini and Mrs Cartner, having ignored my instructions, were now standing on either side of me.

'I must say, Mr Holmes, I had no qualms about taking these men into custody the instant I saw what they were up to. They were a vicious lot, and I'm glad we didn't waste a moment. One of them gave Sergeant Crumley a very nasty cut on the arm with this.' From one of the pockets of his frogged jacket, Bradstreet extracted a bloody knife with a broken tip. I snatched it from his grip.

'Thank you, inspector,' I said. 'One of your colleagues in Pangbourne will be glad to get his hands on this.'

Bradstreet appeared somewhat bewildered by this, and Holmes took the opportunity to set upon him again. 'The plan was not that those devils be allowed to escape, Inspector, but that they should lead us to our objective. Your impatience may have caused us many days of hard work.'

'I don't know anything about any "objective", Mr Holmes. All I know is that some bloodthirsty foreign swine attacked one of my sergeants with a knife, and behind bars is the best place for 'em.'

'We are just wasting more time!' wailed Santini. 'We must begin searching now!'

Bradstreet noticed our companion for the first time. 'Why, you look like you might be one of them!' he snarled.

'Steady, Inspector,' I advised. 'Mr Santini is a client – of sorts – and he has a vested interest in uncovering whatever is hidden in that house. I suggest that from now on we direct all our attentions to that problem. Does that arrangement suit you, Holmes? Inspector?'

'I appreciate your agreeing to remain with us, Bradstreet,' said Holmes, who had regained his composure by this time. 'It would be best if an official witness were on hand to prevent any ill-considered actions.' Here he looked pointedly at Santini, who was preoccupied contemplating his surroundings.

The hallway of Croftlands was somewhat larger than that of Field House, and I assumed that Mrs Cartner had no hand in its decor, which I considered in hideous taste. Even from this limited vantage point, it was clear that Hector Miras and his associates had wreaked havoc throughout the house; paintings were pulled from the walls, sliced to bits and their frames smashed, every item of furniture lay in pieces, even the banister had been pulled to the ground and apparently cut up with a saw. Mrs Cartner said nothing. Her mouth remained open, as though on the point of emitting an expression of horror, but she seemed unable even to do this. I placed her hand within mine, but if she even noticed the gesture, she gave no indication. Clearly, Croftland's most recent occupants had had a good deal of time in which to conduct their search, and they had been quite thorough. I wondered whether Sherlock Holmes might fare any better.

'Well, Mr Holmes,' said Bradstreet, rubbing his large hands together, 'it seems pretty clear to me that we are looking for something that has been secreted somewhere in this house. From the outside, I imagine there must be a dozen rooms at least.'

'Fifteen, if memory serves, Inspector,' volunteered our client.

'Where do you suggest we begin?'

Holmes's eyes shone with the amused exultation he reserved for his moments of greatest confidence.

'I believe that we should begin with a question for the owner of Croftlands. Mrs Cartner, this building appears slightly larger than Field House and is – save for the damage done by your knife-wielding tenants – in no better or worse state of repair to my eye. Why then did you favour one house over the other?'

Demurely, the lady replied: 'A woman's whim, Mr Holmes. The truth is, I detested the wallpaper here and I had not the money to redecorate. Normally, I have no objection to the colour yellow, but the addition of brown stripes I find quite – '

'Hideous?' I suggested.

'Just so, Doctor.' Mrs Cartner graced me with an attractive smile and disengaged her hand from my grasp.

'Was the house always decorated so?'

Santini began to protest about the relevance of this line of questioning, but Holmes silenced him with a raised palm.

'I could not say, Mr Holmes. Mr Sawyer always took care of such matters.'

On his haunches, Holmes began to run his fingers over the paper. We three watched in silence for a good minute before the detective spoke.

'Tell me, Mr Santini,' he asked, 'what are the colours of the San Pedro flag?'

'Why, green and white of course, as any schoolboy knows.'

'And before the ousting of President Murillo?'

'As I have told you, Mr Holmes, brown and yellow – '

Santini came to an abrupt halt. As one, we considered the wallpaper as though it had somehow changed before our eyes. Then, the foreign diplomat hurried to Holmes's side, attempting to gain some purchase at the very edge of the decoration.

'Carefully, if you please, sir,' said Holmes, calmly. 'My client's reward is at stake.'

Both men rose, pulling the paper away from the wall slowly. As it fell before me, I observed attached to its reverse side, several dozen pieces of paper. They were slightly smaller than the English equivalent and the print colour was a deep red, but there was no mistaking the fact that these were bank notes of a high denomination.

'The missing San Pedro treasury,' explained Sherlock Holmes.

'Murillo absconded with it, leaving his country virtually bankrupt. Bradstreet, would you be so kind as to assist Mr Santini in the recovery of this treasure trove? Judging by the extensive use of this paper, there would appear to be a good deal of it.'

'Good Lord!' I cried. 'Holmes, when did you deduce that this is what Santini was truly searching for?'

'You will remember, Watson, that I had suspected he was not in earnest when he called wishing to consult me. But I confess that the truth of the matter did not become plain until Mrs Cartner related Valentine's preposterous tale. Where he had purposely laid hints in his speech, calculated to cause Mrs Cartner to involve me in her largely fictional predicament, Santini did so accidentally, sprinkling his address with words related to financial worth – "valuable", "treasured", and so on. Try as he might, he could not discipline himself sufficiently to expunge all thoughts of the stolen treasury from his mind. In fact, he so far forgot himself at one point as to describe the object of his search as "the notes" – bank notes, in fact, which Murillo stole from his country and stored in this house during the brief period in which he rented it from the representative of the late Mr Cartner. I doubt Santini or his countrymen would find anything remotely amusing in the notion that one of the Hanging Tyrant's final acts should be that of *paper* hanging.'

'But could not the new San Pedro government simply print more money?'

'Which would then become next to worthless if Murillo's hoard ever came to light. The Stockholm Banco caused financial disaster for Sweden in the Seventeenth Century by issuing too many notes. The same problem occurred in France less than fifty years later. Why take such a risk when all that is required is to identify the location of Murillo's reserve? It is certainly more ingenious than a buried chest, and I suppose that we should congratulate him for that. The money is needed desperately in San Pedro. I am advised by a financial expert of my acquaintance that if the promising San Pedro tin mining industry is to succeed, it will require the assistance of the government, as well as a few discriminating investors.'

'And one must have money in order to make money,' I reminded him.

'So I am told. There is, of course, one exception: our client. She has no money at present and yet, if the exchange rate with the San Pedro dollar is good, she will doubtless change from a needy widow to one of the richest heiresses in the country.'

I considered this beautiful young woman as she stood silently watching Bradstreet and Santini frantically tearing the paper from the walls and extracting large handfuls of banknotes. If I had spoken to her at that moment, I do not believe that she would have heard me.

'Really, Watson,' snapped Holmes, 'don't tell me that you were considering making a chivalrous gesture?'

'Do not be absurd, Holmes,' I replied, grimly. 'There will never be a second Mrs Watson.'

'I am delighted to hear it. I did not rise from the dead, so to speak, in order to resume a solitary existence. And now, since no one here will notice our departure, we should return to Baker Street at once. I believe you have some unpacking to do, old fellow.'

The North Walk Mystery

DENIS O. SMITH

Violent murder will always excite both horror and fascination in the public mind. When the victim of the crime is a well-known public figure, the case becomes a sensation, and leaves little space in the newspapers of the day for any other subject. Such was the mysterious death of Sir Gilbert Cheshire Q.C, senior bencher of the Inner Temple and the most eminent criminal lawyer of his day. But the matter never came to trial, and those involved were reluctant to discuss it, so that despite the many newspaper columns devoted to it at the time, and the countless number of articles written since, there are some facts in connection with the case which have never been fully reported, and I have even seen it described as an 'unsolved mystery'. Having been privileged to be present during the investigation of the crime, I can state categorically that this description is false, and it is my hope that the following account will clear the matter up once and for all.

It was a dark evening, late in the year. The morning had provided a brief glimpse of watery sunshine, but the weather had taken a turn for the worse about lunch-time, and a dense fog had rolled across the city, filling every street and alleyway with its thick, greasy coils. I was glad on such an evening to be in the warm seclusion of our sitting room, where a fire blazed merrily in the grate.

Sherlock Holmes had been seated at the table for several hours, occupied in pasting newspaper extracts into his commonplace books, and carefully cross-indexing each entry. Eventually, as the clock was striking nine, he put down his pasting-brush with a weary sigh, stood up from the table and stretched himself.

'So,' said he after a moment, turning to me, as he rubbed his hands together before the fire; 'you have seen your friend, Anstruther, and he has told you that he is postponing his holiday until the spring.'

'He hopes for better weather then,' I replied. 'But I do not recall mentioning the matter to you, Holmes.'

'Indeed you did not, Watson, but it is clear, nevertheless.'

'I cannot imagine how that can be, for he only informed me of his decision this afternoon; unless, of course, you heard it from someone else.'

Holmes chuckled. 'I have not left these rooms all day,' said he. 'Fortunately, the materials for a simple little deduction lie conveniently upon the table by your elbow.'

I glanced at the table. An empty glass, a saucer, my pipe and a book I had been reading were all I could see there. My face must have betrayed the puzzlement I felt, for my friend chuckled anew.

'In the saucer is the end of a cigar,' said he, 'and by the side of it lies your old copy of Clarendon's *History of the Great Rebellion*. To anyone familiar with your habits, the inference is plain.'

'I cannot see it.'

'No? You went out at lunch-time, and returned a while later, smoking a Havana cigar. You do not generally permit yourself such extravagance, save on your visits to the American Bar at the Criterion, and you do not frequent the Criterion these days, save to meet your friend, Anstruther. I therefore feel on reasonably safe ground in inferring that such was your occupation this lunch-time. You mentioned to me some time ago that he had received an invitation to stay with relations of his near Hastings, either later this month, or in the spring, and you had agreed that, in that event, you would attend to his medical duties for a week, as you did for a few days earlier this year. Today is the twenty-sixth: the last week-end of the month is almost upon us, and thus the last likely opportunity for Anstruther to begin his holiday. When you returned today, however, you gave no sign of any impending change in your circumstances, nor of any preparations for imminent medical duties. Unlike the previous occasion when Anstruther called upon your professional assistance, you did not immerse yourself in your old medical text-books, but in your old friend, Clarendon, in whose company you proceeded to fall asleep. I could only conclude, then, that your assistance was not, for the present, required, and that Anstruther had postponed his visit to the Sussex coast until the spring.'

'How perfectly obvious!' said I. 'I believe I was still half asleep when you spoke to me, Holmes; otherwise I am sure I should not have found your remark so surprising.'

'No doubt,' said he, sounding a little irritated. 'If so, you are not alone. One might suppose the whole of London to be half asleep, so few have been the calls upon my time in recent days! It is certainly a dull, stale and unprofitable life we lead at present!' He stepped to the window and drew aside the curtain. Filthy brown drops glistened on the outside of the window-pane. 'See, Watson, how the fog creeps about the houses and smothers the street lamps! What opportunity for criminal pursuits such conditions present! What a lacklustre crew our modern criminals must be if they fail to take advantage of it!'

'I doubt if your professional appreciation of the opportunities would be shared by many of your fellow citizens!' I had responded with a chuckle, when he held up his hand.

'Here is someone, and in a tearing hurry, too,' said he sharply, as the muffled clatter of hooves came to my ears. 'Perhaps our services will be required at last. Yes, by George!' he cried, as the cab rattled to a halt outside our door. 'But, wait! The cab is empty! Ah, the jarvey himself springs down, with a letter in his hand! Your boots and your heaviest overcoat, Watson! Unless I am much mistaken, villainy has at last shaken off its torpor and walks abroad in the fog!'

There came a sharp ring at the doorbell as he spoke, and moments later the landlady brought in a letter addressed to Sherlock Holmes. He tore open the buff envelope, and a moment later passed me the single sheet it had contained, on which I read the following:

Come at once if at all possible. North Walk, Inner Temple. Most savage and puzzling crime. – D. STODDARD

'No reply, Mrs Hudson,' said Holmes in response to the landlady's query. 'We shall take the cab which brought the note.'

A moment later we were ready to leave, when my friend stopped abruptly in the open doorway of our room and stepped back quickly to the long shelf which held the reference volumes he had compiled over the years. He selected a volume, thumbed through it for a few moments, then tossed it aside and took down another. He turned the pages over rapidly, until with a cry of satisfaction he brought the book across to show me.

'Look at this, Watson! It is as I thought!' said he, pointing to a yellowing paragraph cut from the *Standard* and dated ten years previously. It was headed '**EMINENT BENCHER MURDERED IN TEMPLE**', and ran as follows:

The murder of Sir John Hawkesworth Q.C, upon the evening before last, at the North Walk Chambers, Inner Temple, seems likely to prove as perplexing as it is shocking. Sir John, one of the most senior benchers of the Inner Temple, and a man as

personally popular as he was professionally respected, was bludgeoned to death upon his own door-step, by an unknown assailant.
His door-key was still in his grasp, and it is conjectured that he
was on the point of entering his chambers when the assault took
place, which perhaps indicates that the assailant had been waiting there for him to return. This would increase the likelihood
of the criminal's presence having been witnessed, were it not
that the recent very foggy conditions which we have been experiencing make it difficult for anyone to see even those who wish
to be seen. Who the assailant is, and what the motive for such a
terrible crime might be, no-one can suggest; and we can only
hope that some clue to the matter will quickly be discovered.

'In fact, nothing ever was discovered,' Holmes remarked as I
finished reading, 'and the case remains open to this day. It was
before my own practice was established, but I recall it very well.'

Beneath the extract from the *Standard* was a second item, cut from
the *Pall Mall Gazette* of the following evening:

A correspondent, Dr J. Gibbon of South Norwood, writes to
inform us that the spot upon which the shocking murder of Sir
John Hawkesworth took place has witnessed once before the
spilling of blood. Almost six hundred years ago, on a similarly
foggy night in 1285, when the property was still in the hands of
the Knights Templars from whom the area takes its name, one
Edmund of Essex was found fatally stabbed in the North Walk.
Officially, the crime remained a mystery, and the spot upon
which it occurred was said to have been cursed since ancient
times; although most modern authorities concur in regarding the
Grand Commander of the Order himself as responsible for at
least instigating, if not indeed perpetrating the terrible deed, it
being common knowledge at the time that the two men had
quarrelled. It was the increasing frequency of such scandals
which led to a decline in the reputation of the Knights Templars,
and, eventually, to the suppression of the Order altogether, less
than thirty years later.

'The North Walk of the Inner Temple certainly has a sinister
history,' said Holmes; 'and now Stoddard reports another "savage
and puzzling crime" there! Come! Let us waste no more time!'

In a moment we were in the waiting hansom and rattling through
the fog.

'You remember Inspector Stoddard?' queried my friend, as we passed down Regent Street.

I nodded. Stoddard was one of the senior detectives of the City Police.

'I have been able to help him once or twice recently,' continued Holmes, 'and he promised, in return, to keep me informed of any interesting case which came his way. This must be a serious matter indeed, for him to call us out at this hour, and on such a night!'

In the Strand, Holmes called instructions to the driver, and we drew to a halt opposite the entrance to a narrow lane. Some distance ahead of us, a police constable stood on duty by a gateway, and before him, motionless upon the pavement, was a large group of people, forming a strange tableau in the drifting fog.

'It is murder, by the size of the crowd,' remarked Holmes as we stepped from the cab. 'Come, let us slip in this way.'

I followed him down the dark, dripping lane, where the muffled ring of our feet upon the wet cobbles was the only sound to be heard. Our route took us by narrow alleys, round abrupt and unlit corners, and through small, hidden courtyards. The fog was even denser here than elsewhere, and quite a degree colder, as it rolled across the Temple Gardens from the river, and brought the chill reek of the Thames to our nostrils. We could see scarcely five paces ahead of us, but Holmes pressed forward without pause through the murk, and I hurried after him. Though I knew we were passing among the jumble of old brick buildings which make up this ancient lawyers' quarter, so dense was the fog that save for the occasional fitful glimmer of a lamp in an upstairs window, I could make out nothing at all of our surroundings.

Abruptly Holmes turned to the left, into a narrow alleyway between two tall buildings. On the right, a door stood open wide, casting a bright rectangle of light across the dark alley.

'The North Walk,' remarked my companion.

Just inside the brightly-lit doorway stood a tall, thin man with black hair and moustache, whom I recognised as Inspector Stoddard. He was in conversation with a rough-looking man of medium build, with close-cropped ginger hair and beard. The policeman stepped forward as we approached, and greeted us warmly.

'I am very glad you were able to come,' said he, in an agitated voice. 'Sir Gilbert Cheshire has been murdered. This is Mr Thomas Mason, the gate-keeper of the Fleet Street Gate,' he continued, indicating the man by his side, 'who first brought news of the tragedy to the police station. He was also one of the last people to see Sir Gilbert alive in his chambers, when he brought in some coal at about twenty to seven, although Sir Gilbert was seen later by several of his colleagues in the dining hall, where he dined as usual between seven and eight.'

'The attack occurred on his return from dinner, then?' queried Holmes.

'Exactly. I can give you the essential details in a few sentences, Mr Holmes. That will be all for the present, Mason. I'll call you if we have any further questions. Poor fellow!' Stoddard remarked, when Mason had vanished into the fog. 'He is terribly affected by what has happened.'

'He appears an unlikely character to find in this quarter,' observed Holmes.

'There is a story there,' Stoddard responded as he led us into the building. 'He was once on trial himself, about fifteen years ago, accused of murdering his wife. He might have found himself on the gallows, but Gilbert Cheshire was the defence counsel, and got him acquitted. Since then he's been as devoted as a dog to him. It was Sir Gilbert who found him the fairly undemanding post of gate-keeper and general factotum, about eight years ago, when he was down on his luck.'

We followed the policeman into a room on the left of the hallway. All the lamps were lit, and revealed a shocking scene. In the centre of the square, book-lined room was a large desk, and behind this, in a chair, was the lifeless body of a large, broad-chested man. His head was tilted back, so that his thick, wiry black beard thrust upwards, and his eyes stared blankly at the ceiling. On the left side of his neck was a savage wound, which appeared to have bled profusely, while the front of his garments were thick with blood which was still wet and glistened in the glare of the lamps. The surface of the desk was strewn with bundles of papers, tied up with red tape. Lying amongst them was a large, brass-bound cash-box, its lid hanging open. Beyond the desk, two uniformed policemen were examining the floor by the fireplace.

Stoddard consulted his notebook. 'As you're probably aware,' he began, 'King's Bench Walk, where many of the barristers of the Inner Temple have their chambers, is just round the corner. This is the only set of chambers with its entrance on this side. Sir Gilbert Cheshire has been head of chambers for ten years, since the death of the previous head. He has two junior colleagues here, and two clerks – I have already sent messages to them all. The other two barristers share the office directly across the corridor from this one, the clerks' office is along the corridor to the rear. Upstairs, there are two rooms, Sir Gilbert's private study and his bedroom, for these chambers were also his residence.

'As far as I have been able to learn, the others all left for home at the usual time, after which Sir Gilbert was working here alone. He went over to the dining hall as usual, at about ten to seven – dinner is at seven – but did not linger over his brandy and cigar, as was his habit, but excused himself on grounds of work as soon as the plates were cleared from the table, and was back here by eight o'clock. At around quarter past eight, a barrister by the name of Philip Ormerod, who has chambers in King's Bench Walk, was passing the end of the alley outside – the North Walk – on his way to Fleet Street, to get a cab home, when he saw the door standing open, and light streaming out. A short time before that, he had heard the sound of running footsteps in the fog, somewhere ahead of him. Concerned that something might be amiss, he had a look in and saw it as you see it now. In a few moments, he had run to the Fleet Street gatehouse, which is only a short distance, and sent the gate-keeper round to Bridewell Place Police Station to get a constable. They communicated with Snow Hill Station, where I happened to be, and I was here within fifteen minutes.'

'There is no sign of a forced entry at the front door,' remarked Holmes.

The policeman nodded. 'It seems probable that the murderer rang at the bell, and was admitted by Sir Gilbert himself. The chambers would, of course, have been locked up while he was away at the dining hall. The only people with a front-door key, other than Sir Gilbert himself, are the two other barristers, the chief clerk, and the gate-keeper, who is responsible for attending to the fires and the like. There is much of value here, and, of course, many of these papers are of the most confidential nature.'

'From your information it appears that Sir Gilbert was attacked very soon after his return from the dining hall,' remarked Holmes. 'It is possible that someone was waiting for him outside these chambers and entered at the same time as he did. Was he quite dead when this man Ormerod found him?'

Stoddard hesitated before replying. 'May I inquire, Mr Holmes, if you recall the Hawkesworth case?' he responded at length, an odd expression on his face.

'Very clearly.'

'Then you will understand,' said Stoddard, 'that Sir John Hawkesworth, who was Sir Gilbert Cheshire's immediate predecessor as head of these chambers, was also murdered. He was bludgeoned to death on just such a night as this, exactly ten years ago. He was attacked as he stood on the front door step of these very chambers. His assailant was never discovered. I was a young officer at the time, and was not directly involved with the case, but of course I knew all about it, for it was the single topic of conversation for some considerable time. There was much talk then, in certain parts of the press, of an ancient curse which was said to lie upon this part of the Inner Temple, and of how a man murdered many centuries ago returned from time to time to exact vengeance for his own death. Now, I'm not, as you know, much taken with such stories generally, but it is not the sort of thing you forget. I suppose I have not thought about it now for seven or eight years, but this business tonight has brought it afresh to my mind.'

'I am aware of the story,' said Holmes, a trace of impatience in his voice, 'and was struck by the fact that little had been heard of it before Sir John Hawkesworth's murder. I do not think we should permit our thoughts to become confused by ancient history, Stoddard.'

'Of course not, Mr Holmes,' the policeman returned, 'but I thought I had best mention the matter to you. In most ways this appears a brutal but unremarkable crime, and I should not have sent for you were it not that it has a couple of unusual features. The eminence of the victim, for one thing – '

'The victim's station in life is not in itself of any interest to me,' interrupted Holmes. 'What was the other unusual feature?'

'When Mr Ormerod entered these chambers and discovered what had happened,' Stoddard explained, 'he thought at first that Sir Gilbert Cheshire was dead. But as he mastered his horror, he heard a slight murmur escape the poor man's lips. He raised Sir Gilbert's head a little, and bent closer to listen. He says that Sir Gilbert coughed and spluttered a little, then murmured "It was he – " followed by more coughing and attempts to speak, then " – Sir John Hawkesworth." A moment later, all life had passed from him.'

Stoddard pursed his lips and regarded Holmes with a querying look, as if wondering what the other would make of this strange information.

'What a very singular pronouncement!' said Holmes at length. 'Is Mr Ormerod absolutely certain on the point?'

'He says he would take his oath on the matter.'

'Where is he now?'

'I sent him home in a cab. He was very badly shaken up, as you can imagine. I have his address – Montpelier Square, in Knightsbridge – if we need to speak to him again.'

Holmes nodded. 'You are not aware of any other Hawkesworth?' he queried. 'No brother or cousin of the late Sir John, who might bear the same name?'

'None but the man murdered ten years ago. His nephew, oddly enough, is a member of these same chambers, but his name is not Hawkesworth, but Lewis. He is the son of Sir John Hawkesworth's sister, who married Sir George Lewis, the well-known society solicitor. He is here now, in the other office.'

Holmes's features expressed surprise.

'He must have answered your summons with great dispatch,' he remarked.

'I had no need to summon him, Mr Holmes. He was here before we were. Just after Sir Gilbert breathed his last, but before Ormerod had left the room to summon help, in he walked through the front door of the chambers.'

'I understood that everyone had left some hours previously,' said Holmes. 'What is his explanation for his reappearance?'

'He left just before six o'clock,' said Stoddard, 'took a bit and sup in a tavern in Fleet Street, and set out on foot to pay a call on a friend of his who lives at Brixton. This friend turned out not to be at home, however, so Lewis walked all the way back to town again, and was on his way back to his lodgings in Bedford Place, near Bloomsbury Square, when he passed this way and saw the door open.'

'It is a dreary evening on which to undertake such long walks,' remarked Holmes. 'He might have saved himself trouble by taking a train back from Brixton to, say, Ludgate Hill Station, and arrived back in town somewhat earlier.'

'He says he felt in need of physical exertion. Do you wish to speak to him now, Mr Holmes?'

'His testimony will keep for a few moments,' returned Holmes. 'I should prefer to have a look round while evidence of the crime is still fresh.'

He took off his overcoat, laid it carefully over the back of a chair, and began a methodical examination of the fatal chamber. For some time, he examined the dead man closely, the desk and the chairs, then squatted down to examine the carpet. After a few minutes, he rose to his feet and stood, his chin in his hand.

'The artery has been severed,' he remarked at length. 'There are two chairs behind the desk, the second of which was moved to its present position beside that of the dead man from its usual place at the far side of the room. There is one clear impression of a footprint, and traces of several others, not so complete. As they all appear to have been made after a copious amount of blood had flowed, they were probably made by Mr Ormerod. As he has now gone home, however, and taken his shoes with him, we are unable to confirm the matter.'

Stoddard conceded the point in an apologetic tone. 'I had thought we had learned all we could from Mr Ormerod,' he said. 'It is fairly certain they are his prints, though,' he added. 'As I see it, the assailant was probably on the far side of the desk from Sir Gilbert, and leaned across it to stab him. From the position of the wound, it is clear he is right-handed.'

Holmes did not reply at once, but regarded the dead man and his desk in silence for a minute, as if picturing to himself what had occurred earlier. Then he came round to the front of the desk. 'And yet,' said he, 'the desk is a broad one, from front to back. I am not convinced that an average man could reach across it sufficiently to inflict the wound.' He picked up a pencil from a tray on top of the desk, then leaned across the desk-top and attempted to touch the side of the dead man's head with it, but fell short by a good nine inches. 'Unless you are prepared to put out the description of a seven-foot giant, or a man whose arms are four feet long,' he remarked, 'I think we must reject the theory.'

'But the dead man's chair is now pushed back a little from the desk,' Stoddard persisted. 'It is also the sort of chair which turns on its base, and he has turned it so that he is sideways on to the desk. If it were tight up to the desk, and facing forwards, you might be able to reach him.'

'The chair may have swivelled round as he was attacked,' Holmes returned, 'but it was not pushed back then, or since, for there is blood all around the foot of the chair legs, but none beneath them. The base of the chair has not moved since before the attack took place.'

'What do you suggest, then?'

'That the assailant was on the same side of the desk as his victim. What is this cash-box? Hum! Two or three drops of blood inside, so it was open before the attack took place. Nothing in it now but a few cheques, made out to Sir Gilbert Cheshire.'

'All the money has gone,' said Stoddard. 'That is evidently the motive for the crime. This is the account book which relates to the cash-box,' he continued, lifting a ledger from the desk. 'I found it in the clerks' office.'

'The last entry in the book indicates a credit balance of eighteen pounds, twelve and seven,' said Holmes, 'so that is the amount which should be in the box. Hum! It does not seem a very large sum for which to commit murder.'

'I have known murder committed for less.'

'That is true. Let us now examine the corridor outside.'

We followed Holmes out into the hallway, where he crouched down and examined the floor closely. A long strip of coconut matting was laid along the length of the corridor. After a moment, he took out his lens and examined a dark smudge more closely.

'It is blood,' said he; 'no doubt left by the passage of Mr Ormerod's shoe. There is little else visible on this coarse matting. Halloa! What is this?' Carefully, he picked up a small object which had lain on the bare floor, just to the left of the matting, almost tucked under the edge. He held it out on the palm of his hand and I saw that it was the charred stump of a match.

Stoddard had bent down with interest as Holmes had spoken, but now he straightened up, an expression of disappointment on his features. 'Someone has used it to light the gas,' said he in a dismissive tone.

'But there is no gas-jet near this spot,' returned Holmes, his eyes darting round the walls of the corridor. 'There is one near the front door and one at the very back, just outside the door to the clerks' office, but not just here.' He turned his attention to the floor once more, his nose scarcely an inch above the matting, as he moved from side to side, like a dog casting about for a scent. In a moment he uttered a low cry of triumph.

'What is it, Holmes?' I queried, leaning forward to see what had aroused his interest.

In answer, he pointed with his long thin forefinger to a small, circular greasy mark on the matting, perhaps three-quarters of an inch across.

'Oh, it's just an old smear of tallow, dropped from a candle,' said Stoddard dismissively.

'On the contrary,' said Holmes in a severe tone; 'it is a very fresh smear. See how it shines in the light!' He took out his lens again, and bent very low to the floor. 'There is not the slightest trace of dust upon its surface. In this foul weather, and with the fires smoking away all day,' he continued, gently passing his finger over the surface of the tallow, 'this splash could not remain in this state for more than a couple of hours.'

'You may be right,' said Stoddard without interest. 'I think I shall see how my men are getting on.'

Holmes did not reply, but continued his careful examination of the corridor, for all the world like some gaunt bloodhound on the trail. A few feet further on, he stopped once more, his brow furrowed with intense concentration, and called me over.

'Look at this, Watson,' said he. 'The candle has dripped again. See how the shape is different.'

'It is more oval than the previous mark,' I observed, crouching down.

'Precisely. What does that tell us?'

'That the candle from which it fell was moving,' I suggested.

'Precisely, the long axis of the splash giving the direction of travel. At the first mark, the candle had just been lit, and was stationary. At this point, however, whoever was holding it was moving along the corridor, towards the rear of the chambers.' He crawled a little further along the corridor, to the point at which a carpeted flight of stairs led off to the left. 'See if you can find any tallow on the staircase,' said he; 'I shall carry on to the end of the corridor.'

I did as he asked, and examined each step carefully. The stair-carpet was dark, with an intricate pattern upon it, which made my task the more difficult, but in a few moments, I had discovered a very small blob upon the fourth stair, near the right-hand edge of the carpet. I called to my companion.

'There is nothing more to be seen in the corridor,' said he, as he examined with his lens the drip I had found. 'Another oval,' he remarked after a moment, 'but this time, there is also a tiny pin-head of the same substance towards the back of the step. Here, take a look, Watson! The extra drop indicates that the splash occurred when the candle was being carried up the stair rather than down it, and suggests that it was moving at a slightly faster rate than before. Evidently our friend with the candle went upstairs, so let us follow in his footsteps!'

At the top of the staircase was a narrow, dark landing. Holmes struck a match. Immediately ahead of us was a blank wall, on which hung a large painting depicting a full-rigged man-of-war of Nelson's day. To left and right were doors, both closed. Beside the left-hand door was a gas-jet, which Holmes lit and turned up. The door to the right was locked, but that on the left opened easily, and as it did so, I saw that the wood of the door-jamb was splintered. Holmes bent down and examined this, and the edge of the door.

'Forced open with a flat metal rod,' he murmured, 'the end of which was about an inch across. Another drop of tallow on the floor,' he continued, pointing to a spot slightly to the right of the doorway. 'Circular this time, indicating that the candle was motionless.'

'No doubt the candle was placed upon the floor while the door was being forced open,' I suggested, but my companion shook his head.

'It is an isolated little gout, and perfectly circular,' said he, 'which indicates that it dripped from some height. The candle was still being held.'

We pushed the door wide open, and entered.

'This chamber is evidently the private study to which Stoddard referred,' Holmes observed, as he struck another match and lit the gas which was immediately behind the door. It was a large room, perhaps fifteen feet across from the doorway to the wall opposite, but nearer twenty-five feet from right to left. To the right, by the fireplace, stood tall bookcases, and to the left, a number of tables, cupboards and bureaux. Holmes lit a lamp which stood upon a small writing-table, and made a circuit of the chamber with the lamp in his hand, eventually stopping before a large, double-fronted cupboard.

'These doors have been forced, too,' said he, 'with the same implement as before; and on the floor to the right is another little gout of tallow.' Carefully, he opened the cupboard doors. The interior consisted entirely of narrow shelves, all stuffed tight with papers. 'There does not appear to be anything of value in here,' he remarked, 'and yet our intruder has directed all his energies to this one cupboard – none of the other bureaux shows any sign of his attentions.'

'There is no obvious sign that anything has been removed,' I observed. 'Perhaps the damage to the doors was done some time ago.'

Holmes shook his head. 'Where the wood by the lock is splintered, the exposed surfaces are pale and freshly revealed. This cupboard was certainly the focus of the intruder's interest.' He pulled a few papers from the shelves at random, and examined them. 'Personal documents,' said he at length; 'old receipts and accounts, private correspondence, letters from Hoare and Co, the bankers in Fleet Street, all jumbled together. It does not appear that the precise habits of mind for which Sir Gilbert Cheshire's professional life was noted were applied with such rigour to his personal affairs. These documents are in a very disordered state!'

In this cold-blooded, detached and businesslike manner, my companion sifted carefully through the documents for some time. For my own part, I could not but think of the man so recently and hideously murdered in the room below us, and feel a distinct sense of unease at rifling so freely through his private papers.

'There is nothing of interest here,' said Holmes at length, 'and no obvious reason why anyone should be so keen to gain access to this press.'

He pushed back the last bundle of papers, and stood in thoughtful silence for several minutes, until there came the sound of a footstep on the stair, and a moment later Inspector Stoddard entered the room.

'Ah! there you are, gentlemen!' said he. 'I thought you would wish to know that Mr Oliver Brown, the deputy head of chambers, has now arrived, as has Elijah Smith, the chief clerk. The junior clerk, Peter Russell, will not be coming. He has been ill all week, and has spent the last four days in bed, attended by a doctor.' Stoddard paused a moment, then added in a lower tone: 'I must also tell you that there has been another odd development. Mr Justice Nellington has just called in with some surprising information.'

'Nellington the High Court judge?'

'Indeed, Mr Holmes. He says that he was passing these chambers at about five past eight, and heard raised voices. He paused for a moment, and as he did so he heard a loud voice say "I have returned!"'

'Nothing else?'

'He says he is a little hard of hearing, and, besides, he did not linger, as he was already late for an appointment at Lord Justice Beningfield's lodgings, in Mitre Court. He has been there all evening, and heard only a short while ago of the tragedy which had occurred here.'

'How very curious!' said I, as my friend shook his head, his brow furrowed with thought.

'Yes – if one can credit it,' remarked the policeman, in a doubtful tone. 'Might I inquire what has brought you up here, gentlemen?'

Holmes described briefly the trail of tallow, and the forced doors to which it had led us, and Stoddard nodded his head.

'That's one for you, Mr Holmes!' said he. 'I had had a glance up the staircase of course, but did not notice the damaged door, and so did not believe that the intruder had ever been up here. Still, the fact that someone has been rooting around for anything he might find accords with what I had already decided about the matter.'

'Which is?'

'That the assault was made by some low ruffian on the prowl in the fog, who just chanced to pick on these chambers, perhaps because he saw Sir Gilbert entering. No doubt Sir Gilbert offered resistance, and received the fatal wound in the struggle. Between you and me, gentlemen, unless we're fortunate enough to light upon some tell-tale clue, which I doubt, or hear something from one of our informers, I don't think we have much chance of ever bringing the crime home. These random burglaries are the very devil to solve!'

'My view of the matter is somewhat different,' Holmes interrupted in a serious tone. 'You say that the evidence of the intruder's presence in this room accords with the view you had already formed. I should have thought it would alter it.'

'A little, perhaps,' Stoddard conceded.

'I should say it alters matters entirely,' Holmes persisted.

'The intruder was obviously a cool hand,' Stoddard began, in a hesitant voice, evidently unsure what the other was driving at, 'to come up here, ransacking the place, when his victim is lying downstairs!'

Holmes shook his head vehemently.

'It will not do, Stoddard!' said he in an emphatic tone. 'How does your theory explain Sir Gilbert's dying words, to which you drew my attention, and the words overheard by Mr Justice Nellington?'

'I mentioned Sir Gilbert's words to you because they were curious, Mr Holmes, but it is obvious that his mind was wandering in delirium, and the words are probably of no significance whatever. As to what Mr Justice Nellington says he overheard, I think it very likely that he was simply mistaken. He himself admitted that his hearing is poor. But what, then, may I ask, is your own view of the matter?'

'I should prefer to reserve my opinion for a few more minutes,' replied Holmes. 'It is an interesting case, Stoddard, with some features which may be unique, and I am grateful that you called us in. It is well worth leaving one's fireside for! Let us now go down and hear what the other members of the chambers have to say, and then perhaps we can shed some light upon this most unusual mystery.'

The clerks' office, at the rear of the chambers, contained one large desk in the middle of the room, and a smaller one to the side, with a great number of cupboards and cabinets stacked tightly round the walls. In this room, Holmes and I seated ourselves, and a moment later Stoddard entered, accompanied by a tall, portly man, about forty years of age, with thinning hair and a small moustache, whom he introduced as Mr Oliver Brown.

He had left the chambers at about half past six, he informed us, at which time nothing was amiss, and there was nothing to indicate that the evening would prove to be at all out of the ordinary. Sir Gilbert Cheshire had been sitting at his desk, reading through a brief, when he bade him good night. No visitors had been expected in the evening, so far as he was aware. After leaving the Temple, he had walked along the Strand to Rule's restaurant, in Maiden Lane, where he had dined alone, leaving shortly before eight o'clock. He had then walked on towards Charing Cross, where he had picked up a cab in the street, and driven directly home to his house in Half Moon Street, off Piccadilly.

Holmes then asked him if Sir Gilbert Cheshire had shown any apprehension of danger recently, but he shook his head at this suggestion.

'Not at all,' said he, 'although any such apprehension might not have been apparent, for Sir Gilbert was not one to display emotion at any time. He was a very close man. I have never known him appear either happy or unhappy. He simply pursued his own unswerving course through life.'

'You and he were not on terms of personal friendship?' inquired Holmes after a moment.

'Our relations were purely professional,' the other replied, with a shake of the head. 'I do not believe that Sir Gilbert was ever on terms of personal friendship, as you put it, with anyone. There were a couple of men with whom he would sometimes smoke a cigar after dinner, but that, to the best of my knowledge, was the extent of his social recreation. It was not popularity he desired, but professional success, and his desire for that was unbounded. It was for that reason that I was confident, when he assumed the headship of these chambers, ten years ago, that our practice would quickly recover from the tragedy of Sir John Hawkesworth's death. Sir Gilbert was very highly regarded at that time, professionally speaking, and had always had very great ambitions. It had been apparent to me for years that he greatly desired the headship, and also to become a bencher of the Temple. He and Sir John had quarrelled frequently, for it was his opinion, often forcibly expressed, that Sir John was deliberately holding him back, by reserving all the most attractive briefs for himself.'

'And your opinion?' queried Holmes

'I did not agree, but I kept my thoughts to myself, for I was the junior at the time, and my opinion would not have been welcomed. Sir John Hawkesworth was a fine man, as highly regarded for his personal qualities as for his professional excellence. He was always extremely kind and encouraging to me, and I cannot believe he would ever have acted meanly to a subordinate. His whole character forbade such a thought. Since his death, however, our chambers have acquired a reputation for grim efficiency. "North Walk Chambers will win your case for you," people say, "but do not expect to be much cheered by the experience."'

'Presumably, you will now become leading counsel in these chambers,' observed Holmes.

The barrister hesitated a moment before replying. 'I am not at all sure that I want the position,' said he at length. 'There seems a curse upon the place. No man, surely, would be eager to remain upon the scene of such terrible and inexplicable bloodshed.'

'Did such thoughts ever trouble Sir Gilbert Cheshire?' queried Holmes.

'He never once spoke of Sir John's murder to me,' replied Brown, 'and I cannot therefore say what his thoughts upon the matter may have been. As he was such a cold and unemotional man, it may be that he was quite unmoved by thoughts which would have troubled other men.'

Stoddard accompanied Brown back to his office, to fetch the junior barrister, and we sat in silence for some minutes. My friend's brow was furrowed with thought, and it was clear from the fleeting expressions which chased each other across his features that his swift and agile brain was sifting and re-sifting the evidence, and weighing and re-weighing the facts, to find an arrangement which would balance the scales of probability to his satisfaction.

For myself, I confess that the dark events which had occurred seemed like something from an evil dream, and I was still shocked by the horror of the scene in Sir Gilbert Cheshire's chamber. For such a tragedy to have befallen the North Walk chambers once was a most terrible misfortune, but for such a thing to have occurred a second time seemed incomprehensible. My thoughts were interrupted by a remark from my companion.

'You realise, of course,' said he in a quiet voice, 'that Mr Brown could have left his restaurant at, say, ten to eight, walked back here and murdered Sir Gilbert at five past eight, retraced his steps to the other end of the Strand, and picked up a cab there, as he says.'

'Holmes!' I cried. 'You surely cannot be serious!'

'I merely point out the possibility, Watson. In this fog, much can happen and be observed by no-one.'

'But the empty cash-box? Surely therein lies the motive for this terrible crime?'

'I think not, Watson. These are deeper waters than was at first apparent.'

Stoddard returned before I could question my companion further, accompanied by a young man of about seven and twenty, introduced to us as Stephen Lewis, junior counsel of the chambers. He was a tall, remarkably thin man, with dark hair, and a clean-shaven face which was as white as paper. It was apparent from the nervousness of his manner and the tremor in his voice as he spoke that he was in a state of some considerable agitation. He took a silver cigarette-case from his pocket as he sat down, extracted a cigarette and lit it.

'Such a terrible thing to have happened,' said he after a moment, 'and to such an eminent and highly-respected man.'

'Indeed,' responded Holmes in a sympathetic tone. 'I understand, however, that for all his professional eminence, Sir Gilbert was not an especially popular man.'

'That can scarcely be denied,' replied Lewis after a moment's hesitation, in a cautious tone. 'He was known by many people, but intimate with none. I know of no-one who considered himself a particular friend of his. He conducted his relations with people at arm's length, so to speak.'

'Was there, then, anyone who might be considered an enemy?'

'None that I am aware of. He had occasionally received abuse from criminals whom he had failed to save, but nothing of the sort recently. For several weeks – almost all the Michaelmas term, in fact – we have been appearing for the defence in the Brockwell Heath Case, which finally reached its conclusion on Tuesday, and in which we were completely successful. One might imagine that that would be a cause for celebration, but Sir Gilbert's mood appeared unaffected. His character was saturnine and dark at the best of times, but recently he had seemed in an even darker mood than usual, and for the last couple of days he had been as limp as a rag, and unable to concentrate on the next brief.'

'Do you know anything of the death of your uncle, Sir John Hawkesworth?' queried Holmes after a moment.

'Very little,' Lewis replied, shaking his head. 'I was a mere school-boy when it occurred, away at Rugby. I know no more of it than anyone might who read his newspaper. The accepted theory, I under-stand, was that Sir John was assaulted by a thief, who had intended to take his door-key and use it to gain entry to these chambers, but who fled upon realising that his attack, intended to incapacitate his victim, had in fact killed him.'

'And yet, the assault was an exceptionally ferocious one, as I recall,' remarked Holmes, 'Sir John being bludgeoned again and again, in a manner suggesting that the assailant intended more than merely to temporarily incapacitate him.'

'Then it is inexplicable.'

'You have heard, I take it, that Sir Gilbert's last words were "It was he – Sir John Hawkesworth"?'

'Indeed. That, too, is inexplicable.'

'What, if I may ask, brought you back through the Temple this evening, Mr Lewis? I understand that you were walking back from Brixton, to your lodgings in Bedford Place. But surely a more direct route would have taken you across Waterloo Bridge, and up Bow Street?'

'That is true,' the other conceded; 'but, as you correctly perceive, I made a detour. I was disappointed at missing my friend, and determined to seek out another, a fellow-barrister, who has chambers in King's Bench Walk. Alas, he was absent, too. I therefore resigned myself to a solitary evening, and set off, finally, for home. But my way from King's Bench Walk to the Fleet Street gateway brought me past the end of the North Walk, and when I saw the door of our own chambers standing wide open, and the light streaming out of it, I hurried to determine the reason.'

'You suspected something amiss?'

'Very definitely. I knew Sir Gilbert to be a most careful man. He would no more leave his front door open at night than he would leave his wallet at the foot of Nelson's Column.'

'And you can shed no light on what has happened?'

'I'm afraid I can't.'

Elijah Smith, the chief clerk, was next shown in. He was a medium-sized man of about fifty, with a pale, clean-shaven face, and a nervous manner. He informed us that there were just two keys to the cash-box, one kept by him, and the other on Sir Gilbert Cheshire's watch-chain. He also confirmed that the amount of money missing was as stated in the ledger which Stoddard had shown us.

'Is there any reason why Sir Gilbert should have been looking in the cash-box this evening?' inquired Holmes.

'None at all, sir. He always left all such matters to me. Every Friday morning I take round to the bank any cheques received during the week, and any cash which is surplus to our immediate requirements.'

'At what time did you last speak to your employer?'

'Just as I was leaving, sir; shortly after half past five. His manner was exactly as usual.'

'And you have not seen him since?'

'No, sir. I ate at home with the family, then went round about seven o'clock to see my brother, who lives a short distance away, in Clerkenwell, and was there until the police constable called.'

After Smith and Stoddard had left us, Holmes sat a while in silent thought. Then he stood up abruptly, as if having reached a decision, and took a few sheets of blank foolscap from the desk.

'Come,' said he. 'Let us see if we cannot make more definite progress.'

'Do you see any likelihood of ever apprehending the criminal?' I asked.

'I have hopes,' said he. 'It rather depends on the statements I shall now take, in the other office.'

In the hallway we met Inspector Stoddard who had just come in through the front door of the chambers.

'I have had another word with Mason, the gate-keeper,' said he. 'He says he remembers now that he saw someone he did not recognise, loitering in King's Bench Walk at about half past four, just as it was getting dark; but as that way through the Temple is used by all manner of people simply as a short-cut from the Strand to Blackfriars Bridge, he did not think it worth mentioning before.'

'That is interesting,' said Holmes. 'Would you be so good as to ask Mason to step across here, Stoddard?'

The junior barristers' office was similar in size to Sir Gilbert Cheshire's, but of a somewhat more cluttered appearance. The fire had been banked up, and blazed fiercely in the grate, so that the room was free of the dank, chill atmosphere that pervaded the rest of the chambers. Oliver Brown sat at his desk, a brandy-glass in his hand, staring gloomily across the room, and did not look up as we entered. Stephen Lewis was sitting beside the hearth, his head in his hands. The chief clerk, Elijah Smith, was perched on the edge of a chair beside the window, a nervous expression on his face.

'Do you think that we might be permitted to leave soon?' Brown inquired of us. 'It's getting very late, and I can't think that there is anything more we can tell you.'

'Very shortly,' returned my companion. 'If you would just be so good as to sign a formal statement as to when you last saw Sir Gilbert Cheshire alive, and your subsequent whereabouts this evening.'

Stoddard had entered as he spoke, accompanied by the ginger-haired gate-keeper.

'There is no need – ' began the policeman, but Holmes interrupted him.

'As you say Inspector, there is no need to wait until tomorrow. We may as well get it over with now, and then we shall not need to trouble anyone further. You say you left these chambers at half past six,' he continued, addressing Brown, 'at which time Sir Gilbert was alive and well, walked to Rule's, where you passed an hour, and then took a cab home.'

'That is correct,' the other replied.

'Would you mind signing this paper to that effect, then?' said Holmes, who had scribbled a few lines on one of his sheets of foolscap.

Brown took the sheet from him with a suspicious narrowing of the eyes. 'I do not understand the purpose of this,' said he, glancing at what Holmes had written, and making no move to pick up a pen, 'nor what you suppose its legal status might be.'

'Its legal status,' returned Holmes, 'is simply that it is a statement of the facts, according to you, and, as such, you can scarcely object to signing it.'

The other man grunted, and with a show of reluctance, took a pen and signed the paper with a flourish. Holmes then repeated his questions to Lewis, who also signed the paper. He then turned to the chief clerk, scribbled down a couple of lines, and passed across the sheet, which Elijah Smith signed slowly and carefully.

'Now, Mr Mason,' Holmes continued, turning to the gate-keeper: 'You last saw Sir Gilbert Cheshire alive at about twenty to seven, I understand.'

'That's right; when I brought in some coal, and raked the grates out.'

'And you did not see him again?'

'No, sir, I didn't. I met a friend of mine in the "Cock", just afore seven, and was there till twenty to eight, when I came home.'

'Very well. If you will just sign this?'

Mason appended his signature to the few lines which Holmes had written, and returned the paper to him. Brown drained his glass, set it down on the desk-top, and wiped his moustache.

'Will that be all?' said he in a weary voice.

'We have finished here now,' said Stoddard. 'My men can find no clue, so we may as well lock up, Mr Holmes, and let these gentlemen get off home. We can do no more tonight.'

'I would wish to give you my view of the matter first,' said Holmes, in a tone which commanded attention.

'Very well,' responded the policeman. The others, who had stood up and begun to put on their coats, sat back down again, their expressions a mixture of curiosity and resignation.

'This brutal and shocking crime,' began Holmes, 'appeared at first to be the work of an unknown assailant, someone to whom Sir Gilbert Cheshire had probably opened the door himself, and who had then, at the point of his knife, forced Sir Gilbert to open the cash-box, and had, in the course of a struggle, inflicted the wound which killed him.'

'That must be so,' observed Brown, nodding.

'However,' Holmes continued, 'our investigation of the premises has revealed a number of features which cast doubt on such an interpretation. In the first place, there is no evidence of a struggle having taken place. In the second, it is apparent that the intruder lit a candle in the hallway and passed upstairs with it, where he forced entry to Sir Gilbert's private study and broke open a press there, containing personal documents and records.'

There was a murmur of interest at this information, and then a silence fell upon the chamber once more, as Holmes continued.

'Once Sir Gilbert had returned from the dining-hall, all the gas would be lit – as indeed was the case when Mr Ormerod passed and saw the open door – and it would therefore have been perfectly pointless for anyone to have lit a candle. Nor, once the downstairs gas was lit, need the intruder have feared that lighting the upstairs gas-jets would increase the chances of his being detected. It seems clear, then, that the intruder lit his candle when there was no other illumination in the chambers, that is to say, before Sir Gilbert returned from dinner. No doubt he lit a candle in order to keep the light to a minimum, and hoped to have finished what he was doing before Sir Gilbert returned. But it follows from this, that he was not admitted to the premises by Sir Gilbert, but admitted himself, there being no-one else here at the time. It further follows from this that the intruder had his own key, for the door would certainly have been locked.'

There was an odd stillness in the chamber, as those present absorbed this information. Each must have realised, as did I, that the four men who possessed a key to the North Walk Chambers were all together in the room at that moment.

'Now,' continued Holmes, 'we know that Sir Gilbert left the dining-hall a little earlier than was his habit, in order to return here to work. We may suppose, then, that the intruder, believing himself to have time in hand, was surprised when he heard the unlocking of the front door. He must have extinguished his candle, descended to the ground floor, and, in his turn, surprised Sir Gilbert in his office. We do not know what Sir Gilbert's reaction was, but it is clear that he knew the intruder, for a second chair was moved behind the desk, and placed beside his own: it does not seem likely that a stranger, threatening Sir Gilbert with a knife, would have troubled to procure a chair for himself. The two men evidently sat in discussion for some time. The fact that the cash-box was open before the attack took place suggests that money came into this discussion. What happened next we cannot say for certain, but it seems likely that there was a disagreement, as a result of which the intruder inflicted the fatal wound upon Sir Gilbert.

'The evidence of the wound itself is in my view inconclusive as to whether the assailant was right-handed or left-handed, although I incline to the latter. The evidence of the tallow which dripped from the candle, however, indicates clearly that the man who held it is left-handed. A man may generally carry a candle in the right or left hand with indifference, but if he has work to do – especially work which involves the application of force, such as the bursting open of a door, or a cupboard – he will always pass the candle to his weaker hand. For most people, who are right-handed, this will be the left hand, but tonight's intruder held the candle in his right hand, while forcing the locks with a metal rod held in his left. He is therefore, beyond a shadow of a doubt, left-handed. Having conducted a little handwriting experiment, I am now in a position to state that there is only one man who both possesses a key to these chambers, and who is left-handed.'

As Sherlock Holmes spoke these last words, he turned to Thomas Mason, the gate-keeper, whose face had assumed the colour of putty.

'It's a lie!' cried he in a hoarse voice, springing unsteadily to his feet. 'I was never in here!'

'In that case,' said Holmes, 'you can have no objection to a search being made of your quarters.'

'You've no right to do that!' retorted Mason, in a loud, strident voice.

'We'll see about that!' Stoddard interrupted. 'Thomas Mason: I am arresting you on suspicion of having been involved in the death of Sir Gilbert Cheshire. You will accompany me to your lodgings where a search will be undertaken for evidence.'

The inspector and two constables escorted their prisoner from the chambers, leaving the three others in a dazed state, their features displaying the shock and amazement they clearly felt. Sherlock Holmes lit his pipe, and sat smoking in silence for several minutes, his brow furrowed with thought.

'It may be that the right man has been arrested,' said Brown at length; 'but the whole affair is still dark to me. I have a feeling that we do not yet know all that there is to know of the matter. Can you enlighten us any further, Mr Holmes? Do you believe there was any meaning in Sir Gilbert's dying words, or was the poor fellow simply raving?'

'Sir Gilbert's words,' Holmes replied, 'as reported by Mr Ormerod, began, if you recall, "It was he", and ended with "Sir John Hawkesworth", with a gap of a few moments in between, during which he struggled for breath. I suspect that in those words Sir Gilbert was attempting to name his murderer.'

'But that is madness!' cried Brown. 'Sir John was himself murdered ten years ago.'

'Quite so. I therefore suggest that a phrase is missing from the sentence, which Sir Gilbert was unable to articulate. The likeliest candidate is something such as "the man who murdered", so that the whole sentence would be "It was he: the man who murdered Sir John Hawkesworth".'

'Good Lord!' cried Lewis.

'However,' continued Holmes, 'if it was Sir Gilbert's intention to identify his assailant in this way, it follows that he himself was aware of who had murdered his predecessor. This raises the question as to how he knew this with such certainty, and, if he did, why he had never made public his knowledge.'

'It could be that Mason informed him this very evening that he was the murderer of Sir John,' I suggested.

'Yes, that is possible, Watson, but on the whole I incline to the view that Sir Gilbert already knew the truth behind Sir John's death, had known about it, in fact, for ten years.'

'I find that suggestion quite incredible,' said Brown in a tone of disbelief.

'No doubt,' said Holmes. 'Nevertheless, the indications are there. In the first place,' he continued, in his precise, methodical manner, like a specialist delivering a lecture, 'it is well known that fifteen years ago, Sir Gilbert secured Mason's acquittal on a charge of murder. Presumably Mason felt some gratitude for this. But then we hear that, about eight years ago, Sir Gilbert, actuated by sympathy at Mason's plight, secured him a distinctly undemanding post as gate-keeper here. There seems something wrong with this: Sir Gilbert was not known for any great degree of sympathy; and the favour seems the wrong way about. It is as if there is some link missing from the chain of cause and effect, as we have it at present.'

'Just what are you suggesting?' said Brown sharply.

Before Holmes could reply, the door opened, and Inspector Stoddard entered. He informed us that the search of Mason's quarters had revealed a large sharp knife, its blade caked in blood, and a long thin chisel, both wrapped in a blood-stained shirt, and hidden under a sink. An amount of money exactly matching that missing from the cash-box had also been found, in a canvas bag inside a coal-scuttle. Mason had offered no resistance to the search, and had shown no surprise when the above articles had been discovered, but had made one surprising request, that he be allowed to make a statement to the gentlemen awaiting his return in the North Walk Chambers.

'I am sure we should have no objection to that proposal, if you do not,' said Holmes.

'Very well, then,' said Stoddard. 'I have already cautioned the prisoner that anything which he chooses to say in his statement may be given against him in court.'

The prisoner was brought in then, his wrists manacled together, and, standing before us, made the following voluntary statement. In the interests of clarity, I have made one or two very slight alterations, but otherwise the statement is exactly as Thomas Mason made it to us that night.

'Yes, I killed Sir Gilbert Cheshire. I see there is no point in denying it, and I'm not proud of it. But you ought to know that whatever they say about him in the newspapers, and whatever people might think, he weren't so marvellous, neither.

'I first met him when I was accused of murdering my wife, and he was assigned to defend me. I was in Newgate when he came to see me. "Don't worry," says he; "I'll get you off." He knew I'd done it, although he never asked me outright. Things was looking black against me, and I'd given up thinking about ever getting out; but somehow, in the court, it all came out different. One or two of the witnesses seemed to change their minds about what they were going to say, and Sir Gilbert spoke for such a long time and in such a confusing way, that in the end the jury decided I hadn't done it after all, and I could go free.

'I was grateful to Sir Gilbert. I didn't know how he'd done it, but I knew it was him I had to thank for the fact that I wasn't swinging on the end of a rope. But things wasn't so rosy with me even if I was free. I was a slater by trade, but now I couldn't find any work nowhere. The trouble was, a lot of people – all the wife's relations, and half the district – knew that I had done it, really, and they wasn't likely to employ me, and I couldn't blame 'em for that. I tried all sorts of different lines, went half-way round the world in a clipper, one year, but was still no better off when, about four year on from my trial, I was coming along Carey Street one afternoon, when who should step out of a bookshop in front of me but Sir Gilbert Cheshire.

' "Hallo, Thomas," says he, cool as you like. "How are you keeping yourself?"

' "Not so well as I'd like, sir," said I. "I haven't had more than a tanner in my pocket any time in the last four year."

' "I'm sorry to hear that, Thomas," says he, in a thoughtful voice. "You are still grateful for the little favour I did you the other year?" When I said course I was, he says "Then I have a little favour to ask of you in return, Thomas. Be under the Holborn Viaduct at seven o'clock this evening," says he, "and I'll tell you what I'd like you to do." He slipped two bob into my hand then, and walked off.

'When I saw him later, he told me what was in his mind. It seems there was someone standing in his way, professionally speaking, and preventing the light shining on him as he'd like. "If he could be put out of the way for a time," says Sir Gilbert in that slow cunning way of his, "I might find it convenient. And you might find, Thomas, that there was something in it for you, too."

'To make the matter brief: the party's name was Hawkesworth, Sir Gilbert told me exactly what to do, and I done it. He'd given me some money beforehand, and told me to lie low for a while afterwards, then come back after a year or so, and he'd find me a job. Which I did.

'That was all ten year ago. Things have been all right since, but I've never had much money, and when I asked him, the other week, if he could let me have a bit more, he says I couldn't have none. Well, I said this, and he said that, and it got so we was almost at each other's throats; and then I said I could stir up plenty of trouble for him if he didn't do right by me. 'Oh? How's that?' said he in a cool voice; so I told him: I'd saved a note he'd sent to me in connection with the Hawkesworth job, which he'd told me to burn. I've always found that when someone tells you to burn something, it generally pays to hang on to it.

' "That note won't prove anything," says he; "I didn't commit myself in it."

' "Perhaps not," says I, "but it'll certainly start some rumours off."

' "You'll condemn yourself if you produce that," says he.

' "Oh no I won't, see, 'cause it's not got my name on it, and I'll send it anonymously to his Honour, the Head of the Bench."

I could see that this had worried him. He bit his lip, and thought for a while.

' "When I saved you from the gallows," says he in a quiet voice, "some evidence came my way which ended up locked in my private cupboard. If you threaten me, Mason, that evidence will come back out of my cupboard again, and you'll swing for it."

' "I know the Law," says I. "I've been tried once and found not guilty. I can't be tried again, whatever you come up with."

'At this he laughed. "Dear me!" says he, cackling like a hen. "Dear me, Thomas! You know the Law, do you? Well, let me tell you, my man, that I'm the expert, and I tell you that with the evidence I've got hidden away, you could be re-charged, with slightly different words on the indictment, and you'd hang as sure as you're standing here now! If you give me any more trouble, that evidence comes out of my cupboard!" '

'That was a lie,' Brown interrupted: 'You could not be charged again with the same crime.'

'Mebbe it was, but it put the wind up me, anyhow. I didn't say nothing then, but I made my mind up to break into his blessed cupboard one night when he wasn't there, and see if I couldn't find his precious evidence. I've had a bit of a wait for the right time, 'cause the gentlemen have all been working late recently, but tonight looked a fair chance, so in I went. I thought I'd have plenty of time, but – curse my luck – he came back early from his supper and heard me moving about, so I had to go down and face him out. He got a surprise when I walked into his office.

' "What the devil are you doing here, Mason!" he cried in a loud, unpleasant tone. "I thought I'd seen the last of you for today!"

' "I have returned," I shouted back at him, "to find that evidence you've got against me."

' "What!" says he in an angry voice. "You've been in my private rooms? This is the last straw, Mason! It's time for you and me to part company altogether."

' "Give me some money and I'll go as fast as you like," says I, as hot as he was.

' "Very well." says he; "and then I never want to see you again as long as I live."

'He fetched the big cash-box and opened it up with the key on his watch-chain, but there was little enough in it.

' "I thought there'd be more than this," says he.

' "Oh, did you?" says I, thinking he was trying to play a game, with me as the fool. I had my knife out and at his throat before he could move. "You find some more," says I, "or you won't leave this room alive."

' "You can't threaten me," says he, and made a grab at the knife. But quick as he moved, so did I, and the knife went straight into his throat. I didn't mean to do it, but he brought it on himself, and that's the Gospel truth, if I have to swing for it.'

We all sat in silence as this remarkable and terrible tale ended with these words, and remained in silence after Stoddard had taken his prisoner away. Then Sherlock Holmes stood up, took his hat and coat, and we prepared to leave.

'Can all this be true?' said Brown, in a tone of stupefaction.

'I rather fancy it is,' said Holmes, 'and that Sir Gilbert Cheshire learnt too late that he who conceals a serpent within his bosom will at last feel the serpent's bite himself.'

The following morning's newspapers had been printed too early to include news of Mason's arrest, and it was left to the evening papers to apprise their readers of the latest developments. But by then this remarkable case had produced a further surprise, and I remember vividly the shock with which I read the heading in the *St James's Gazette*:

TEMPLE MURDER: ESCAPE OF CHIEF SUSPECT

It appeared from the account given beneath this heading that very soon after he had left us the night before, Mason had suddenly broken from the grasp of the policemen who held him, dashed away, and vanished into the dense, swirling fog.

For twenty-four hours he was sought in vain. But late the following night, a police-constable saw a man crossing London Bridge whom he recognised from the description as Mason, and gave chase across the bridge. Summoned by the first man's rattle, a second officer made his way on to the bridge from the Southwark side, and Mason, seeing that there was no chance of escape in either direction, threw himself from the parapet of the bridge into the blackness of the river below. The River Police were at once notified, and an organised search made, but no trace of the fugitive was discovered.

Three days later, Sherlock Holmes received a letter by the last post which he read and passed to me without comment. It ran as follows:

MY DEAR MR HOLMES – This is to inform you that a body was washed up by Wapping Old Stairs early this morning, which has now been identified as that of Thomas Mason. The doctor says that his skull is fractured, which was the cause of death, and it is thought likely that he struck his head on one of the stone piers of the bridge when he jumped. I have now made a full report to my superiors of all the facts of which I am aware, and both the Cheshire case and the Hawkesworth case are now officially closed. Thanking you for your great help in the matter, I remain –

Yours very sincerely

DAVID STODDARD

The Case of the Vanishing Barque

JUNE THOMSON

Looking through my notes, I see that 1889 was a particularly busy year for my old friend Sherlock Holmes. In addition to those cases such as the mystery of the five orange pips or the Reigate squire, accounts of which I have laid before my reading public, there were others where, for various reasons, I withheld publication. These include the inquiries into the Paradol chamber, the Amateur Mendicant Society, the adventures of the Grice Patersons on the island of Uffa, the Camberwell poisoning case and, finally, the investigation into the disappearance of the British barque, the *Sophy Anderson*, in which I played a small part and of which I have kept the records.

The inquiry began, I recall, one morning in April of that year, some time after my marriage to Miss Mary Morstan and my return to civil practice. I was on my way home from visiting a patient in the Baker Street area when, on the spur of the moment, I decided to call on Holmes, whom I had not seen for several weeks. As I turned into the familiar road, I saw a stocky, heavily-built man on the opposite pavement walking in the same direction as myself but more slowly, for he frequently halted to glance up at the numbers on the doors before consulting a piece of paper he held in his hand.

His appearance was so striking that I decided to play the game with which Holmes often amused himself as well as me, that of judging an individual's character and profession by his clothes and his demeanour.

The man in question was in his fifties, I estimated, and even at a cursory glance it was easy to guess from his pea jacket and peaked cap that he was a sailor. His rolling gait and weather-beaten face bore out this impression.

I hurried ahead of him, eager to reach Holmes and lay my deductions before him so that, by glancing out of the window, he could confirm my conclusions. I was so eager, in fact, that I took the stairs two at a time and, bursting into the room, seized my old friend by the sleeve and drew him across the room. The man was now directly opposite the house, staring straight across the street at it.

'Look, Holmes!' I cried. 'I am right, am I not, in thinking the man is a sailor who has spent most of his life at sea?'

'You are quite correct, my dear Watson,' Holmes replied, looking down appraisingly at the man. 'He is indeed a sailor. But more to the point, what *sort* of sailor is he?'

'I do not quite understand,' I began, rather chastened by Holmes's response.

'Come now. Is he an able seaman, for example? Or a naval officer? Or perhaps a stoker? One must be precise about such details. My own assessment is that he is a merchant seaman, someone of rank, probably a mate rather than a captain, that he has sailed extensively in the southern latitudes and that he is left-handed.'

Seeing my expression, he burst out laughing.

'It is really quite simple, Watson. His bearing tells me he is a man used to authority but of a lower order. He lacks the demeanour of an officer of high rank. His skin is tanned but the wrinkles round his eyes are paler on their inner surfaces, suggesting he has spent considerable time with his eyes screwed up against bright sunlight. As for his left-handedness, that, too, is obvious. He is holding the piece of paper in his left hand. He is also a potential client,' he added, 'a deduction for which I claim no credit at all for the man has, at this very moment, crossed the street to our front door.'

As he spoke, there came a peal on the bell and, seconds later, the sound of heavy, deliberate footsteps mounting the stairs and the man in question entered the room.

Seen at closer quarters, he bore out those particulars of his appearance which Holmes had specified but which I had failed to notice. His bearing did, indeed, have a stamp of authority while the network of fine lines about his eyes showed the paler skin which lined their inner surfaces which Holmes, with his amazingly keen eyesight, had already remarked on.

However, what he had not apparently noticed and which I, as a medical man, immediately discerned, was the unhealthy flush about our visitor's face and the difficulty he had in regaining his breath after mounting the stairs. If ever I saw a man suffering from heart disease, it was he.

In addition to these physical symptoms, there was an aura of profound melancholy about him which seemed to sit upon him like a large, heavy weight, bowing his shoulders and making his movements slow and cumbersome.

At Holmes's invitation, he lowered himself ponderously into an armchair, bringing his two great hands, which put me in mind of shovels, to rest one on each knee. He had already removed his cap, revealing close-cropped grey hair and a deeply furrowed brow.

'I'm sorry to call on you like this, Mr Holmes, without writing to you first to fix an appointment,' he said in a gruff voice which had an unmistakable North country accent, 'but I had to speak to someone about the affair and I daren't go to the police with my tale.'

As he spoke, he glanced dubiously in my direction under heavy eyebrows, a look which Holmes intercepted.

'This is my colleague, Dr Watson,' he said briskly. 'You may speak as frankly in front of him as you would to me. Now, sir, tell me about this affair which I see is causing you great disquiet. But first, I would like to know a little about yourself, including your name. You are a seafaring man, are you not?'

'Indeed I am, sir. As for my name, it's Thomas Corbett and I'm the mate on board the *Lucy Belle*, *a* four-masted barque which trades mostly between Newcastle and the Far East.'

At this point in his narrative, he hesitated and I saw him clasp his two huge hands convulsively together.

'Leastways, sir, that is the name the ship has carried for the past three years. Before that, she used to sail under a different name.'

Although I was considerably taken aback by this last statement, as well as confused about exactly what it might imply, Holmes seemed to understand, for he gave a little inclination of his head.

'And what was her original name, may I ask?' he inquired.

'The *Sophy Anderson*,' Corbett replied, his voice husky with emotion as if he were naming a dead child.

'If I recall correctly, she sank with all hands, did she not?'

'Aye, sir; or so it was believed. She was supposed to have gone down in January three years ago off the coast of the Outer Hebrides when she was making for Glasgow from Valparaiso carrying a cargo of nitrate.'

I saw Holmes's features sharpen and he murmured under his breath as if to himself, 'Ah, an insurance fraud!'

Corbett heard him, for he replied, his expression grave, 'Aye, it was, sir, and one I bitterly regret taking part in.'

'Tell me about it,' Holmes said, settling back in his chair and directing a sharp, attentive glance in Corbett's direction.

'That I will, Mr Holmes. But first I must explain a little about the circumstances behind it. The *Sophy Anderson* was built on the Clyde in 1876 and was owned by a small shipping company, called the White Heather Line, based at Glasgow, which ran three or four other barques. The owners were a pair of brothers, Jamie and Duncan McNeil, and the captain was Joseph Chafer, a relative of the McNeils by marriage.

'It seems the McNeils owed a lot of money and were close to going bankrupt, which was why the scheme was put in place. The plan was this. The *Sophy Anderson* would pick up a cargo of nitrate from Valparaiso but no passengers on the return voyage. Months before this, the crew had been carefully looked over and anyone Chafer thought couldn't be trusted to keep his mouth shut over the plan was turned off and a new crew member taken on his place. You see, they wanted men who would be willing to disappear, so to speak, as if they really had been lost at sea, and would take up new lives and new names. So they had to be men with no families to question their whereabouts. They'd be paid, of course, with a cut of the insurance money.

'When the scheme was put to me, I agreed to it like a shot. My wife's been dead these many years and my only child, Tom, named after me, had died when he was twelve, so I had no close family to worry what had become of me. A sum of several hundred pounds, my share of the insurance money, would come in very useful. I was getting close to retiring age, you see, Mr Holmes, and I had this dream of owning a little farm somewhere south where it's warmer, in Cornwall maybe, but near the coast so that I could still be in sight and sound of the sea. As for the details of the plot, the claiming of the insurance money and the re-registering of the *Sophy Anderson* under a new name, I left all that to the McNeil brothers. For that was the idea, Mr Holmes. She'd go on trading as the *Lucy Belle*, but not from those ports where the *Sophy* had traded in the past, like Liverpool, Glasgow or London. That way, the vessel would still be making money and the men would earn their usual wages, plus their share of the insurance which, taking into account the value of the ship and its cargo, would add up to a fair sum, more than most of them would see in a year's sailing.

Like I said, we took on a cargo at Valparaiso, but no passengers, set sail for Glasgow on January 17th, and with a good wind behind us, in 128 days we were in sight of the small island of Duncraig to the south-west of the Outer Hebrides. Chafer and I knew the island well because we'd taken shelter there from a storm several years before. It's an uninhabited island with steep cliffs rising straight from the sea on its western coast, a treacherous shoreline for any mariner who doesn't know the tides and currents. But to one who does and has the courage to take a ship between the rocks, there are several sheltered inlets where a vessel can lie up for weeks out of sight of other shipping. And to give Chafer his due, he didn't lack for neither skill nor courage. So with my help and the rest of the crew's, Chafer took the *Sophy Anderson* into one of those inlets, where we dropped anchor.

'When we'd loaded up the nitrate, I'd taken on board extra stores at Chafer's orders in the way of lengths of timber and tins of paint, and, once we were safely anchored, the whole crew set about changing the look of the ship, painting her dark blue down to the water-line instead of grey and giving her a white line round the hull. The ship's carpenter, Morrison, also changed the trim round the edge of the deck housing which, too, was painted white. We renamed her as well, the *Lucy Belle*, which was written in dark blue letters along her prow.

'When all that was done and the paint was dry, Chafer called us all up on deck and made a speech welcoming us aboard the *Lucy Belle* and wishing us God speed on all her voyages. He then re-christened the vessel in a little ceremony, pouring a tot of rum over her fo'csle. When that was done, every man jack of us from me, the mate, down to the least on board, young Billy Wheeler, a deck-hand, was handed a glass of rum and his new papers and the old ones were torn up and burnt there on deck in an old iron cooking-pot. More rum was handed round and we went from one to the other, getting used to our new names and those of the rest of the crew. Chafer's was Michael Lofthouse, mine Joseph Nully, but I only use it when I have to. It don't seem to sit easy on me like my old one, Thomas Corbett.

'I think the handing out of the new names and the getting rid of the old ones made everyone realise there was no turning back. Like the papers, we had burned our bridges and it was too late to change our minds. Some took it hard, especially Billy Wheeler, the young deck-hand. I was told later that on his last trip to Glasgow he'd met a lass he fancied, but that was all finished and done with now.

'Anyways, whatever the reason, he drank too much of the rum and lost his nerve. Or perhaps he found it. He ran up and down the deck telling everyone that when we got to Rotterdam, the port we was to make for after we'd got under sail again, he'd sign on with another vessel and make his way back to Scotland. "I want to go home!" he kept shouting. As for the insurance money, it could be dropped in the sea, as far as he was concerned. He wanted none of it.

'Well, Mr Holmes, what with him running about and shouting like a madman, it was like putting a spark to a powder keg. Several of the men, including Morrison, the ship's carpenter, set about him like madmen themselves and began hitting him, not just with their fists but with anything that came to hand. I think I know what was in their minds. They, too, were wondering if they'd done the right thing and at the same time they were fearful that Billy might blag and then not only would the fraud come to light but their part in it. They'd lose their share of the money and perhaps finish up in gaol. By the time me and Chafer managed to drag the men off Billy, he was lying on the deck, his face and head covered in blood.

'Chafer knelt beside him and felt for the pulse in his neck. Then he stood up and said in a loud, harsh voice, "Now listen up, my lads. Billy's dead. There's nothing we can do for him except set him adrift."

'The sound of his voice and the sight of Billy's dead body brought the men to their senses. They drew back and one of them, Newton, started to speak, the tears standing out in his eyes.

'"We didn't mean to . . . " he began but Chafer cut him short. "Shut your mouth and get below," he ordered him. "Find a length of canvas and some rope."

'When Newton came back, he and another man wrapped the body in the canvas and tied it up. They were lifting it to carry it over to the side ready to tip it overboard, when I stepped forward.

'I don't know what made me do it but I couldn't let them chuck him into the sea like a dead sheep. He was fifteen, Mr Holmes; a pleasant lad, always laughing and joking. Many a time he'd put me in mind of my dead son with his fair hair and blue eyes. I just couldn't see him thrown overboard with nothing to mark his going.

'When I first went to sea, my mother gave me a silver St Christopher on a chain which I'd always worn round my neck for good luck on my voyages. I took it off and, just as they had lifted the body up on to the rail and had it balanced there, I put my hand through the folds of the canvas and laid it on his chest.'

At this point, Corbett broke off his account and stared fixedly down at his huge hands which he was kneading together as if trying to squeeze the life out of them. Then just as suddenly, he lifted his head and looked directly at Holmes.

'He was still alive, sir!'

'Are you sure?' Holmes asked sharply.

'As sure as I'm sitting here. I felt his chest rise and fall under my hand. I looked across at Chafer who was standing by the rail ready to give the order to throw Billy overboard. He looked back at me, Mr Holmes, and he knew, sir! Oh, yes, he *knew* all right! He stared me straight in the eyes and then he drew one finger across his throat, meaning "I'll kill you if you don't keep your mouth shut."'

'About Wheeler still being alive?'

Without speaking, Corbett nodded his head in agreement. Then, swallowing hard, he continued, 'The next second, Chafer looked away to give the order and Billy had gone overboard. It all happened so quickly, Mr Holmes, I didn't get a chance to stop them.'

A terrible silence fell over the three of us as we pictured the scene, Holmes and I in our imaginations, Thomas Corbett all too vividly in his memory.

Then Corbett continued in a husky voice, 'I've thought of what we did that day thousands of times since and gone over and over in my mind what I could or should have done. I've tried telling myself that, if we'd kept him aboard, he wouldn't have lived. The injuries to his head were too severe. He'd've died sooner or later. But thinking that don't make it any better. The truth is, sir, we committed murder and it's been lying on my conscience ever since like a stone. That's why I've come to you, Mr Holmes. I can't bear the burden no longer and I want you to ease my soul by reporting what happened to whoever needs to be told. I'm willing to make a full confession and take whatever punishment the law thinks fit for me.'

'That is highly commendable of you, but it is easier said than done, Mr Corbett.' Holmes said in a brisk, matter-of-fact manner which I thought a little brusque under the circumstances, although Corbett seemed to accept my old friend's comment, for he lowered his grizzled head in a humble, compliant manner.

'I'm in your hands, sir,' he said in a low voice.

Holmes took a turn or two up and down the room, deep in thought, eyes lowered and arms folded tightly across his chest. Then, spinning round, he confronted Corbett, his mind clearly made up.

'Before I go any further with this matter,' said he, 'first let me establish the facts of the case and, in order to do that, I need to learn from you what happened after Billy Wheeler was put overboard. You continued on your way, I assume?'

'Yes, we did, Mr Holmes. Once we were clear of Duncraig, we threw some debris into the sea – bits of wood, some rope, a lifebelt with the name *Sophy Anderson* painted on it, so that anyone finding it would think the vessel had gone down with all hands. Then we set course for Rotterdam. We had all the necessary papers to show the officials there, for the McNeil brothers had already registered the ship as the *Lucy Belle* with a shipping company based in Panama. No one questioned the papers. The McNeils had already set up a buyer in Rotterdam for the nitrate we were carrying, so we unloaded it and took on a cargo of coal which they'd also arranged in advance. We then set sail for Bergen where we sold the coal and took on another cargo. And so it went on for the next three years, going to and fro between the Baltic and the Dutch ports where we'd never traded before and where the crew was not known, as well as the Far East where we were likewise strangers.

'In the meantime, a passenger ship had picked up the debris we had thrown overboard and the *Sophy Anderson* was duly posted missing by Lloyds, presumably lost at sea with all hands. Later, the insurance money was paid out and all seemed sealed and settled, but I couldn't put it out of my mind. In fact, Mr Holmes, as the years have gone by, it's got worse, not better.'

'And where is the *Lucy Belle* now?'

'In the Port of London. We were on our way from Bremen to Shanghai when one of the crew fell down a companionway and broke his leg and we had to put in there to get him to a doctor. Chafer went off to find a replacement for him and I took him by cab to the London hospital in the Mile End Road. While I was there, I got talking to one of the porters and, without telling him what it was all about, I asked him if he knew of a detective, not a policeman, who could look into a private matter for me. It was him who mentioned your name. "Go and see Mr Holmes," said he "at 221B Baker Street. He's the best in the business."'

'Indeed!' murmured Holmes, raising his eyebrows. 'A hospital porter, your said? Was his name Reynolds, by any chance?'

Corbett looked abashed.

'I didn't ask his name, I'm afraid, Mr Holmes, but he was a little man with as much hair on his head as a billiard ball.'

Holmes threw back his head and laughed heartily at this description.

'Excellent, Mr Corbett! You have caught Reynolds exactly!' Seeing my baffled expression, he turned briefly to me in explanation. 'I met Reynolds two years ago. A lady, a Mrs Dawlish, wanted me to find her husband who was missing. To cut a very long story short, I found him in the London hospital, thanks to Reynolds's co-operation. The man had been knocked down by a hansom and had lost his memory temporarily as a result of head injuries.'

Turning back to his client, he added, 'Pray continue, Mr Corbett.'

'There is not much more to tell, sir,' he replied. 'I took a cab straight here from the hospital to ask for your help. There may not be much time to spare, Mr Holmes. At this very minute, Chafer is looking about for a new crewman to replace the one who's broken his leg. It's his intention to sail early tomorrow morning with the high tide. If it's possible, I'd like to have this business settled before we leave. God knows when we'll be back in London. Perhaps never.'

'I take your point, Mr Corbett,' Holmes said gravely. 'But before I agree to act in this matter, I must explain the serious nature of the situation. We are dealing here with murder on the part of Chafer, the ship's captain; for, if your account is correct, and I assume it is, then he gave the order for Billy Wheeler to be thrown overboard knowing he was still alive. Then there is the part played by those members of the crew who attacked the young man, against whom charges of grievous bodily harm could be brought. In addition, there is the question of your own responsibility in the affair. Supposing the case came to court with you as witness against Chafer? A clever counsel could argue that you, too, knew Wheeler was alive and yet did nothing to prevent his death by drowning.'

'I had no chance, Mr Holmes!' Corbett broke in, the sweat standing out on his brow. 'On my oath, he was thrown over the rail before I could stop it from happening!'

'On your oath!' Holmes repeated. 'That is another important point to consider, Mr Corbett, before you decide to take action. It is your word against Chafer's that Wheeler was still alive. There are no other witnesses to that fact. Chafer, who is obviously no fool, will swear to the contrary – should a trial be held – that when he felt for the carotid artery in Wheeler's neck, there was no pulse. The man was undoubtedly dead. Who is a jury most likely to believe, you or Chafer? Are you prepared to take that risk? For whatever way the decision goes, you are certain to suffer. If the vote goes against Chafer, then it is murder in which you are implicated. And if the verdict goes the other way, then you could be charged with perjury and, even if it does not come to that, your reputation will be ruined. What shipping company would be willing to take you on as mate when the imputation is you lied on oath against a senior officer? Apart from all that, there is matter of the insurance fraud in which every one of you is involved. Have you thought of that?'

As Holmes put the question, I saw Corbett's right hand make a small, involuntary movement towards his chest as if, by physically reaching for the region of his heart, he wanted to reassure himself that the decision he was about to make was the right one, despite the strain it would cause him, an action which confirmed my earlier supposition that the man was suffering from some chronic, and possibly life-threatening, cardiac condition. His reply was a further ratification, if any were needed.

'Mr Holmes,' said he in the tone of a man who has come to a decision, 'I've carried this burden for nigh on four years and I have no wish to go to my grave with it still on my conscience. Whatever the outcome, I want the truth known at last.'

'Very well, Mr Corbett!' Holmes replied, his voice as resolute and vigorous as his client's. 'Then there is only one problem left to be solved.'

'And what is that?' Corbett asked.

'The matter of proving Chafer's guilt. As I have already pointed out, it is a question of your word against Chafer's as to whether or not Wheeler was still alive when he was thrown overboard. From what you have told me about the captain, I doubt very much if he would ever confess the truth of his own volition. What is needed therefore is a witness who is prepared to support your account of the events on board the *Sophy Anderson* the day Wheeler was murdered. Is there any among the crew who was present on deck and saw what happened?'

Corbett was silent for a moment, rubbing his chin.

'Well, there's Harry Deakin, the ship's cook,' he said at last. 'He was there at the time.'

'He saw the attack on Wheeler?' Holmes asked sharply.

'He did, sir. In fact he tried to stop it, but he was outnumbered.'

'And he was there when Wheeler's body was wrapped in the canvas?'

'He was, sir.'

'And saw you put the St Christopher on Wheeler's chest?'

'Aye. He helped me fold the canvas back so that I could get my hand in. And I'm pretty sure he saw Chafer make that cutting motion across his throat because, after he made it, Deakin looked hard at me as if to ask what was going on. But nothing was said either then or later.'

'No matter. If Deakin would be willing to make a statement, that would be enough corroboration to persuade a jury you are telling the truth. Is Deakin still on board the ship?'

'Aye, he is, Mr Holmes.'

'Could he be persuaded to speak up for you in court if need be?'

Corbett looked doubtful.

'I wouldn't like to swear to that, Mr Holmes. Deakin likes a quiet life and he's afraid of anyone in authority. If it came to choosing between me and Chafer, he'd be more inclined to pick the Captain or, at best, refuse to say anything.'

'Then he must be forced to speak up on your behalf,' Holmes replied.

'But how?' Corbett asked with a hopeless air.

Without replying, Holmes got to his feet and strode up and down the room several times, before swinging back to face Corbett.

'Who has left the crew since Wheeler's murder, preferably someone who is himself dead?' he demanded.

Corbett seemed bewildered by the question.

'Well, there's Tommy Brewster, a deck-hand. He was killed when he fell from the rigging last February on a voyage to . . . '

'Never mind the details. Was the man literate?'

'Literate?' Corbett stammered, his bewilderment increasing.

'Could he read and write?'

'Aye, sir. He could.'

'Splendid!' Holmes exclaimed, rubbing his hands together with satisfaction. 'Now only one problem remains. Can you arrange for Dr Watson and myself to come aboard the *Lucy Belle* without arousing any suspicion?'

'Yes, I could, sir, provided it's after dark. If you could get yourselves up to look like seamen and make your way to Picott's Wharf in St Catherine's dock by ten o'clock tonight, I'll be on deck with a lantern. I'll wave it three times when the coast is clear for you to come up the gangplank. Is there anything else I can do?'

'Yes. Make sure Deakin is on board. Perhaps you could also arrange for a cabin to be available for Dr Watson and myself, equipped with paper, pen and ink. And now, Mr Corbett, I wish you good morning. We shall meet again at ten o'clock.'

'But your plan . . . ?' Corbett began as he rose to his feet. However, his protest was to no avail. Shaking hands firmly with him, Holmes conducted him to the door.

'Yes, what *is* your plan, Holmes?' I asked when he had returned to his chair.

But I fared no better than his client.

'You will find out tonight, my dear fellow,' he replied with a smile. 'All I will tell you for the moment is that what I propose using is one of the oldest tricks in the world and, if Harry Deakin is deceived by it, as I have every reason to suppose he will be, then we will have a witness to testify to all that Corbett has told us. I suggest you call here again at nine o'clock tonight. And, by the way, make sure you bring your revolver.'

And with that, he picked up the Morning Post and, giving it a shake, retired behind its open pages.

Feeling dismissed, I, too, left the house to return to Paddington, where I was kept busy for the rest of the day with my medical duties. Although the practice was not yet a large one, having been neglected by the previous owner, I was determined by sheer diligence and hard work to make a success of it.

However, despite my professional preoccupations, whenever I had a spare moment, my thoughts turned to Holmes's parting remarks. What was this trick he had mentioned, I wondered. And why was he so sure it would deceive Harry Deakin, whom he had never met?

I also had certain arrangements of my own to make with regard to the coming appointment with Holmes later that evening. Not wishing to alarm my wife unnecessarily, I did not speak of his advice to bring my revolver with me, but mentioned only an inquiry in which he had asked me to take part. My dear Mary, the most generous and understanding of women, raised no objections. In fact, she urged me to go.

'You deserve a change,' she said. 'You have been working far too hard recently and are looking quite pale. An evening spent with your old friend will do you the world of good.'

The only other person who had to be consulted was my neighbour Jackson, a fellow doctor with whom I had a reciprocal arrangement to act as locum should the need arise. Having gained his agreement to be on call that evening, I set off by cab for Baker Street, my heart beating high at the prospect of the adventure to come. For, although I was happily married and would not have changed my life for all the money in the world, I must confess that there were times when I missed that tingle of excitement which taking part in any of Holmes's investigations always roused in me. Part of it was the intellectual stimulation of such occasions, but mostly it was the thrill of the physical challenge which stirred the blood, and I could not help smiling as I felt the comfortable weight in my pocket of my army revolver, a relic of my days in Afghanistan serving with the 66th Berkshire Regiment of Foot.

Holmes was waiting for me in my old Baker Street lodgings with our disguises in the form of pea jackets and peaked caps, very like those which Corbett had been wearing, and once we had we put these on, we took a cab to Picott's wharf.

It was a damp, overcast night with low clouds and therefore there was very little light from either the moon or the stars. Once we had passed from the well-lit streets of west London into the meaner byways of the East End, the only illumination was the subdued yellow gleam of the street lamps, which glistened fitfully on the wet pavements and the brick façades of buildings. Even the passers-by seemed diminished by the weather and slunk furtively along like sad ghosts, huddled in mufflers and shawls against the chill night air. The only bright islands in this sea of murky darkness were garishly-lit taverns and public houses which shone like beacons beckoning the inhabitants of the dingy streets to their warm, glittering interiors.

After travelling along Leadenhall Street for some distance, the cab turned right into a labyrinth of narrow side streets behind St Katherine's Dock, until at last it drew up at an arched stone entrance from which a cobbled lane gave access to the wharf. It was poorly lit by a single gas lamp fixed to the brickwork by an iron bracket, and by this dim glow we made our way between high walls of blackened brick towards the river Thames, led by our ears and noses rather than our eyes, for although we could see little, we could smell the unmistakable odour of river mud mingled with the fainter tang of the sea, and hear the heavy, rhythmic, liquid slop of water against wood and stone.

By that time, the drizzle had turned into a fine rain which lay over the scene like a sombre wash over a pen and ink drawing, so that everything, the wharf, the vessels, the river itself, seemed to blur and run into one another, the dark hulks of the ships at anchor melting into the river, the tall masts and rigging merging with the sky. As for the river itself, it had turned into a dark, sliding mass, like thick oil, in which the glow from the ships' lanterns was smeared into long, shifting patterns of light.

We felt our way gingerly along the wooden planking of the wharf, so sodden with rain that the sound of our footsteps was deadened as, stepping carefully round casks and barrels and over ropes which lay like coiled serpents in our path, we approached the vast bulk of the *Lucy Belle* which towered above us, the lower part of its four masts just visible before the upper sections and the rigging were swallowed up by the lowering darkness.

There were few lights aboard the ship and no sign of any human activity. Indeed it had the ghostly air of a vessel abandoned by its crew after some terrible tragedy at sea, and I instinctively reached into my pocket to feel for my revolver as a talisman against some unknown danger.

It was a moment of foolishness which quickly passed. Moments later, we heard a distant bell strike ten o'clock and, on this signal, the yellow gleam of a lantern sprang up on the darkened deck above us, hung motionless for a second and then gently swung from left to right and then back again.

This was our signal and we groped our way forward towards the gangplank, which we mounted slowly, for it was treacherous underfoot, until at last we reached the top and were hauled on to the deck by Thomas Corbett who loomed out of the blackness to meet us.

He led the way towards the stern of the ship to a flat-roofed wooden construction housing the passengers' accommodation and down some steps into a dimly-lit passage lined with doors, one of which he opened before ushering us into a cabin furnished with a bunk bed and a number of lockers, as well as a small table and a chair screwed to the floor. As Holmes had requested, a pen, inkwell and several sheets of paper were lying on the table, above which a lantern was hanging from the ceiling, swinging gently with the movement of the ship and casting glinting lights and shadows over the polished mahogany and brass fittings with which the cabin was equipped.

Thomas Corbett waited until we had settled ourselves, Holmes on the chair, I on the edge of the bunk, before announcing, 'Since you seem satisfied with the arrangements, Mr Holmes, I'll fetch Harry Deakin to speak to you.'

Holmes nodded to show his agreement and, as Corbett left, we divested ourselves of our seamen's outer garments, Holmes first producing from the pocket of his pea jacket a large envelope containing a sheet of stiff paper covered with legal-looking writing that had an official seal of red wax affixed to the bottom, stamped with what appeared to be the impress of a coat of arms.

Having laid this sheet of paper alongside those provided by Corbett, he looked across at me and chuckled.

'Here, Watson, you see the stock-in-trade for performing the old trick I mentioned to you.'

'But where on earth did you get that letter?' I asked.

'From a dealer in Charing Cross Road who sells second-hand books and old legal documents. If you examine the one I have here, you will see that it is connected with the lease of a property drawn up many years ago.'

'But suppose Deakin realises what it is?'

'He will not be given the opportunity to look at it, my dear fellow, as you will shortly see. Ah, here he is now!' He broke off as there came a knock on the door and Corbett ushered in a nervous-looking, middle-aged man, the very antithesis of the conventional image of a ship's cook. His features were thin and melancholy, his stature small, and his general air was one of wary suspicion as he stood just inside the door, his eyes darting between Holmes and myself before shifting down to the table where the papers were laid out.

'Mr Deakin?' Holmes asked, his voice as clipped and austere as a prosecuting counsel's.

The man nodded.

'Mr Harry Deakin?' my old friend persisted.

'That's me, sir,' Deakin replied in a hoarse voice.

The impact of this opening move was evident in Deakin's demeanour. He seemed to shrink in upon himself, and shifted from one foot to another in a manner which suggested extreme unease.

'I have reason to believe,' Holmes continued in the same terse voice, 'that three years ago you served as cook aboard the barque the *Sophy Anderson* and that . . .'

At this point he broke off briefly to consult the document with the wax seal as if to confirm his facts before continuing ' . . . and that you made the acquaintance of a deck-hand called Billy Wheeler, who later was attacked in a brawl on board the same vessel.'

The effect of this statement on Deakin was immediate and dramatic.

'That's a flaming lie!' he shouted, starting forward so violently that, thinking he was about to attack Holmes, I jumped to my feet to seize my revolver. But Holmes waved me back with a masterful gesture of his hand.

'Is it indeed a lie? Well, we shall see,' he told Deakin, tapping with a long index finger on the official-looking document. 'You will no doubt recall Tommy Brewster, the deck-hand who was killed by a fall from the rigging? Then let me inform you that the year before that accident, Brewster made a statement to a lawyer about those events aboard the *Sophy Anderson* and the death of Billy Wheeler. So there is no use your denying the facts. I have them here in black and white, signed and sealed. Do you still deny that such an incident took place?'

At once, all the fire went out of Deakin, who seemed to shrink in upon himself, his shoulders bowed and his expression one of utter defeat and despair.

'I ain't denying nothing, sir,' he mumbled. 'It all 'appened as Tommy says but I swear on my mother's 'ead I ain't guilty of Billy's death. I never touched 'im. It were the others 'oo set on 'im and beat 'im. I tried to stop 'em, but what good was one man against five?'

'You were also a witness to other events on that same morning, I believe?' Holmes continued, scanning the document as if reading from its contents. 'You saw, did you not, Captain Chafer feel for a pulse in Wheeler's neck and then pronounce him dead?'

'I did, sir,' Deakin replied in the tone of a man who realises he is defeated.

'And you witnessed the mate, Thomas Corbett, placing a St Christopher medallion on Wheeler's chest?'

'I saw that, too, sir. I 'elped 'im put it there.'

'You also saw Corbett look across at the Captain?'

'Aye, sir.'

'What did Chafer do when Corbett looked at him?'

Deakin ran his tongue over his lips before replying.

'The Cap'n drew a finger across 'is throat as if with a knife,' the man replied without any prompting.

'Indicating what?'

Again Deakin hung his head, refusing to meet Holmes's eyes.

'I don't foller you, sir.'

My old friend flung himself impatiently back in his chair.

'Do not trifle with me, my good man!' he cried. 'You know perfectly well the meaning of the gesture. It suggests that the person whom it is intended for, Mr Corbett on that occasion, should keep silent or he would have his throat cut, does it not? Does it not, Deakin?' he repeated, his voice rising.

The wretched man glanced up briefly.

'Aye, it does, sir.' he agreed softly.

'In other words, Chafer was threatening to murder Corbett?'

'I suppose so, sir.'

The words were dragged out of Deakin.

'There is no "suppose" about it,' Holmes retorted.

He paused for a few seconds but, receiving no further response from Deakin, he pressed on.

'Do you know what Corbett was supposed to keep silent about?' When Deakin shook his head dumbly, Holmes looked down at the document in front of him, his eyes scanning it as if he were looking for a particular passage. Then, raising his head, he looked directly at Deakin, his gaze fixed and implacable.

'Then allow me to inform you, Mr Deakin. The truth which Chafer was so anxious Corbett should not divulge was this: Billy Wheeler was still alive when he was wrapped in that canvas shroud and put over the side of the ship. In plain words, he was murdered!'

For several seconds, there was a dreadful silence which seemed interminable and then, without uttering a word, Deakin's head fell forward and he began to weep. It was a pitiful sight to witness. I doubt if Deakin had wept since he was a child and the tears were wrung out of him in a series of harsh cries, more like the death throes of an animal in torment than a human being.

I was considerably relieved when Holmes, getting up from his chair, came across to whisper to me, 'Find Corbett and tell him to signal again with the lantern.'

As I left the cabin, I glanced back to see the tall figure of my friend standing over the crouched form of the ship's cook, his arms folded and an expression on his lean features as hard and as implacable as if they had been carved from granite. He put me in mind of some grim statue personifying Vengeance itself.

I had no difficulty in finding Corbett. He was anxiously pacing up and down in the passageway outside the cabin and, as soon as I gave him Holmes's instructions, he seized his lantern and made for the companionway which led up to the deck. I followed at his heels, wondering who or what the second signal was intended for.

It soon became clear. As soon as Corbett had swung the lantern, several human forms emerged from various hiding-places among the shadows below on the wharf and began to mount the gang-plank. At their head was the unmistakable figure of Inspector Lestrade dressed in unofficial tweeds, his sharp, sallow features turned up towards the light of the lantern, his dark eyes glinting suspiciously. Behind him tramped half a dozen uniformed men, their black waterproof capes reflecting the light like the oily surface of the Thames.

Lestrade seemed as surprised to see me as I was to see him.

'What's going on here, Dr Watson?' he demanded.

'Did not Holmes explain matters to you?' I countered.

'No, he did not. He called at Scotland Yard this afternoon when I was out and left a message asking me to come here with half a dozen men at half past ten this evening on what he called a very serious matter. What is this matter, may I ask? And it had better be serious.

I don't take kindly to requests to take myself and a posse of my officers out on a wet night to the back of beyond unless it is a very serious matter indeed. If it wasn't Mr Holmes who asked, I'd've stayed at the Yard in front of the office fire.'

'I think you had better wait and ask Holmes himself,' I replied, a little uneasy at Lestrade's obvious annoyance. 'This gentleman, by the way, is Mr Thomas Corbett, the mate of the vessel the *Lucy Belle*, or rather the *Sophy Anderson*.'

'Make up your mind, Dr Watson,' Lestrade snapped, nodding briefly at Corbett to acknowledge his presence. Realising the situation was too complex to explain to Lestrade in a few sentences, I led the way towards the passengers' accommodation.

Leaving the six uniformed officers outside the door, only the three of us entered the cabin. Even so, there was hardly room for all of us, and Corbett and I were crushed against the bunk bed while Lestrade approached the table where Holmes and Deakin were standing, Holmes looking bright-eyed and confident, Deakin cowed and nervous.

'Ah, Lestrade!' Holmes exclaimed as the Inspector came towards him. 'I am sorry to call you out on such an inclement evening. Allow me to explain the situation.'

This he proceeded to do in a few concise sentences, while Deakin shuffled his feet and hung his head in shame, and Lestrade's mouth dropped open in amazement at the account.

'So you see,' Holmes concluded briskly, 'what we have here is a case of murder, as well as fraud on a massive scale. And this is what I propose should be done so that the case may go to court. Thomas Corbett is willing to give evidence on oath to those counts of murder and fraud which I have just reported. That evidence will be corroborated by Harry Deakin, the ship's cook, from whom I have just taken a statement,' Holmes continued, picking up a sheet of paper from the desk and brandishing it in the air. 'I now suggest that Mr Deakin signs it in your presence, Lestrade, after which I shall add my signature as witness.'

The little ceremony was carried out in silence as Holmes gave the pen, already dipped in ink, to Deakin who, awed by the gravity of the occasion, signed his name with a trembling hand before Holmes, recharging the pen with ink, added his own signature with a flourish and handed the statement to the Inspector.

'And now, Lestrade,' he concluded, laying down the pen, 'I suggest you arrest Chafer and charge him with the murder of Billy Wheeler.

The rest of the crew involved in the assault on the young man and the insurance fraud may be rounded up later. But I do most earnestly advise you to put a guard on the gang-planks so that none of the crew can escape. Meanwhile, Mr Corbett, the ship's mate, will show you the way to the Captain's cabin.'

Much bemused by Holmes's masterly control of the situation, Lestrade, who under the circumstances had no other option, followed Corbett out of the cabin and we heard the tramp of their feet and those of the accompanying uniformed officers proceed along the passage on their way to arrest Chafer, Deakin taking the opportunity to scuttle out after them like a frightened rabbit released from a trap.

'You see what I mean about the oldest trick in the world, Watson?' Holmes remarked as the door closed behind them.

'You mean, of course, Brewster's supposed statement?' I replied.

'Of course, my dear fellow. If you want someone to confess, all you have to do is declare you have irrefutable proof of his guilt. Unless the suspect is unusually hardened and, in my experience, he is most often not, then he will invariably crumble and confess all. It often works. There is a story, probably apocryphal, of telegrams being sent to various members of a gentlemen's club stating quite simply, "Flee the country. All is discovered." It is claimed that half a dozen of them did exactly that.

'You may also have noticed that it was not necessary to lie directly to Deakin. I simply asked him if he knew that Tommy Brewster had made a statement about the events on board the *Sophy Anderson* before he died.'

'At the same time drawing his attention to the legal document,' I pointed out.

'Oh, that is perfectly acceptable under the rules of the game,' Holmes replied with a shrug and a smile. 'Any conjurer or stage magician uses exactly the same ruse when performing a trick. He makes sure the audience's eyes are directed towards what he wants them to observe. Anyway, whatever the method employed, it has been a good night's work, do you not agree? I suggest we return to Baker Street and celebrate its conclusion with a whisky and soda in front of the fire.'

Of course, it was not the end of the affair. After months of investigation on the part of the police in rounding up all the original members of the crew of the *Sophy Anderson* who could be traced and who had agreed to the insurance fraud and been present at the murder of Billy Wheeler, they as well as the main participants in the events, were sent for trial at the Old Bailey and were sentenced to various terms of imprisonment, including the McNeil brothers who had set up the scheme in the first place. Because of his direct participation in the murder, Captain Chafer was sentenced to be hanged.

Thomas Corbett, like most of the others, was found guilty of conspiracy to defraud and was given ten years in gaol.

It is with mixed feelings that I have to report that he did not live to serve out this sentence. Eighteen months later he died of a heart attack while in prison; a sad end for a man of such courage and honesty, but probably one he himself would have wished for.

In recognition of these qualities of his, I have decided not to publish this account but will place it among my other papers in my dispatch box, a decision, I feel, which would also have met with his approval.

Sherlock Holmes and the Ghost of Christmas Past

DAVID STUART DAVIES

It was approaching the season of Christmas in the year 1899 that Sherlock Holmes was presented with one of his strangest adventures, a case which he solved in a unique fashion. How well I remember that bleak December afternoon when we received Miss Caroline Harrison in our Baker Street rooms. It had hardly grown light all day, and after lunch the sky had darkened further as a precursor to snow. As I lit the lamps, I gazed out of the window and watched the white flakes patter silently on our panes. It was then that we heard the bell below, and shortly Mrs Hudson ushered in our visitor: a young lady of considerable beauty. She was tall, with well-defined features, a porcelain complexion framed by a tumble of rich, raven hair, and was in possession of two of the most startling blue eyes that I have ever encountered. Although it was clear to me that she was an assured and confident young woman with a strong independent streak, as she took a seat by our fireside one could not help but observe that she was in some state of distress.

Of course this fact had not been missed by Holmes's searching gaze and as he addressed her, he used his softest and kindest of tones. 'I am Sherlock Holmes', said he, taking a seat opposite the young lady, 'and this is my friend and colleague, Dr Watson.'

I nodded my head in greeting. She acknowledged this with a gentle smile.

'My name is Caroline Harrison,' she said.

'Now then', announced Holmes in a more businesslike fashion, 'any young lady who is so distracted that she dons two odd gloves before setting out in such inclement weather and has walked a fair part of the way to Baker Street . . . '

'How do you know that?' she asked more with suspicion than surprise.

Holmes smiled indulgently. 'The toes of your boots are already whitened by the damp conditions and your outer coat is heavy with moisture. No doubt you had difficulty hailing a cab in the snow.'

'Quite so,' she agreed.

'Now then, Miss Harrison, if you will be so kind as to relate what is troubling you enough to bring you to my doorstep on such a harsh winter's day, then perhaps I may be able to help you'.

She nodded and took a deep breath, summoning up the courage to commence her narrative. She stared into our fire as though she derived inspiration and comfort from the flickering flames.

'The matter concerns my father, Septimus Harrison, a successful stockbroker in the city. He is being haunted and I fear for his sanity.'

With a groan, Holmes flopped back in his chair. 'Miss Harrison, forgive me for being blunt, but I am a detective. I do not deal with hauntings. Ghosts and spirits from the grave are beyond my purview and interest. May I suggest you consult a priest or a spiritualist.'

'Holmes, that's a little harsh,' I said, observing how my friend's rather brittle outburst had further distressed our visitor.

'Please, at least hear me out. The matter is not a straightforward one: there is a mystery involved which, should it be exposed, I believe may alleviate my father's oppression.'

'Very well, Miss Harrison. I have no wish to be rude, but as I intimated, I confine my activities to this world.'

I shot Holmes a warning look. 'Let us hear your story, Miss Harrison,' I said.

'It really began a year ago. I live with my father in a town house in Kensington, my mother having died of a fever some eight years ago. I had been in the country for a week staying with friends. On my return home I found that a stranger had moved in. He was a stranger to me, that is, but my father introduced him as Oscar Leyland, an old friend from his youth. Apparently Leyland had been in Australia for the last thirty years, where he had made his fortune. He had now returned to this country to settle down in his old age. It seems that he had persuaded my father to let him move in with him until such time as he could find a suitable property to purchase for his own. He was a vile man, Mr Holmes. He had thick coarse features and even coarser manners. He spoke with a harsh guttural Australian accent and was not averse to swearing even in the presence of the servants and myself. He wore gaudy checked jackets and smoked little cheroots constantly that filled the house with an unpleasant smell. I could see that my father was unhappy to accommodate such an unsavoury individual but I suppose he felt obliged to help out an old comrade.'

'Had you heard your father speak of this man before?'

'Never. As you may gather, my father and I are very close, and I know all about his life and history, but until last December I had never heard of Oscar Leyland.'

She said the name with such disdain that her lips twisted in an unpleasant fashion, robbing her face of its beauty.

'I know this is fanciful, gentlemen, but it was as though Leyland had some hold over my father. The man had only been with us a fortnight and I was beginning to find the situation intolerable. He would leer at me over the dining table and on one occasion he tried to steal a kiss when we were alone together. I slapped his face but all he did was laugh, revealing two rows of ugly broken teeth. When I complained to my father he just passed the incident off as an example of Leyland's high spirits.'

'How dreadful,' I murmured.

'Matters came to a head two nights before Christmas. Leyland had remained in the house all day drinking brandy. I had been out Christmas shopping and had lunch with an old school friend and of course my father had been at his office. Dinner that evening was a nightmare. Leyland, barely sober, slobbered over the food, hardly able to hold his knife and fork. I absented myself early and went to my room. Later I became aware of loud voices. It was the first time I had heard my father raise his voice in anger. Nevertheless Leyland's booming voice brayed the loudest.'

'Did you hear anything of the conversation?'

'A few snatches only. I remember my father saying, ' . . . you promised, you devil, you promised.' And at one point Leyland roared, 'but she's mine, that's all that matters.'

'Did you take the reference to 'she' to mean you?' asked Holmes.

'I honestly don't know. Events came to a tragic climax that night. I was awoken sometime in the early hours by the sound of gunshots and cries. They were coming from my father's private office on the ground floor. When I got there Sheridan, our butler, had also arrived carrying a small candelabra. He ventured into the room, gave a gasp of alarm and emerged again quickly saying that I should not enter. I ignored his plea, brushed past him and went inside. The sight that met my eyes nearly caused me to faint. There lying on the floor were the bodies of Oscar Leyland and my father. Both had been wounded. The safe was open and the window had been smashed. It seemed that the two men had surprised an armed burglar and had been shot.

The police and the doctor were sent for. As it turned out my father had only been injured in the left arm but Oscar Leyland had been shot through the heart and was dead. The police found the gun in the shrubbery beneath the window. When my father recovered sufficiently, he recounted the incident. Apparently, he had persuaded Leyland to move out of our house to rented accommodation and was arranging to pay him one hundred pounds for his inconvenience. They had gone down to the office to retrieve the cash and seal the deal and had surprised the armed intruder, who without hesitation fired, wounding my father and killing Leyland. The burglar made a swift escape without taking anything. Despite the police investigation, he was never found.'

'Mmm,' said Holmes, 'burglars have a remarkable facility for disappearing into thin air. But pray continue, Miss Harrison, there is more to your story, I am sure. We haven't reached the haunting yet!'

Apparently oblivious of my friend's pointed remark, Miss Harrison resumed her narrative. 'My father recovered from his injury by the early spring and he returned to work, although now he only goes to the office three days a week. I said that he had recovered from his injury. Physically he had, but mentally he became a changed man. He seems to carry around with him an unseen burden of sorrow. He jumps at the slightest noise and keeps a light burning in his room at night because he has become frightened of the dark. But just recently he has grown much worse. As the anniversary of that fateful night nears – two days before Christmas – he has begun to have delusions. He claims that he is being haunted by Oscar Leyland.'

'In what manner?'

'Apparently he appears to him in the mirror in his room. Last night I listened at my father's door and heard him talking to the ghost.'

'I assume the ghost did not reply?'

Miss Harrison shook her head. 'Of course not. I am entirely of your persuasion, Mr Holmes. I do not believe in ghosts. I am convinced that this apparition is a figment of my father's tortured imagination but it is generated by some secret he shared with that foul creature Leyland. I have tried to raise the subject with him, but at the mere mention of his name my father shakes his head, refusing to talk, and leaves the room. I had thought that with your special investigative powers you could find out what this "secret" might be.'

Holmes beamed. 'Now I see why you have consulted me. There is certainly a case here.'

For a brief moment the suggestion of a smile touched the young woman's tired features. 'Do you think you can help me, Mr Holmes?'

My friend steepled his fingers and brought them to his lips as he lost himself in contemplation for some moments. 'I believe so. A plan of action is forming, but I will need time and further thought before it is fully engendered. Would you call here at noon tomorrow and then we can take the matter further?'

Now the smile became a reality and Miss Harrison's eyes lit up with pleasure and relief. 'I will be here at the appointed hour.'

'Two further points. May I ask how old you are?'

'I am in my twenty-ninth year,' she replied without shyness.

'Thank you. And do you happen to possess a photograph of Oscar Leyland?'

Caroline Harrison shook her head. 'I do not have a photograph, but . . . ' She paused and opened her handbag and withdrew a large sheet of paper. 'Here is a sketch of the devil, which I did from memory for you. I thought it would be useful if you could actually picture the man.'

Holmes gave a chortle and took the sketch from her. 'Excellent. This I am sure will aid us into bringing this matter to a head. Now Miss Harrison, I suggest you wrap yourself up well and good friend Watson here will endeavour to secure a cab for you, eh, Watson?'

When I returned to our rooms after seeing Miss Harrison safely into a hansom, to my surprise I found Holmes engrossed once more in the book he had been reading all the morning.

'Does this mean you have already solved the mystery?' I said sitting opposite him by the fire.

'Not quite, but I believe this book may aid me in my investigation.'

'What is it?'

'It is Sigmund Freud's *Interpretation of Dreams*. As a medical man you will have heard of it.'

'Indeed.'

'It really is a fascinating analysis of how the brain can affect and indeed control our emotions, thoughts and actions.'

'You really think it can have some bearing on this case?'

'Yes, I do, Watson. I do.'

The next day dawned cold and bright. The snow had ceased to fall, but it had left behind a crisp white covering that decorated the city in readiness for Christmas. Holmes had gone out on some errand or other shortly after breakfast, and I spent the morning alone. He returned just before noon, at which time Miss Harrison arrived with an eagerness to learn what conclusions my friend had reached concerning her dilemma. In typical fashion Holmes had not discussed the matter with me and so I had no idea what he was about to say to his client.

'With your permission I should like to conduct an experiment this evening, Miss Harrison, on the anniversary of the death of Oscar Leyland', he said, once the young lady was seated by our cheery fire. 'And to carry out this experiment, I shall require your assistance.'

'I'll do anything, if it will resolve matters,' she said firmly.

Holmes gave a quick smile. 'I thought you would say that. I need to gain access to your father's bedroom this evening without him being aware. Could that be arranged?'

Miss Harrison hesitated a moment while she thought the matter over. 'We usually dine at seven-thirty, after which it has become my father's habit to retire to his bedroom. I believe he reads a little before going to bed. I could make sure the back door is left open during our meal, which would present you with the opportunity of entering the house and slipping upstairs to his room.'

Holmes rubbed his hands together. 'Excellent! You can provide me with a sketch map of the house. I must be sure that I enter the correct room.'

'Of course.'

Suddenly Holmes's face became very serious. He reached out and took the young woman's hands in his. 'I have a strong belief that this evening I can uncover the truth, the secret, as you call it, which has brought distress to your father. However I shall be using the most unconventional methods in order to do so. I have to warn you that should I be successful, I cannot guarantee that the outcome will be joyous.'

She nodded gravely. 'I understand. I feel that anything, any truth will be easier to bear than this dreadful uncertainty that is driving my father to an early grave.'

'This is one occasion when I shall not require your services, my dear Watson. I must carry out this little investigation on my own,' Holmes informed me after our visitor had left. Seeing my disappointed expression, he smiled and patted me on the shoulder. 'Fear not, I will present you with all the details on my return. And there is one thing you could do which would be of the greatest assistance . . .'

'Anything.'

'I estimate that it will be between midnight and one in the morning when I return. I will not have had dinner and so a little late supper would be most welcome. As it will be in the early hours of Christmas Eve something festive would be most appropriate, with a good bottle of claret to wash it down. Would you be so kind as to arrange that?'

'Yes,' I said with some disappointment, not happy at being on the sidelines in one of Holmes's investigations.

He spent most of the afternoon in his room, emerging at around five o'clock. He had retired as the tall, upright, clean-shaven fellow-lodger with the keen aquiline features and dark swept-back hair that I knew so well, but he reappeared as a bloated grotesque fellow with a balding pate and fiery side-whiskers. He shambled towards me, dressed in cord britches and a vivid checked jacket.

I gasped at this transformation. I had seen Holmes in many disguises but this, I believe, was his greatest triumph. He was the very image of Oscar Leyland as sketched by Miss Harrison.

Holmes smiled at my astonishment, revealing a row of ugly and broken teeth. 'Well, I must leave you, my friend; I have some haunting to see to.'

Without another word he swept from the room. I moved to the window and saw him emerge into the snow-bedecked Baker Street, moving swiftly down the pavement in search of a cab.

I spent the night between bouts of reading one of Clark Russell's seafaring tales and skimming through the pages of Freud's *Interpretation of Dreams* in an attempt to determine what my friend had planned this evening. As the clock chimed midnight I was no wiser. As the minute crept past the quarter hour, I gazed at the festive cold supper on our dining table that Mrs Hudson had prepared for us, along with the inviting bottle of claret, and I was tempted to start the meal without Holmes. As my hand reached for the corkscrew, I heard a foot on the stair. The door burst open, and a dishevelled fellow, half in and half out of his disguise, crossed the threshold.

'Holmes,' I cried, relieved to see him.

He grinned at me, and I was pleased to see that he had discarded the grotesque dentures he had worn earlier that evening.

'It is over,' he said.

Some five minutes later, with all vestiges of his disguise removed, Sherlock Holmes was his old sleek self again. Wrapped in his mouse-coloured dressing gown, he was seated opposite me by the fire, sipping a glass of claret.

'I beg you, keep me in suspense no longer,' I said eagerly.

Holmes nodded. 'It has been a most instructive affair, my friend. As you are well aware, from the outset I knew that whatever kind of dark shadow haunted Septimus Harrison it did not have its origin in the realms of the supernatural; rather it was some real and tangible ghost from the past. And quite obviously that ghost was Oscar Leyland. He disappeared from Harrison's life over thirty years ago, and then he suddenly returns posing a threat to the stability and serenity of his household. Why? What was the hold Leyland had over Harrison? One could only surmise and certainly I came up with several theories to explain the situation. But those snatches of conversation which his daughter relayed to us helped me narrow down the matter. You remember, she heard her father exclaim, 'you promised, you devil, you promised'; and Leyland responded with 'but she's mine, that's all that matters.' I deduced that the promise was for Leyland to leave Harrison and his family alone. Why? Well because in some way 'she', that is Miss Caroline Harrison, was his. In what way, you might ask. In the only way possible given the thirty year absence and the fact that Miss Harrison is twenty-nine.'

'She is his daughter!' I gasped.

'That's how I read the riddle. This morning I visited the various shipping lines to check the passenger lists from Australia to this country in the November and December of last year. I discovered that the SS Gerontes docked at Southampton on 25 November 1898 with a certain Oscar Leyland on board. However, the gentleman in question was travelling third class – hardly the means of travel for a rich man. Obviously he had returned to this country penniless and was intent on securing a home and finances from Septimus Harrison because he had some hold over the poor devil.'

'Caroline was really Leyland's daughter.'

'Yes. It has the hallmarks of a Greek tragedy, doesn't it? It also became clear to me that the scenario of the attempted robbery was a set up in order for Harrison to kill Leyland. And so it turned out to be.'

'How do you know for certain?'

'Because Harrison told me tonight. In reading Freud, I became convinced that the apparition of Leyland that Harrison claims to have seen was merely a projection of his own guilt, and so I reasoned that if I could impersonate this ghost I could elicit a confession from the man, thus relieving him of his terrible burden. That is what I did. When Harrison retired to bed, I was waiting for him in his room, secreted behind a curtain. He nearly fainted when I emerged from my hiding place but he was soon pleading for forgiveness. With gentle prompting on my part, he revealed the full story of his tragedy.'

'Over thirty years ago Harrison and Leyland sought the affection of a young woman called Emily. She was torn between them but one night Leyland forced his attentions upon her. He then deserted her once he knew she was bearing his child. Septimus Harrison offered to marry the girl and take the baby as his. He also paid for Leyland's passage to Australia and gave him the sum of five hundred pounds to help establish himself there on the promise that he would never return to England. Then last year, like some dark phantom, he returned to blackmail Harrison into providing him with shelter and money. He threatened to tell Caroline that she was in fact his daughter if Harrison did not comply.'

'The situation became intolerable for Harrison and so he lured Leyland to his office in the house in the small hours with the promise of more money. He had already faked a burglary scene when Leyland entered. Harrison then shot his tormentor dead before wounding himself to add to the authenticity of the burglary story.'

'It is fantastic.'

'We often forget how often the thread of the fantastic runs through what are perceived as ordinary lives,' said Holmes, draining his glass. 'Harrison confessed all to my disguised persona. Then it was time to reveal myself. By now the fellow was drained of emotion and my revelation prompted little reaction. I could see that by his open confession the weight of guilt had been lifted from his shoulders.'

'But the man is a murderer.'

'In the eyes of the law, yes. Man-made law. But what he did was done to protect the happiness and sanity of his innocent daughter, to protect her from the clutches of a heartless and evil man. I for one cannot condemn him for that. I believe that he has suffered enough. I promised him that I would keep his secret. I told him that neither his daughter nor the authorities would ever learn the truth from me.'

I raised my eyebrows in surprise.

'Apart from this one act, Septimus Harrison has lived a good and blameless life, and certainly he will not transgress again. And after all, my dear Watson, it is the season of forgiveness. Now, pour me another glass of this excellent claret and then let us attack this excellent cold supper that you have arranged for us.'

As we repaired to the dining table, I asked Holmes what he had told Miss Harrison of the case.

'Nothing. As I left the house I informed her that the matter was settled, but that detectives like magicians have their procedures which must remain secret. I assured her that her father will be haunted no more. That brought a smile to those careworn features. Now, my dear fellow, as we have passed into the hours of Christmas Eve, may I raise my glass and wish you a very merry Christmas.'

The Dragon of Lea Lane

MATTHEW BOOTH

I have remarked elsewhere that from the years 1894 to 1901, Mr Sherlock Holmes was a very busy man. During those years, he distinguished himself in a number of investigations which I have subsequently made public. By way of example, the terrible death of Black Peter will no doubt recall itself to students of these demonstrations of my friend's peculiar talents. I also remain hopeful that I will gain approval in time to provide full details of the terrible affair of the Kensington Plague, the solution of which was given to Holmes by a close examination of a dead man's handkerchief.

Another enquiry recalls itself to my mind, which was so remarkable in its details and displayed my companion's gifts so acutely, that I feel these chronicles would be incomplete without some record of it. I refer to the brutal murder of Lawton Fields, and the terrible truth surrounding the Dragon of Lea Lane.

It was in the latter part of the second week in October 1895, that we were sitting together at the breakfast table when our landlady brought in a telegram. Holmes tore it open, perused it, before tossing it to one side. He rose from his chair and paced up and down the sitting room, although it was evident from his expression that the contents had intrigued him. He rang for the landlady, scribbled a response to the telegram, and ordered her to dispatch it at once. As she closed the door behind her, he turned swiftly to me.

'Cast your discerning eye over that, friend Watson,' said he, pointing to the telegram. 'When you have done so, get your hat and coat and meet me downstairs.'

Such curt instructions were not uncommon from him when the possibility of a problem had presented itself to him, and he had walked briskly from the room before I had even had the opportunity to digest the contents of the telegram. It was itself a terse communication from our old comrade, Inspector Lestrade, and ran as follows.

TERRIBLE BUSINESS AT WHYTEDALE, LARGE VILLA IN NORWOOD.
MURDER. PROMPT ASSISTANCE REQUIRED. MUCH IN YOUR LINE.
SEND REPLY, WILL MEET AT LOCAL STATION. LESTRADE.

Within quarter of an hour, I was seated beside my companion in a hansom, rattling through the early morning streets towards our destination. The sun had yet to rise, and the lamps were still lit, giving a dull orange tint to the grey buildings which lined the London thoroughfares. Early risers and working men were making their way through the darkened streets to wherever their day was to take them. For ourselves, we had no notion of the business upon which Lestrade had engaged us. Holmes, with his usual reticence, refused to speculate upon the purpose of our journey. We were fortunate in catching a train promptly, and were in Norwood in an acceptable time. At the station, we had no difficulty in recognising the small, alert bulldog of a man, who hurried forward to greet us warmly. He shook Holmes's hand with reverence.

'It is good of you to come, Mr Holmes. I apologise for the brevity of my telegram.'

'It was rather short on detail, Lestrade.'

'I thought it best to tell you the full facts as we drive to the house. It is only a fifteen-minute journey.'

He had hired a dogcart, and we climbed into it, leaning back in the seats, whilst Lestrade sat opposite us, checking off the points of his tale on the fingers of his left hand.

'Whytedale is a large villa situated on Lea Lane, a little under a mile from here. It is owned by Mr John Carlton, whose name may be familiar to you as one of the most respected art historians of recent years.'

'His name has not escaped my notice,' said Holmes. 'His analyses of the works of Caravaggio, though eccentric, were not devoid of some interest.'

'I wouldn't know too much about that, Mr Holmes, I must confess. What I do know is that Mr Carlton lives in the villa with his wife, Victoria, and a small number of domestic staff, including the maid, a girl by the name of Sarah Harte.

'Mr Carlton is writing a learned book on the influence of art in modern culture and society, and in order to assist him, he employed a man called Lawton Fields, fresh from the University, who seemed eager to develop a relationship with his famous employer. His duties were varied, but consisted mainly of researching references and illustrations, and taking dictation when necessary. His references were excellent, and for the last six months, the two men have worked closely together. It all came to an end at about ten o'clock last night, however, when the maid, tidying away after dinner, heard a terrible shriek from the hallway. This is a long, narrow passageway leading from the front door and stretching the length of the house. A stairway extends from the centre of it, and on either side of it there are doors leading to various rooms including the dining room, the study, and the drawing room. Do I make myself clear?'

'Perfectly so.'

'Mrs Carlton had retired to the drawing room, and her husband was reading some proofs in the study. On hearing the scream, Sarah, the maid, ran from the dining room into the hallway, and found Lawton Fields lying on his back, his body convulsing violently. Seconds later the master and mistress came into the hallway, disturbed also by the cry. Fields gripped Sarah with such force that she was unable to move, and was much distressed, as you can imagine.'

'The man spoke to her?'

'Just so, Mr Holmes. She is prepared to swear to the words.'

'And they were?' prompted Holmes, eagerly.

Lestrade shook his head, as though he himself did not believe the maid's story. 'She says he muttered, "The dragon – my God, the dragon." '

It seemed a fantastic revelation, and I found myself sharing Lestrade's scepticism. I looked across at Holmes, but his face was impassive.

'She is certain?' he asked.

'Positive. The proximity of her to his lips convinces her that there is no doubt as to the words themselves.'

'And this remarkable statement of a dragon was heard by Mr and Mrs Carlton?'

Lestrade shook his head. 'They heard nothing. The man whispered the words into the maid's ear.'

'Quite so. Does she offer any explanation?'

Lestrade shook his head. 'There is an obvious explanation for them, however.'

Holmes gave a wave of his hand. 'Speak plainly, Lestrade.'

The little official gave a sharp intake of breath, and sighed heavily. 'Mr Lawton Fields was stabbed to the chest, as I have told you. The weapon used, however, was an ornate silver letter opener, which belongs to John Carlton himself. It was kept in the study.'

'I see no connection.'

'The handle is delicately carved,' continued Lestrade, 'into the shape of a resplendent dragon.'

Our conversation had continued throughout the course of our journey, and by the time Lestrade had given us his final revelation, we found ourselves at the villa gates, where we alighted from the trap. Whytedale was a large, modern villa of white brick, consisting of three stories, each with latticed windows which peered out from sprawling ivy. It stood in its own grounds, set back from the road, and with the exception of the policeman standing at the wrought-iron gates, betrayed no evidence of the violence which had been committed within it. We walked up a grassy pathway, lined with laurel bushes, and stopped at the large, wood-panelled door. Holmes pointed to the door with his stick.

'Was this door locked last night?'

'Yes, Mr Holmes. Mrs Carlton herself did so.'

'And you have left everything undisturbed, for our inspection?'

'I have touched nothing, though John Carlton is not too happy about his secretary lying in his hallway still, as you can imagine.'

Holmes gave a snort of derision. 'Well, his inconvenience cannot hinder the course of justice. Some of these rich men must be taught that the world cannot always bend to their desires.'

Lestrade led us into the long hallway of which he had spoken. It was a lofty passageway, with wooden floors, and an impressive spiral staircase winding heavenward from the centre. The inspector had been as good as his word in leaving everything untouched, for the door to the study was ajar, and on the opposite side of the hallway, two doors also stood open. These no doubt led to the drawing room and the dining room of which we had heard. The walls were lined with excellent portraits of cavaliers and noblemen from the previous century, as well as a particularly striking image of the crucifixion, all of which paid testament to the occupation of the owner of the house.

These details I noticed afterwards. For now, my attention was directed to the tragic figure which lay on its back in the centre of the passageway. It was the body of a man of no more than thirty years of age, whose face had once been handsome, before a terrible death agony had twisted it beyond the recognition of those who had known him in life. He wore an evening suit, his starched shirt front stained crimson by his loss of life. One arm was stretched out to the left, and the other lay across his stomach. From the centre of his chest there protruded a magnificently carved letter opener, whose blade was thrust into the man's body to the ornate hilt. The design on the handle, cast in silver, was of the creature of legend known as a dragon, its head raised in almost noble fashion, and its huge wings coiled around its body.

'The dragon of Lea Lane,' I could not help but say.

'A remarkable instrument,' said Holmes, kneeling down beside the body and peering at the dragon's form through his lens.

'Its splendour is diminished by what it has been used for,' I remarked.

Holmes beckoned me closer to the body. 'Observe the depth to which the blade has been plunged. It took some force to do that. A man's doing, would you say?'

'A suitably enraged woman, if she were strong enough, might well be able to inflict a similar wound.'

Holmes rose to his full height, and placed his finger to his lips. He shook his head like a man who is far from convinced, but was prevented from elucidating, for we heard footsteps coming from the great staircase which towered over us. I had no difficulty in recognising a man who is master of his own house. He was a tall, noble man, around forty, with the first glimpse of the blanching of the hair at his temples which shows a man's journey through life. His thick, dark moustache had delicately waxed tips, and a short Imperial beard gave his strong chin a jutting prominence of patrician determination. He wore a sombre black suit, with a claret-coloured satin waistcoat and corresponding cravat which enhanced the elegance of his ensemble. He looked from one to the other of us and after a moment's consideration approached my companion.

'You are Mr Sherlock Holmes?' My companion bowed. 'My name is John Carlton. My wife, Victoria.'

Mrs Carlton was a woman of equal nobility to her husband. Her face was proud, her features delicate, though the poise of her head gave some intimation of arrogance. She held her husband's arm, and when she gave a slight inclination of her head by way of a greeting to us, I could not help but wonder at the grim determination behind her eyes that the tragedy which had occurred would not blight her reputation.

'I understand you have a reputation for speed and discretion,' her husband was saying. 'I trust you will endeavour to employ both in this matter.'

Holmes adopted his brisk, businesslike tone. 'I shall certainly do everything I can to assist a swift conclusion to this tragedy, Mr

Carlton. It would help me to do so, if I could clarify a number of points with you.'

Carlton gave a grunt of irritation. 'If you must, you must, but I have told the police everything I know.'

His wife released her arm from around his. 'For heaven's sake, John, have sense. The sooner we co-operate, the sooner this can be behind us.'

'This is our private sanctum, Victoria, damn it! How sordid it is to have something so unaesthetic as murder over our threshold.'

She turned to face my companion. 'Forgive my husband, Mr Holmes. Unless someone wishes to talk about art with him, or congratulate him on his collection, he tends to have no interest in them.'

Sherlock Holmes smiled, though his eyes were fixed on the art historian. When he spoke, however, his manner was cordiality itself. 'I can appreciate dedication to one's pursuits. Mr Carlton, I wonder if you could give me an account of what happened last night?'

'Perhaps we can go to my study,' he said. 'Looking at that thing in front of me is hardly conducive to conversation.'

'Certainly,' replied Holmes. 'Lestrade, I should like to speak to the maid. Perhaps you would be kind enough to fetch her? Thank you. Now, Mr Carlton, I am at your disposal.'

With a dismissive nod of his head, John Carlton led us across the hallway to the study. It was a small, cluttered room, lined with shelves of leather-bound volumes. There were display cases in the corners of the room, each one filled with artefacts and curios ranging from bronze sculptures to ancient drawings on parchment, the exhibits in Mr Carlton's personal museum of art. A large desk stood in the centre of the room, with papers strewn across it, and various notes scribbled on bits of scrap paper. Behind the desk was a leather-backed chair in which Mr Carlton now sat. There were other, smaller chairs in the room, but he did not invite any of us to sit.

Mrs Carlton was the first to speak. 'I must apologise for the disarray in this room, but John forbids me to clean it. I tried this morning but he wouldn't let me near the place.'

'They're not interested in that, Victoria.'

'I am sorry,' she said. 'This business has affected my nerves, I'm afraid, as it has all of us.'

'Of course,' I said, nodding sympathetically.

Holmes's tone was impatient. 'The events of last night . . . ?'

'As I said to the police,' Carlton began, without preamble, 'I was in here, sitting at this very desk, reading over some proofs that Fields had written up for me, when I heard a loud cry of agony.'

'The cry came from the hallway?'

'Obviously. I went out and met Sarah – that's the maid. Simple girl, but efficient nevertheless. Anyway, she was coming out of the dining room – heard the scream herself I imagine. Victoria rushed out of the drawing room at the same time. We all saw poor Fields there, lying in his own blood.' He stared into the distance suddenly, as though he had instantly forgotten our presence. 'I shall have to find a new secretary now, I suppose.'

'A man is dead, Mr Carlton,' I felt obliged to say.

Holmes's interruption was immediate. 'These words which your maid claims to have heard Mr Fields utter – did you yourself hear them?'

He shook his head. 'I saw him try to mumble something to her, but I didn't hear it. No more did Victoria.'

'I heard only a horrible murmur,' said the lady. 'It was incoherent to me.'

Holmes was walking around the room, his eyes taking in every detail in one of his all-encompassing glances. 'You know what she alleges he said?'

'Some delirium about a dragon,' the art historian replied. 'A reference to the letter opener, no doubt.'

'That is your idea, is it?' asked my companion.

'I don't attempt to explain it, Mr Holmes. I would have thought that was more your province than mine.'

Mrs Carlton evidently feared an altercation between the two men, for she walked purposefully towards her husband and laid her hand on his shoulder. 'John, please, Mr Holmes is only trying to get to the truth.' She turned to my friend. 'I must apologise for my husband's abruptness. I blame his Latin blood. With regard to the strange words spoken – surely Mr Fields could only have meant the letter opener?'

Holmes gave a brief smile. 'I hardly see it as likely. It is a very queer thing to assume. This letter opener belonged to you, Mr Carlton, as I understand it?'

Mrs Carlton provided the answer. 'It belonged to John's father.'

Carlton rose from the desk, slamming his hand against the arm of the chair. 'By the Lord Harry, Victoria, the man was speaking to me!' He seemed to regret his outburst as soon as it had occurred. He squeezed his wife's hand with a sigh, and walked past her towards Sherlock Holmes, his noble face contorted with anger and frustration. 'Look here, sir, I apologise for my manner if I appear somewhat brusque, but unlike you murder is not a way of life for me. It is a tension, and I cannot afford any extra strain upon my heart at present. If I offend you, I am sorry.'

Holmes waved the apology to one side. 'Murder is never a welcome visitor, Mr Carlton. You speak of speed and discretion. I can achieve both with your frankness.'

The noble head bowed in supplication. 'Then ask your questions, Mr Holmes. I will hold nothing back.'

'Can you think of any reason why anybody should want to harm this secretary of yours?'

'None in the world,' came the reply. 'He was always a well-mannered young man.'

'Conscientious in his work?'

'Admirably so.'

'Do you yourself have any theories regarding the tragedy?'

Carlton stiffened, his lips pursed in concentration. 'My own belief is that it was a foiled burglary.'

'Indeed?'

Mrs Carlton seemed anxious to interrupt. 'John, I have warned you against this!'

'Blast it, Victoria, the man asked for frankness! Now, Mr Holmes, there is a man by the name of Maclachlan Hamer, a fellow art historian. The fact is that he is jealous of my own collection, which you will no doubt perceive to be of immense value. I've long wondered whether Hamer had the audacity to break the law to get his paws on my treasures!'

'A serious allegation, sir,' said Sherlock Holmes.

'The man is a leech!'

'And yet there is no sign of a break-in?'

The colour flushed to the historian's cheeks once more. 'I don't presume to do the police's work for them, Mr Holmes. Maybe Sarah left the back door open and he got in that way. Maybe he is adept at picking locks. It is not my province to solve puzzles, it is yours.'

He walked past my friend, his steps betraying his irritation and the strain on his health which had been brought upon him by the tragedy. He pulled open the door, signalling that the interview was at an end. As we crossed the threshold of the study, Carlton touched my companion upon the arm. 'What I do know is that no one in this house had any reason to kill Fields, so the culprit must be an out-sider. Add to that the fact that Hamer wants my collection for himself, and you find yourself looking at a burglary which Fields foiled and lost his life for.'

'A beauty, eh, Watson?' whispered Holmes, as the study door closed behind us.

'The man is a monster.'

'Ah, but he is an illuminating one. He has told us a number of factors which are vital to this case.'

'I saw nothing of value in what he said.'

'Very likely not. Ah, here is Lestrade with young Sarah.'

The official detective was approaching us with a girl of no more than nineteen, with a timid expression, and hands which shook as she held them to her breast. Her cheeks were sallow, the horror of her experience plainly visible upon them. The girl pleaded to us with her eyes.

'I've said everything I know about all this already, sir. I swear I have! I swear on the book!'

Holmes, who had a remarkable gentleness with women when it was required of him, spoke in his softest voice. 'I am sure you have, Sarah, but I have a fancy to hear things for myself. You were tidying away after dinner?'

'Yes, sir. About ten it was. The mistress was next door in the drawing room, and the master in his study.'

'And you heard this terrible scream?'

'I never want to hear anything like it as long as I live, sir,' sobbed the girl. 'He was a-moaning and a-groaning when I got to him, and grabbing at me with his blood-stained hands. Oh, it was too awful, sir!'

'How long was it before Mr Carlton and his wife arrived on the scene?'

The girl dabbed her eyes with the handkerchief I had given her. 'Only a matter of seconds, sir, no longer. Mr Carlton almost fainted away at the sight. He's not well, sir, as you may know, and Mrs Carlton was flushed to the face and breathless with shock.'

'There was no one in the corridor? No possibility of concealment?'

'None, sir. There was no one in the place.'

Holmes patted her on the arm, placed his hat upon his head, and turned to the door. He had taken only a few steps before he stopped, and turned back to the frightened maid. 'One final point – you are certain of the words Mr Fields spoke to you in his last moments? "The dragon – my God, the dragon!" '

'I've tried to make sense of it, sir, thinking maybe I was wrong, but I can't make any other sense from the words other than what I've already said.'

'Excellent,' said Holmes, and he turned on his heel and left the house.

We enjoyed a brisk walk along the lane, having ascertained Mr Maclachlan Hamer's address from Lestrade. The official stayed behind, having business to attend to in writing up his report. Holmes promised to be back at Whytedale by the evening, and requested that Lestrade meet us back at the villa at six. The lane was lined with huge oak trees, which were so large that they seemed to form a shelter over Lea Lane. It gave me the impression of the vicinity being hidden from the elements, guarded by the branches and leaves of the remarkable foliage which encompassed it. It was a place of great natural beauty.

Mr Hamer proved to be a small, dapper man with a neatly trimmed beard and hair freckled with grey. He was younger than John Carlton, but possessed a bearing of his own which belied his years. He wore a Chinese smoking jacket and velvet slippers, and was smoking a small clay pipe. He was not impressed with Holmes's introduction to our purpose.

'Carlton's suggestion is monstrous, Mr Holmes!' he protested. 'I didn't even know this man, Fields.'

'Nevertheless, the accusation has been made. I detected some hint of animosity between you and Mr Carlton, Mr Hamer.'

'Despite his honourable reputation, Carlton's a blackguard. Pompous, arrogant, concerned only with the value of his own collection.'

'And yet, you are a collector yourself, Mr Hamer. Do you not cherish your own treasures?'

The little man drooped his eyes in condescension. 'Art should be shared with the world, Mr Holmes, not hidden away in a secluded villa like Whytedale.'

'Mr Carlton indicated some envy on your part over his collection.'

Mr Hamer threw his pipe to the table in a petulant show of disgust. He walked to a small tray on the sideboard, and poured himself a large glass of brandy. When he spoke again, his voice was tremulous, though it had lost none of its passion.

'Was it I who tried to leave this very house with a valued jade Buddha in his coat pocket? No, sir! It was not.'

'Mr Carlton did such a thing?'

'The snake! Do not be fooled by the apparent nobility of his bearing, Mr Holmes. There is as much nobility in the slums of Limehouse.'

This new revelation seemed to surprise Sherlock Holmes, and he was silent for a moment, his brows drawn together in thought.

'Now, sir,' said he at last, 'this letter opener, the one with the dragon handle. You had seen it before?'

Hamer gave a slight shrug of his slender shoulders. 'It had never intrigued me. It is neither intrinsically valuable, nor very tasteful.'

'Yet it pleased Mr Carlton?'

'I suppose it must have done. He never spoke to me of it, but he owned it, so I assume he liked it. Each to his own, of course.'

'Every man is entitled to an opinion,' remarked my friend. 'It is the basis of our existence. Am I to assume, then, that you were not at Whytedale last night?'

'Certainly not.'

'Might I enquire whether you have any corroborative evidence?'

Hamer chuckled slyly. 'Must I assume, in return, that I am under suspicion?'

'I seek only the truth, Mr Hamer.'

'Then I can assure you, Mr Sherlock Holmes, that I have no such corroborative evidence to provide.'

Holmes stared at the art collector for what seemed like a long while, his grey eyes probing the petulant but sly face for some indication of guilt. After some moments, however, he rose from his chair and thanked the man for his assistance.

'Our way lies elsewhere, Watson. Come, we shall travel back to town, and see if we cannot find the truth of the affair.'

We were fortunate in getting a train to London swiftly, and in the corner of a first-class carriage, Holmes settled down in silence, with his fingertips together. His knitted brows and abstracted eyes told me that he had returned mentally to Lea Lane, and I knew well enough that a labyrinth of theories and suppositions would be formed and discarded inside his mind. For myself, I tried in vain to extract some clue from the web of facts which had been woven before us. I was unsuccessful, however, and the truth of the case remained as far from me as ever.

That afternoon, Sherlock Holmes spent his time rummaging in files of old daily papers and his own personal indices of people and events which he had amassed over the years. By the end of two hours, our sitting room was littered with discarded papers and memoranda which he had tossed aside. Finally, with a sharp and sudden exclamation of satisfaction, he leapt to his feet, clutching to his breast a page torn from a newspaper.

'I have it, Watson! A quick telegram to Lestrade with final instructions, and we can lay the dragon of Lea Lane to rest!'

It was late afternoon, the light slowly fading under the onset of an autumn evening sky, when we found ourselves in Lea Lane once more. In the impending darkness, I had a growing sense of excitement as we walked up to the front door of the house, caused in part by the alert glittering of my companion's eyes, as the lights of the house flickered on his lean features. He rapped on the door with his stick.

'An ugly business, Watson, but an instructive one,' said he. 'Do you see any light in the darkness?'

'I confess that I do not accept the theory of Mr Hamer's being responsible.'

Holmes gave a snort of derision. 'The suggestion is nonsense, and Mr Carlton's attempts to implicate his rival speak for themselves. How can he expect us to believe that this fellow Hamer could enter the house, murder Fields, and disappear without being seen? It was only seconds after the murder that this maid and Carlton found the body.'

'What then is the truth? And what is the explanation of the man's dying reference to a dragon?'

My questions were to remain unanswered, however, as the front door was opened by Lestrade himself.

'I got your telegram, Mr Holmes,' said he, 'and I've assembled people in the hall as you instructed. The body has been taken to the mortuary. I must confess that I am still in the dark about the business.'

'All will become clear, Lestrade,' said Holmes, walking past the inspector into the familiar hallway.

Mr John Carlton was sitting on the bottom step of the immense staircase, his wife standing to his left. Sarah stood timidly to one side, her eyes fixed in wonder on my companion. Holmes removed his hat and coat and faced the three of them, his voice and demeanour displaying their most authoritative and judicial manner.

'Mr Carlton, you asked me for speed and discretion,' said he. 'I think you cannot doubt that I have provided you with both.'

'I don't see any progress has been made at all,' grumbled the historian.

'Nevertheless, I hold in my hands the truth concerning the murder of Lawton Fields.'

'I see no clue,' confessed Lestrade.

Holmes turned to him. 'That is because you have started this case with a preconception, rather than with an open mind. I make it a rule never to be allowed to deviate from where facts lead me by any preconceptions.'

'What on earth are you talking about, sir?' snarled John Carlton, rising to his feet.

Holmes held up a warning finger. 'No interruptions from you, sir. Your time for remonstrance is over, and now you will listen to the truth. There were three vital clues in this case – one given by the dead man himself, one by Sarah here, and one by you, Mrs Carlton.'

The woman put a hand to her breast in shock. 'Me?'

'You mentioned to me that your husband had Latin blood in him, which was a vital clue to the solution of this crime. No doubt you thought it a trivial comment, but my friend Watson will tell you that I dare call nothing inconsequential.'

Lestrade walked over to my companion with an air of impatience. 'I don't know whether you are playing a game with us, Mr Holmes, but surely we can get to the point?'

'There is a very succinct point to be made, Lestrade. Mr John Carlton is not the man he pretends to be – that is the point.'

The man in question strode over to my companion, his eyes ablaze with fire, and his fists clenched. I was ready to spring to Holmes's defence, but I could see from his cool exterior and defiant eyes that no attempt to aid him was necessary.

'Do not be noisy, Mr Carlton, any pretence is useless. My suspicions were already directed towards you by your clumsy attempt to implicate Mr Maclachlan Hamer. As you said, Watson, it is impossible that Mr Hamer should be considered as being complicit in this affair. He could never have entered the house at all, as the house had been locked, by Mrs Carlton herself.'

'I told you, Holmes!' roared Carlton, pointing to Sarah. 'She probably left the back door open!'

Sarah made an attempt to plead her innocence, but Holmes spoke before her, his voice rasping with ferocity. 'Do not play games with me, sir! You told us she was an efficient servant. I do not think you are a man to provide false praise to anyone, which inclines me to believe in the girl's efficiency. Now I ask you, Mr Carlton, whether it is likely that such an efficient servant would leave a door unlocked at night?'

Never have I seen a change come over a man as the one which affected John Carlton at that moment. He glanced back to his wife, and it seemed to me that something died between them in that instant, a flicker of hope which had finally burnt itself out.

'The biggest clue of all, of course, were the final words of the dying man. "The dragon – my God, the dragon!"'

'That was the maid's clue you spoke of?' asked Lestrade.

'Not at all,' replied Holmes. 'Sarah's vital clue came later, as I shall explain in due course. Those final words, the dying allusion to a dragon, provided not only the most stimulating aspect of the crime – but the motive for it also. You assumed, Lestrade, simply because of its convenience, that the words referred to the decorations on the weapon. But I was not able to agree with you. I told Mr Carlton myself that I considered it a strange and unlikely possibility. Why should a man use his final breath of life to convey something which can easily be determined by whoever finds the body? It is unthinkable. It occurred to me that Fields was attempting to convey something much more important to us than the method of his death.'

'Who knows what passes through a man's mind when he is dying?' sneered Carlton.

'John, do be quiet,' I heard Mrs Carlton whisper to him. She sounded tired, as though the strain of the events were wearing her down.

Lestrade had failed to hear the exchange, however, and his attention was fixed on my companion. 'What, then, did Fields mean by his words?'

Holmes held the piece of paper he had taken with him from Baker Street into the air. I began to see the sense of a vague outline of the truth.

'I believe that a specialist in crime should always be aware of the criminal activities of other countries as well as his own, however far in the past they are,' said he. 'This is a newspaper clipping of a report of the murder of a tyrant in South America some thirty years ago. The man was Jose Roderigo Diego, a horrific sadist who ruled the province of Los Kernos in South America with a fist of iron. He would murder, maim, and mutilate any who opposed or betrayed him. His speciality was torture . . . by fire.'

'By fire?' I exclaimed, the horror of it striking me at once.

'For this reason, those under his regime in the Latin province called him the Dragon. Diego's stronghold was stormed by rebels three decades ago, and he and his wife were slaughtered by the intruders.

The rebels freed themselves from the power of the Dragon, but themselves were killed in an act of vengeance by some of his more loyal supporters.'

'What is the connection between this foreign tyrant and the murder, Mr Holmes?' asked Lestrade.

'Diego suspected that some misfortune was likely to befall him very soon. Some word of the uprising may have reached him. As a precaution, his only child, a teenage son named Juan Carlos, who was a promising artist, was sent away before the massacre.'

'He dispatched his son to a place of safety?' I guessed.

'Quite so. Juan Carlos buried himself away. The son, as well as being a talented artist, resembled his father remarkably, as this photograph in the clipping of them both shows. Thirty years is a long time, and can change a man, but you can see the similarities between the son, and the man standing before you.'

'Juan Carlos,' I murmured, looking back to the man standing before us. 'John Carlton.'

'A man is seldom able to sacrifice every detail of his name when altering his identity,' said Holmes. 'In addition, Juan Carlos was an artist. The link is obvious.'

The arrogance and the anger had vanished from John Carlton. He now looked a broken man, his eyes heavy with the memory of his own past, and the burden of his guilt. He nodded slowly, lowering himself with dejection to sit back on the stair. His wife's loving hand went slowly to his shoulder. His gave it a gentle kiss.

'One of the few memories I have of my father was the letter opener he had had fashioned for himself,' he said. 'He gave it to me as a symbol. He believed he was a strong man, a powerful man, never once able to see his own wickedness. He gave me a memory of him to induce me to have some power in a land of strangers. That, and some journals he left for me, written in his own hand.'

'Oh, John,' said Mrs Carlton. 'My poor John.'

Carlton looked back to Sherlock Holmes. 'I swear to you, I had no idea what my father really was. I had a secluded life. Only when I read about him in those journals, when I read in his own words what sort of man had raised me, did I understand. He played with me in the gardens, read me stories before I slept, who held me in his strong arms. He killed, murdered, and terrorised. I wanted nothing more to do with him.'

Lestrade stepped forward. 'In his researches, Lawton Fields somehow discovered your family history. He threatened you?'

Carlton nodded. 'Fields threatened to expose my lineage. I am a hard man, I know that, and maybe you yourselves have seen some of it. A man who wishes to succeed must be hard to some degree. Maybe there is something of my father in me. But my reputation in this country is an honest one.'

'You were frightened that Fields would reveal your family history and damage your own reputation,' continued the official policeman.

'I could not risk it, even the threat of it. And so I killed him. With my father's own souvenir to me of his memory.' Carlton looked up at his wife. 'I am so sorry, my darling.'

There was the sudden, stark sound of a foot against the wood of the floor. We all turned round to find Sherlock Holmes staring back at us, his eyes like steel and his jaw set in determined defiance.

'This charade will *not* do!' he scolded. 'It is a noble action, Mr Carlton, but it will not serve you well. The guilty must be punished!'

'Mr Holmes!' said Lestrade, sudden confusion clouding his face. 'Have you gone mad?'

Holmes pointed an accusatory finger. 'You cannot allow your husband to make the sacrifice, madam.'

I turned back to where John Carlton stood in his wife's arms. The change on her face was terrible. Her lips had become set like stone, her eyes insolent, and her features rigid with resolve. Holmes remained transfixed upon her, however, and I have never met a man whose power of will was as strong as his. Under his glare, she softened, her possession of mind failed her, and her lips began to tremble.

'It was not your husband Fields confronted with the secrecy of the lineage. Fields knew that Carlton was a man of strong character, perhaps even of a hereditary violent temperament. He turned to you as a safer, more compliant subject. It was you, Mrs Carlton, who stabbed Fields to the chest, horrified that your husband's secret might be revealed. It was you who suffered the terrible threat of blackmail. And it was Sarah who provided the clue.'

I had forgotten, in the drama of the confrontation, that Holmes had mentioned the maid's evidence as being crucial. 'How so?'

'You recall that Sarah said Mrs Carlton was flushed in the face, and was breathing heavily when she approached the body? Why was that, do you suppose?'

I saw it at once. 'It was not the shock! She had been running!'

Holmes gave a cry of satisfaction. 'Precisely, my dear Watson! She had been running – running from the drawing room to the hallway, stabbing Fields, and running back to the drawing room, before the scream revealed her presence on the scene. She then returned to the hall, under the pretence of having just heard the cry. Her flushed face was a result of the exertions, themselves fuelled by the adrenalin of the crime itself.'

Carlton kissed his wife's hand again. 'God bless you for trying to protect my honour.'

'Mrs Carlton lay in wait in the drawing room for Fields to pass through the hallway,' said Holmes. 'She had taken the letter opener when she tried to tidy the study that morning, as she told us.'

'But why the false confession from Mr Carlton?' asked Lestrade.

'When he saw what had happened, and the weapon used, Carlton himself suspected his wife's guilt. His transparent attempt to implicate Maclachlan Hamer was his way of shielding his wife. When it failed, he saw that the evidence might implicate him as much as her, and sought to save her from the gallows that way.'

'He is a noble man,' said Mrs Carlton.

'And you are a noble woman, my darling,' her husband replied. 'I love you for it.'

Mrs Carlton looked at her husband for a long moment in his eyes, their tears falling as one, before she kissed him softly on the lips. I heard him sob under the weight of the embrace, before she slipped her hand from his grasp. She turned to face us, her emotions concealed beneath the mask of pride we had witnessed that afternoon.

There is little more to be told. Mrs Carlton was condemned to death at the winter assizes; Sherlock Holmes attended the trial, but did not speak to me of it. The details of John Carlton's history were forced out in the proceedings and although no adverse association with his father affected him, the loss of his wife forced him into isolation. We heard no more of him until a brief note arrived last month from Mr Maclachlan Hamer. It stated only that John Carlton had reunited himself with his wife in the only way he knew, by ending his life with the same weapon with which she had so violently fought to protect his honour.

Jerusalem Keep

MARK VALENTINE AND JOHN HOWARD

I have often thought that if Sherlock Holmes had not made his name in the annals of detection, he might have secured some equally notable fame as an antiquary. For his questing mind, relentless eye for the significant detail, and intense powers of concentration, would all serve him admirably in the tasks of the historical scholar. Indeed, in the intervals between such cases as caught his attention, it was my custom to try to engage his interest in some such absorbing matter, for I knew that only thus could the dangerous lethargy that sometimes took hold of him be avoided. I have spoken elsewhere of his interest in out-of-the-way subjects – medieval music, the Cornish language – and I recall with particular fondness a case that enabled my friend to indulge both his interest in the archaic and his investigative skills.

I should own at once that it may not appear to be a case played for the highest stakes – here was no instance of a threat against our country, nor the machinations of a brutal criminal mastermind, nor the theft of a precious treasure, nor any of the tragic and pitiable matters often brought to our door. And yet, in some ways, it was indeed about the highest and rarest thing a man may own – his honour.

It had been a simmering summer in London and all the air was still and stagnant. There had been no matter of any consequence for Holmes's restless spirit for several weeks, and I had begun to see the signs, both as a friend and physician, of that dark *ennui* that was apt to seize him and drive him toward the cruel stimulants that alone could assuage his soul. I listened keenly for the approach of a carriage to our door, or the sound of footsteps pausing outside, and I scoured the pages of *The Times* for the slightest indication of the untoward. There was nothing: it was as if the great city had sunk into a torpor.

'My dear fellow, do put that newspaper down,' said Holmes. 'You are even more restless than I feel. Your hands will be even blacker from the newsprint than they already were, and that will be no way to greet our visitors.'

I folded *The Times* somewhat roughly, and left it on the breakfast table. As I did so I glanced at my hands. They were indeed rather grimy, and the newspaper could not be wholly to blame.

'Already were? Really, Holmes – '

He looked up from the chair where he had been sitting in contemplation. 'I observed that the window was not quite closed. Of course, the noise of the traffic was also slightly louder in consequence. The dust on the windowsill was slightly disarranged. And when you poured your breakfast cup of tea, I saw what I already expected to see: that your hands were somewhat dusty from resting them on the windowsill when you opened the window and peered out.'

'Very well,' I replied. 'I did open the window and look out of it earlier.'

'And what did you see?'

'Nothing. The usual scene.'

'Now, Watson,' said Holmes, 'that is no answer. Baker Street is out there. It is not "nothing". And it is certainly never "the usual scene".'

'Well, I must grant you that point.'

'So then? You were leaning out of the window. Did you not see our visitors, from Lyonne's Lodge?'

'Lyonne's Lodge? Holmes!'

He laughed. 'I will put you out of your misery, old friend! Among many other things, you saw a hired carriage, scarcely more than a cart really, of the sort kept by the landlords of public houses and small hotels in more remote districts. As you know, Watson, these vehicles are retained for the use of guests in areas where the railway has not penetrated, or for ferrying guests to and from the nearest railway station.'

'Indeed,' I said. 'There are always innumerable carriages in Baker Street. There may well be one of the type you describe.'

'If I am not mistaken there is only one, however, from Lyonne's Lodge. Or to be more precise, from the Lyonne's Lodge Inn, situated in the village also of that name. If you would please pass me the gazetteer . . . '

A few moments later Holmes had found what he was looking for. He handed the book back to me with a palpable glow of satisfaction.

'It is as I thought, Watson. Lyonne's Lodge is in Hertfordshire, in the old Verulam Chase, a Royal Forest. It does not boast a railway halt, and the nearest station is some ten miles away. But there is an inn or hotel. So our visitors have borrowed the inn's carriage, in order to get to us all the faster.'

'My dear fellow!'

'I have no doubt that you observed the carriage pass by when you looked out of the window. It drove past when I was looking out a short while ago, although of course I did not actually open the window and lean out. I think that if you were to look out of the window now, you will see it again. Or, rather, actually observe it for the first time.'

I did as Holmes said. And sure enough, a rather dusty and slightly dilapidated carriage had pulled up on the other side of the street. There was an ornate lion, somewhat bedraggled, painted on the door, but even I could tell that it was the sign of an inn or hotel, rather than the arms of a noble and ancient family who were permitted to use such a device.

'The occupants are still in debate I assume, then, Watson?'

'It would seem so. They are making no attempt to get out and come to us.'

'The other black mark, Watson – apart from those on your hands of course – is that in your perusal of *The Times* you did not notice the mention – a very small mention, I grant you – of a forthcoming and rather intriguing court case concerning a certain family from near Lyonne's Lodge in the county of Hertford. I felt sure that the defendant and his solicitor would approach us.'

I sighed, and put the gazetteer back on the shelf, then hastily wiped its spine with my handkerchief.

'Ah,' I said. 'The carriage door is opening.'

A minute later we heard footsteps on the stair.

'Come in, come in!' Holmes called.

A short and rather plump man entered, followed by a tall and slender woman. As the gentleman fussed with his hat, which I prised from his grasp and dropped on the table, Holmes jumped to his feet and held out his hand in welcome. Our visitors greeted him with relief.

'My name is Arncote, and I am a lawyer. This is Miss Alexandra Urishay, my client.'

'Quite, quite,' said Holmes. 'And this is my associate, Dr Watson. Won't you please sit down? You must be in need of refreshment, after your demanding journey. It is a fair distance from the Chase to London.'

I rang for tea.

'Mr Holmes,' said Mr Arncote, 'I have explained your reputation to my client – even though I did not really have to – but I fail to see how you know where we came from.'

'My dear sir,' laughed Holmes, 'it really is absurdly simple. You travelled in a carriage rented for the journey from your local inn. It is a distinctive carriage, now parked outside, across the street. By the way, pray have no anxieties concerning its security. Certain of my little friends, some street Arabs, will have observed your arrival and the fact that you are visiting me. Your carriage and any contents, and the horses, will be absolutely safe. In fact, the horses may receive an apple or two.'

The lady took out a shilling from her bag. I noticed that Holmes glanced at her fingers as she handed it to him.

'For the boys . . . '

'My dear madam, you will have friends for life whenever you visit London!'

'We also read a paragraph in *The Times*,' I added.

The tea arrived. When it had been poured, our visitors drank gratefully.

'You will know the reason for our visit, if you have read the newspaper,' said the solicitor.

'It was but an all-too-brief notice,' Holmes said. 'Nothing more. I look to you for the full story. Then I will see if I can help you. You have, of course, come for a consultation'.

'Oh yes, Mr Holmes,' said Miss Urishay. She was a young and captivating woman, with a keen glance and dusty gold hair, worn long.

'Well, begin in your own time, when you are quite ready.'

She put her cup down. I hastened to refill it, and Mr Arncote's. Miss Urishay raised her cup and sipped more tea.

'You are a keen needlewoman, I see,' observed Holmes.

Our visitor replaced her cup and raised her fair eyebrows. 'I like embroidery, it is true – indeed, that is the offence with which I am charged. It was a shrewd guess on your part, sir.'

I saw my friend's nostrils quiver at the unintended slight. 'Oh, I never guess. Forgive me . . . ' Holmes took her pale hand gently and turned it palm upwards. 'You observe, Watson, a delicate furrow in each of the forefinger and thumb, where the needle is held – and these minute punctures where at times it slips. You are – forgive me, madam – scarcely of the breeding to be a seamstress by profession – but only much diligence in the art would leave such insistent traces. I wonder you do not use a thimble, though?'

'It is too cumbersome for the work I do.'

'I see. Well, now, how has such a gentle pursuit led you to a career in crime?'

Our visitor laughed at this little sally, but her rotund companion cleared his throat and remarked in disapproval, 'Now, Mr Holmes, let us be clear. This is not a criminal, but a civil matter. That is well established.'

Holmes waved the objection aside. 'Come, then, let us have more.'

'I am arraigned before one of the highest courts in the land, Mr Holmes – as is my brother. We have been summoned by the Earl Marshall himself, and he will try us – in the Court of Chivalry.'

'Or a Surrogate he shall appoint,' put in the elderly lawyer.

'It is a quaint matter. On what charge?'

'On the part of Mr Urishay,' Mr Arncote explained, 'that of unlawfully assuming arms . . . '

'Arms?' I put in 'Why, that surely is a serious and a criminal matter. It sounds like treason. There is so much conspiracy abroad, that any caches of weapons are rightly regarded as suspicious . . . '

My friend roared with laughter, and his two clients permitted themselves to smile.

'I fancy,' said Holmes, 'that the arms are heraldic, are they not?'

'Quite so,' responded the beaming lawyer, 'Yet it is not only Mr Urishay who is to be tried. Miss Urishay, too, is accused. The charge against her is that of uttering arms.'

'Uttering arms?' I repeated, 'Why, the whole thing sounds quite medieval.'

'So it is, Watson. Come, let us have the full story.'

'Certainly, Mr Holmes,' the young woman replied. 'There is very little to tell. Last year my brother came into possession of a small but ancient property near Lyonne's Lodge. It was an inheritance from our great-uncle Tom, who had lived to a very advanced age, outstripping his brother and his nephew, our grandfather and father, who predeceased him by some measure. The property comprises a single great tower, the Jerusalem Keep, of medieval foundation, and some parcels of land stretching out from this old, hoary citadel. It had long been a place of romance to us, Mr Holmes, a place that might be found in the pages of Walter Scott. Old Tom, our great-uncle, had a fondness for us, and we stayed there whenever we might: but we knew, too, that his predilection was to the solitary, so did not often trespass upon his domain.

'It is a great grey stone, thick-walled edifice, and I thought that it wanted colour and brilliance to relieve this somewhat. I had found in various parts of the house and in the papers that great-uncle Tom had left, some illuminations of an old shield, in glorious glowing colours, and I thought to embellish the house with these. I have made in the course of the year, a wall-hanging, cushions, and other dainty things, until, wanting some more demanding matter, I assayed to embroider a great silk flag. For we have a staff upon the turret, and it has always been bare. My brother affixed a lanyard and ran my work up to the top, where it flew very proudly indeed. There was the start of our trouble.

'We have a neighbour, a Mr Malligo, a saturnine gentleman, who fancies himself a great antiquary and chronicler of all the area, and who is also a zealous litigant, forever resorting to the courts – against the local yeomen for infractions of his land, the parson for whiffs of popery (as he sees it), the trustees of local charities for deviating from the exact terms of bequests, etc. Oh, how his eyes must have gleamed when he saw my gay flag a-flying . . . he at once reported us to the College of Arms who, although reluctant, felt obliged to act under his repeated threats and representations. To give him his due, he also called upon us, most civilly, to tell us all about it, and assure us he bore no malice, but merely wished to uphold the great traditions of the country.'

'He sounds just like Mr Frankland, Holmes, ' I suggested.

'Indeed. I fear the type is not uncommon. What precisely was Malligo's objection, Miss Urishay?'

'Oh, it is a very studiously proper one. We have been caught displaying arms when we have no right to do so. We are not an armigerous family, duly entered in the great court rolls.'

Holmes smote his hand upon his knee and laughed once more. 'It is certainly one of the rarest, if not perhaps the gravest, of offences I have been called upon to consider. Now I assume, Arncote, that you are well read-up in the precedents. Give them to us briefly.' Holmes leant back in his armchair, let his eyelids droop, and placed his fingertips together.

Mr Arncote adjusted glinting little glasses, and (with much waggling of his fingers) did as he was bid.

'It was established as long ago as the fourteenth century, in Scrope vs Grosvenor, that the King alone had power to grant or confirm arms, and that he was the authority to determine disputes about arms. By the seventeenth century, the College of Arms asserted his authority in Visitations, where it would seek out and prosecute those bearing arms to which they had no right, and those artists, engravers, painters who had purported to design arms that had no authority. Miss Urishay here is accused of the same offence as these, for she has uttered, in her flag, arms that do not exist – while her brother, in flying it, has 'assumed' arms without the monarch's authority.'

'Dear me,' said Holmes, 'the case seems quite clear. But it is a most archaic matter, is it not? I wonder that the authorities have allowed it to proceed.'

'It is hard for them to resist a persistent and well-informed complainant, Mr Holmes. The law still stands. Furthermore – well, a certain august personage has made it known since his recent ascension that he expects more punctilio in matters of this kind. The Earl Marshal may have little option.'

'I see. That does rather darken the matter for Miss Urishay here, and her brother.' Holmes drummed his fingers. 'Yet surely, Arncote, even the most ancient families cannot all show a written title from the King, with the Great Seal and all affixed?'

'That is so, but there are other means of asserting arms. It is possible, for instance, to establish that a family has borne them since "time immemorial", in a continuous line. Carminow of Cornwall claimed he had owned the same arms as Scrope since the time of King Arthur, and that claim was accepted: unlike Grosvenor, he was allowed to keep his. But more usually "time immemorial" is taken to mean "since the time of King Richard I".'

'Is it now?' enquired Holmes, 'That may be of significance . . . well now, Miss Urishay, and what were these arms you are alleged to have uttered, and where did you find them?'

'Oh, they were very simple. A golden cross with sort of forked ends, on a silver background. They are to be seen in several places in our home – the keep, I mean.'

I saw Holmes's interest quicken further. 'That is most interesting. Well,' he said, 'I think that we must inspect the Jerusalem Keep. And the sooner the better.'

I handed Holmes the Bradshaw, our usual handbook for travel out of town.

Holmes handed it straight back to me. 'No, no, Watson! Thank you all the same; but I wish to move decisively on this case, and we cannot wait for the railway companies. Madam, I take it that Dr Watson and I can accompany you back to the county immediately in your carriage? I dare say that the landlord will also be glad of its speedy return.'

'That is very kind of you, Mr Holmes,' Miss Urishay said. She then looked enquiringly at her solicitor. 'Mr Arncote?'

'If it is acceptable to you, Miss Urishay, I will research a little further while I am here in London, and catch a train this evening and join you as soon as practicable. In any case, I have to say that a return journey in that carriage would not be very appealing to me. I am no longer a young man.'

Miss Urishay inclined her head graciously. 'Of course, Mr Arncote. Please return at your convenience.'

Holmes jumped up. 'Excellent! Come, Miss Urishay, Watson! I am already relishing our little trip out to the old Royal forest!'

Mr Arncote puffed his way out of our rooms. Holmes and I gathered together some clothing suitable for the journey. No doubt it would be a dusty one. Holmes thrust some papers into his travelling bag, and I grabbed my black doctor's bag.

We made our way to the carriage, Holmes bestowing ample silver upon the ragged youths who had kept ward. 'It will be a hard journey,' he said, 'Do you wish to drive again, Miss Urishay? I must say that you are clearly highly proficient.'

'Surely Mr Arncote drove?' I said. 'I am perfectly prepared to take the reins, Holmes.'

Miss Urishay smiled most charmingly as she took the reins and we climbed into the carriage. 'Thank you, Dr Watson,' she said, 'but I did drive and we will make good time, I assure you.'

'I will let you spare my blushes, Watson,' Holmes said as he sat down next to me. 'The marks in the dust on the floor where the driver sits. They match the smaller size of a woman's boots, and the fair sex's lighter tread.'

During the journey, I busied myself with the latest issue of a medical journal, but from time to time I glanced across to Holmes. He was, as usual, giving the impression that he was looking at nothing in particular, although of course, as I usually found out, he was observing absolutely everything.

We were soon heading north out of London on the Uxbridge Road. The attractive countryside sped past at a satisfying rate. Miss Urishay drove smoothly and confidently; the carriage was under the control of an expert.

'Middlesex is a most pleasant county, is it not, Watson?' Holmes remarked. 'And yet, I can envisage the day when the growth of our mighty capital will overtake this rural Eden. All these fine villages will become joined to the metropolis. Perhaps a splendid great avenue, linking them all with the city, will be constructed one day. People will be able to go about their business with more despatch, but I for one am not so sure that I wish it would be so.'

'Have you been reading the latest story by Mr Wells again?' I asked. 'It would certainly seem so.'

Holmes continued his meditations as the fields and farms flew by. The hot sun was often thankfully obscured by the great and ancient trees overhanging the road, but there was still plenty of dust. Eventually, after over three hours of driving, with a few brief halts to rest the horses, Miss Urishay called out to us.

'It will soon be quicker for us to take small side-roads and lanes,' the lady said. 'My brother and I have explored far and wide through them.'

The sun was definitely in the western part of the sky when we neared our destination. The landscape was bathed in a rich, golden sunlight, which deepened the myriad greens of the gentle, rounded hills, the patchwork of fields, and the old broad oak trees, all against a sharp blue sky that was almost imperceptibly darkening towards the eastern horizon. The country was in one way unremarkable: quiet, undramatic, pleasing rather than striking; and yet I felt somehow that it was the very heart and soul of England.

After we had travelled a little while longer in the most obscure and charming by-ways, 'We are almost at Lyonne's Lodge,' Miss Urishay called out. 'Look! There is the inn.' We had driven past a few houses of old, rose-hued brick and grey thatch, scattered apparently at random around the crossroads where the inn stood. She brought the carriage to a stop outside the small hotel that seemed to be also Lyonne's Lodge's only inn.

A young man in dark trousers and a white shirt ran out into the yard, shading his eyes against the strong light.

'Alexandra!' he shouted.

Miss Urishay jumped down from the carriage and flung her arms around his neck. 'Peter! Here we are!'

'I assume that this man is Miss Urishay's brother,' I remarked.

Holmes smiled. 'I think that we need have no worries on that account,' he said. 'Their bone structure is all but identical.'

Holmes and I got out of the carriage. Holding her brother's hand, she led him to where we were waiting.

'Mr Holmes, this is my brother, Peter. And Peter, this is Dr Watson.'

We all shook hands. 'Honoured, gentlemen,' Mr Urishay said. His voice was cultivated, and he seemed to be of a somewhat graver mien than could be discerned from first appearances. 'Thank you for coming so swiftly. You must be tired. Shall we . . . ?' He gestured vaguely.

'It is not far to walk from here, Mr Holmes,' Miss Urishay said. 'I would like to walk after all that driving. But if you and Dr Watson want to wait, I can secure the carriage for a while longer.'

'I won't hear of it, Madam,' Holmes said. 'Watson and I will be glad to stretch our limbs. It is a very short walk, I believe.' He pointed at a footpath leading away from the other side of the road.

'But you have not been here before!' I exclaimed.

'Watson, you really do sometimes astonish me. Look at the dust on Mr Urishay's boots. It is not the dust of the road, but that of the footpath. The colour and texture is distinctive. There is only one footpath in sight from here. Mr Urishay is holding a stick cut a little earlier today. It is hawthorn. The trees and bushes lining the footpath up there, towards the summit of that hill, are hawthorn.'

'Holmes!'

'And besides, Watson, there is a sign with an arrow by the gate there. It says "Jerusalem Keep".

'Lead the way, please,' Holmes said to brother and sister. 'I perceive that the tower is just out of sight on the other side of the hill. No doubt it will look splendid, with its flag flying, when we see it.'

'How did you know that we would have the flag flying?' Miss Urishay asked.

'I felt you would be sure to,' I said. 'If only to show defiance to your un-neighbourly persecutor.'

Peter Urishay nodded in fierce approval. 'You are right, Dr Watson. Nothing will make me take down the banner my sister has so beautifully made. I do not care what Court challenges me on the matter. They shall not!'

'Yes, quite so, Watson, admirably correct,' said Holmes. 'However, did you not also notice the fresh grazes on Mr Urishay's hands? Just as his sister is a capable needlewoman, a pursuit which leaves its traces, so Mr Urishay is a not quite so capable flag-raiser. He will have cause to improve, I am sure. But the marks left by the rope betray that he has had but little practice up until now. You would do well to observe hands much more carefully, my dear fellow.'

The Keep was indeed but a short distance further. Miss Urishay had described it perfectly. A great staunch stone tower, with small number of narrow windows; it was partly covered by creepers and a few twining roses. Over the great door, a deep and elegant arch, a stone lintel bore the deep-graven legend in simple, antique, somewhat indistinct characters: 'R L I', together with a carven shield bearing a forked cross. Holmes paused and remarked upon the letters.

'Yes,' replied Alexandra Urishay, 'Uncle Tom always used to tell us as children that they stood for Richard Lionheart I, and that he lived here once. Of course, that was just a fairy story, but it was certainly thrilling for us then.'

'There may be something in it, though,' put in her brother, 'For Lyonne's Lodge has the same reputation. It is claimed Richard I had a hunting lodge hereabouts in the Chase. Great Uncle Tom was fascinated by the tradition and devoted a great deal of his later years to looking into it. When we visited, he would often be found at his desk poring over old papers. '

Holmes eyed the lintel curiously, then nodded and we entered the ancient edifice. A short while later, suitably refreshed, we sat in the magnificent main chamber of the Keep, in old but comfortable chairs, richly upholstered. I looked around the great room. I sipped my tea and gazed at the areas of the floor not obscured by furniture or rugs. There was a design, but it was largely hidden. The background consisted of blocks of a pale grey or worn silvery-white; the floor around the walls, where the panelling met it, was of a very dark brown or even of a time-worn gold. Then I realised that I was looking at the same design of cross as formed the flag flying outside far above our heads – a fine foundation!

'Ah, Watson, I see that you have worked out the floor design,' exclaimed Holmes. 'Glorious, is it not? Fit for a king, one could almost say!'

'I am so glad you like it, Mr Holmes,' said Peter Urishay. 'I hope that you will be able to help us to maintain it and all of its manifestations here.'

'Well, now, sir,' said Holmes, 'the case is from one point of view very much against you, as you know. You have done well to call me in, for I fancy there are few with so keen an interest in matters of this kind. I cannot hold out any great hopes, but I see a possible glimmering. Tell me first all you know about this place and your family connections to it.'

'I am very grateful to you, Mr Holmes. We are not a wealthy family, but if you can find some way to defend us against this foolish charge . . . '

Holmes held up his hand. 'I assure you the interest of the matter will be reward enough for me. Now, pray, your history, please.'

The young man sighed. 'I am afraid there is so little I can tell. Uncle Tom took a great interest in these matters and quite buried himself in his researches, but though he would sometimes throw out teasing little remarks to us, I never heard what was the point of them. One thing only is clear: we have certainly been here for about six centuries, and not many families can show such continuous succession – and yet we have never been granted any title or distinction, or indeed – I confess it – arms. It is a mystery to me why not, especially when there are such relics in the house. But it has not concerned us. There are many thoroughly decent families of which the same could be said.' Peter Urishay set his jaw and glared at us as if we were the very court sitting in judgement of him.

'Quite so,' said Holmes. 'Certainly no full set of arms, with crest, supporters, motto and all. And yet you do have this emblem here, which Miss Urishay has so adroitly copied.'

'Oh, and not only here,' she put in.

Miss Urishay got up. 'Mr Holmes, perhaps you and Dr Watson would like to see some of the other little heirlooms?'

'We would be honoured,' said Holmes.

The Urishays allowed us to see some of the most fascinating arte-facts that I have ever seen. There was an exquisitely carved crystal chalice; and a round box, of gold, that their Uncle Tom had said once contained the Seal of the Keep. But now the cross-design on its lid was the only evidence of the connection. We were also shown a carved marble eagle, only three inches in height, which clutched the cross in its talons.

'However, Mr Holmes,' the young woman concluded, with a fine shining in her eyes, 'what do you make of this?'

She produced an ornate staff or tall walking stick of brightly polished wood, bearing a silver lion's head and a small enamel shield bearing the same sign of the gold cross upon a silver ground. Holmes examined it carefully.

'This is a remarkable object,' he remarked, 'for it is quite modern.'

'Modern, Mr Holmes? Surely not. You see, Uncle Tom told us, on one of our last rare visits here, that it was our family's greatest treasure of all. He always kept it by him, he said. With this caution in mind, we have kept it locked away and barely touched it since we came here.'

'And yet, Miss Urishay, the assay mark on this silver lion's head is for just seven years ago. And the glazing on this fine enamel shield is also contemporary. I have examined enamel in medieval relics and the effect is quite different. Think carefully, both of you – do you recall this staff from your childhood visits at all?'

The Urishays looked at each other and then slowly shook their heads.

Holmes subjected the staff to a further, minute scrutiny, looking closely at the seal between the lion's head and the polished wood.

'Forgive me,' he said, and rapped the stick sharply upon a desk. Our clients looked shocked. Then, with a savage twist, Holmes tore off the glinting lion's head and paused as he caught the look on each of our startled faces in turn. His long, keen fingers were intruded into the hollowed-out stick, and drew out a yellowed, gnarled scroll. With a smirk of satisfaction, Holmes carefully unrolled this, and his eyes darted across its dim, intricate characters. Then he lifted his gaze towards us all.

'Oh, your great uncle was perfectly correct, you know. This is a most precious thing indeed.'

Seldom can there have been in recent times a court hearing of such stately splendour and solemnity as the Court of Chivalry, in the case of In Re Urishay and Urishay, presented when it was convened some few weeks later in the Great Hall of the College of Arms.

Although I have often hastened past the College of Arms on pressing business, and scarcely ever given the building more than a glance, I have always admired its gracious brick and stone exterior. As Holmes and I hurried down Godliman Street and turned the corner, I glanced at the building again.

'I do like Georgian architecture, Holmes,' I remarked. 'It is so fine and harmonious.'

I caught the glint in Holmes's eye. He smiled. 'Ah, Watson, I can foresee the need for another monograph! The architecture is indeed fine, but it dates from the late seventeenth century, a good quarter of a century before Her Majesty's Hanoverian ancestors ascended the throne. Nevertheless, it is a not unattractive edifice. I fancy that we shall be seeing more of it than most people ever do.'

The Great Hall certainly deserved its name. It was richly panelled and galleried. The ceiling was gorgeously coffered, and painted cream and gold. I had been expecting stained-glass windows, as of something restored by Mr Butterfield or Mr Ruskin; however, the windows were of clear glass and admitted enough light to see the Hall and its furnishings and appointments in all their splendour. Against the far end of the Hall stood a great throne.

In between the high windows hung banners and tapestries. From what I could see, the tapestries depicted scenes of chivalry and legend: medieval knights, kings, and ladies, together with the occasional dragon, or monster of even worse aspect. The banners were heraldic shields and other devices, worked in gold and silver against sumptuous backgrounds of purple and red.

'My dear Watson, you are acting quite like a child at the cinematograph,' Holmes whispered.

'It is a magnificent sight,' I answered. Then I looked along the galleries. They were also brightly lit by the great windows, but, alas their denizens did not cut such a fine show as their surroundings. I recognised a group of journalists and scene-sketchers; for upon our entrance I had noticed that these gentlemen were being firmly but politely asked to leave their photographic apparatus in the custody of the Earl Marshal's Sergeants-at-Arms. They had all pushed back their bowler hats on their heads and sharpened their pencils. The press contingent was expecting a good story.

There were also several people who seemed to be doing nothing at all in particular, and doing it very well. Top-hats and frock coats were also in evidence amongst the sharply-tailored check; these proceedings seemed to have been transformed into a crowded spectacle, an excursion worthy of one of Mr Frith's canvases.

'I smell tobacco, Watson,' Holmes whispered. 'Yes, definitely. And far from good, at that. The Sergeants-at-Arms will soon put a stop to that! Smoking has never been allowed in the Court of Chivalry.'

'I say! Why?'

'This ancient Court was founded long before the discovery of the New World and what has possibly become its most famous export. Therefore it has never been accepted. No, Watson, I fear that we will have to do without the consolation of smoking for the duration.'

There was a subdued scuffle in one of the galleries, and a muffled exchange. But the smell of tobacco had faded away.

'Bermondsey,' said Holmes.

A hush fell over the Hall.

'At last,' Holmes whispered.

Counsel for both sides appeared from a side door, and took their places. Then the door on the right-hand side of the throne opened, and two tall men in scarlet, black, and gold emerged and stood on either side of it. They raised silver horns to their lips, and a few intense and penetrating notes rang out in the great Hall.

'It is said that the fanfare originated in the tunes composed by the Psalmist, King David, himself,' Holmes observed, as we got to our feet.

I thought that I would hear those notes for the rest of my life, or if I ever forgot them, I would always be seeking to remember them.

The Lord Surrogate of the Earl Marshal walked slowly out into the Hall, past the heralds, and mounted his throne. He was wearing robes of scarlet, black, and gold. A gold chain of office hung around his neck, and glinted in the rays of sunlight that illuminated the throne. He wore no wig, but his fine white hair was worn long. He was accompanied by two other men of distinction, chiefly adorned in white and scarlet: the Garter Principal King of Arms, our Chief Herald of England, and Clarenceux King of Arms, the herald with responsibility for the South of England. Behind these walked two young men in black and silver, one carrying a silver sword and the other a silver helmet. As the Lord Surrogate stood at his seat, these they placed on embroidered cushions on either side of him. Then they stepped backwards, down the steps, and back into the chamber behind the great throne.

The Lord Surrogate's voice called out. It filled the Hall.

'The Court of Chivalry is convoked. Be seated, and let us have a beginning!'

The Earl Marshall had appointed the eminent and learned Lord Fremlingham as his High Surrogate, a man of stern mien accentuated by expressive steel-grey eyebrows. Behind the great oak daïs on which he was raised there hung a magnificent banner. Above him were the Royal Arms, with its fierce-tongued lion and gracile, pure white unicorn.

I can do no better than to quote from the official proceedings, with my own occasional interpolations. Counsel for the plaintiff, who had somewhat the air of a reluctant combatant, began with his main witness: 'You are Mr Edward Malligo, of Moor Hall, in the county of Hertford?'

'I am not.'

Counsel visibly drew back, and looked at him incredulously.

'You are not?'

'Mister is a form of address reserved for tradesmen. I am Edward Malligo, Esquire.'

There was a subdued spluttering in court.

'I see. Would you tell the court what you were doing on the morning of 18 August last?'

'Yes. I was travelling on the turnpike that traverses the estate called Jerusalem Keep.'

'And what did you see?'

'I observed a banner flying from the turret.'

'What did you do?'

'I reined in, and trained my scrying glass upon it.'

'What did you then observe?'

'A flag that displayed arms.'

'Could you see the design?'

'Yes. It was Or crusily and a cross argent.'

'In other words, a gold cross on a white background.'

(I observed the heraldic officers wince at this crude simplification of their fine High French vocabulary).

Mr Malligo pursed his lips.

'Simply put, yes.'

'What did you do next?'

'I called upon Mr Peter Urishay, the occupant of the Keep.'

'And what passed between you?'

'I told him he was at fault in displaying a flag bearing arms, and I should have to report it.'

'What was his reply?'

There was a hesitation.

'He said I could go tell the devil for all he cared.'

'And did you? . . . I beg your pardon, did you in fact report the matter to the authorities?'

'Yes. I wrote to the High Sheriff, Garter King of Arms, and the Earl Marshall.'

'Thank you. No more questions.'

'Counsel for the defence?'

Mr Portwin, an eminent barrister, and a friend of ours from certain other cases, rose languidly to his feet.

'Squire Malligo,' began Portwin, smoothly, 'have you ever seen the decorative silk you describe as a flag displayed anywhere else?'

There was a pause. 'No, I have not.'

'So it has only been visible in the private grounds of Jerusalem Keep?'

'Yes: but publicly visible.'

'You have never seen the defendant Peter Urishay bear arms in any other place?'

'No.'

'He has not, for example, to your knowledge, taken part in a tournament, flourished a shield, gone about with an escutcheon painted upon his coach, nor worn a signet ring displaying arms?'

'I am not aware of any such things.'

'So: you have seen a flag flown on top of Jerusalem Keep; and that's it, is it?'

'No, sir. I have seen arms displayed on a flag, by a man with no right to claim arms: that is it.'

'No further questions.'

Counsel for the plaintiff rose.

'How often have you seen the flag flying?'

'Every day since I first noticed it: some thirty days or more.'

'So you would say the arms have been persistently displayed?'

'Precisely'.

The next witness was summoned.

'You are Colonel Henry de Vere, and you are the High Sheriff of Hertfordshire?'

'Correct.'

'In that capacity, you are familiar with all the old families of the county, including those that may bear arms?'

'I am.'

'Are you aware whether the family of Urishay may bear arms?'

'I have never known that to be so.'

'Thank you,'

'I should like to add, however, that the family are undoubtedly of ancient and gentle origin and of high esteem in the county.'

'Thank you, Colonel, though that is not germane.'

Mr Portwin rose.

'Your writ runs right across the county, Colonel?'

'It does.'

'Are you sure?'

The Colonel looked baffled. 'Sure. Why?'

'What are you powers as sheriff?'

'Largely honorary.'

'Indeed. But is it not the case that you may call all able-bodied men under forty to practise with the bow if you require?'

'It not a power I have had occasion to exercise lately.' [laughter].

'And you may also levy a duty for the entertainment of the monarch during a Royal Progress in the shire?'

'Yes – I believe so.'

'With exceptions?'

The military man's bewildered expression gave way to realisation.

'Ah, yes. My powers do not run – I remember being told this on my appointment, by the clerk – to those with benefit of clergy, foreign princes, peculiars and the lands without.'

These last were said in a rush, like a schoolboy recalling a lesson.

'The lands without being certain properties outside parish boundaries?'

'Yes, that is so. I see what you are driving at. Jerusalem Keep is indeed a land without.'

'Thank you. You have answered my next question. And there are no more.'

Counsel for the plaintiff sniffed.

'Colonel, do your powers include determining who may or may not bear arms?'

'No.'

'That is a matter, in your understanding, reserved to the Crown, and exercised by the Garter King of Arms?'

'Certainly not by me, anyway.'

'So those four exemptions to your own powers do not necessarily apply to other Crown powers?'

'I suppose not.'

'You have no reason to think they do?'

'I have not.'

It was then the turn of the defence, and at first both brother and sister were called to give an account of the flag, winning much sympathy for their frankness and loyalty to each other. Mr Portwin also called an expert in parochial law who confirmed that there remained parcels of land which lay outside civil boundaries and were held to be exempt from certain obligations. Counsel for the plaintiff, in cross-questioning, again established that there was no clear evidence that this applied to the Law of Arms. Mr Portwin then paused, before sounding his last trump.

'My Lord, I call Sherlock Holmes.'

There was an appreciative murmur throughout this most curious of courts.

'Mr Holmes, as well as your reputation as a great servant to this country, you are also an antiquary?'

'Yes: I may claim that.'

'You identified the missing crown of Charles I at Musgrave Hall, as well as solving the unhappy mystery there?'

'I did.'

'And your identification was confirmed by the chief authority?'

'By the British Museum, certainly.'

'You have written a monograph upon the Polyphonic Motets of Lassus?'

'I have.'

'And you studied numerous medieval manuscripts, in Latin, for this purpose?'

'Many.'

'Your conclusions were approved by other scholars?'

'The few capable enough to comment did so kindly.'

Counsel for the plaintiff rose.

'My Lord, if it will help the Court, I am prepared to say that we accept Mr Holmes's credentials in the general sphere of antiquarian research.'

The Surrogate nodded. 'I am grateful. Continue, Mr Portwin.'

'Mr Holmes, you had occasion to examine the device shown upon the banner flown at Jerusalem Keep?'

'Yes.'

'Please tell the court your conclusions.'

'The device appears to derive from the earliest known examples of the arms of the *Rex Latinitas Ierosolimitanus*.'

'The Latin King of Jerusalem? The Crusader Kings, as we might know them?'

'Quite so.'

'On what do you base that conclusion?'

'The arms are to be found on coins, vessels, monuments and other images, all clearly associated with the Kingdom. I have made a study of the matter, and the identification is indisputable.'

'Who would bear such arms, other than the Kings of Jerusalem themselves?'

'His seneschal, who ruled for the King in his absence: his constable, who might lead his army. His bailiff, who might enforce homage and taxes on his behalf. And the castellans, who held his possessions for him.'

'Besides its name, is there any other connection between the Keep and the Kingdom?'

'Certainly. What I take to be an original lintel stone bears the king's ceremonial sigil – R L I.'

'Anything else?'

'Yes. There are several relics, indisputably medieval, that bear the King of Jerusalem's device.'

The Lord Surrogate cleared his throat.

'This is a most diverting matter, Mr Portwin, and I think I see the drift of your questioning. But I do not yet quite see how it assists you. The Kingdom of Jerusalem has been dead some five hundred years, has it not?'

'One further question, My Lord?'

'Very well.'

'Thank you. Mr Holmes, will you now tell the Court about what you found at Jerusalem Keep?'

Sherlock Holmes turned to face the Earl Marshal's Lord High Surrogate. 'My Lord, it is my clear conclusion, based on a document I shall make available both to the Court and to the finest scholars, that Jerusalem Keep, in, but not of, the county of Hertfordshire, was made an inalienable fief of the King of Jerusalem, in perpetuity, by Richard I. It was made by that great King a shrine for the success of his Crusade for the recovery of Jerusalem, and a treasury for the riches raised to support the Crusade. The charter in question has an easily attested mark of the King and is witnessed by the Bishop of Lincoln and by the Constable of the Kingdom. To answer your question, My Lord: the Kingdom of Jerusalem may have been banished from the Holy Land many centuries ago, as you say; but it has lived on here under the protection of England for ever after. May we always guard and honour it.'

There was a great hubbub in the Court which the Lord Surrogate, his brows of tarnished silver raised appreciatively, did not subdue for some moments. Mr Portwin could not contain himself, and called out, with a flourish of his papers, 'My Lord, the defence submits that Peter Urishay and his kin are hereditary Castellans and most devout servants of the Kingdom of Jerusalem, and that as such neither the Keep nor its family are subject to the Law of Arms of England.'

And that was indeed the finding of the Lord Surrogate, after several adjournments and conferences between the most learned of lawyers. The Urishays had gained the sympathy of the Court and of the public: and the picturesque quality of their claim, together with the authority of Sherlock Holmes and other scholars upon the ancient deed their ancestors had cherished, quite won the day. And as Autumn began to bring its ancient splendour of crimson and gold upon the old Keep and even upon the parks and gardens of the great city, my friend took himself to his study to begin the monograph that later earned him so much esteem, and is known to this day as *Holmes Upon the Heraldry of the Latin Kingdom of Jerusalem*.

The Adventure of the Haunted Showman

CHRISTOPHER SEQUEIRA

When I look back at the enquiries my friend, Mr Sherlock Holmes, was asked to make in the year 1897, I recall his complaint that European crime had become unremarkable. Holmes claimed that villainy had largely slipped back into a catalogue of brutal assaults and straightforward (if skilful) burglaries. He believed the glory days of criminology had ended with the removal of Moriarty and Moran, and the more recent failure of the resurrected Baron Gruner to ensnare London in a spiritual terror as hideous as the Baron's own acid-ruined face. For Holmes, of course, the selfish aspect of his complaint was that this lack of a felonious challenge meant that he, Holmes, might go quietly mad from boredom – never mind that for the rest of us it meant living in a safer world. However the year did not close before one case came my friend's way that suggested he still had many a daunting investigation before him.

It was a cold October morning and Holmes and I were finishing a late breakfast. My friend had turned to a small white mountain of his unopened correspondence. I fancied I heard a carriage pull up below our window and was going to venture a remark when the next moment the doorbell rang and we heard Mrs Turner's shuffling gait respond. Holmes listened for some moments, and then chuckled.

'Mrs Hudson's sister is trying to rebuff a potential visitor until she thinks we have concluded our breakfast,' said Holmes. 'There have been no further steps into the house, nor has the front door been heard to close, yet the chill air must be quite the incentive for a visitor to depart – so, clearly, they do not wish to do so, but they are not being allowed to advance.'

He paused and we both listened. Finally the door slammed shut and we heard a familiar, brisk tread ascend to our floor, accompanied by a lighter step, while Mrs Turner's footfalls plodded off below stairs. 'Lestrade is accompanied by a woman,' said Holmes.

Holmes put his correspondence under the breakfast dish cover, glanced about the room and spotting his volume of *Catullus* on the table near the gasogene he snatched it up and hid it in the new umbrella stand the Reverend Walter Jekyll had presented to him with the adventure of the Surrey Terror. Before the knock could sound Holmes called to Lestrade to enter and the little inspector stepped into our rooms.

'Mr Holmes, Doctor Watson, good to see you both again. Please, let me introduce Mrs Lillian Myers.'

Mrs Myers was a tall woman of perhaps thirty years, of graceful demeanour. Her dark clothing immediately informed us that she had suffered a cardinal loss. She spoke with a strong voice.

'Mr Holmes, the Inspector tells me that your reputation is not unearned. He says that in cases where the official forces would not be able to pursue an investigation, you can, and that sometimes your efforts then allow the authorities to bring a felon to justice. Mr Holmes, I believe this makes you my best hope!'

Holmes ushered both Lestrade and Mrs Myers into chairs near the fire, and set the woman at ease.

'Mrs Myers, the good inspector does not exaggerate. If you wish me to look into the situation at Islington in conjunction with the circumstances of your husband's death, I will consider it.'

Our visitor's hand sprang to her face as she gasped in shock.

'Mr Holmes, you know of my case? Inspector Lestrade has informed you?'

'Not at all, Madam,' said Holmes. 'But, you are a widow, obviously, by your dress. You arrived with Lestrade, and it is clear that although the day is not old you have both been visiting some location together this morning; for your shoes and the inspector's bear small mud-stains identical in colour, ergo you have been to the same location together before coming here. I know that Lestrade currently rooms near the Yard, but when he removed his hat I noticed that he had a North London Railways ticket to Highbury tucked in it – he has retained his ticket so that the Yard will reimburse him – so I can safely venture that he met you in the Highbury and Islington vicinity. That the meeting was not resolved to your satisfaction I deduce from the fact that you both then took a cab ride here, to see me. Lestrade has joked that I have some small value as a "second opinion" in police matters. Finally, Mrs Myers, there is the top edge of a small printed handbill of some kind protruding from your bag, and though I cannot make out the words I recognise that typeface and border well – it is of a type often used for a fairground amusement or illusion show, and the only shows currently open close to Highbury are those at Islington, although I am unfamiliar with their current slate of attractions, I must say.'

Lestrade's face was screwed up in impatience. He had long learned that Holmes's earliest words to a client that Lestrade referred to him could make our poor Scotland Yard friend look like Goethe's apprentice in the presence of his sorcerer, and today was sadly no exception. Mrs Myers looked hypnotised by Holmes.

'Very good, Mr Holmes,' Lestrade said. 'We were indeed at Islington, at a show called the Phantasmosphere, where we spoke to the owner, but in my official capacity I could do little or nothing. No crime appears to have been committed.'

'Exactly,' said Holmes. 'Yet Mrs Myers was insistent on further action. I hypothesised that could only mean the matter for investigation relates to her recent loss, for, what else could overshadow that for her at the moment? So, my dear lady, I must ask you to explain your problem.'

Mrs Myers nodded and then seemed to choke back strong emotion before she spoke in a calm voice.

'Mr Holmes, my husband was quite wealthy. His parents had made their money in the Australian goldfields and he never had to work particularly hard. So he invested some of his spare capital in entertainments. He had been interested in legerdemain and magician's tricks as a child and so he very much enjoyed the ghost shows that provide much entertainment to Londoners and tourists. He was well known at many of these attractions, and he became very friendly with the owner of the Phantasmosphere, an attraction currently on show at Islington, run by Mr Carstairs Bidman.'

'My husband formed a business partnership with Mr Bidman a little over a year ago. Thereafter the two of them would meet every month and they would review the takings of the Phantasmosphere and Mr Bidman would issue a cheque to my husband. My husband was delighted with his investment, Mr Holmes. He said it was proving better than he expected.'

Holmes interjected gently. 'Mrs Myers, if I may – were all of Bidman's cheques honoured?'

'A good question, Mr Holmes,' said Lestrade, 'but one I have answered. Mrs Myers has a letter from her bank that says they indeed were.'

'I do not resent the question, Mr Holmes, and in fact our family's finances appear completely healthy,' said Mrs Myers.

'Excellent. Pray continue, then,' said Holmes, leaning back and closing his eyes.

'Well, sir, all went well, or appeared to,' said our visitor. 'I even visited the Phantasmosphere with my husband, and I must say I found it a clever and engaging series of illusions – I cannot imagine how they achieve some of their effects! Disappearing faces, colour-changing objects, creatures that appear to be weird hybrids of man and beast – all done with smoke and mirrors, so they say, but it looks startling! My husband adored it all, and would often chuckle when he believed that he had discerned how one or illusion or another was being achieved – but I could never divine such things myself.'

'Then, last month, my husband passed away in his sleep. It was not a melodramatic event, sir, not rendered bizarre in any way. We had used separate rooms, for I am – was – very sensitive to my husband's rather pronounced snoring. Normally he awakens me, and has tea brought in, but this morning he did not. I went in to see him and was shattered to find him hours cold and seemingly at peace. The doctor advised it was some sort of heart failure, so sudden he would not have experienced any pain. Horrible, but not unheard of, and his comfort-able life had made exercise rather foreign to him. I was shocked, but completely satisfied about the doctor's view of cause of death. Indeed I understood his father to have died in an identical fashion.'

'My worries about the Phantasmosphere began when I received no correspondence in return to the note I sent to Mr Bidman about attending the funeral, and indeed he did not appear, although a very pleasant show-hand, who I only know as Old Jimmy, did attend. I was not able to speak to him at the funeral as he remained at the rear of the church, and when I tried to approach him at the burial he darted off.'

'I determined, however, a couple of weeks ago, to settle my hus-band's affairs with Mr Bidman. However, my solicitor could find no copy of any contract between them. Although the will also made no especial references to Bidman or the Phantasmosphere, I decided that any investment that had been made by my husband should be left to the Phantasmosphere and Bidman, as they were clearly a favourite of his.'

'I wrote to Mr Bidman advising him of this intention, but a few days later I had no reply, which I considered somewhat curious given the news it contained. I was keen to seek action to help assuage my grief, gentlemen, so I went to Islington. Mr Holmes, I attended the grounds with my husband's broker, Mr Summersby, and we were treated in the rudest fashion. Bidman handed me a cheque covering all outstanding monies and ordered me to leave the property immediately! Then he called two surly old workers and had them escort us out. I was dumbfounded. He had previously treated me in a polite and chivalrous manner. There seemed to be no explanation why he should now behave so roughly and discourteously. Mr Summersby suggested commencing an action against him, but I told him not to.'

Holmes eyes twinkled. 'I can safely conclude, madam, that this cheque must have cleared as the others did, or you would not be here. A man who returns money, with ill-concealed hostility, when he does not have to, just so he can keep you from the premises – that is intriguing! Watson, I do believe it is unique in my personal records, so please note it as such. I take it, Mrs Myers, at that point you sought the services of my friend, Lestrade, here.'

Lestrade smiled, but in clear consideration of our guest he moved to his part of the tale quickly.

'Indeed, Mrs Myers did, Mr Holmes, and I will admit to being concerned. I took a couple of men with me, and we went down to the grounds, and saw Mr Bidman. He is a funny chap, and a few local inquiries I made might also be of use to you. Before we entered the grounds I noticed there was a public house right over the way from the Phantasmosphere, and questioned the owner. I soon learned two interesting facts. Firstly, that Bidman was fond of the grape of late and had bought more than few bottles to take back to his caravan. And secondly, a number of the workers had become very unhappy, shaken they were, and left. The show was actually in quite dire need of new hands, for it seems Bidman's brusque attitude was not confined to Mrs Myers – it was helping to drive men off the job.'

'Capital!' cried Holmes. 'Lestrade, you are entering the top of your class. Now go on – your encounter with Bidman, himself?'

Lestrade looked at our guest and she nodded, so he continued.

'Bidman was initially angry to see me, but when I showed him I was with the Yard he soon calmed down. At first he refused to explain himself, but then he became apologetic, said he was upset at Mr Dontanville Myers's death, and he offered to write an apology to Mrs Myers. Then he said business was falling off and he was thinking of selling the whole concern. He said unfortunately he now had a show to prepare, and we were welcome to come and see it that night.'

Holmes looked at Lestrade's face, intently. 'And you did not believe a word of his story, did you, Lestrade?'

The Scotland Yard expert gave a small grin. 'Glad to see you know me, sir. No, I did not believe him. He was lying about something, that much I have little doubt – he is a poor liar, too. I informed Mrs Myers as much.'

The widow looked at us and there was a steely glint in her eyes that informed me that this was a very determined woman. 'Inspector Lestrade's report made my mind up. I needed to know why my husband's trusted partner was acting so strangely. I mentioned Old Jim, Mr Holmes, well, I made up my mind to see him at least and find out what was going on. I did not tell the Inspector this, and instead told him I would consider things and call upon him again if I needed his help.

'You will think me mad, and perhaps I was, perhaps made temporarily so by grief, but I had my driver, Edmond, take me to the Islington Phantasmosphere's grounds after dark, and I slipped in, a dark lantern with me. No one was about, and I needed the light I'd brought to look for Old Jim's quarters – he had a small caravan and stayed on the grounds most nights. I found the 'van, but it was empty – I feared Old Jim had run off and I would never be able to find out what the matter was.'

'Then I heard a voice cursing, and so I darted inside Jim's empty caravan. I peered through a slit in the flimsy door and saw Mr Bidman, swinging a lantern. He was striding towards the Phantasmosphere itself, and I realised that he also carried a bottle and was quite drunk, as he muttered and stumbled along. I followed him but soon realised that I was in little danger of discovery, as he was so very inebriated.'

'He approached the Phantasmosphere. It is a curious structure, Mr Holmes. It is made of wood, and is essentially a large, octagonal, wooden shell of a building, built simply to house the show, a year ago or so ago. The audience is led into the building through a single doorway at front and then the show is conducted by an attendant, often Mr Bidman himself, leading that audience of up to a hundred people, through the eight separate chambers of the building. Each chamber houses a different optical trick or apparition. Some of the chambers have seats for the audience to sit upon whilst the attendant sets the stage for the illusion, which might at first be concealed with a curtain, or be a transformation trick that is displayed, then curtained, then revealed. Finally the audience is allowed to exit the building through a doorway from the eighth chamber; therefore they exit to the right of the door and chamber they first entered.'

'I followed Mr Bidman into the building and I must confess that my heart drummed in my throat as I went through the darkened confines, with only a sliver of light from my lantern guiding me. A hideous, purple-faced dummy swinging from a wire in the second room almost made me shriek, but I recognised it as the "ghost of an unjust hanging" that featured prominently in the scene of that room. Clearly they had brought it out for cleaning after the crowd went home.'

'Bidman kept moving through the Phantasmosphere, passing distorting mirrors and electric lights and the stage and wardrobe cabinet of the Great Medium that performed in one chamber, until he entered the eighth chamber. I stayed back at the doorway between chambers, obscured in shadow, watching Mr Bidman. He could not have seen me. That last chamber was empty save for a battered wooden chair leaning against one corner and on this he sat, and while I watched he simply sat and drank, cursing and muttering, and, it seemed to me, waved his fist, not at any person, but perhaps at fate itself. I did not understand what he was talking about, although I listened astutely, perhaps expectantly; I caught no name or reference I recognised.'

'I was about to leave when Mr Bidman suddenly stood up and began shouting and I thought I had been caught. But he was not looking at me; he was looking at a man who had suddenly appeared in the room.'

I leaned forward when Mrs Myers reached this portion of her story, Lestrade concentrated his gaze on Mrs Myers, and Holmes actually opened his eyes.

'I assumed the man must have stepped in from the exit door beyond where Bidman sat, and I had somehow failed to see him enter in the gloom. He wore a black suit and frock-coat and hat. He was facing Bidman, standing. I could not see his face. Bidman stared at him, then turned his head away and covered his face with one hand. I had a horrible certainty about the man – from his ample frame. I called out "Please, who are you?" '

'The figure turned and looked at me and, I swear, it was my Dontanville. His face looked somewhat sad. I thought I was going to cry. Then, before my eyes, as I advanced to reach out to him, he disappeared – he literally disappeared from view as if he were a candle-flame that blinked out. A solid, real person, who was standing in front of me, was gone.'

A log hissed in the grate at Baker Street. I studied Mrs Myers' face, she was resolute. I feared that at any moment, Holmes would be unable to prevent himself – he would offer a rebuke that was too harsh for this poor, grieving woman. He was studying her now, she had his full attention.

But our visitor spoke first. 'Mr Holmes you doubtless think me a foolish female, but before you send me on my way I will quickly conclude. I confronted Bidman but he angrily turned on me, babbling that nothing had happened, when it was plain he was frightened out of his wits, and then he fled the room. I ran after him and found Old Jim approaching the Phantasmosphere. He was shocked to see me in this place at that hour, but he was kind and considerate, as he always had been. His words were the most surprising part of the night's strangeness, for he said that he thought my dead husband was haunting the show. He saw me to the gate and to my carriage without another word.'

'Well, then, Mr Holmes,' said Lestrade, 'You see my predicament. I received a letter yesterday from Mrs Myers and accompanied her and her solicitor to the Phantasmosphere this morning. I talked to this Old Jim fellow, and Bidman, but all I got was a confirmation that Mrs Myers had been on the grounds, after hours. I have also explained to Mrs Myers that perhaps Mr Bidman was playing some sort of trick on her; perhaps some sort of revenge for some grievance he secretly nurses against her or her late husband, but it's a weak notion, I know. What do you think?'

Holmes sighed and spoke in a tone that I had seen him use to great effect in the past to calm a troubled client.

'Mrs Myers, I know this will distress you, but I am afraid Lestrade's theory is likely to be the correct one, unless further facts are forthcoming. A hoax of some kind is most probable – however, and this is crucial, a motive seems unfathomable.'

'Mr Holmes, I would accept your conclusion, save I saw the man's face. He was Dontanville's ghost, or the most amazing case of a resemblance I have ever seen,' said our visitor.

Holmes looked at her, rubbed his hands together and smiled. 'Mrs Myers, your insistence, and your demeanour are the only reasons I will even consider this case, but, I must advise you I am engaged in a pressing affair involving an unclaimed rare book recently auctioned after the sale of the Al Hazred Collection, and I shall not be free until a courier returns from Amsterdam with a message I require. I shall not give you false hope, but in four days you will learn if I will take your case.'

I knew nothing of this case of which Holmes spoke, but remained silent. I don't know if Lestrade or Mrs Myers looked the more relieved as they left. As soon as the two had left our dwelling Holmes bounced to the window with great energy, obviously making sure they had hailed a carriage and departed.

'Watson, there appears to be at least one unique feature in this business, would you not agree; this question of motive?' Holmes said.

'Unless she is somehow correct about a ghost, which I am sure you will say is impossible. However, I have told you of how my aunt swears to this day that her own mother visited her in her rooms after she died. And in India I saw things, that, well, let us say, rather than you mocking me, that they were deucedly hard to explain.'

'Good, old fellow, good, you have an open mind, though we shall perhaps beg to differ on how open it should be. I suggest we rummage through one of my steamer-trunks, for I feel our own trip to Islington is called for, in the disguise of two unemployed roustabouts. That will be our occupation, not any fabrication about awaiting Dutch couriers.'

So it was that later in the day Holmes and I wandered into the public house Lestrade had mentioned, attired as two working men in less than favourable circumstances. We were soon referred to the Phantasmosphere where we encountered the infamous Bidman, who was a square-shouldered, pale-faced man of perhaps forty years. When we explained our purpose he beamed, and soon had us engaged in washing and sweeping the public areas, and tending to a large horse-drawn caravan that was hitched at the rear of the Phantasmosphere building. Under the guidance of Bidman – a guise a little too close for my liking, for the man reeked of drink – Holmes and I had to unhitch the horses, clean the 'van, and then re-hitch the team of steeds. Holmes cleverly peppered the show proprietor with questions about the Phantasmosphere, and obtained a few answers. A lanky individual named Grames who appeared at Bidman's side was the chief operator of the illusions, together with three performers who only arrived at the Phantasmosphere just before the evening's shows. These three, two men and a woman, acted in roles either clownish or dramatic; they were the human element of the show. Bidman laughed when we asked how the tricks were done, he said he was asked that same question a hundred times a day by customers, and he was hardly going to reveal anything to two ne'er-do-wells whom he had only just employed. We both laughed in agreement with him.

At one stage Holmes was able to use his extraordinary affinity with equines to a useful advantage. Warning me of his plan first, he loosened the rig on one of the horses and it cantered away, and he yelled out to Bidman for help. As the ghost show owner ran after Holmes and the animal I darted inside the Phantasmosphere, directly into the eighth chamber where the strange appearance Mrs Myers had described took place. As swiftly as I could, I surveyed the room, and studied the lock on the entrance door, the walls and floors, looking for hidden mirrors, doors, traps and the like. For maddening moments I could find nothing out of the ordinary. It was clear, though, that the interior of the room did not match the shape of the exterior; the room had obviously been shaped a certain way with interior walls to appear rectangular; not an octagonal segment. There were no seats in this room but there were some fixed railings, which I perceived would keep a flowing crowd from crossing from one side of the room to the other. If there were hidden panels or other trickery concealed it was all cunningly fashioned and I could not reveal any. Too soon I heard Holmes's voice. I quickly put my head outside the door and saw the men and the horse returning, Bidman and Grames were deep in discussion and not looking towards me so I was able to dash outside and around the building and out of sight, reverse my steps and then appear as if I was meeting the men. No one noticed my subterfuge. The remainder of the day passed uneventfully, and Bidman paid us without quibble.

That evening, at Baker Street, Holmes and discussed the day's efforts over a late dinner. Based on my report, Holmes believed that he would have little trouble breaching the door-lock on the Phantasmosphere after dark.

'While I do not think it essential that I examine the room, it will be useful. Clearly, there are two elements to the artifice described by Mrs Myers, the first being an accomplished make-up artiste's disguising of someone to resemble her husband, the second being the disappearance illusion. That illusion is most likely, from her description, to be a variant of Pepper's Ghost trick.'

'Yes,' I responded, 'I have seen it used in other ghost shows. Quite clever. As I understand it, the audience looks at something, through a forced viewpoint of a doorway, or window. Let us say the scene they see is an empty chair and a real man sitting on another chair, reading a newspaper or doing some other task. The crowd does not know they are actually viewing this through a floor-to-ceiling glass pane. The audience is also unaware that facing this tableau, at an angle, is a hidden room, out of their line of sight; another small room painted black, wherein a man stands. This man then steps forward, still within the black room, still out of sight of the audience. His reflection, however, appears on the pane of glass. He sits on a chair identical to the one in the other room, placed in a precise spot corresponding to the other chair, and *voilà*, it appears as if a man has appeared from nowhere to sit on a very real chair. He stands up and walks back in the direction he came and disappears completely. The railings in the room keep the audience from reaching to a position where they might see the black room.'

'Indeed,' said Holmes, 'the devising of the illusion took place a few decades ago, and has been a staple of Ghost Shows and theatrical novelties since. There are variations, where the pane of glass and reflection are mounted horizontally, and an audience seated above the apparatus, and smaller scale versions exist also. If you could find no evidence of the glass or the black room, then I would conjecture that Bidman only assembles that part of the equipment before show time, and fastens it into position then. He is clearly not fool enough to allow his workmen any chance whatsoever to examine his secrets, which may be a telling trait.'

'We could see the show ourselves, tonight,' I suggested.

'No, I think a man as cautious as Bidman, a man we can suspect of having accomplices adept in disguise, will soon see through any false whiskers and paint we might apply to our own faces, faces he now knows quite well, so must forego that pleasure.' said Holmes.

'Since we shall still need, however, to occupy ourselves until the Phantasmosphere has closed, allow me to persevere with Saint-Saens' *Violin Concerto No. 3*,' said Holmes, taking up his Stradivarius and bow.

*   *   *

It was eleven-thirty when Holmes and I reached the fairgrounds at Islington. We had travelled by cab and deliberately created the impression that we were staying at the public house near the Phantasmosphere. Dressed in dark clothing and carrying lanterns we entered through the main gate, which was secured only by a length of chain which was easily unravelled.

We approached the Phantasmosphere in the gloom, listening and watching. I saw the horses sleeping in their lean-to as we neared the attraction, but couldn't see the large caravan we had cleaned; it had obviously been moved to another part of the grounds.

Holmes gripped my lapel, and I pulled up short, as the light of a lantern suddenly appeared in the dark. We were in the open, so the only thing to do was flatten ourselves on the ground. We lay there, squinting up as the light bobbed quite briskly several yards in front, between us and the Phantasmosphere. As Holmes and I watched we saw that it was Old Jim who wandered along, smoking a clay pipe and moving towards the horses, until he was out of sight.

'Quickly,' Holmes whispered, jumping to his feet, and we ran to the building.

Holmes had me hold a steady light on the door, but it proved no difficulty for my friend's bunch of lock tools, a gift from a grateful burglar.

Soon we were inside.

I did not expect an apparition, so what we observed the moment we entered was something of a shock. A loud voice was intoning, resounding through the walls, muffled but clear. We reduced our lantern-lights to the thinnest of beams and moved carefully towards the source.

I made a point of counting in merest whisper to myself as we moved through the premises, going through room after room, seeing nothing of importance but a couple of puppet-like mannequins and a few silken turbans and scarves, presumably left in haste by the performers. Eventually we had traversed seven rooms, and reached the origin of the noise. It was a pathetic sight. Carstairs Bidman sat on the floor in one corner of the chamber before us. His shirtfront was awry and covered in stains, wine and food I thought. Clutched in his hand was a wine bottle. He was dirty and dusty as if he had been rolling around the floor. He swigged from the bottle and uttered a string of terrible oaths. As we watched an awful feeling settled over me of violating the man's most private shame. I wanted to withdraw from that place. No matter what Holmes desired to investigate, this was too wretched a vision.

Then Bidman began to laugh, and talk animatedly. I realised he was having some sort of delirium, a not uncommon fate of those whose souls are prisoners of the bottle. He gestured and giggled between sentences that were largely incomprehensible.

Then a man appeared, not from any door, but it seemed from out of the air itself. The figure appeared to slide into view vertically, as if entering from behind some partition, but a non-existent one. It was a rotund man of medium height, dressed in town clothes, and I knew it must be the figure that Mrs Myers had seen. Even knowing how such conjurings were created I was transfixed by what I saw.

Bidman began to whimper, and yelp the name "Myers", and I briefly wondered whether this strange affair involved some sort of hoax being played on the Ghost Showman, rather than his late investor's widow.

Holmes seemed unmoved. His eyes were bright with the ferocity they exhibited when was hot on the scent; I had seen that look at Stoke Moran; and I had seen it on moors near Baskerville Hall. He was studying the floorboards.

He gripped my arm and we dashed forward 'Now, Watson, this way!' he said and we darted forwards and to the right.

The figure turned, and stood staring at us, absolutely impassively. Bidman screamed and fell like stone. I reached for the stranger's arm.

My arm closed about nothing, empty air. Holmes was standing at my side. He too was confused, halted where he was. We were alone with Bidman.

'I – I have misjudged my mark,' Holmes snapped. 'I was calculating the location of our reflected ghost from the floorboard's pattern, but I appear to have made an error.'

He turned to Bidman. 'You hear me, Mr Bidman? Your accomplice made his escape from this room, but when I can show Mrs Myers how, your little effort shall be at an end.'

Bidman said nothing. Holmes clucked with disgust. 'Clearly he saw through our charade today, and prepared a little show for us. He may even be genuinely drunk as part of his act. See that he is not actually injured, would you?'

I moved to the man and examined him. He was definitely under the influence of alcohol, but appeared otherwise unhurt, and his pulse and respiration seemed strong enough.

I turned to Holmes and watched as he began to inspect the room, much as he had asked that I do when we were in disguise. As I did so I witnessed a curious change come over my friend. At first he was calm and methodical; he paced the room, measuring its internal dimensions, examining joins and cracks for hidden seams and studying the room's geometry. He darted outside and returned, a worried look on his face. He left again and returned with a large sledge hammer and to my amazement began to smash panels in the walls.

When he had punched through these he shone his lantern into the darkened apertures. They were all empty. And this fact seemed to make Holmes more agitated.

Bidman began to stir, and I suggested to Holmes that we leave, but he began pounding a hole in the only unmarked wall. The swings grew more and more savage as he took out his frustration. He finally broke through and gazed into the darkness. He turned to me his features a mixture of puzzlement and grave disappointment.

'We have to go,' I reiterated and he nodded in agreement.

'Now, how on Earth did he do that, how did he do it?' muttered Holmes as we rode back to Baker Street in the first cab we found.

*   *   *

I have described in the various accounts of my friend's investigations something of the complex personality of the man himself. Long has he chided me for this, but I feel it is inevitable, for Holmes's processes were inextricably linked to the strengths and limitations of his remarkable intellect, and very much to his impressive willpower. He was a man who would spurn an invitation to a foreign noble's court, in favour of locating a missing street urchin's father; he had refused a high position in Scotland Yard although he lamented their resistance to the suggestions he sent to the Commissioner of Police every year. On the day after the incident at the Phantasmosphere Holmes was in as black a mood as I had ever beheld him.

He took neither food nor drink save pot after pot of coffee and he smoked five of the foulest pipes of dottles and remnants of tobacco I'd seen him assemble, before throwing his pipe into my fez and opening a box of Egyptian cigarettes which he then smoked, chain-fashion. He refused to engage me in conversation, other than to make one plaintive request that I 'Understand that the case makes no sense! The motive defies the opportunity!' I eventually realised that I was testing my own patience and went to my club for the morning.

When I returned, Mrs Turner was attempting to amble upstairs with the late post so I retrieved the envelopes from her. Only one was for Holmes who sat sullenly by the fire. He barely grunted as he took it and tore it open.

I had been firm in my abstinence of late, but the day had wearied me, so I reached for a tumbler and the whisky decanter on the sideboard. A cry from my companion halted me in my task and I turned to see him waving the letter angrily.

'Maddening, maddening!' he said, 'I have been threatened with legal action by Bidman's solicitor if we trespass again!'

'Then,' I said, 'The man has something to hide! You have rattled him, Holmes, don't you see?'

Holmes actually threw the letter in the fire with much venom. 'No, Watson, no! He cannot have anything to hide! He is a carnival owner, he is a showman! He runs a ghost show with a ghost, but there are no such things as ghosts! He was never suspected of any wrong-doing in Bidman's death, or with Bidman's money – the case is impossible!'

In that moment my rising anger at Holmes's difficult nature was turned away, and channelled into a heated dislike of Bidman. I blamed Bidman for seeing my good friend distressed like this, and I felt the need to demonstrate my feelings.

'This is Bidman's work – whatever it is, Holmes, do not be harsh on yourself. But he will fail, and you will lay his dashed ghost! If Bidman has had a black hand in his investor's death then Sherlock Holmes, the specialist in crime will find him out – I have unshakeable faith in you, my friend!'

Holmes did not react, but I knew he heard me. Then a curious expression lighted upon his features and he looked at me, sharply. 'A specialist in crime, the only one in Europe, yes, that is my trade, is it not?'

Before I could answer Holmes threw off his dressing gown and headed for his room as he did so. He returned seconds later, wrestling with his frock coat.

'I shall send some telegrams, directly from the Post Office in Wigmore Street, and I have some records to inspect. I think you have provided me with the missing element in this case – and that element might be something missing in myself.' And with that he was gone, out of the door and down the stairs.

Holmes did not return all afternoon and I had just finished a solitary evening meal when Lestrade's tread sounded on the stairs, with a companion. Our client Mrs Myers was with him. The two were surprised to discover that Holmes was not at home. Lestrade showed me a note he had received at the Yard requesting him to collect Mrs Myers and meet Holmes at Baker Street. I was puzzled and embarrassed until a messenger arrived, bearing a note for Lestrade from Holmes. But this missive only made the mystery deeper, for it contained a message from Holmes stating that he was making a late-night assignation with the doctor who signed the death certificate for Mrs Myers's husband, after which he would be conducting an experiment in the laboratory at Bart's Hospital (where certain courtesies quite especial had been extended to him over the years). The final instructions in his note were underlined, and quite clear and detailed; they included the fact that Holmes required that Lestrade, Mrs Myers and I meet him at nine o'clock in the morning at the Phantasmosphere, where a resolution to the case could be determined.

Mrs Myers looked quite concerned and said she did not understand this at all. The talk of her husband's passing then agitated her
to the point where Lestrade decided to take her home. After they had
departed, I sat heavily in my chair – wondering whether I should fly
to Bart's, then recalling how Holmes disliked company when he was
engrossed in his more complex researches.

I retired near midnight, with no sign of Holmes. When I approached the breakfast table in the morning my friend had still not
returned, but I prepared for the day and the unequivocal following of
his instructions.

I took a cab to Islington and as I stepped down I saw Lestrade and
Mrs Myers walk towards me. They had been awaiting my arrival for
only a few minutes. Together we walked into the grounds through
the open gates. A couple of workmen, including the thin Grames,
wandered about. His glance told me he recognised me, but surprisingly he didn't seem to be troubled by the fact that a man who'd
washed dirty caravans for his employer was now dressed as a London
gentleman. The three of us approached the front of the Phantasmosphere even as Bidman strode over from the direction of his own
caravan and intercepted us just outside the front door to the attraction. He was angry and red-faced.

'I have had my solicitor write to your friend, Doctor Watson, and
he has made my position very clear,' said the Showman. 'Your presence here is not wanted. I have a good mind to call for the police.'

Lestrade took a step forward. 'It may interest you to know, sir,' he
announced in a gruff manner, 'that I *am* the police. Inspector Giles
Lestrade of Scotland Yard.'

At this pronouncement Bidman lost most of his bluster.

'Now sir,' continued Lestrade in a stern and confident manner, 'I
have an appointment to meet Mr Sherlock Holmes here at nine. In
fact his instructions were to have Mrs Myers show me to the spot
where she alleges she saw a man who looked just like her husband.
So, I think that's where I'm going to go. And if you obstruct me,
sir, I may not arrest you right now, but I will be back this evening
with a brace of some of my sharpest – my sharpest, I say – officers.
Because you never know; there might be pickpockets and such-like
frequenting an attraction like this, mightn't there? Might scare your
customers away? And we can't have that?'

Bidman was defeated. He produced a ring of keys and let us in
to the Phantasmosphere. We moved through its seven rooms until
we reached the last chamber. Bidman regained some of his surly

manner as we entered that final chamber. 'Well, then, Inspector, we're here, what do you and your friends expect me to do now? Summon some ghosts?'

I truly expected a confrontation of some sort, as Lestrade was losing his patience with Bidman, and I felt the Showman's rudeness was too provocative for the Scotand Yarder to contain himself, but what occurred next was most startling and surprising. A voice – Holmes's voice – boomed with anger, filling the air around us. 'Carstairs Bidman, your time has come!' it bellowed, and we looked behind us in anticipation of Holmes entering from the previous chamber.

But the voice sounded again – from *in front* of us. Everyone turned and Holmes appeared, in the room, as if walking out from behind some invisible wall – Holmes materialised from thin air, right before our eyes! I was astonished – even knowing it was a deception of some kind, but Bidman and Mrs Myers were open-mouthed in surprise! Bidman turned to flee the room, as, surprisingly, did Mrs Myers, but Lestrade blocked the way.

'I think I want to see the rest of this show,' said Lestrade.

From a doorway so expertly concealed that I could not discern its outline from the wooden slats of the walls, Holmes stepped into the room, not a ghost but a flesh-and-blood man. As we turned and moved towards him we could see how the illusion had been performed, and we spilled outside as a group to examine the situation properly.

The eighth chamber of the Phantasmosphere was a Pepper's Ghost trick, but with an ingenious variation. The 'black room' and glass pane were not in the actual Phantasmosphere, they were in a completely separate wooden construction that was concealed in a large caravan that had been backed against the outside of the Phantasmosphere. This of course had been drawn by the horses. Before an audience entered the chamber, the carriage had been put into place, the moveable walls secured to flooring with dowels to provide a seamless finished appearance. What had happened the other evening when Homes and I had searched the eighth room was that the carriage and horses had been led away so that there was nothing to reveal this part of the trick – the 'mechanism' of the illusion had been removed before Holmes was able to 'open it'. Old Jim and Grames stood outside, watching over the apparatus, both men clearly in league with Holmes on this occasion, if the looks the three men exchanged were any indication, while Bidman, Mrs Myers, Lestrade and I looked at Holmes only for more answers, which were forthcoming.

Holmes turned to Bidman, but he swept his arm across at Mrs Myers, also, inclusively. 'You are both to be congratulated!' my friend said to them.

Lestrade was confused, and so was I. 'What is this, Mr Holmes? Mrs Myers is involved? Is this all about some conspiracy – her husband – his death, his fortune? I confess, you have me at a loss. Please be more specific.'

Mrs Myers herself provided part of the answer as she stepped forward and in a dramatic gesture looped an arm around her Carstairs Bidman. 'I am sorry,' she said, her voice harsh with emotion. 'My name is really Irma Bidman, and this is my husband,' she cried with fierce pride. 'You have seen through our little performance. Bravo, Mr Holmes.'

My friend turned to Lestrade. 'They had only one purpose, and that was to fool you and me. In the Ghost Show business there is one advertisement that brings crowds from miles around, and brings them back, again and again. Imagine the enormous earnings of the Ghost Show that can claim to be really haunted. No matter if the official owner says there is no ghost! *For, Scotland Yard and Sherlock Holmes themselves investigated and couldn't find anything! They gave up!*'

Holmes explained, nodding at the Bidmans as Lestrade's eyes bulged. 'Your wealthy banker was pure misdirection – to create a case reeking of foul play and covered-up death. But it was all a fiction. And I was slow to determine this. I believed Dontanville Myers must have died, for his wife said she discovered his dead body herself, thus eliminating – in my mind – an initial possibility of a faked death by him, in collusion with his Showman friend. What I should have questioned at the outset, was that there really *was* a Mr and Mrs Myers in business with Bidman. This was where your ploy could only resist scrutiny so far.

'And you were clever and thorough in your plans, so I wonder, how long ago you first conceived them, patiently waiting for the elements to fall into place? For there *was* a Dontanville Myers who died a month ago in this city. I must admit, when I examined records of death and found that such an individual had died of heart failure, I almost dropped the case, but Watson had convinced me that the motive lay in some sort of public manipulation of my own reputation; so I switched my queries to the wife instead of the husband. Imagine my pleasure at learning that this lady was fifty-eight years old and had relocated to Switzerland. Therefore she could not have been the same woman who visited me in Baker Street with Lestrade.

'I have to admit that I admire your efforts. There was an unstinting patience, and a devious turn of mind in evidence here. You left clues that were entirely tantalising to me, which leads me to believe, Watson, that your records of my cases give too many of my secrets away. I think, Mr and Mrs Bidman, that you truly honour your profession as showpeople; you exercised some courage in testing Scotland Yard and myself, especially considering the potential consequences.'

In response to this last remark our Inspector friend rounded on the Bidmans and Grames. 'You three . . . scoundrels!' he said with controlled anger. 'You will find the law takes a dim view of such . . . '

Holmes cut him off with a huge gust of laughter. 'My dear Lestrade, the last thing I wish to do, and I'm sure the Yard's official position might be similar, would be to provide these people with further publicity. Might I instead suggest that Mr Bidman provide a written undertaking that ten percent of his revenues be turned over to a local children's charity that I shall name? Otherwise, my brother Mycroft might be inspired to have a word to his associates working for Her Majesty's Income Tax Collectors, who may well be prompted make some troublesome enquiries which would prove injurious to one's profits?'

Bidman replaced his grin with an earnest, deferential expression, and quickly agreed. With some reluctance Lestrade agreed to Holmes's suggestion.

'Quite a case,' said Holmes as we left the grounds, 'and a cause for giving thanks to the powers-that-be. Bidman would make a formidable criminal if he had chosen to use his talents for ill, rather than entertainment.'

'Indeed,' I said, 'and prior to this case I'd venture to say that Sherlock Holmes would never have thought that a fairground would be a satisfactory place to alleviate his intellectual boredom'.

Sherlock Holmes and the Reichenbach Secret

DAVID STUART DAVIES

'Stand with me here on the terrace, for it may be the last quiet talk we shall ever have.' The words are those of my friend Sherlock Holmes. They were spoken to me on that fateful evening in August 1914 just after we had captured the German spy, Von Bork. You will find details of this adventure in *His Last Bow*, an account I penned myself but presented in the third person in order to achieve a more dramatic effect. As it turned out it was not the last occasion on which Holmes and I had a 'quiet talk'. That occurred some two summers later.

I had heard little of Holmes since the capture of Von Bork and then, out of the blue, I received a note from a neighbour of his, informing me of my friend's failing health. Shocked at this news, I determined to travel down from London to his retirement cottage in Sussex to see him. I was aware that this was probably the last opportunity I would have to meet with my old friend – a last chance to say goodbye.

I wired ahead to ascertain whether my visit was possible and received an instant, impish response from Holmes:

PLEASE COME IF CONVENIENT; IF INCONVENIENT, PLEASE COME ALL THE SAME.

I travelled from London by train and hired a taxi cab from the local station to take me to his cottage. The cab dropped me by a dusty lane, at the end of which I saw a whitewashed cottage almost perched on the cliffs, overlooking the sea.

I found Holmes sitting in his garden in the afternoon sun, gazing across the great blue expanse of the English Channel. He wore a pale linen suit and a sand-coloured Panama hat and for all the world looked like a retired colonial. His face, however, was pale and gaunt and those bright eyes, although still sharp and piercing, had sunk deeper into their sockets. He rose to greet me and I found his handshake as firm as ever.

'My dear, dear Watson, by all that's wonderful, you are a sight for sore eyes,' he said warmly. 'Still practising a little medicine, I see.'

'Why, yes,' I replied in some surprise.

He grinned and pulled up a garden chair for me to sit on. 'Iodine stains on the fingers and the telltale shape of a thermometer case in your top pocket.'

I chuckled gently. 'You can still surprise me with . . . '

' . . . my little observations. I'm pleased to hear it.' He leaned forward and rang a small bell on the table beside him. 'I am sure that you would find a cup of tea refreshing after your long journey.'

In response to the bell, his housekeeper emerged from the cottage, took my overnight bag and set about arranging for the tea.

'Martha is no longer with you?' I asked when the lady had returned indoors.

'Sadly, no. She has retired and returned to her native Scotland. "My old bones are not up to serving you any more, Mr Holmes." He mimicked the faint Scottish tones of our redoubtable landlady.

'It was a wrench to both of us for her to go. She has served me well and truly.'

'Served us both.'

Holmes paused and gave me a thin smile. 'Served us both,' he said softly.

How strong are the memories of that afternoon: Holmes and I sitting in the bright sunshine, drinking our tea, the faint breeze off the sea, the hum of the bees and the conversation. The conversation, which began with talk of the war but then drifted inevitably into discussions of our past cases. As is the way with old men, we relived our youth, talking of Milverton, John Clay, the Baskerville affair and countless other cases in which Sherlock Holmes and I joined together to counteract the forces of crime. Once again we were in our Baker Street rooms, hearing the distressed pleas of a desperate client or rattling through the streets in a hansom cab on our way to Paddington, Euston or King's Cross to catch an express which would bring us to some great house in the shires where there was another mystery to unravel.

I felt pangs of sadness when we discussed the Agra treasure business, a case which brought me my own greatest treasure, Mary, my beloved wife. At first, Holmes seemed unaware of my discomfort but, as he moved on to discuss another of our adventures, he narrowed his eyes, gave me a brief nod and patted my arm.

As we talked, I felt my heart grow light and the spirit of adventure rise within my weary bones. I marvelled at the realisation of what we had done and achieved. To think that I was the companion of the man who had turned detection into an exact science.

Suddenly my friend laughed out loud. 'The irony of it, Watson, the irony of it.'

'I'm sorry, I don't quite understand.'

'You remember how I used to rail at you about your overly romantic accounts of my cases that were published in the *Strand Magazine*?'

'Indeed I do.'

'Well, now I find my memory somewhat . . . unreliable, so that I have had to purchase a whole bound set of the magazine in order that I can bring to mind all the details of those cases.'

He burst out laughing and I joined him.

We sat conversing until the sun had almost set, sending warm, crimson fingers of twilight across the still, sparkling waters.

That evening we dined quietly. Holmes's new housekeeper, Mrs Towers, a local lady who didn't live in, provided us with a simple but appetising meal, and Holmes had dug out a very good bottle of Beaune from his modest cellar. The cottage was illuminated by oil lamps, electricity not yet being available in such an isolated spot. There was also a small fire lit in the dining room to ward off the chill of an English summer evening; the flames added to the soft amber glow of the chamber which, in essence, reflected my own inner glow. Here I was with the best and wisest friend I knew, chatting amiably about old times. For the moment I felt cocooned in this pleasantly primitive dwelling against the harsh realities of the terrible war which was being fought across the channel whose blue waters we had been gazing upon that afternoon.

Mrs Towers served us pudding, assured my friend that she would attend to the washing up in the morning and bid us both good night. By the time Holmes and I were tackling the brandy and coffee, we were in a very relaxed mood indeed.

Holmes lit his pipe and stared at me quite sternly for some moments. 'I think the time is right to confide in you a secret that I have held close to my chest for a long time – something I wished I could have told you many years ago. I tell you now, my dear Watson, so that I can ask your forgiveness.'

I looked at my companion in surprise. 'Surely there can be nothing . . .'

He held up his hand to silence me. 'Pass judgment when I have finished.'

'Very well,' I said, somewhat sobered by Holmes's change in demeanour.

'You will remember with great clarity the Moriarty case.'

'Certainly.'

'The way his thugs sought to kill me and how he visited me in my Baker Street chambers to warn me off? How I fled to Switzerland and he followed me? How we fought on the brink of the Reichenbach Falls? How he fell to his death in the roaring torrent and I escaped? You remember all that?'

'As though it were yesterday.'

Holmes paused and swirled the brandy in his glass before taking a drink. 'I was fooled, Watson. We all were. I did not actually meet Professor Moriarty for the first time until a month after the Reichenbach incident.'

'What! But you told me that he came to see you in London.'

Holmes shrugged. 'I believed that he did. I was a gullible fool. Someone came to see me. He told me that he was Moriarty and he bore a close approximation to the description that I had been given of the scheming professor – a description which also turned out to be false. In truth, the man who came up the seventeen steps of 221b was an impostor hired by Moriarty. If I had had I my wits about me at the time, I should have realised that. The great man was not going to place his own person in such danger by visiting his arch-enemy in his lair. He could not know what I would or could have done. Moriarty did not take those kinds of risks, so he sent along a consummate actor to play him. The message was genuine: it was the messenger who was a fake.'

'I cannot believe that you were taken in by this charade.'

Holmes shook his head sadly. 'But I was, my friend. The phrase is "hook, line and sinker", I believe. But the fellow played his part well. Even now my flesh begins to creep when I consider that encounter. The trick worked beautifully, as Moriarty knew it would. He had a powerful intellect and created his own certainties out of mere possibilities. One more brutish attack from his agents and I came to realise that my best plan was to leave the country until Scotland Yard moved in on the Professor's organisation.'

Holmes smiled. 'And what a pleasant time we had of it – until we reached Rosenlaui.'

'But you were aware of the shadow cast over our sojourn.'

'Yes. I tried to protect you from it, but I knew that your sensibilities would alert you to the danger we were in. It was I who arranged for the boy to bring you the message about the dying Englishwoman at our hotel. I knew your stout heart could not refuse such a patriotic summons.'

'You wanted me out of the way.'

'I wanted you out of danger. I believed I was about to face my nemesis by the Reichenbach Falls. I feared the worst. But what I didn't know – what, as a detective, I failed to deduce – was that we were being trailed by trained assassins in the pay of Moriarty, under the leadership of Colonel Sebastian Moran. And not, as I assumed, by Professor James Moriarty himself.'

I took a gulp of brandy. My mind and my senses were now clear and alert. All feelings of drowsiness and inebriation had been expelled by my friend's narrative. Although these revelations were shocking and new, they only presented a fresh interpretation of events as I knew them. It was an interpretation which was frighteningly plausible.

'Where was Moriarty?' I asked at length.

'That comes later. Suffice it so say that he too had left London for the safety of foreign shores. You see, he was far more concerned about preserving his own life and salvaging what he could of his organisation than dealing with an irritant like me.'

'More than an irritant, surely? It was your work which brought about the collapse of his empire.'

Holmes grinned broadly. 'You still have a way with words and the use of a telling phrase, Watson. You are correct, of course, but Moriarty was far too intellectual to lower his sights to personal revenge. I had to be removed, there was no uncertainty about that, but for a long time it was not a personal vendetta. That would be too . . . '

'Emotional – and emotion clouds the intellect.'

'Yes. You see, we were twins – of a kind.'

I leaned forward on the table and gazed at my friend for some moments before I spoke. 'Then who . . . who did you meet on the path above the Reichenbach Falls?'

For an instant, Holmes seemed to be overcome by a strange emotion. He closed his eyes and lowered his head. 'In truth,' he replied at length, 'I do not know. He was yet another agent of Moriarty. Not the same man who visited me in Baker Street but of similar appearance. At the time, I really believed that this was *the* Professor Moriarty, the Napoleon of Crime, but he was not. However, I soon discovered that this fine fellow was skilled in martial arts. Never have I fought so hard and so desperately as I did on that precipitous ledge overlooking that yawning chasm. Our struggle was exactly as I reported it to you in your consulting rooms on my return to London three years later.'

'With your knowledge of *baritsu* you managed to overbalance him and he fell over . . . '

'That terrible abyss,' he mouthed my own words back at me.

I did not smile.

'You see why I found it hard to tell the truth.'

'But these are lies upon lies. You kept me in the dark for three years – three whole years – believing you to be dead and now you are telling me that you never met Moriarty at all and did not bring about his death.'

'I am not saying that. The truth is always darker and more complex than we would have it.'

'Is it?' I replied tersely, reaching for the brandy bottle and pouring myself another drink.

'The account I gave you of my escape was true. After my opponent had dropped into the swirling waters below me, I knew I could not retreat down the path without leaving tracks. My only resort was to attempt to scale the cliff wall behind me. I struggled upwards and at last I reached a ledge several feet deep and covered with green moss where I could lie unseen. I felt I had reached the end of my dramatic adventures for that day when an unexpected occurrence showed me that there were further surprises in store for me. A huge rock, falling from above, boomed past me, struck the path and bounded over the chasm. For an instant, I thought it was an accident; but a moment later, looking up, I saw a man's head and shoulders silhouetted against the darkening sky; and another stone struck the ledge within a foot of my head. The meaning was plain: another of Moriarty's minions was on the scene. I had to act quickly unless I wished to remain an easy target. I scrambled back down on to the path. I don't think I could have done it in cold blood. It was a hundred times more difficult than getting up. But I had no time to think of danger, for another stone sang past me as I hung by my hands from the edge of the ledge. Half-way down I slipped but, by the blessing of God, I landed, torn and bleeding, on the path. I took to my heels, did ten miles over the mountains in the darkness, and a week later I found myself in Florence, with the certainty that no one on the world knew what had become of me.'

'This much I know.'

'Then it is time I told you what you do *not* know.'

Holmes threw another log on the fading fire and it retaliated with a crackle and a spray of sparks. I sat impassively awaiting the recommencement of his narrative, unsure of my own emotions. I had believed that I had passed the stage of being surprised or angered by my friend, but I had been wrong. To the end, he was an enigma. And a devilishly frustrating one.

'Florence is a magical city. I fell in love with it at once. I might have stayed there if events had turned out differently. There is a warmth and a sense of wellbeing there which I have seldom encountered anywhere else. Walking its streets is like coming home. The light is hypnotic and those wearied sand-coloured edifices soothe and inspire.'

'Cut the poetry, Holmes.'

Holmes raised his brows and gave me a wry smile. 'I soon found myself lodgings and started to acquaint myself with the great city. I supplemented what money I had by selling sketches. '

'I never knew that you could draw.'

'Sufficiently well. I have art in my blood. You will remember that the painter Vernet was a distant relation of mine. Indeed, I was known as Martin Verner during my stay in the city. I drew the Duomo and the Ponte Vecchio countless times and sold them to eager tourists. I could have made a healthy living there had it not been for certain developments.'

'Developments?'

'Indeed. I had been in Florence for about a month and I had become a regular artist by the Ponte S. Trinità with its exquisite statues of the four seasons – it is upstream of the Ponte Vecchio and an ideal vantage-point. I was even on nodding terms with some of my fellow artists, most of whom were Italian.

It was late one afternoon and the tourists had not been coming to view the wonderful bridge that day. I had been alone sketching out another canvas and was thinking about packing up for the day when my concentration was broken by cries for help. The voice was that of an Englishwoman. I looked up from my easel and saw her, not fifty yards away, struggling with two swarthy fellows, footpads I assumed. One of them was pulling at her handbag. I raced to her assistance, shouting terms of abuse at her attackers.

After a month in Italy, my knowledge of the vernacular was fairly comprehensive. On seeing this tall stranger bearing down on them, the cowards fled, leaving the lady slumped on the cobbles but still clutching her bag.

'I helped her to her feet and enquired if she were hurt. She shook her head and thanked me for my intervention. She was not a young woman, Watson, probably in her late thirties, but she was a handsome one. She possessed pale skin, iridescent blue eyes, and strongly defined features, with a nose that was perhaps too large for a feminine face but which gave her features a strange attractiveness.'

'You sound like me,' I said.

'The result of reading all those *Strand Magazine* accounts of yours, no doubt.'

Holmes puffed on his pipe and for a moment his eyes took on a dreamy, faraway look, as though he was conjuring an image of this woman in his mind, and then abruptly he returned to his narrative.

'She introduced herself to me as Hilda Courtney from London. I offered to escort the lady to her destination and she smiled. 'My destination is a restaurant. I am only in the city for one night and I wished to experience dinner *al fresco* at one of the open-air restaurants here rather than the stuffy dining room at the hotel. Please join me as my guest, a small gesture to thank you for your chivalrous rescue.' I accepted her offer and suggested we dine at Santo Spirito on the Via Michelangelo.

I can tell you, Watson, it was a delight to converse with someone English once again. The lady was spirited and intelligent and our conversation meandered through politics – British and European – the merits of Pre-Raphaelite paintings and Babbage's computer, a subject upon which Miss Courtney was very knowledgeable.'

'What was she doing in Florence?'

'I was coming to that. Apparently, she was working as a courier for Carmichael's, the auction house in Bond Street. Two weeks previously, a London agent acting for Count Mario Bava had acquired the Belvedere Stone, a precious 22-carat South African diamond, at a sale and Miss Courtney was bringing it from England for him. The Count had a villa in the hills above Florence and was due to rendezvous with Miss Courtney at her hotel the following morning.'

'You mean to say that she kept the diamond in that handbag?'

Holmes nodded.

'Then possibly those fellows were not simply common thieves . . .'

' . . . but informed felons? The thought had struck me also.'

'Why didn't she leave the damned thing in the hotel?'

'Safes in Italian hotels are notoriously vulnerable.'

'Did she show you the Belvedere Stone?'

'Indeed she did. Discreetly of course, but nevertheless I can tell you that it appeared to be a very handsome lump of carbon.'

'Why on earth did they send a woman on such a precarious errand?'

'Because a middle-aged lady is less likely to be suspected of carrying such precious cargo than a pale-faced, dark-suited Englishman clutching a sturdy attaché case.'

'I suppose so.'

Holmes took another sip of brandy and laughed. 'What do you know of disguise, Watson?'

I was somewhat thrown by this unexpected question and its vague nature. I shrugged in response.

'Clothes, various properties and subtle make-up are fine,' said Holmes. 'I have used them all myself, but to the trained eye certain natural aspects cannot be disguised.'

'The ears,' I suggested.

'Quite so. The ears and the hands. And something else.'

'Is this relevant?' I asked.

Holmes ignored my query and returned to his narrative. 'The time came for Miss Courtney to return to her hotel. We had talked long into the evening and I had enjoyed the occasion enormously, but the hovering waiters were hint enough that our departure was overdue. The lady insisted on paying. Gloves are a nuisance in dealing with *lire*, aren't they? Miss Courtney had to remove them to ensure that she paid correctly. It was a perfect Italian evening: warm with a faint breeze from the hills and a star-spotted blue sky . . . '

'You sound like a romantic, Holmes. Don't tell me you were falling in love with this lady?'

'I will not tell you that. But I cannot deny that I experienced a certain . . . excitement in her company. We made our way back along the Ponte S. Trinità, chatting in a desultory fashion, when I heard footsteps behind us. I turned and saw three dark shadows advancing stealthily in our direction. There was no doubt that their purpose was malevolent. As they drew nearer, I saw that each carried a weapon. I knew what they were after.'

'The Belvedere Stone!'

Holmes shook his head. 'Oh, no. They were after me! The lady gave a cry of anguish as one of the fellows lunged at me with a stiletto.'

'What on earth did you do?' I asked, finding myself now sitting on the edge of my seat.

'I did what I had to do. I grabbed Miss Courtney around the neck and pulled her in front of me to take the force of the blow.'

My blood ran cold. Could I believe what I was hearing? Did my friend, my honourable friend, really use a woman as a shield to protect himself from armed thugs? Was this the terrible secret that he had waited all these years to reveal? Was this why he had delayed his return to London and sought counsel with the head lama in Tibet? I stared at those strained, chiselled features with a mixture of disbelief and horror.

'It was only a glancing blow and caught the creature on the wrist. Miss Courtney gave a very unladylike oath. By this time I had my own knife out and, pulling away her high scarf, I held the blade to her neck – to the slight lump in her throat, to be precise.'

'The slight lump in the throat . . . My God! an Adam's apple! She was a man!'

Undeterred by my outburst, Holmes continued his narrative. 'I yelled at the thugs to disappear or their accomplice would die. They obeyed with remarkable alacrity.'

'It had all been a plot to trap you.'

'Slowly sinking in, Watson, old fellow?'

'Moriarty's men?'

'Of course. Like an organism under a microscope, I had been observed closely all the time. The Professor had waited patiently until he had decided that my guard was down and then he played the most remarkable of stunts. You see, he is so like me in many ways, Watson. He cannot resist a touch of the dramatic: hiring actors to portray him and then finally, when his criminal pyramid had been reduced to dust, he came after me with typical guile and flair. No doubt he could have had me killed by hired assassins at any time in that hot, teeming city. But that would have been so impersonal. And he approached this scheme, as he did his many others, with ingenuity and originality. There were no thespian alter egos in this charade, just a cool killer dressed as a woman, a subtle diversion which might well have worked.'

I laughed aloud. 'This is incredible,' I cried, 'and you will not be surprised to learn that I am utterly amazed. So, what happened?'

'It is a simple tale to tell. The assassins, having fled, left me alone on the bridge with my strange antagonist. I relaxed my guard moment-arily. This was sufficient for him to slip free of my grasp and aim a blow at my face. I dodged, but his fist caught me on the jaw. I staggered backwards, my knife dropping from my hand into the dark swirling waters below. The fellow rushed at me, throwing his long arms about my body. I fell back against the balustrade and, as we struggled together, he managed to hoist me up in an attempt to tip me into the river. My head and shoulders were hanging dangerously over the edge high above the gushing torrent. It was then that I brought into play my knowledge of *baritsu*. I relaxed my body like a rag doll as my opponent forced me further over the edge. Believe me, Watson, I had to judge this with tremendous precision. Then, on the point of losing my balance, I stiffened my body, flexed it violently, and pulled and heaved this creature over my head. Rather like a dark shooting star, he flew past me with a piercing shriek and fell into the blackness. There was a splash and a cry. And then there was silence.' Sherlock Holmes paused and puffed on his pipe. 'No doubt you will find the fellow's remains lodged on the silted bed of the River Arno in the lovely city of Florence.'

I was lost for words. I knew not how to respond to this amazing story and yet Holmes made it clear by a telling gesture that his tale was not yet complete.

'I lodged in a large block in the Via Matteo di Giovanni,' said Holmes, leaning forward to stir the fading embers of our fire. 'My rooms were on the second floor and were reached by an exterior stone staircase. It was a simple and basic apartment but it was self-contained and afforded me the privacy and seclusion I needed. On the following morning, I was having my second pipe of the day and idly reading Boccacio when my door opened and a visitor stood on the threshold. The figure was virtually a silhouette, like a dark angel, with the fierce morning sun rippling behind him, dispersing bright beams of light around him into my room. I could tell that he was a young man dressed in a linen suit and, as he removed his hat, his dark hair tumbled over his forehead.

'Despite the sunshine and the warm morning air, I suddenly felt a chill as I gazed on this apparition.

' "So, Mr Sherlock Holmes," he said softly, "we meet at last." The voice was cool, relaxed and had the sinister charm of a hissing snake.

' "Do we?" I replied casually. "How can I be sure?"

'The stranger allowed himself a dry chuckle. "Oh, you will have to take my word for it, but I assure you that there is no deception on this occasion. I really *am* Professor James Moriarty."

'I believed him. I strained my eyes to get a better look at him, but his face was in deep shade with the yellow light of the sun in bright relief behind him. But I could tell that he was young, Watson. Some ten years younger than I. Here was no ancient professor with a balding pate and stooped shoulders – that was all a hoax.

' "Why are you here?" I asked.

' "To congratulate you and to warn you."

'I said nothing but waited for him to explain.

' "You are a remarkable man, Mr Holmes. It has almost been a pleasure to encounter your opposition – an intellectual pleasure, you understand. However, now I am tired of the game – a game which you have come very close to winning."

' "With your organisation in ruins and your need to flee the country, I would say that I *was* the winner."

'Moriarty responded quickly to my jibe, but the voice remained calm and unruffled. "The game is far from over, Mr Holmes. It is true that there must be some years spent in the wilderness – for both of us. But in due course, like the phoenix, I shall rise. For the present I think it is time that I enjoyed my riches and travelled the world. So resilient have you been in foiling my little plans that I have decided to leave you alone. I admire your brain and have no wish to harm you now. There would simply be no point, so I can assure you that there will be no further attempts on your life or liberty. You may cease looking over your shoulder."

'He paused for effect. When I failed to reply he continued in a more businesslike tone. "But this must be a reciprocal arrangement. You must eliminate from your mind all thoughts of revenge or plots to bring me to justice. As far as the world at large is concerned, they must believe that I perished at the bottom of the Reichenbach Falls. And just to make sure that you accept these conditions, I have arranged for a watch to be placed upon Dr Watson. Dear Dr Watson, your closest friend and ally."

'I felt my hands gripping the arms of the chair in impotent anger as the devil unveiled the details of his plan.

' "If I even hear or suspect that you are making enquiries about either my whereabouts or my plans, I will arrange for the good doctor to meet with an accident – something suitably nasty."

'I jumped to my feet, the chair tipping over behind me, and was about to pounce on him when he flashed a revolver at me. I heard the click of the hammer being cocked.

' "Now, do not act in haste or anger, Mr Holmes. Should anything befall me here, Watson will be dead within twenty-four hours. Not *all* my colleagues were arrested, you know. There is a slender framework to my organisation still in place in London. Be sensible. Leave me alone and I will leave you and the good Watson alone. However, one false step and . . . well, need I go into detail?"

'I was lost for words, Watson, and, indeed, words were useless on this occasion. There was nothing I could say or do. In that sense, he remained the victor. Whatever success I had in destroying his organisation, when the dust settled he still held the upper hand. A wave of fury surged through my veins but I was incapable of action.

' "We will have our time in the wilderness, but in due course we shall return to our respective professions. It has been good to know you, Sherlock Holmes, but I hope that we never meet again."

'Without another word, he turned, pulling the door quickly behind him, cutting out the bright sunlight and plunging the room into comparative shadow.

'I stood for some time staring at the door, my mind turning over his words. For all my cleverness, I had been placed in a situation where I could do nothing. I could not risk your life to pursue him further.'

'If only I had known . . . I am an old campaigner, after all. I could have looked after myself,' I said with some passion.

'Against a foe that was visible and recognisable, I am sure you could. But not against Moriarty. Remember airguns, Watson? One cannot be prepared for the unforeseen.'

'Why didn't you tell me?'

'I couldn't. I knew how you would react – much as you are doing now. I had to keep it a secret. I could not risk the consequences of such indiscretion.'

Despite my sense of disappointment and uncertain emotions, I knew in my heart that Sherlock Holmes had taken the only course of action open to him.

'I understand,' I said at length, and then added, 'What became of Moriarty?'

'He never quite revived his organisation, but some years later he commenced operations again in London for a short time. Although I never became actively involved in the investigation of his crimes, mainly robberies, I did pass on information about them to Scotland Yard secretly. Then there was silence. Whether he is dead or he just grew weary of his calling and has retired I cannot say.'

Holmes and I sat in quietly for some time. Eventually, it was my friend who spoke.

'I hope you can forgive me, Watson.'

As I responded, I felt the prickle of tears in my eyes. 'I can forgive you. Of course, I can forgive you. I only wish . . . '

'I know, I know.'

We both smiled, but they were mirthless smiles.

I drained my glass and sighed. It was a sigh for lost opportunities, for the passing of a lost world and for the final revelation in my long relationship with Sherlock Holmes.

'I think, said I, stretching my weary limbs, 'it is long past my bedtime. I am not as young as I believe I am.'

Neither of us mentioned the Reichenbach secret again. At breakfast the following morning, it was as though nothing had been said the night before. As we sat with our coffee and toast, with Mrs Towers bustling around us, our conversation did not flow very easily and to be honest I was relieved when my hired car came to collect me at eleven. We stood, Holmes and I, for the last time, at his wooden gate, shaking hands and smiling. We both knew that our paths would never cross again and so it was with some difficulty that we parted. 'Thank you for everything,' I said.

Holmes smiled faintly, leaning on his stick for support. 'It wouldn't have been the same without you, Watson. It would not have been the same.'

As the car sped away and I turned to wave through the rear window, the spare figure of my old friend was already fading into the distance.